Fire from the Wine Dark Sea

Fire from the Wine Dark Sea

Somtow Sucharitkul

Illustrator: Lindahn/Artifact

STARBLAZE
EDITIONS

Donning
Norfolk/Virginia Beach

Dedication

To Hank Stine, who was crazy enough to buy this book.

The Donning Company/Publishers,
5659 Virginia Beach Boulevard,
Norfolk, Virginia 23502

Library of Congress Cataloging in Publication Data:

Sucharitkul, Somtow.
  Fire from the wine-dark sea.

  1. Science fiction, American. I. Title.
PS3569.U23F5   1983   813'.54   82-12827
ISBN 0-89865-252-9

Printed in the United States of America

Contents

Fire from the Wine-Dark Sea

And now for the first story, Fire from the Wine-Dark Sea, *which was inspired by the Geithner boys, a real pair of twins similar to the ones you will encounter in the story. It's also about myth and reality and other academically juicy subjects. I have chosen to begin with this story because I believe that it is written, more or less, in my own voice, as much as is possible, at least, within my need to tell lies for a living.*

Once upon a time there was a man who had two sons, twins; they had wild wheatfield hair that rustled in rough winds and was bleached still whiter in summer, and pale freckles, and snub noses, and smiles that burst out, teethcrooked and all, like sunlight after a stormfall, and great dark darting daunting eyes.

People would stare at them, searching for a difference, and they usually couldn't find one. They also stared because they were shockingly beautiful kids. Of course the man could tell the difference; he was their father.

For the man, what was difficult was another thing—having two such beautiful children, and knowing that he loved one of them better....

I've started this all wrong, haven't I? When you've got the Poetry Chair at some obscure New England university, you feel an obligation to talk this way, to write this way; it's the literary syndrome. Because words are in themselves beautiful things. Like gems. Like clothes. Like coffins. Hiding the hurt.

Well. Shit.

You see, this man I'm writing about. It's no fairytale. It's not an archetypal hypothetical mythopoeic paradigm out there in a house by the sea, scribbling ironic Byronic laconic verses into a tattered notebook. Maybe this man exists, but the man in this story isn't him.

He's me.

So I think I'll desist from this "universalizing" crap now. I only began that way because it's so scary, trying to write about something real, something that happened. You want to escape into "he did this," "he did that." And yet....

It's because of this very story that I don't ever want to run away from anything again.

First person.

Summers we lived by the sea, in our estate two miles down from the village of St. Joan—it's pronounced "Sin-jun"—in an old house ghosted with grandfathers, on Delenda Circle that curved off Moore Avenue that ran from the village and route 311, past Charley's Cliffs and along the Cape for many miles. From my window and from the boys' window you saw the sea mostly, a ribbon of beach at high tide, and a fuzzy Tuckatinck Island, white and gray-green.

Mornings Sandy and Claude would go running before I woke, up the avenue a bit and then into DuPertuis Lane, twistier than a cat-pawed yarnball and smelling of old earth and moss and tall woods peering over the mist....

One morning I was meditating on the sunny side of an egg when Sandy burst through the kitchen door. Everything always exploded from silent black-and-white to technicolor sensurround whenever he came into a room....

"Harry!" he yelled. "Harry! We've found a friend!"

"Who—?"

"Coming up behind us! Running behind, up DuPertuis Lane, rounding the corner...C'mon, Harold, Mr. Vance, come see!"

He stopped for a breath. Christ, what a kid! With a grandly unselfconscious movement he swept back his hair. It remained a mess, moss-sprinkled and mussed up by the morning wind. Then he shucked his sneakers over the table. They arced over the eggs and crashed on the stoneware tiles, and he smiled a little.

"Sandy, who is he?" I said.

"We don't know, Harry."

Then Claude stood quietly in the doorway, his face gridded by the screen, and the sunrise shooting sparkdarts through his hair.

The room temperature seemed to drop a notch.

"Hi, Dad."

It's funny, how Sandy never called me that. Always—with a wryness concealing awkward tenderness—'Harold,' or 'Harry,' or 'Mr. Vance.' Kids that age hate to give anything away...and yet it was Sandy I loved the most, wild Sandy.

"Sandy—" I touched him but he slipped through my fingers like sea spray.

Claude said, "Dad, he's very strange, the man. I don't know if I like him. He keeps babbling on about...oh, weird stuff."

"He's terrific!" Sandy said.

"Yah," said Claude, coming in and pressing against the door-hinges to make them squeak. He came and sat down at the kitchen table. He moved unsteadily, the way a thirteen-year-old usually does; he was different in this from Sandy, who moved with his whole being, elemental, like a wild animal. He took off his sneakers very carefully and put them down on either side of a tile-

3

crack, so that it would be a completely symmetrical pattern.

I watched them both for a while. What kind of weirdo had they picked up at the beach or in the woods? I looked from one to the other: Sandy's eyes seemed to trust you so blindly, while Claude's were never innocent, they had a way of shaming you, of putting you in the wrong.

Then I heard a voice form outside. "Phew! These bare beet are no good for running along your roads." It was a rich voice, like someone playing the cello in a marble bathroom....

"Oh, Jesus Christ," I said. "Do you guys have to bring in everyone you meet? Can't a fellow eat his breakfast?"

"But Dad—" said Claude.

"Harry, you'll like him," Sandy said, and I swallowed my exasperation for a second, and then the room went dark because the stranger filled up the doorway completely.

He was tall, fair, with a torn white tunic on, and a trim beard. He was sunburnt. He didn't smile. I looked at him, rather belligerently—

And he transfixed me with his eyes, dark and formidable as my sons' eyes could be sometimes, and cold as a winter wind. And then I noticed that his hair was streaming behind him like fire. But there was no wind in the room at all. I started to say something angry but my mouth was chilled shut....

Then the coldness melted away and he seemed all friendliness. "These... sneakers, you call them," he said, half-laughing, "a fabulous exotic treasure indeed! Hermes could not be swifter than a stripling shod with these...." He knelt down to look at Sandy's Adidases, carelessly thrown there on the brown tiles. He picked one of them up and began to poke it, as though he'd never seen one before.

I got my voice back then. "Of all the nerve!" I said. "Marching into a stranger's house like this, peering at his things—"

He rose up then, and stared at me very seriously until I felt guilty—the way Claude could always do—and said, "I've come an awful long way." His hair never stopped billowing. "Thousands of miles. Would you turn me out, Mr. Vance? You boys have been most kind to me...."

"Who are you?" I said, more quietly.

"I am," he said, "Odysseus, King of Ithaca."

"See, Dad?" said Claude, laughing suddenly. "I told you he was weird."

"Now look here...." I was desperately scanning the newspaper in my mind. There had to be some kind of headline like PSYCHOPATH FLEES EMERGENCY WARD, something like

4

that. I floundered for something to say, and came out with: "Okay, so you're Napoleon—whoops—Odysseus. How come you're not speaking classical Greek, then?"

"I am."

And then I saw it.

When he spoke, it wasn't in lip-synch. I mean what I was hearing didn't synchronize with what his mouth was doing. I mean my God, it was like watching a Godzilla movie. And then there was the hair. And the tunic, too...lashed by a still tempest.

Now I was really frightened.

Claude said, "It's being translated straight into our minds. Like, you know, telepathy, some kind of radar, something—"

But Sandy didn't say anything at all. He seemed just to accept the stranger, to know he was all right, without looking for an explanation.

"I've left Ithaca for good," the stranger said. "After ten years of war, ten years of high adventure, who can stay home? And that Penelope..so perfect, so patient and everything. Every time I so much as looked at her she would accuse me with her eyes, never meaning to of course, but you just knew she was swallowing her suffering and trying to look beautiful for you. She has her loom now, and I—I wander over the sea, landing in new countries and new epochs, exchanging gifts with the strange new people...."

"Either that, or you're a hell of a good actor," I said. The eggs had grown cold now.

"Harry, can he stay here?" Sandy pleaded. "He has to get supplies, and—"

"Well..." I saw that Claude had turned away and was staring at the wall. There was so much eagerness in Sandy's eyes....

"It would please me much, sir, if I could call you my guest-friend," Odysseus said.

I didn't know what to think.

Claude got up suddenly and said: "Dad, I'm going up to the den to use your typewriter." He had this craze for doing concrete poetry, picked up from a whacky creative writing teacher at his school...."

I watched my son cross the living room and run up the stairs, his fingers skimming the banister. Not looking at the man, I said, "If only I could believe your story...but it can't be happening. You can't be real."

Odysseus said, "Mr. Vance, you are a poet. You of all people should know how tenuous the line between reality and fantasy is...if the line itself is a fantasy, then fantasy must of necessity be real...."

"You talk like Odysseus should talk," I said. "Wily, word-twisting, devious. You should do well in our century." It was easy to fall right into what he was saying. He made it sound all so plausible.

"So can he stay, huh, Harry?"

I saw them exchanging a look. He had my son quite hypnotized. Well, that wasn't surprising. And I scrutinized his face, still avoiding his eyes, searching for a trace of deceit, and I couldn't find anything at all...and the wind on his face never stopped blowing.

I knew his eyes were on me, and without meaning to I was raising my eyes to meet his...they were so dark. Even in the morning light they were crystals of night.

"Wait till you see his ship!" cried Sandy.

Odysseus laughed. "It isn't much of one, judging by the monstrosities I have seen, breasting the tides in the middle of nowhere...."

"He has a *ship*?" I gasped.

"You can see it from the window!" and Sandy had run to the stairs and was springing up them like a cat.

Odysseus said to me, "Beautiful child. Beautiful...'sneakers'." He was holding one of Sandy's, hefting it from hand to hand. And then he smiled a broad sunny smile, and gathered up his tunic more tightly around him, bracing himself against the wind I couldn't feel, and we went up to the boys' room on the second floor.

I could hear Claude tapping laboriously on the typewriter from my den.

Sandy was gazing out of the window. Without turning around, he beckoned for me to come and stand by him. I stood over him and he didn't push me away; and I saw a little boat moored on the beach, on our private dock, next to our own boat. Nothing very strange about it....

"That's it?"

"No, Dad," he said—he never called me that!—and pointed. Out over the sparkle-kissed dark water, to where Tuckatinck Island blocked the horizon. "Don't you see it?" That boat's only his little shuttle."

I couldn't see anything at first. "What do you mean, Sandy?"

And then I saw a vague white outline, as though a cloud had settled on the distant shoreline. Perhaps a mast. Perhaps a sail. Perhaps a prow chiselled into a nude woman with wide-open arms. I couldn't tell...."

"See, Harry?" He was yelling excitedly. "There are people walking the decks, the sails are flapping...."

"Damn it, I don't see anything! I guess you just have better eyesight than me."

"You suck shit, Mr. Vance!" he said, childish suddenly.

I shrugged. "I guess your peculiar friend will be with us for a few days, huh?" I looked at the man expectantly. Then I turned around and tried to turn the cloud that hugged the Island into a firm-outlined ship, with planks, masts, rivets, but the haze would not resolve...."

"Just long enough to look around," said Odysseus. "Already I long for the sea, for tastier adventures. But I'd like to take something with me, a souvenir perhaps...at every port I take some gift from the inhabitants. After all, I am a King."

He and Sandy exchanged a look.

In that moment I knew that I was jealous.

"Sure," I said.

Claude's typing pelted the silence.

* * *

Claude woke me up by putting on one of Laura's records. The one of Beethoven's last piano sonata, the opus one one one, with the long impossible trills that seem to stretch from your guts to the end of the sky. Laura had played it at her last concert.

(Laughing Laura! The arms like wild cranes in flight. Sweeping up from the keyboard like Sandy springing from the diving rock by Charley's Cliffs. Laughing alone in the Albert Hall before the audience came on, confounding the ushers. Darting from the underground at Piccadilly Circus. Stepping in front of a double-decker bus.)

"Dad...?"

(Coming back to the States. Clearing the coffin through customs.)

Claude: a slim shadow crossing the bed, bisecting the triangle of dawn light from the half-closed shutters.

(Really? Four years ago?)

"Dad...."

I felt a pang of guilt, suddenly. I couldn't think why, except that I'd neglected the kid, as always. "Hey, why aren't you out running with Sandy, Claudius?"

"He took Odysseus with him." Then—the anguish in his voice all out of proportion with what he was saying—"Dad, he lent him *your* sneakers!"

I suppressed the unreasonable, un-adult annoyance I felt.

"Besides," he said, "I hate to run. I only do it to be with him."

"And now—"

"He's with the immortal stranger."

—the piano had reached the first of the long trills—

"Daddy, I think he's surrounded by some kind of time-shield, you know, like a force field. It keeps him locked away from our universe, you know. And we don't know what he's really saying either. It's all dubbed, but the translation could be wrong, you know like in Swedish movies when they're really saying 'oh, fuck,' or something, and it comes out 'jeepers.' Or he's come bursting through from an alternate universe—"

"Yeah."

I didn't really know what he was saying; you know faculty kids. Smart as hell, old before their time. Smartassed, too. He was hiding something though, under the froth of words. I said, as gently as I could, "What's up, kid?"

He sat down on the bed then. I could feel him against my knee, and I could feel the tension between us like a jack-in-the-box ready to burst. "You love him a lot, don't you, Dad?" he said. "More than me."

I was silent.

"That's all right, Dad. I want you to know that. I do too." He was talking at the shutters, trying not to see me. "But sometimes I don't think he's really here at all. He's like a wind or a fire, not a person. Like Odysseus."

—the long trill went on and on, the piano strained high, high, touching the sky—

"Jesus Christ!" he said. "Why do you have to be deaf to write such great music?" And I saw he'd been crying.

It wasn't like him. He was always the one with no emotions. The brick-walled one.

"All right, Claudius. Get your clothes on. You and I are going to drive to Hyannis. Right now."

"How come?" But his face lit up. I sat up on the bed and threw open the shutters. Light exploded across the waxed oak floor.... "Do we have to wait for the others?"

"No." He was really smiling now, but he looked like he hadn't had any sleep. "Look, Odysseus wanted a souvenir, didn't he? Maybe we can get him something really nice, and then maybe he'll go away."

Downstairs, Laura's record clicked.

* * *

In the afternoon Sandy made me drive him and Odysseus to Laura's grave, which was five miles past the last of Charley's Cliffs. Claude had already hidden the parcel we had bought in my den, in the desk drawer under the typewriter....

We were in our ancient Austin, with Claude nestled against me as if terrified, and Odysseus in the front seat too, watching the view, and Sandy in the dog seat. Claude pushed hard against me the whole time. Odysseus seemed preoccupied: his eyes flitted from cliff to pebblestrewn roadside to forest wall. We took a left into the cemetery and I saw the grave.

I walked ahead, not wanting to be too close to the stranger, and Claude was huddled against me the whole time. The cement path was broken by moss-veins and tufts of grass, and the sun shone so fiercely that the newer gravestones, the ones that had been washed recently, blazed blindingly.

Claude whispered, "Do you think it'll work? The present, I mean." We walked on quickly so as to be out of earshot.

"For thirty-nine ninety-five," I said, "It better." Then I said, "Christ, I'm scared." We came up to the grave and stopped suddenly. I knelt down and saw that there was a clumsy wreath of wild flowers on the ground. "Did you do this?" I asked Claude.

"No."

I turned around and saw Sandy; he looked away. And then Odysseus was behind us, his shadow eclipsing the gravestone.

Claude said, under his breath, "You shouldn't have brought him here. This is *our* place."

In the heat-haze, in the oppressive bright stillness, still the stranger's hair caught fire and flamed. Still his tunic rustled; and still his lips moved differently from the sounds we heard....

"Wives," he said, sighing. "I have a wife, too."

"Then why don't you go back to her?" I said, angry. Already he'd lured Sandy into his power and he'd driven Claude to near hysteria. "What's your game, stranger? All right, so you're not an escapee from a mental home, but what do you want from us?"

"Nothing that you would not give freely...."

Sandy said, "I told him about Mom, Harry. We ran down to the very end of DuPertuis Lane this morning, maybe three miles. He loves your sneakers...I played him Mom's records." His light blue teeshirt was plastered to him, the hair glistening-damp. "He wanted to pour a libation here, that's all." He looked at me, his eyes seeming to conceal nothing.

I picked up the crude wreath and put it on top of the gravestone. The marble had already worn away some; you couldn't read her name unless you got the exact angle of sunlight.

"I have a wife too," said Odysseus. "She sits at home and weaves enormous tapestries. And sometimes she rips them up, and begin again, and rips them up, and begins again...."

"Don't you feel sorry for her?" I said.

"No," he said. Not very convincingly, though. "I like the sea and the changings and the constant new strangenesses of new shores. To be at home is to be rooted, like rocks, like trees: I don't feel *real* in that way. Sometimes I feel more like a wind, something that slips through people's fingers.'

"Oh?"

He went on: "You should all be thankful to my wife Penelope, though. If she were to stop weaving, you'd all come to an end, most likely...because a millenium or two ago she was sick of all those scenes of heroes and titans and beasts. She became a little more creative, a little...how do you people say it these days... *science-fictional*. And everything she weaves comes true, of course."

"That's bullshit," I said. "The world has existed far longer than your Greek mythology ever did...."

"When a good writer writes, doesn't the story seem to stretch beyond the writing itself? Don't the characters seem to have histories from long before the first page? But they don't, you know."

Claude said, "So did you spring into being when Homer sang, then, Odysseus?"

Odysseus' face clouded for a moment. Then he said: "Homer?" He seemed very puzzled. "Now who is that?"

"You can't see where you come from," Claude said, "unless you stand outside where you came from."

Odysseus said in a hurry, "Let's talk of other things. It hurts me to think of my wife alone at her loom. I've never stopped feeling guilty...you know, one of you boys should come with me when I leave."

He said it so casually. It was much *too* impromptu. I knew at once that this was why he had come. I stared at my two boys, and saw they were both terrified.

"But think of it!" Odysseus cried out. "Think of the open sea, the wind on the wine-dark waves, the giants and the cyclopes and the golden princesses and the enchantresses...and of being immortal. For we are not real as you are; we are more than that. We are the old things that do not change."

"I won't leave my father," said Claude hesitantly.

"I'll say you won't!" I said.

We all looked at Sandy. He was so small.... Suddenly

Claude said, "Maybe one of us is *meant* to go. If so, I'll go, Dad. If one of us has to. I know you'll never want to lose Sandy, and it's the only way—"

"Hold it, kid!" I said. "Nothing's going to change, nobody's going anywhere! Except Odysseus. He's going straight back to the nuthouse."

Sandy was shaking with anger, struggling to get something out, and then—

"Fuck you Odysseus!" he screamed. "Leave us alone! Just get out of our lives, just fuck off!"

In the appalling silence I saw—

(Laura's arms, anger-hammering the dead piano, Laura tearing the music, Laura's eyes from the coffin depths—)

—Sandy backing away into the dead stone.

"It's all right," Odysseus said gently. "I don't insist...."

And then there was more silence. And behind the silence, from behind the cliffs across Moore Avenue, came the whisper of the unseen sea.

* * *

And so in the evening we went to the beach and sat on the sand and ate broiled hamburgers and watched the sun setting behind us, partly over the cliffs, partly over Tuckatinck Island, a little over the open sea.

He was going to leave in the morning.

After the afternoon's explosions I just wanted to relax. I knew that he was leaving and that there was nothing to worry about anymore.... Odysseus sat with his feet just touching the water, telling tall tales. He looked out to sea the whole time; and though I knew his ship was meant to be docked by the island, I still could see nothing. Only a haze that enveloped the rocks and rose and shifted in color from white to blue-gray, like a Siamese cat's fur.

We were waiting for Claude. Sandy was away in the water, jumping up and down.

Claude came clutching the parcel, running out of the house. He made a breeze with his running, he made the sand fly, for a moment I thought he was Sandy.

"So you still don't see my ship?" Odysseus was saying. "Your son there, he does."

Claude crashed down beside us. The sand poured into my cutoffs...he thrust the parcel at me. I caught his eye for a moment. His look said, *This won't work.*

11

"Come back, Sandy!" I hollered. "We've got something to do!"

He ran over the dark waves, a dark streak in the pink and gray...and tumbled in front of us. Sand and water on my face.

"We're sorry to see you go." It was a ritual. The words were meaningless.

"I know you are not," said Odysseus, not playing the game. I handed him the parcel wordlessly.

He opened it and took out the sneakers...soft suede Adidases, fawn with pale blue stripes, size ten, nesting on layers of tissue...he seemed very thoughtful.

"Thank you," he said. There was so much sadness in his voice. "I will wear them often, when I tread strange shores, and I will think of your beautiful children, the ones who would not come with me, the ones who loved their father better than the wild wide ocean."

"Tell us another story," said Sandy. "Tell us about Troy."

"You don't want to hear about it." A wind had sprung up; for once the billowing of his hair seemed to match reality. He stroked the sneakers. Behind the habitual coldness of his eyes I thought I saw...some indescribable yearning. It was truly terrible, and I was afraid.

"I can show you," he said, "the fires of Troy, I can show you if you can see them. Look there at the island, over by the ship...."

And all I could see was the shifting haze, pinker now in the twilight.

"Don't you see the fire across the wine-dark sea?" said Odysseus. "Don't you see the slaughter, don't you see the screaming women being dragged to the ships?"

The haze twisted. But I saw nothing.

Then Sandy burst out: "I see it all, Harry! I see everything! I see the walls crumbling and the horse standing behind the walls, and the fire burning the houses and the children screaming in the streets...."

"Cut the crap, Sandy!" said Claude tightly. He was trembling all over.

"Your son has vision, then," Odysseus said. "He is like one of us...."

Sandy said, "It's terrible, Harry! Now they've dragged a child from its mother, they're going to throw it down from the walls, and the walls are falling, falling—"

The sky was fireblood-red, but I saw nothing—

Claude was shaking Sandy. "It's all lies, Dad! He's just making it up! He doesn't see those things!" he screamed. And Sandy's eyes were frozen like Laura's eyes, crystallized and cold

12

watching me from the coffin—

I put out my arms and covered the boy's eyes. He pushed me away. "I've got to see, Harry, I've got to!" he whispered. And I saw that Odysseus no longer seemed interested in us. He had stood up and had put on his new sneakers and was springing lightly up and down on them, laughing for joy.

Red rays like fire fingers grasping the water—

"This is enough," I said. I lifted Sandy up in my arms. He held me so tightly I couldn't breathe.

"Harry," he said, "you've got to come running with me."

I saw that Claude had gone into the house, and so I walked Sandy to the front of the house, where our sneakers were, and then we set off down Delenda Circle, into the redstreaked darkness.

It was hard at first. Mostly I watched the pavement. When I looked up Sandy was running free, pounding the ground and leaping in smooth curves and looking straight ahead. The woods were so much taller than him. We crossed Moore Avenue and turned into DuPertuis Lane.

"Don't tailgate!" Sandy hollered.

We ran on. I felt lost in the leaf-moist stillness. The rhythm of foot-thuds became a heartbeat. We ran flat out and the lane corkscrewed, it was alive, it was a snake's gullet, we were flowing into its gut, flowing like blood, like bile.

"Wait for me, damn it!" I shouted.

He was into the wood now, darting from shadow to shadow, and I was so tired I could hardly think. My sneakers crunched on twigs and winced away from pebbles.

And then we stopped.

Why had he made me do this? Later I realized: he was showing me that he possessed me. That I belonged to him, no matter what.

We sank down on the wet ground, against a tree.

Sandy said, "Dad."

He said it shyly. He wasn't used to calling me Dad. But defiantly too. Because I was his father. He shook something out of his hair and smoothed a crease in his teeshirt and a moonbeam fell on his face....

Even in this darkness his eyes could still flash, like sunlight out of a gap in a thundercloud. I waited. It was his show. I didn't know what was coming. It could have been a storm. Or nothing at all.

—Laura's eyes breaking out from behind the crook of the piano—

"Dad, will you love me forever?"

"Of course, Sandy," I said, tense.

"And Claude? You're going to stop pushing him away from you?"

"I don't know what you mean," I lied.

A leaf fell.

"Christ, Dad...can't you think of her as a human being? Can't you remember the human things about her? I make you think of her, don't I, Dad? But she isn't real anymore. And I don't think I am, either...you never did see the ship, did you, Dad, or the fire from the sea...?"

"Let's talk about something else," I said.

The forest pressed us in. We really were in the serpent's gut. And Sandy seemed so far away. Even though I could smell the fabric softener on his tee-shirt, through the sweet boy's sweat odor.

"I have to go with Odysseus, Dad."

"No, Sandy, please," I said, "don't play games with me, you'll kill me...."

"I saw the ship. I saw the walls crumble. I saw the fire." He spoke without emotion. "I'm part of his world, Harry, But that's not why I have to go."

I waited.

"If I stay here I'm going to go on breaking your heart, forever," he said, talking into the ground.

"How can you say that?" I said.

"You're so ashamed about feeling one way about me and one way about Claude. Your guilt's a scary thing. And it's only that you're afraid of him...because he's so like you. People think they love the things they can't be. That's all you see in me, Dad."

He had drained me. I couldn't talk. All I could think of was him, leaping from diving rocks, running in the darkness, sliding down the banisters....

"Daddy, before I go, I have a gift for you too."

This was his gift: he laughed me Laura's laugh until the trees laughed in the close darkness, until his laughing dried up, and then I caught the laugh from him and laughed too, laughed hysterically until I couldn't stop crying.

Then he said, "Let's go, Dad."

In the moonlight I saw that his lips didn't match his words.

* * *

There's a little bit of the stereotype that's true. I do possess a tattered notebook and I do go around writing in it: lines that become poems, sometimes, but usually are just lines that go nowhere, smoke-trails of a skywriter that disperse in the wind....

I carried the notebook out to the beach.

I saw two sets of sneakerprints. Size ten and size six. They led to a point in the sand and stopped.

"I think the stranger was Death," I whispered to myself.

Claude said, startling me—I didn't know he was there—"No, Daddy, no. Sandy went away because he loved us. To kill your mourning, to give me a chance." He looked so serious. He hadn't slept.

As we looked out at the sea a high wind sprang up and blew the fog away from Tuckatinck Island, and the fog drifted, skimming the water still, toward the sunrise, blushing against the gray sea and sky.

"It's the ship!" Claude yelled. And he jumped up and down frantically and waved, "Goodbye, goodbye, Sandy!" and rushed out into the low tide....

"Do you see the ship?" I called out to him.

"No."

We turned and went into the house. Claude had left the record on. The one of Laura playing the opus one one one.

Jesus Christ! Do you have to be deaf to write great music?

And then I saw that we are all deaf, and blind too. If we were not, if we could see, we would be like Sandy. We wouldn't need visions, or art. We would run after the truth until we melted into a breeze, into sea water, into sunlight.

That's why art is all lies.

I saw my son in the doorway, I thought he was Sandy for a moment. Then I crushed him against me as though it were the last time.

Claude said, "I'm not Sandy, Dad, but some day..." behind the grief, his eyes sparkled briefly..."someday, can we go running in the woods?"

I wrote another line in the book:

art is the dark glasses a blind man wears

—*Cape Cod and Arlington, 1978*

15

The Thirteenth Utopia

The Thirteenth Utopia *was my first...what you might call professional...sale. I was sitting on a roller coaster at Busch Gardens, Virginia, when I got the idea for this one. Later it turned out to be the seed from which the entire Inquestor Universe sprang, but I had no idea at the time that the story would spawn a series, let alone an—ahem—five book trilogy, complete with fully conceived artificial language with 100 pages of background notes on usage, and so on, and so on. It's amazing to me, how this child of mine grew and grew. Perhaps it's elephantiasis.*

In any case, the story that follows, exactly the way it appeared in Analog *in 1979, is no longer, strictly speaking, part of the Inquestral canon at all; but those who would learn more about Davaryush and what happens to Shtoma are advised to read* Light on the Sound, *Book I of the trilogy, and its forthcoming sequels.*

I am putting it in this collection because as a solo story it seemed to attract quite a bit of attention (missing a Hugo nomination by two votes, damn it! If only I'd conned my parents into voting) and I thought it would be a shame not to see it in one of my books.

Here goes...The Thirteenth Utopia.

He came to Shtoma in the cadent lightfall, his tachyon bubble breaching the gilt-fringed incandescent clouds like a dark meteor.

Some feelings are never unlearned. Some wonders never fade with experience. So he reflected, Ton Davaryush, master iconoclast, purger of planets, transformer of societies. Especially one: the thrill of power, of potentiality... of a virgin utopia, ripe for the unmasking of its purifying flaw.

Every utopia has its flaw. Ton Davaryush wished it were not so. He was sad—but only for a moment—that he must wreak havoc on this planet, even though it lay at the very limits of the Dispersal of Man; but he had learned not to compromise. With the destruction of twelve deceptive utopias, experience had at least banished misgivings. For Davaryush was two hundred and thirteen years old, and at the height of his analytic powers.

He closed his curiously heavy-lidded eyes to the shimmering of the cloud-banks and the extravagance of the alien landscape that grew constantly as he fell, with its strange sharp-angled trees like gigantic pink spiders, their photosynthesizing pigment having a ferric, not a magnesium base, and its whimsical spiral dwellings of transparent plastic, jutting up at irregular intervals from the blanket of dense vegetation, crimsons and vermilions. He ignored them, and the savage thrashings of the wind as his translucent sphere automatically adjusted to the gravity, softening his fall for landing on Shtoma.

And thought of the covenant: *for the breaking of joy is the beginning of wisdom.* And thought, pathetically: I, Ton Davaryush, expelled from the mainstream of human society by time dilations and the gulfs of space, am too alone. He tried to bury himself—eyes still closed to the atmospheric turmoil—in analyses of what he had been told about this world. How they had fallen into a pattern, an ecological stasis, from which he must release them, whatever the cost. And this was no backward, back-to-nature primitivistic planet, exulting in its own self-conscious apartness and ignorance, but a world whose technical sophistication rivaled his own; exceeded it, in at least one respect, for Shtoma alone, in the entire Dispersal of Man, knew the secret of gravity control. For which they had no use, except for the manufacture of toys. And which they guarded with such miserliness and irrational fervor as to belie their much-vaunted saintliness, their notorious lack of greed and every other human quality. And the rumor that Shtoma was a utopia was more than could be tolerated.

If it was a utopia it could be destroyed. This he knew. He understood every facet of the utopian heresy. He was a master iconoclast, dedicated to the perpetuation of change. *Every utopia has its flaw.* He clutched this knowledge to him like a secret prayer.

I may be a savior.

He opened his eyes finally. And saw the incredible wildness, the intractable angularity of the landscape, the lurid carmines and scarlets of the trees that lurched toward him with their arachnoid arms outstretched. His bubble slowed itself, gradually, to bring him to the field of rust-colored grass. Alien buzzings and high-pitched song-snatches assailed his ears.

He deactivated his tachyon bubble with a flick of his mind— the keys were cybernetically brain-implanted—and was now at the mercy of the alien environment. At some indeterminate future, he would be rescued—when the computer on homeworld decided.

I may be a savior. This was more important to him than why they had jealously hidden their secret from a galaxy where knowledge was not for concealing, why they had not used their secret for conquest, as was their right. But this would come. *I am bringing them their human nature,* he thought. The thrill of it lived in his heart. (For this thrill he had joined the Inquest.)

He drew his shimmercloak over his shoulder. It absorbed the fresh air and began to radiate in the safe range, as he knew it would: he stroked it softly as it blushed, pink against the aquamarine fur; wishing, as always, that it was not a dumb semisentient. For he was alone.

Turning in the direction of the nearest habitation, he reviewed once more all he had been told about Shtoma.

A planet unaccountably close to its primary, a white dwarf, yet environmentally anomalous: Earth-sized, temperate, with the wrong atmosphere. With incredible potential for economic power, yet with no armed forces, which ignored the rest of the Dispersal of Man, the galactic authority—leading inexorably to the heretic suspicion of utopia! He began walking. It was not the Inquest's way to arrive conspicuously, gaudy with the trappings of salvation.

But then a stranger stood in his path, unmoving. An oldish man, clad severely in a brown tunic; clearly a peasant or slave. He was looking at the ground, and Davaryush had come quite close to him.;

The stranger looked up at Davaryush and sang, in a clear tenor, the first alien words he had heard since his arrival, words he was to hear so many times on Shtoma:

qithe qithembara
udres a kilima shtoisti.

Davaryush signalled to his polyglot implant, then closed his eyes to see, as though inscribed on a white page before him, the words

"soul, renounce suffering;
you have danced on the face of the sun."

It appeared to be a form of greeting. But the strange words, with their opaque and patently sinful meaning, strengthened his suspicions; and he approached the stranger diffidently. There was one other thing experience never banished: fear.

Activating his implant so that it would intervene in his speech functions, he said: "I am from another world. Who may I address?"

The alien's gaze chilled him, though it contained no malice. "You are Inquestor Davàryush, of the Clan of Ton. Welcome." Abruptly the stranger beamed and stretched out his arms to embrace Davaryush. The Inquestor yielded ungracefully. He had misjudged; this was no peasant. "We were expecting you."

"Yes. I come to investigate Shtoma's utopian possibilities, so that it may be considered for the honor of being named a Human Sanctuary." Davaryush did not blush at the lie, for it came easily to him by now.

"So! How delightful." His eyes laughed themselves into a hatchwork of wrinkles. "I am your host, Ernad. You must be weary; come."

Who was this man, poorly dressed and without a single attendant, who dared to address a Master Inquestor by name and who knew his mission? Again the alienness of the world unnerved him. The clouds had parted to reveal the white dwarf unnaturally close. The rough wind tousled the grass, blood-red and tall. He started to answer Ernad, but the old man had turned, expecting Davaryush to follow him.

A stony path, pebbled with shiny stones, led to the first recognizably human artifact: a displacement plate, metallic and incongruous in the middle of the field. He was unprepared for this. He was forced to remind himself that this was no primitive world—in spite of the absence of war or, apparently, slavery. "When can I begin my investigation? The Inquest must know soon, in time for the Grand Convocation," he said.

Ernad beckoned Davaryush onto the plate. "Frankly, we have so little involvement with the worlds outside—" he began, then stopped himself. "Well, as you wish; whenever you wish." Davaryush was suspicious of the warmth in his voice, but it appeared convincing. Clearly he was dealing with a master of ambiguity. But the impropriety and unashamedness of "little involvement" compounded his bewilderment.

They materialized in what appeared to be one of the structures he had glimpsed during the landing.

He reeled with the vertigo of it—the crazy swirlings and spiralings of transparent walls, the cacophony of chimings and chirpings that bombarded his senses. How could they live amid such a wilderness of sensual stimuli? Where was their discipline, their culture? A woman nearly ran into him, then trotted away, laughing, children and young people sauntered by, gaily calling out "qithe qithembara; udres a kilima shtoisti!" completely without respect. "You must forgive them," said Ernad, interrupting his dismay. "You are an off-worlder, and...well, it is especially exciting for them now. It is almost time for the festival of Initiation, and anything can spark their enthusiasm." He said this matter-of-factly, with no trace of criticism in his voice, again pointing up his alienness.

"They are your attendants?" Surely someone important enough to be his host would have servants of a kind.

"No; neighbors, relatives, friends. My house is theirs."

But Davaryush was thinking: what of the initiation ceremony? Perhaps that was the flaw. Perhaps there was some unspeakable rite, some trauma they were all forced to go through...perhaps this would be the handle he could use to save this misguided people.

"Ernad, I must rest," he said. "But after, I would see everything on your world: your games, your pleasures, your prisons, your criminals, your asylums, your places of execution."

"Ah. Yes, I have heard of madmen and criminals. I am not uneducated, Inquestor Ton," replied Ernad mysteriously. They turned down a corridor of glass that swerved upwards into the air, and Davaryush felt a sudden dislocation, as though he had changed weight or *down* had become sideways, and he found they were walking upside down, on the ceiling. "What is happening?"

Ernad laughed mildly. "It is the same principle, you know, as the varigrav coasters. You must have seen them, our principal export—"

"Buy why fool around with gravity inside your dwellings?"

"Why not? Would you not be bored, if all directions remained constantly the same...?"

Up became *down* again. They reached a large chamber that seemed to be perched, precariously, on the point of a translucent pyramid in the sky. "Your resting place. It is my own chamber, Inquestor; I trust you will find it comfortable."

Davaryush's eye alighted on the only adornment of the room, apart from the resting-pad. It was a huge, capelike sheet of some sheer material that hung on one wall, like a rainbow sail, rippling softly in the ventilating breeze. It was beautiful, he conceded, but bewilderingly complex, uncivilized. "This cape? What is it for?"

"Oh. My wings," Ernad said.

Davaryush knew then how addicted they must be to the varigrav coasters, those toys they had inflicted on the rest of the galaxy. And he looked at the old man, who seemed utterly ingenuous, and wondered if it were possible that this sincerity were not, after all, the product of a trained deviousness, but merely a product of his lower mentality.

For here was a toy, hanging on the wall as though it were a god.

"Leave me, Ernad," he said brusquely.

He was trying to establish authority, the distancing proper for an Inquestor. He needed to preserve his mask of sternness, for he was already sad. He was vulnerable, he realized, even after twelve successful missions.

For he was nothing if not compassionate.

You have compassion, Davaryush.

"Yes, Father." He was twelve years old, veteran of three wars, and now an initiate. And alone, in the small room, with the Inquestor, whose eyes glared fire and millenial wisdom. Now after more than two centuries, the scene returned, vivid.

When you came to kill the condemned criminal, you did not torture him or play with him, as was your right, an essential part of the initiation. You killed him cleanly, in a matter of seconds, slicing him into two congruent parts with your energizer. It was artistically done. But why?

"Father, it was necessary to show skill, not cruelty. I have already killed many people." He feigned an assurance that was

22

far from his true feelings.

Very well. I name you to the Clan of Ton.

Davaryush started, gasped audibly despite his knowledge of proper conduct...he had come expecting to fail, to be returned to homeworld. The Clan of Ton...that would mean seminary, long lonely years on harsh, inhospitable planets, unwelcome, thankless labor for the sake of pure altruism. "Father—"

You are unworthy. I know. Nevertheless, the Inquest takes what it can get.

His first mission was the planet Gom, a hot planet of a blue-white star. The people lived in tall buildings, thousands to a building, fifteen billion to the planet. But they were happy. They were quite ignorant of their responsibilities as a fallen race; reliant on automata, they pursued their hedonistic existence without regard for their true natures. They suffered from the heresy of utopia.

He remembered how he found the flaw to that utopia. Every year, in a special ceremony marked by compulsive gratifications of the senses, all those over the age of fifty intoxicated themselves and then committed suicide, leaping by thousands into the volcanic lava lakes that boiled ubiquitously on every continent.

He had saved them. Whispering to only one or two: *And what if you did not die?* he had created civil wars, revolutions, unhappiness. People ran mad, setting fire to the machines that had succored them. Then the ships of the Inquest came, bringing comfort with them, comfort and truth.

But the happiness had tempted him. *Remember, man is a fallen creature, Davaryush. Utopias exist only in the mind, a state to which it is given us to aspire. But to imagine we have attained that state—that is to deny life. The breaking of joy is the beginning of wisdom.*

Now he was no longer tempted. For he had seen such as the planet Eldereldad, where the happy ones feasted on their own children, which they produced in great litters, by hormonal stimulation; and the planet Xurdeg, his most recent mission, where the people smiled constantly, irritatingly, showing no face except the face of rapt ecstasy, until he finally learned that the penalty for grief was dismemberment, to feed the hungry demands of the degenerating bodies of five-thousand-year-old patriarchs...yet when he had asked one of these ancients, what he most desired, he had replied: *To feel grief. But I am afraid to die for it.*

Ton Alkamathdes, Grand Inquestor of his Sector, who had watched his initiation and had chosen him out for the Clan of

Ton, had said to him that day when he was a young boy facing his new destiny: *Never forget the lie. This lie is the sacrifice that you must make, the little sin that you must commit, for the sake of saving countless millions. The lie is this: the Inquest is seeking a perfect utopia, a planet that will be designated a Human Sanctuary, for the edification and glory of the Dispersal of Man. You will tell them that always, and always you will understand in your heart that there will exist one tragic flaw.*

And always, the ships of the Inquest would follow him. And after, in a year or two, or perhaps a few decades, they would awake to their true natures, and they would fight wars and exhibit avarice and pitilessness, like all the other worlds. Man is a fallen being.

Remember: you are a guardian of the human condition. He felt the eyes of Ton Alkamathdes on him, even two centuries away and countless parsecs, boring into his soul, purifying him; and in their sternness he drew a kind of comfort. But then he awoke, long before dawn, and was on Shtoma and frighteningly alone, exposed to the alien sky under the structures of glass and clear plastics. He found a young girl singing to him, "*qithe qithembara,* Lord Inquestor."

He sat up abruptly, reaching for a nonexistent weapon. "Who are you?"

"I am Alk, daughter of Ernad." (The voice haunted his thoughts for many days, reminding him of the whispering sea on homeworld.) "Will you be pleased with me? Of all the children who saw you, I was most taken by you, Inquestor."

They were depraved, shockingly amoral! They sent their own children to sleep with strangers! "No!" he cried out, and the severity of his own emotion startled them both. "On our worlds we do not do things like this."

"But father said to show you our love, the love of *udara.*"

Udara? (Their name for the dwarf star, their sun, whispered his polyglot implant. Again he was puzzled.)

"Leave me, please." He tried to exclude the pain from his voice. Shame flooded him. In the starlight he saw disappointment on her face, and thought: they do not even hide their emotions! what savages, what innocents! And without a further word she rose and left him, noiseless as a breeze.

Quickly he ran through what he had learnt in those few hours. They dressed severely, denying all rank and pomp and self-importance; they made curious fetish of their wings, they were morally loose, they did not make any effort to conceal their feelings, but were like children, wholly innocent of the need for

24

tact and diplomacy—and this last thing, the love of *udara*. That could mean anything. Every perversion, every practice of perversion was possible, because of the human condition.

And, under the strange constellations, knowing that he had no weapons and that he could not know when he would be rescued, he began to recite the first prayer he had ever learnt. Its meaning, for its language was no longer spoken, was a sublime mystery to the Inquest, but all who went through the seminary could repeat it, as a solace, in times of emotional turmoil. The nonsense words—perhaps little more than gibberish distorted by man's long history—were a kind of bond between the members of the Inquest, all solitary men: "pater noster, qui es in inferno...."

"But—what is *in* these black boxes? I have seen several during my stay here," Davaryush demanded of the heretic priest.

The white-bearded old man—a magnificent mottlement of wrinkles and discolorations, without the common decency of cosmetics—smiled beneficently at him. "*Udara*," he said. "*Udara* is in them."

"Will you not touch it?" the priest said, beckoning to him. The temple's black box—it was perhaps a meter square—stood in the center of the transparent hall which could have held ten thousand people without any trouble. It was the only object in the chamber. "Come, touch; you will feel *udara*."

Hesitantly, Davaryush went up to it with his hand outstretched. He felt wobbly-kneed, as though his weight were constantly shifting, as though he were losing control of his limbs. Gingerly, he brushed the cool metal with his fingertips.

Overwhelming joy coursed through his thoughts for a moment. He saw homeworld fleetingly, and ached for it, heard the music of the sea, saw vividly the faces of his parents, whom his own time dilation had stranded in an unreachable past...they smiled at him, he was a child half their height, reaching up to touch their faces, laughing....

And snatched away his hand as though he had been burnt. This was dangerous, clearly some powerful hallucinogenic device. He stared at his hand in terror.

The happiness he had just felt echoed in his mind. He was tempted to reach out again, and he controlled himself with tremendous difficulty, and knew he had stumbled upon one of the key clues to what was wrong with Shtoma.

They were self-deluders, obviously, intoxicating themselves with false memories and artificially induced joys.

"Did you not feel the love of *udara*, stranger?"

"No, priest. I felt—I remembered something I thought I had lost forever." He turned to leave.

"You do not wish for more? Ah, but you have not danced on the face of the sun."

He turned again, saw the look of pity in the priest's face, the expression of *ah, but you are incapable of understanding.* So he walked hurriedly out, not bothering to acknowledge the priest's hearty "*qithe qithembara.*"

Ernad was waiting for him, and the girl Alk, who was—by daylight—a creature of striking beauty, not in her facial features but in the way she moved and spoke; and another of Ernad's children, Eshly, a little boy of about six, who prattled and asked questions as though he were much younger, and was quite devoid of discipline. They walked on to the next displacement plate: Ernad smiling, the girl and her brother running excitedly, then lagging behind, Davaryush moody. Ernad told him more about the Shtoikitha, the people of the dance (and they called their planet Shtoma, *Danceworld.*)

"Yes, we're a very thinly populated planet, only half a million souls...what do we eat? There is fruit in the forests, small animals too, crustacea of fantastical shapes in the rivers; we don't have agriculture here. The fruit of the *gruyesh* falls to the ground and ripens, and when it turns mauve we tap it for the *zul*, that mildly fermented sweet juice that you drank this morning...."

"Crime?"

"Why should anyone commit it?" Ernad laughed gently. "We have *udara*, you see, so it isn't necessary."

"I don't understand. My polyglot implant translates that word simply as "sun"; but I have heard it in at least a dozen meanings since I came to Shtoma. I know that semantics aren't perfect, but could I be missing something? You can't tell me that your people, in all their evident complexity, attribute all your fortunes to some mythical property of your sun!"

Davaryush was exasperated now. It was becoming a strain to maintain his investigator's pose. Clearly the problem on this planet had to do with some fundamental misunderstanding of the workings of the universe.

They had come to a small clearing, having vanished and rematerialized several times: it was level, dotted with pink shrubs...the two children, or rather the young woman and the boy, had run forward, breathless, and had collapsed, exhausted, on the grass...*by now, they would both be warriors, in the real world,* he thought. How sad, that they were trapped in a permanent preadolescence.

26

The boy he felt compassion for: he was like a retarded child who is nevertheless extremely beautiful. But Ernad was talking again.

"Still you don't see, you don't comprehend the elegant simplicity of it. Relax! Feel the singing in the sky: one cannot commit evil here."

He tried to feel, sensing, in the absurdity of the old man's beliefs, some core of faith that he would never be able to alter... the soft susurrant rustlings of the red forests sang to him, but in their singings was mingled, chillingly, an image of homeworld... he tensed, instinctively, knowing he was playing with fire.

"Have you ever ridden a varigrav coaster?"

"No!" The thought horrified him. Abandonment to the senses, to utter helplessness! Never would he....

"It is a pity. What *did* you feel, when I asked you to listen to the music of *udara?*"

(Again, some obscure semantic twist.) "I don't know. A memory. It doesn't matter."

"On the contrary; it probably *does* matter. But you will learn at the initiation ceremony, perhaps."

"I am to take part?" Nothing would induce him to take part in any barbarian rite! Why, he might be mutilated, he might have to watch some unspeakable evil...but Ernad smiled the smile that excluded him from those who understood, frustrating him even more. "*Udara* is the key to what you are searching for, you know. Without it, this world would surely not be the paradise it has become."

"Why, that's ridiculous."

The two children of his host had come up and were watching him intently. "Father," said the boy Eshly, "don't be hard on the poor man."

He was so naive, so tactless, so ignorant! But Alk only looked at him, knowing what had passed between them in the night. (He knew now that no stigma was attached to sexual promiscuity; an expression of affection, nothing more. Finally, he had had to concede that this in itself was no flaw.)

"I must show you—" Ernad began.

"Take him to the nearest varigrav coaster, *please*, Father," Eshly cried urgently. He clasped Davaryush's hand—such presumption in a stripling, such undeserved trust—and propelled him toward the nearest displacement plate.

And in an instant they were at the edge of a cliff, sheer and blindingly white, that stretched perhaps half a kilometer down to a cleared and endless plain, without the pink of vegetation. The

plate where they had arrived stood in the shadow of a tremendously tall column of the transparent building material they used.
It was slender—the width of a few men, and it reached up to
vanish somewhere in the vague loftiness of the clouds that hid
udara from view then. This was nothing like the varigrav
coasters he had seen, children's pleasure things. This was over-
poweringly stark, and huge, a quasi-religious luminousness
emanated from it. Its vastness distorted the scale of everything,
so he felt a crazy disorientation, while the two children, in
nonchalant irreverence, were pushing him to the other side,
shouting at him to hurry.

"Quick, come, Inquestor!" shouted Eshly. A lift platform was
descending for them. Turning to watch the sky beyond the cliff,
Davaryush saw black dots and smudges, microscopic in the
expanse of sky and white plain, and he knew what they were. An
ancient fear petrified him, he was like a robot as they buckled
him in to the elevator. Suddenly, with a wild jerk, they were aloft,
racing up to the starting point in the clouds, and the rushing blood
in his brain crashed against the rushing of the mad winds. He was
nauseated; he closed his eyes and muttered his ancient prayer,
longing for an end.

At the top there was a sort of control room, diving platforms
of various sizes, racks where sets of wings were set out, not the
rainbow-colored type that adorned his resting-room, but plain
ones, black or gray. Alk and Eshly each seized a set of wings and
had run to the platforms and leapt off the edge while Davaryush
fought a wild impulse to go to their rescue.

He saw them in the air, falling, falling with dizzying speed,
and soon they had vanished—and then he saw them again, flung
violently upward by the interplay of differing gravity fields,
screeching with delight as the varigravs hurled them into
turbulent whirlpools, and the wind, which was pulled in so many
different directions that it was a distended, distorted tornado
blasting his ears. He found himself clutching the railings in terror,
he who had seen nine wars.

But the squeals of pleasure became fainter. The two became
black dots, joining the rapidly shifting patterns of swirling
specks in the distance. It was more tolerable to look at, pretty
patterns against the sky, but when he thought about what was
happening to them (gravity fields wrenching them in different
directions, stretching their bodies' tolerance to its very limits,
how could anyone find it pleasurable?) he—

"Please, take me out of this."

"As you wish."

They went into the control room. They shut out the roaring of the winds and the silence shocked him for a moment, before he gathered his analytic senses enough to look around him.... It was an empty room, like all the others he had seen on Shtoma, domed in the standard material, so that *udara* shone relentlessly inside, with a half-dozen of the black boxes predictably scattered, haphazardly, across the floor.

"I'm impressed." Davaryush tried to sound sincere. "How does it all work, incidentally?" He labored a little over the casual tone of this question, since finding out the secret would make a great difference to the other civilized worlds.

"The scientific principle, or the technical aspects?" Davaryush was startled for a moment by the man's willingness to reveal.

"Both."

"Well, you know as well as I do that gravity control works by selective graviton exchange...the coaster also manufactures antigravitons, which exist of course only with some difficulty under normal conditions."

"But how *do* you manufacture antigravitons?" Davaryush was excited; uncautiously he let it slip through, was not devious enough in asking the question. Ernad seemed not to be aware of such things.

"I'm simply not a scientist," he said—he did not sound at all as if he was trying to put Davaryush off—"and in any case *udara* controls details like that." He pointed happily to the boxes.

Again the evasive tactics, the semantic deceptions! If the people of Shtoma were able to lie with such easy naturalness, perhaps Shtoma had never been a logical candidate for utopiahood. Perhaps his journey had been wasted.

But the Grand Inquestor had entrusted him, and the Inquest was wise.

He saw the children returning, swung upwards in a golden arc that transected *udara* through the shimmering cloud banks....

"Time to go home. It will be night." Ernad motioned to his guest. "I hope you will feel more comfortable this time, and not be so afraid of the height."

The black boxes glinted in the *udara*-light. They attributed everything to those boxes, Davaryush thought. Was there something in it? Of course not. They were lying to him, creating some enormous joke at his expense.

Walking home through the ruddy terrain, Ernad told him how everybody on Shtoma participated in the initiation ceremonies every five years, almost to a man, because those who had been through it once could be renewed, purified. "You will understand everything, you know, once you have taken part—the black boxes, the *udara*-concepts. I know that you find us strange." He chuckled to himself, then added earnestly, "You will take part, won't you?"

Slowly, with the realization that he might well be falling into a trap, a trap cleverly constructed upon his own curiosity and on the necessities of his mission, he said: "I have no choice." For his mission was to understand, and after understanding to control. Even now, compassion touched him, more than ever before.

The accident happened.

Eshly, the boy, had run on ahead to the next displacement plate. He tripped and stumbled, face down, and the power surged. They were upon him, the resounding clang echoing in the woods. The three of them knelt down by the plate.

He lay like a discarded toy. The displacement field had aborted—it was an accident that practically never occurred, was almost unthinkable—and had wrenched half his body away and then slung it back in a nanosecond, so that he was in one piece, but impossibly bent.

Davaryush waited for the tears, for the signs of grief. But the only sighing was the breeze and the voices of the alien forest. Lightfall was ending.

"Go on, Alk," Ernad whispered to his daughter, "the others will want to know." His voice was icy calm.

Davaryush stood to follow as he lifted up the corpse, which seemed merely asleep until one saw the inhuman angle of the arms, and carried it into the encroaching forest, and returned without it, with the red shadows darkening him. There seemed to be no sadness in his face. Indeed, he almost smiled. Was this some incredible fortitude, even in the face of an impossible tragedy? Davaryush devoured the man with his eyes, seeking some clue to his emotions. And he thought, *I have found the flaw.*

And now it was time to plant the doubt, because the lowest point in a man's being is also the beginning of his ascent. Davaryush thought bitterly: here is a people that blithely throws the bodies of its sons into the forests to rot, that has forgotten grief, that does not value human life at all. Here was the flaw.

Davaryush tried to put a lot of anger into his voice, to exclude compassion while not striving too much for an oracular effect: "You don't care about your child," he said. "Love is not part of your utopia, is it? Humanity is what you have abandoned, isn't it?" *Now you are going to break down. Now your repressed humanity will come rushing to the surface.* It had happened twelve times before, and countless other times with the Inquestors.

Ernad did not collapse. He stared at Davaryush with unmitigated pity.

"Of course I grieve for him. I am desolate, Davaryush. But you do not understand our perspectives, or our overview of life. With renewal my grief will be cleansed. And I grieve for him most, that he did not live to dance on the face of the sun."

And Davaryush knew that he had understood nothing at all, nothing. Never had he felt so palpably the alienness of this world, the total incommunicableness of it. His mind whirled in a wild kaleidoscope of images: strange winds, blood-crimson forests with spider arms, flagrantly immodest buildings open to the elements, a dead child unmourned, a dead child who had been playing games amidst the incomprehensible forces of black boxes that manipulated gravity fields...and this strange man's face, which should be racked with sorrow, yet insulted him with an unwanted pity. *I wish I could kill him.*

The death-impulse rose in him, a monster of the subconscious, and he suppressed it with a superhuman effort. *He is a product of his misguided culture, not to be blamed,* he reminded himself. *I have come to save him; I must never forget that; even if I cause his death, I come as a savior.*

He had miscalculated again. Thinking to elicit from the stranger his hidden guilt, his dormant human responses, he had instead forced his own desire to kill to the surface. This desire should long have been dead, since he had renounced it for the sake of the salvation of the Dispersal of Man; yet it haunted him still, a specter from the buried past. Perhaps the will of the man was stronger than his....

At last he found he could feel a bond between himself and the alien, in this moment of deepest misunderstanding. For they were both men, both fallen beings.

"Ernad," said Davaryush, "I pity you." The two of them walked, through the miscolored landscape, up to the twisted house.

Asleep that night, he was nine years old, celebrating the end of his first war.

And they came to Alykh, the pleasure planet. He and Tymyon and Ayulla and Kyg and the other companions, lost themselves in the cacophony of the crowds.

"Wait till you see *this!*" Kyg shouted, and she leapt on to the plate like a cat. They disappeared—

And Davaryush saw it, a topless tower of brick and stone and concrete and plastic and sparkling amethysts, studding the walls like jewelled knuckle-dusters....

"What *is* it?"

"Daavye, don't you know *anything*?" Tymyon cackled offensively.

Kyg said, with mock primness: "It's a...VARIGRAV COASTER!"

The tower glinted oddly, catching the sunset. "Look," said Kyg impatiently, "you dive off the top, you see, and it sets into action a series of random gravity-field interferences, and you plummet like a hawk and you float upward and you swing dangerously and you curve and then you land where you started, like a feather."

("It's beautiful," whispered Ayulla the silent.)

"Well, let's GO!" Tymyon and Kyg raced each other to the tower, and the crowds were everywhere, aliens, child-warriors brandishing their weapons, pimps, crusader-flagellants, Inquestors and their retinues, slave-hunters, veiled Whisper-shadows from the borders of the Dispersal, dirty children strumming on dreamharps, dissonant alien musics, and an itinerant space opera howling full-blast through amplification jewels, and Davaryush was spellbound, unmoving.

He had never...

The tower held him.

And the little specks that were people, dust-motes in the violet sunset.

"Aren't you coming?" Ayulla's voice was almost lost in the confusion.

"No." He was petrified.

"Come *on!* They're all the rage now, all the way from Shtoma you know, from the limits of the Dispersal...."

"No! No!" (It was said that the greatest thrill, when you fell, was the very certainty of death, suddenly averted by a twist in the field. At the moment of inevitable doom, it was said, you felt so *alive*.)

Ayulla was laughing at him. "How many people have you killed, Daavye? How can you be so scared of *life*?"

(He was ashamed. He resolved, then, to change his circle of friends.) *

Now wake up. Face the hostile planet.

He moved, murmuring "Homeworld."

Shrill cries of children awakened him. And then Alk was at

the entrance to his room: "Initiation, Inquestor; hurry."

He threw on his shimmercloak. It tightened around him, sensing his need for warmth, though it was not cold.

The wings on the walls had gone.

The whole family, a dozen or more of them, trooped without ceremony into his room, heady exhilaration in their faces. Quickly he followed them outside, struggling to keep up with them. His heart had sunk when he saw that the wings had vanished. For he had an inkling, now, of what this rite must involve, and it terrified him.

Many displacements later, they were on a mountain top overlooking a vast plain that glittered silver-gray with a thousand spaceships. The ships littered the fields, end to end so that the red grass was quite covered, all the way to the horizon... he could not imagine what they were for. Shtoma had hardly any commerce with other worlds.

Isn't it breathtaking?" Alk grasped his arm, and he felt himself shivering....

"How many of them *are* there, Ernad?" he said, wonderingly. This ceremony involved a journey, it seemed; perhaps on some satellite, some other planet.

The children were dancing and tugging at him and hollering in circles round him, and Ernad did not seem disposed to answer his questions. "Come," he said, and after another displacement they were at the entrance to a ship. (It was much as he knew them; ships did not differ much, having been perfected many millennia ago, before the Dispersal.) But the number of them! And the mobs of people, their wings tucked under the arms, giggling, chattering away as they climbed into them!

In the mid-distance, some of them had already risen. They rose at even intervals, in perfect order, and he could see a long chain of them stretching into the sky, where they glittered like a jewelled necklace in the early lightfall. Quickly (almost shame-facedly) he stifled his wonder, for he knew he must analyze *everything*, if he was to solve the most taxing problem of his life, the enigma of Shtoma. So he climbed the steep steps into the belly of the ship.

It was only a small cruiser, built for perhaps five hundred; there must be a thousand of them, then, to hold the whole popu-lation of Shtoma. It was impersonal, gray-walled like every ship; and it appeared to be a short-hauler, so Davaryush knew they were not going off-system. People were filing into their chambers, seeming to know exactly where they belonged, Davaryush stood stupidly for a few moments before Alk came for him, and took him to the family's cabin.

After a while, he felt the noiseless lifting of the ship.

Some time later Ernad led him to the viewroom, whose screens afforded an unobstructed three hundred and sixty degree view of space; and he saw how the line of ships trailed behind and before, each an exact distance from the other, links in a metal serpent of space...he asked Ernad where they were going.

"To *udara,* of course!" The old man looked blankly at him.

"Not seriously."

"Are there any other planets in this system? Any moons? We are not a mendacious people, Davaryush; perhaps that has not occurred to you yet." He spoke patiently, as though reproving a favorite child, and the attitude stung Davaryush.

He turned to see, on the other side of the room, that *udara* had swollen and was a blindingly white flameball against the blackness. He knew by now that when the word *udara* came up he would get nowhere; so he tried something else. The ubiquitous black boxes were everywhere; in the viewroom they were stacked neatly in the middle of the floor.

"Those *udara*-boxes: they power the ship perhaps?" he said, only half-skeptical.

Ernad laughed again, enjoying his guest's ignorance. (Again Davaryush felt a bitter hate, a death-lust, for his host). "Not at all; they are quite empty, and our spaceships work in the normal way."

After a moment, he said: "Now look, Inquestor: they are darkening the screen, or else *udara* would become unbearable."

"How can you say we are going there!"

"Just look at the face of the sun. There, look."

Udara was growing rapidly, and Davaryush saw: "There's a black spot on the sun's surface!"

"*That's* where we are going."

The black dot was perfectly round. This was impossible. "It must be artificial!" he gasped. These people, far from being simple utopians, were capable of galaxy-dominating technological feats!

"Artificial? In a manner of speaking." Then he explained, "The dot of course is only black by comparison, obviously; when we get there it will appear white and incandescent."

The screen was cut in half! One side was completely black, the other painfully bright, and there were white flame-tongues that shot up, a hundred kilometers high. They were approaching the sun's atmosphere; in its heart, Davaryush knew, matter was packed into inconceivable density.

"And now...there are tablets you must take, since you will not be able to breathe for a few hours; they will release oxygen into your bloodstream."

"What do you mean?"

"You're going to jump into the sun."

Davaryush understood now. They had led him on, and all the time were preparing this elaborate fiery execution. "I'll vaporize instantly!" he said.

"You don't understand, do you?" Ernad countered with surprising vehemence. "Gravity is under control, heat is under control! This is no ordinary star, this is *udara*. Every five years, we all ride on the gravity-fields here, and become clean...."

Davaryush's mind reeled under the impact of this revelation. The sun filled the screen completely now, unbelievably white .·... "You mean that you *built* this star? You built a *varigrav coaster* on the surface of a *sun?*"

"If only we had the technology!" Ernad smiled a little. "Why, the mind boggles. You are so close to the answer, and yet so far, so incredibly far! Well, we are all bound by the limits of our experience. It is time to live; explanations will follow."

They were in the airlock, then; waves of nausea crashed in his head, and he stood stock-still like a martyr waiting for death (which he felt himself to be) while they put the wings on him and the tittering of the children pelted his brain like painful hail-pellets—

The airlock opened!

There was whiteness, such whiteness. He shut his eyes and fell.

Fell. Fell.

His blood was burning. He was burning, he was falling into hell, plummeting helplessly into the scorchswift firebreath of the sunwind. He screamed, he thrashed his body uselessly against emptiness, he opened his eyes and the whiteness shattered his vision, the featureless whiteness, so he screamed and screamed, until he was no longer aware of his screaming.

He heard voices out of the past (Kill the criminal Daavye no I can't I can't you have compassion my son compassion man is a fallen being).

He reached the limit of his falling. And soared! And was flung upwards, upwards, on an antigraviton tide! And swerved, and fell headlong again, and swooped in tandem with a tongue of flame, and his scream was a whisper in the thunder of the wind (come on Daavye you fool it's the latest craze no! are you afraid of life or something Daavye Daavye?) and fell and fell (pater noster qui es in inferno) and fell....

And soared! And caromed into the roaring flame! And fell. And saw death, suddenly, and came face to face with himself, and knew death intimately...and fell (Kill the criminal Daavye compassion compassion) and fell....

Trust me.

Falling, the voice embraced him. The voice sang through him. The voice made him tingle like a perfect harp-string, dispelling his terror in a moment. He was a nothing touched by love.

(Memories came like endless printouts but there was one memory on the verge of crystallizing, and he was waiting for it, waiting for it to come, clear as a presence—)

The voice was like homeworld. The roaring was the whisper of the sea. He could almost see his parents again: and fell and fell and was touched by love and fell and lost consciousness, becoming one with an ineffable serenity.

"Answers! I want answers!" He woke, sweating, in the room in the twisted house. Ernad was there, and the whole family; he felt their concern, and then he broke down and sobbed violently, hopelessly.

"I think we deserve some answers too, Ton Davaryush," Ernad said softly; there was iron in his gentleness. (He heard the others whispering among themselves: "When he came back to the ship, he was in a trance, unconscious." "He's been like this for weeks.")

"Now understand this, Davaryush," said Ernad, "you are not the first Inquestor to visit our planet. And will not be the last either."

Davaryush did what he never dreamed he would do: between fits of weeping, he told them the whole story, how he had come to Shtoma to save the people from themselves, how he had been defeated, how he understood nothing now, nothing at all.

(They fed him with sweet *zul* and were so kind to him. This, too, evoked a strange wonder and respect in him; for he had wanted to betray them.)

"Well, you were promised an explanation. Listen, then: *Udara* is no ordinary star. Of course we didn't build him: that's ridiculous. But—do you know anything about the origins of sentience? Well, you know how life evolves: how certain arrangements of atoms, certain paradigms, created purely by chance interactions, you understand, becoming living beings, self-aware, sometimes...white dwarfs are created by incredible cataclysms, by a star going nova, dying...somehow, a spark of life was made, after the nova, and *udara* became self-aware. *Udara* is alive, Davaryush! and we have acquired a symbiotic relationship with him that permits us to exist in the scientifically anomalous state...do you follow? In the black boxes, Davaryush: pieces of the sun."

Davaryush lay back, stupefied, his thought fired by the incredible imagery of it.

"Did you imagine that mere people like we could create and uncreate gravitons and anti-gravitons? How much power is available, without the resources of a star? Could we make and unmake gravitational fields? Could we dim the sunlight on one area of the sun, so as to be unharmed by its heat? *Udara* does this, by his own will; his knowledge of physical laws is several orders beyond our understanding. We think that he is aware of himself, not only in this four-dimensional continuum, but also in other continua."

"But with this power," Davaryush said, "with this sun to do your bidding, can't you conquer the galaxy, win wars?"

"You still don't understand! The sun does not do our bidding; the sun does all this because he *loves* us." (Davaryush remembered, suddenly, how love had touched him when he was plummeting towards death.) "You felt it in the sunlight. You would always have felt it, but you were so full of confusion and contradiction, and so many people had lied to you...but when you fell into the sun, when you danced on the sun's face, then you understood. You see, we can't commit evil, because in the act of dancing—what the rest of humanity thinks of as our little children's game—we have partaken of a tiny fragment of his nature....

"But let me plant a doubt in *your* mind. That is what you came to do to us, isn't it? Well: what if the Inquest existed, not for salvation, but for destruction? What if its sole purpose were to perpetuate its leaders' desire for conquest, and its mouthpieces, the "Inquestors," were simply indoctrinated with pseudoreligiousness to make them more fanatical, more serviceable?..."

And Davaryush knew that he had lost his faith. (He wondered what answer he would give them about Shtoma. It would probably be unsatisfactory; they would undoubtedly have to send another Inquestor. But he no longer cared what the Inquest thought.)

Finally there came a day when Alk came running in to him, breathlessly: "Your tachyon bubble, it's hovering above the house!"

He stepped outside. The sun shone on him, bathing him with

inexpressible joy.

Suddenly the memory came to him, the memory that was just beginning to come to him, before he became unconscious—

He was six years old. The ship was waiting to take him to the war. He was standing there with his father, by the sea shore, and his father seized him, on impulse, and threw him into the air, and he screamed for help, half-laughing, and fell for an eternity, into the arms that were for him, for protecting him, for loving him.

At last he understood the love of *udara.*

...But the children of the house had come and were clustered around him, making much of him, and Ernad stood at the entrance, waving to him.

"*Qithe qithembara!*" he yelled frantically, forcing back his tears—

He took one more step towards the bubble.

You have danced on the face of the sun.

                                                              —*Arlington, 1978*

A Child of Earth
and Starry Heaven

   Do you know those decks of cards that have heads, middles, and
bottoms, and you can shuffle them up and stick a pig's head on a
ballerina's torso, and so on? This story is a bit like that: imagine, if you
will, Bergman's The Seventh Seal intermixed with The Bad News
Bears, and you begin to get an idea of the demented genesis of this
movie.

   Despite the rather flippant attitude I'm taking here, though, I'd have
to say that it's not ultimately that flippant a story. I'm very scared of
death, myself; in this story I tried to deal with it as a child might, to take
away some of its sting.

we know that death is evil
if death were good
the gods themselves would die
                    —Sappho

what? death has a sense of humor?
              —Euripides, Alcestis

When I think back to the year when I was twelve and we all skipped school and rode the rails all over Europe with the parents muttering on about value-readjustments and expanding our experiential cosmos—

I see Dad, farting to death on the Athens-Paris Express. And the crammed air getting stinkier and stinkier, and the fields of Yugoslavia unreeling like a sickly-green clothroll, and I hear Mom's knit-knit-knitting. And Sophie too, knit-knit-knitting like a wee color Xerox, them with their black hair bunned up and their dresses faded green floral prints and Sophie with those pink shreds of leftover yarn juryrigging her pigtails....

I'm a hell of a lot older now, and I've read books that tell you how the light falls on the ruins at Sounion and stuff like that. Yah. Jesus. I saw it. It wasn't like that at all. It was—think of the sky as a bright blue safe dropping from a cosmic skyscraper. That's the thing I remember. The ruins...take 'em or leave 'em. But the sky and then the mists at Delphi in the dawn. Creepy. Oh, Greece, Greece, Greece. I'm going to go back.

After Greece the world got sick. I mean, Dad got sicker and sicker and I knew that dying wasn't anything like in *Love Story*. It's as glamorous as a garbage can in the Bronx.

It's nervousness. It's wondering how tactless you can get. It's sitting in nonsmoking compartments in cramped European trains and not daring to get up and leave because he'll think you don't love him. It's the fart that makes you cry.

And it was so inconvenient. Because that year I was

supposed to be at home and practicing to be a hitter for the whatever team I wanted to be a hitter for at the time even though I couldn't hit worth shit. And my world was falling in ruins all around me as we traipsed like demons from hotel to *demi-pension* to inn to YMCA to sleeping cars.

It was so hard to believe he *was* dying. Dad looked like a seedy stevedore from Naples—which is just what *his* Dad was—but in real life he was Professor Emilio Caro and taught comparative lit at some college round the corner and had a string of PhD's that stretched all the way from Cambridge, Massachusetts, to Cambridge, England. Yah. In the compartment he'd have the whole of the seat that was facing the way the train was going all to himself so he could stretch out. And he'd erupt now and then like a noisy volcano spewing brimstone. When he was better he'd sit back and pontificate. It was like that all the way through Yugoslavia.

Mom was Greek and just beautiful. I look a lot like her, but I'm just wiry and muscly enough to look cute and not faggy. If she didn't wear those shabby clothes, and if she didn't sit there just knitting, her eyes downcast, not even noticing her four-year-old daughter's awkward mimicking...I always changed my clothes every few hours. I was compulsive about it. And frankly, I was scared because of all the fart gas, thinking it might have germs. It's so hard to be afraid of being near your own father.

The train wasn't like Amtrak. No way. There were these corridors down the side and individualized compartments with seats like the sofas you donate to the Salvation Army.

When I could—like pretending to go to the bathroom—I'd stalk the corridors. I'd lean out of the windows until I almost fell out or until the guard caught me or until the krauts from the next compartment came out to jabber and smoke. They always treated me like I wasn't there. Well, I was a kid. I was used to shoving off.

A couple hours from the Austrian border and we'd just trundled past one of those Hollywood villages, a little grimier than the brochure, and I was leaning out again and thinking about Greece and baseball and death—

Like, you know, Greece and death. There was this play we saw at Epidauros, there was this drama festival there...it was called *Alcestis* and it was by Euripides. There was this guy Admetos, see, who'd gotten Death to agree to let him off if he could find someone else to buy it in his place. So he got his own wife. Then his friend Heracles (that's Hercules to you philistines) came visiting just in time for the funeral, and he got so mad that he went down to the underworld and wrestled Death to the ground (just like those FBI agents. Yah.) So they all got off scotfree. That was a weird idea and it gave me a nightmare at the hotel. With Dad dying and all. They wore these masks and their voices came echo-howling round and round the enormous arena and the mask for Death was worse than something out of *The Exorcist*....

And baseball? Well. There was this kid called Chet Perkins the Pumpkin who pitched for the Annandale Coca-Cola Tomcats or something. He was (as Dad said in a more lucid moment) "querulous, belligerent, beady-eyed and hirsute." (I wrote it down. Dad's pontifications were pretty damn funny sometimes, when you forgot he was on the verge of croaking.) When he got on the field he turned into a blubbery Baryshnikov, though, and so when he beaned me I knew it was no accident. Next season I was going to bust the Pumpkin into a gooey pulp. So what if they sent me off the field.

Well—I had my head in the wind and my hair was all tangled and dusty and billowing and I was pressed hard against the train and the chugchugging and it felt, you know, sexy....

I felt a stab in the ribs and nearly fell out.

"Don't do that, dummy!" I gasped.

"Mommy wants you back, Jody."

"Sophie-"

"Yeah, I know. I'm a pain in the ath," she chirped sweetly. I slid the door panel open and watched the point of light whisk across the peeling varnish....

"I'm here, Mom." They'd been fighting.

I could tell by the tongue-bitten pent-up smile that froze on Mom's face. I could tell by Dad's staring fixedly out of the window as if the telegraph poles were lines of Dante or pictures of naked women. And the smell hit me hard.

"Yah, can I get Dad something?" I said.

"No. I just thought it'd be nice if we were all together, Jody," Mom said, and went on with her knitting.

In a few minutes Dad had fallen asleep, and the snorting and the farting began to syncopate with the chugging of the train like progressive jazz. Sophie suddenly conked out too. This travelling was a bit much for a kid like that sometimes. And the sun was setting ahead of us somewheres, making the meadows all eerie and bloody.

So it was just me and Mom awake then and I knew something was going to happen. I knew she was going to tell me something. We had a special thing going, me and Mom. Going to Greece had confirmed it somehow. Because...I had *recognized* everything there. I mean like the incredible blueness of the sky. I mean it knew it was the way things are meant to be, and that the smog over Brooklyn and even the sun shining through the palms in Florida...were just imitations. We'd lived in so many places and none of them had ever been home. And this was. Sophie and Dad—well, they were the wop contingent. I'm allowed to say that because *I'm* one, and I don't mean...oh shit.

"What were you fighting about?"

Mom said, "Do you remember Alcestis?"

"The play in Epidauros?"

"Uh huh." Knit-knit. And the sunset in her eyes. "What would you say if I took Dad's place?"

I started. "He'd never let you!" I said. She shushed me quickly and pointed to Dad, who was snoring and smiling in his sleep. "Well he wouldn't, would he?" I whispered. "Anyway you're just torturing yourself over it. Life isn't a play by Euripides, Mom."

"I guess."

"The man in the play was an asshole."

"I guess." Knit.

We didn't talk for an hour after that. I was really disturbed because she'd talked almost like it were possible to switch around and die instead of someone else. I tried to forget about it and sat there in the smelly dark, imagining myself batting the Pumpkin's pitches into his face and the blood spurting. Jesus. Yah.

So we got to the Austrian border and the train stopped for us to get our papers stamped, and then I had to help Dad go to the bathroom.

Well—this old man and this kid come charging out from a cubicle in the station and you know what they're thinking, those slimy Passkontrollebeamterscheissekopf characters with their glittertacky uniforms and pug faces.

Yah, dying isn't glamorous at all. I thought that all the way back to the compartment. It's dirty and disgusting and gross.

* * *

Later—we were stalled at the station for a couple of hours— me and Dad were talking on a bench together. He was wrapped in a gray fur coat even though it was the middle of night. He had his arm around me and I was uneasy. I remember the bench: one of the planks was missing from the seat and it had a green lacquery look in the harsh station lights....

"Dad," I said, "Mom just made a really weird suggestion." (I remembered the Greek chorus moving like dancing dolls across the proscenium...and Death's face. In the nightmare the face would jump up at me and stare me down. There were times when I saw the mask of Death almost emerging from behind Dad's face....)

"Your momma very weird, ragazzo," Dad said in his best spaghetti-sauce-commercial accent that always made me laugh, only I didn't; and then I was afraid his feelings would be hurt so I forced out a chuckle that choked me.

"But what exactly did she mean?" I said, persisting.

"Your mother's a witch, you know. Your grandad always tried to ward off the evil eye when she came to their house. At first. I thought she was going to stop all that—"

He looked at me and then stopped talking, as though he'd said too much. "What am I saying, ragazzo?" he said. "I shouldn't be sitting here badmouthing my own wife now, should I? Well I take it back. She's no witch...even though she thinks she is...but she's headstrong, strong-willed, wilfull, foolhardy."

"That was a clever thing to say, Dad," I said, filing it away.

"Verbal concatenations *are* cool, aren't they?" he said, taking a slug from one of those funny teeny continental Coke bottles. "Especially beginning each word with the previous final syllable...."

I hugged him. It was hard. It seemed like under the big coat there was nothing at all, an emptiness. It felt almost as though he were dissolving under the pressure of my arms. He handed me the bottle and I had to have some, even though it made me queasy.

A breeze whooshed over and lifted the stench a little. "So what did *you* think about Momma's proposal?" he said.

"Dad, you'd never let her anyway! I know you, Daddy! Admetos was an asshole."

Was it the glare from the overhead sodium arcs?

He wouldn't meet my eyes and I didn't want him to try.

* * *

The train rumbled into the dark night. It was our second night on the Express; Sophie and I shared one cabin of the sleeping car and Mom and Dad had one about four cabins down. We sat in 2nd Class in the daytime, understand...but with Dad sick we couldn't compromise about the sleeper.

Well, I couldn't sleep. The moon shone into the cabin which wasn't more than a cubbyhole, and I couldn't close the blinds because it was kind of a night light for Sophie. So I got down from the top bunk and changed my clothes a couple of times and washed my face and hands in the midget basin that only ran cold water, like I wanted to scrub every last germ into oblivion. I'd look into the mirror over the basin and comb my hair over and over. Finally I got out my baseball bat from the satchel and swung a couple of times, and then stuffed it back into the bag.

You'll never be any good, I told me, *in spite of the fancy aluminum bat and the spiffy satchel and the classy fifty dollar mitt that two months on an uphill paper route earned you.*

I went outside in a holey t-shirt and pyjama bottoms.

Mom was there. She was leaning out of the window the way I always did. That pleased me no end, that we had so much in common, even our secret pleasures.

I stood watching her for a while. She didn't know I was there and she was sort of moaning and talking to herself. It was in Greek and I don't know Greek except bad words like *skata.* For some reason the mask of Death came floating to the top of my mind. I choked it back but I must have cried out, because she saw me then. She said something to me, so softly I had to strain to hear anything above the patter of the train. I crept up closer to her.

She smelt sweet, like old oranges.

There was a full moon and it turned up the contrast on her, so her hair was like liquid coal and her face like chalk and her eyes like onyxes polished into cabochons. I could see her figure through the nightgown and I remember it was really firm and strong-looking, not like a forty-year-old woman's at all.

"It's time for me to tell you the family secret, Jody sweetheart," she said, so faintly that it was almost an overtone of the wind that the train made, "and about myths and truths."

"Sure, shoot," I said. I thought she just needed a quiet listener who wouldn't bug her; and I was good at that. Her husband was dying and I knew how it was.

Also, I was scared stiff and I was ready to listen to any kind of voice at all.

"Do you know why we went to Greece?"

"Sure," I said. "To see grandma and grandpa and the other Vlachapouloses and...well..." Jesus. I thought of the sky falling from the sky and the blue that was bluer than blue and I knew that was the real reason for me but I wouldn't ever be able to talk about it, not even with her.

"There was another reason," she said. "Okay. A lot of people think myths are just stories. They are, mostly—but they all come from somewhere. Did you know that my family claims descent from the royal house of Admetos?"

Suddenly I could hear my own heart pounding above the

train-roar, suddenly I knew I was shaking all over and—

She was saying, "It's not like in Euripides. That's just a distorted memory of the truth. There were things called Mysteries that only initiates knew about in those days, mostly mumbo-jumbo about symbolic death and rebirth: well, I'm a Priestess of the Mysteries."

"Dad said you were a witch!" I blurted out.

She laughed very lightly and I couldn't tell if it wasn't the rattle of a chain in the train or the clang of a distant shutter....
"Sure, baby. Italians are very superstitious."

She touched my cheek and her hand was ice cold. Or maybe I was burning with fear.

I heard her say, "Our family...and that includes you, and that's why you have to know this, because I'm going to go away, soon—" *I'm not hearing this* I thought *I'm not. I'm not.* "—our family has the blood of Admetos in its veins, we all have the power to cheat Death, to trade places with other people...because we understand Death. You can see Death whenever you want to, Jody, whenever you look into a mirror and stare, past your own face, into the face within...well, I've decided to do it."

"Dad'll never let you!" I said fiercely. "Admetos was an ass-hole! Nobody would let the person they love commit suicide—"
And I didn't believe it. I *couldn't* believe it.

And underneath I knew it was as true as the blue of the sky over the Cape of Sounion, as true as the mask of Death, as true as the morning mist that tendriled the broken columns at Delphi....

Yah. I'd stared at mirrors before.

I knew I carried Death inside me and I could will myself to face it. I knew that there were secret words that lay in my unconscious, spells that I could use. If the moment came.

I could hear her talking through the tumble of my heartbeat. She was saying how they'd made a mutual decision and how it was better for the kids otherwise she couldn't afford to send them to college on her earnings as a secretary—

She went on talking but it was the chattering of the train like teeth death rattle of wheels iron on iron chittering of unoiled chains thunder of the wind scream dinning in my head—

I made it to the cabin. I slid the door with a slam. I listened to myself breathing. Slower. Slower. Remote.

How could you do it, Dad? I wanted to bawl like a baby and nothing came. I glanced up and the mirror glared back, taunting. I turned to face the wall and it was metal and I saw my eyes reflected like ghost eyes eyes of Death and I squeezed them shut to shut off the eyes and plastered the blanket over my face and lay suffocating in the dark for the whole night, I couldn't sleep because I knew I'd dream and the mask would come for me—

* * *

Morning broke all at once. We were pushing through mountains and the train kept jerking to a halt and hauling slowly, off-rhythm...I found I'd been hugging my baseball glove like a teddy bear.

I took Sophie over to the dining car. We passed the parents' cabin and I walked very quickly. They'd opened the windows and the air smelled of drifting leaves and cold showers. We found a table with a white starchy tablecloth and a plastic vase with a pink rose, half-wilted.

I was facing the wrong way and I was uneasy. But I tried to pretend like there was nothing wrong. For Sophie's sake.

"*Zwei Apfelsaft,*" I said to the waiter. "*Spiegeleier. Speck.*" I pointed to the places on the menu, worn as an old papyrus under the slimy plastic cover, because I knew I'd pronounced it all wrong.

The waiter mumbled something I didn't catch. *Ah well,* I thought, *he has an Austrian accent.* The train was running more smoothly now; a soft pink dawn played over us across the rose-tinted peaks....

I saw Dad in the doorway. A smell of stale apples.... He stood there without moving. The coat was gone. He was wearing fresh clothes. Something was wrong.

"Dad—"

"Jesus, Mary and Joseph," he said—not in the funny accent—"she's done it, I can't think—" He started crying. I'd never heard that before. It didn't sound real. It sounded like the squeaking of the train wheels—

I got up. I was angry. I was hot all over. I stomped over to him. He looked healthy as hell and I thought his crying was phoney and I wished he were dead. He was an asshole just like in the play. I stared up at him and I knew I was scaring him.

"I don't know how you managed to do it," I said. Quietly. "I used to think you were God sometimes, you with your clever colorful phrases and all. But you made her die. Maybe you can live with it. Fuck you."

He'd stopped crying now and his eyes looked like stone. He just gaped at me. "Ragazzo," he said, "God damn it, we need each other now. We made a logical decision, it was all for you kids, we weren't thinking about anything else. Christ, do you think I feel supercool about this or something?"

"Why should I comfort you? I'm your kid, not your mother!" I yelled. Then I pushed past him and went running to their cabin and pulled the door open.

Their cabin was a mirror image of mine; they made them back to back to save on rivets. The walls were metal like ours. The bunks—

I saw her on the lower bunk. She wasn't dead yet. She was still breathing. But something had gone from her. Even though it was broad daylight now the contrast was still turned up on her, as though a different light, a moon-drenched pale light, shone over her....

The white face hid a hint of sky blue.

"Mom," I whispered.

I bent over to kiss the closed eyes. I felt them tremble a little. Then I turned around and saw the mirror over the basin—

You know how in the old days they stuck a mirror over your face to see if your were still alive? They're always doing that in Sherlock Holmes movies....

—breath stains frosting the glass so I could only just see my own face blurring and melting—

(Behind the frost, the train purred past mountains softly furred with green. The brightness hurt. I went and drew the shutters.)

I stared into the mirror. I stared at it angry, because I'd never been angrier in my life. Dad had done the wrong thing. You don't let people die in your place. I wasn't thinking about our family's future and how hard they must have fought over it. I just knew it was wrong.

—the frosting shifted, unfocused, shifted—

My own irises through the mist. Alien. Cold.

I knew she was going fast. In a few hours the spell would be one way. And I was starting to know other things too. I was starting to remember things. Words were welling up behind the dam of my unconscious.

Things I had known all the time.

I hurled all the anger I could dredge up at those eyes. I was going to pull her out of there. My eyes stared back, concentrating my anger.

"Come and get me!" I screamed and the thing inside me leapt clear of me and fell swirling down the irises that spun and twisted and there were tunnels and tunnels and they were skull eyes walled by patches of white bone graying into terrible blackness—

Cold. Cold.

Faintly the train rumbled still.

I guess each person has his own private death. All the images and things he's most afraid of, everything he's pushed down to the very bottom of his mind—

Cold and darkness.

Then cold and light; moonlight without a moon, and I saw I was in a spotlight walking on a field of springy skulls, as though each one were attached to a bedspring, bobbing up and down as I trod. It was an eerie bouncy smoothness....

Then a voice that came from all around me. In a language I didn't know. But I understood it perfectly:

Who art thou, that darest enter?

The voice was echoshifted so I couldn't tell where it came from, it sprang out of the darkness and it made a cold wind with a whiff of methane and rotten egg gas. I suddenly knew the answer to that question, and I spoke a stream of gibberish that sounded like this *gispesimikyeuranuasterondos* and I knew it was Greek: *I am a child of earth and of starry heaven.*

It came out in a blurry kind of way and I was trying to stop myself from bawling or screaming or wetting myself, it was that bad. It was a tall deep darkness and I knew it stretched to forever. The voice asked me more questions and I answered in the same gibberish and sometimes I knew what it meant but sometimes I didn't and it went on for it seemed like hours—

Then *bam!* A flight of stairs in the spotlight and banisters with bony fingers quivering and cobwebs and I walked up it. My own steps. Ping. Ping. Metallic, distant. And the heartbeat. And so far away it was almost like sea waves lapping—the kettledrum of train on mountainside....

I was scared. Shitless. But I was so angry. There was something fake about all this. It was too plastic, too like a horror movie. I knew I had to walk up the steps and I did, and the lightpatch grew a little and there was the music of harps, dry and dissipating quickly into the dusty darkness.

"So you like my show?" A low voice inside my head.

I saw him. The skull face. And purple tights and a green cape and the Greek letter theta in a circle on his chest.

He was standing on a landing on a kind of mezzanine and the harp players were at his feet and they were skeletons and harps of bone with prows of ghoul faces and red crystal eyes. And a low wind moaning. And a chorus sighing. And a string orchestra, sort of a sneering, trilling ostinato of high-pitched squeaks....

"I asked you a question, kid."

"I think it's..." What did you say to Death? "I think it's

phoney, damn it! Give me my mother back!"

There. I'd said it. Now he'd take me and I'd live down here forever.

"Well, well, well," said Death. A grin widened and faded out. "I've seen a lot of people like you...selfish people, the lot of you. Always wanting something. Preferably for nothing."

"I can pay!" I said. "You can come and get me instead! I'm from the blood of Admetos and the bargain stands still, the bargain you made with him—"

"Don't give me that shit," said Death. "I'll do whatever I please." But he was shaking. Maybe there *was* a chink in his armor.

I looked him over. I was scared, sure, but somehow not as badly as I thought I'd be. I was more scared when I didn't know what to expect...the music and the skulls were spooky but plastic. "So bring her back to life."

"God, you're insufferable!" he said, then he did a hideous cackle. I'd been expecting one for a while, so I stood firm and didn't let it faze me. "If I let her go now, I'm still going to have to collect sometime, you know that. Besides, I don't bargain. It's a fixed price store here."

"Heracles didn't think that when he wrestled you to the ground."

"I'd like to see you try."

I stood and listened to the wind. The wind howled but I didn't feel anything. It was dry and cold. When I spoke the air frosted. As I watched him he shimmered and changed into the actor at Epidauros with the mask of Death. It was like the nightmare, close up. The skull face was dead white and the eyes were dead and I couldn't read them....

"Okay," said Death. "If you're going to stand there forever, I suppose we might work out a little something. I don't get much amusement here. I don't suppose you wrestle, but—how about something else?"

"I thought I was just supposed to stay here and you would go wake her up," I said slowly.

The cackle came again. I wasn't afraid anymore. I was in this and I was going to fight it out till the end.

"I love children," he said. "They're so illogical. You won't be around to enjoy her if you die, will you? What would be the point? Oh, don't give me that bull about love and compassion. I don't understand things like that. They don't pay me for my empathy quotient. Anyhow, if you stay here, when your sister grows up she'll come looking for you. She's got the power too, you know.

50

And she adores you."

"How do you know?" Suddenly I felt proud of Sophie. As I'd never done before. I thought of her without me and—

"Play chess?" he said suddenly.

"You saw *The Seventh Seal?*" Mom and Dad always made me watch the serious movies on channel 26. *(Expand your experiential cosmos—)*

"Shit yes. I always watch every movie where I'm the big hero."

"The way I interpreted it you were more like the bad guy. Anyways, I don't play chess."

"...Monopoly?"

"Uh uh."

"Too bad." He started to shimmer again, as though to change shape, then changed his mind and stayed as the play actor..."I've got it! This dude called Orpheus came by once, and...you sing?"

"Oh sure, I tried out for the Brooklyn Boys Chorus and I shattered a 69¢ Burger King glass."

"Oh, get out of here," said Death.

"Baseball?" I said faintly...and tried to choke it back but I knew I'd said it and I was in for it now and as if to play up my helplessness the music of strings and harp welled up and the moan of the wind shrilled to a shriek—

"That's it!" said Death briskly. He clapped his hands. Suddenly I saw that we were overlooking a field of plastic-looking grass and that there were tiers and tiers of spectators and the train rumbling suddenly turned into the murmur of a crowd—

"I'll put your mother on third base," he said. I saw her there. She stood still like a statue and even at the distance I could see how beautiful she was and how the light on her was still moon-light even under the gathering sunlight that was breaking overhead and the sun was yellow and had eyes and a frown like in a kid's painting. "I'll put your Dad on first; he's got farther to go because after all he started it all. Now all you have to do is...."

He took off his mask.

It was Chet Perkins, the Pumpkin. Handing me the expensive bat I'd carried with me across Europe and hadn't used once.

I looked at his slits of eyes squinting at me and his body shaking like a jello that's been left out too long and I hated him. He shimmered back into his superhero costume but now it was topped by a green and purple baseball cap with the big theta on it. Theta for thanatos. The skull face scrutinized me. I saw right through the eyes into the old landing with the ghouls playing harps and I knew that our pavilion overlooking the baseball field was a fakery on top of a fakery.

Then I turned around and looked at the field and the crowd screaming began to make me feel funny and warm inside and I knew I wanted to do whatever it was, even if I died trying....

I felt Death's breath in my back. Cold and slimy.

"Okay, ragazzo," he said, and he suddenly sounded like my Dad and made me twist my intestines..."All you have to do is hit a home run. And I'm pitching."

I gripped the bat and started walking down the steps, I could see that it was like five hundred steps down to the grass below and the sun was hurting my eyes—

Death called after me: "How about second base? Did you have anyone in mind?"

"No," I said, not looking back. I didn't even want to think about it. Aunt Rosie? Poor old Granddad who died of a surfeit of booze? I tried to push the thought back as far as I could. I took three more steps and I heard Death taunting me.

"You humans are all alike!" he cackled. "Selfish, selfish, selfish. Just think what's in your power! You could bring back anyone to life—Jesus Christ, Einstein, Shakespeare—

I turned around. "Damn it, I don't give a shit about those people! I'm just a kid who wants his family to stay in one piece!"

"Charity begins at home, eh?"

"Fuck you!"

* * *

I sort of came to. I saw the tiers all around stretching as far as I could see but sometimes there were holes in the tiers and I saw blackness through them lanced by eerie light. They were like living backcloth, in a seedy off-off-Broadway theater or something, that hadn't been used in a long long time.

I was holding the bat, my own bat, and it was a little-league sized field so I saw Death in his supercostume standing pretty near and licking his chops.

"Where's the catcher?" I yelled.

Death vanished. I swirled round. He stood behind me and I got a whiff of his foul breath as he burst into a villainous campy laugh. "You could do with a good mouthwash," I said. Then I hefted the bat and waited. The crowd's murmur was the same as the pounding of the train...the tiers of living people so I knew it was all a backcloth now. And a wind gusted through the gaps, icy and fetid as Death himself.

I wanted to go find the locker room and scrub myself into

pieces before I came on. But I was there and the crowd was screaming and I saw Mom and Dad, but I saw right through them too so I knew they were shades of people, and the sun shone fierce as anything making me blink over and over and it was cold as anything....

Chet Perkins was up there doing his fancy warm up and— Zing!

Talk about a fast ball. I was still waiting for it when I heard the *s-s-t-r-r-r-i-ke* ONE!

I knew it was all a set up now. I knew it was going to be a dirty game all the way.

Death vanished and popped up all over the field, here an outfielder there a shortstop, and then he'd guffaw and snicker and giggle and the crowd up there would copy him. I looked closer and saw they were all—

Ghosts. Zombies. Headless torsos. Withered shrouds with gargoyle faces. Eye sockets dripping rheum.

It's hopeless, I thought. "God damn it, you've got all the cards," I yelled at Death, who was still in the form of the Pumpkin. "You can make the ball travel faster than light or something and you can rig up this whole Halloween charade to gross me out and give me the creeps...."

"Oh, it's a slow ball you want, huh?"

He pitched.

I waited.

Slow motion. Crowd shrieks dropping an octave like a 78 burbling to a 45 now to 33 now a heart-thump below the threshold of hearing—

The ball hung there for a moment and I saw it was moving dancing in the sunlight, it did three quick figure-eights and somersaulted into swooping sweeping curves and zig-zagged like a hummingbird, hypnotizing me, and then it dangled in front of me—

I swung and it dodged and I swung and it dodged me and then it whooshed right past me into the strike zone and I was still swinging at nothing—

Thwack! Second strike.

Okay. I'd had it. I didn't want to play anymore.

"Okay, Death," I said.

Laughter pealed like funeral bells. "Ha! You can't take it, can you! Well," Death said, stalking towards me, "I let this go on because I wanted to teach you a lesson. You can't win! I am the great leveler, the ultimate nothing in everyone's life! I am totally fair! You can't cheat me!" He was towering over me and his cape was flapping and I saw the scythe sprout out of his bony hand. "I represent justice! Justice!" he shouted. "Everyone dies! Everyone! Everyone!" Holes of eyes burning blackness—

I dropped my bat and stomped towards him in a rage. "If you're so fair how come you don't die yourself, huh?" I screamed. "You're just a God damn hypocrite! Yah! Jesus!"

He stopped cold.

He turned his back on me and walked over and plucked a baseball out of the air. "Have it your way," he said.

He pitched this pathetic pitch that a first-grader could have handled with a plastic bat....

I felt the thunk as I lashed out and then I sprinted without thinking at all and Death just stood there without stopping me. I saw the ball fly through a hole in the big canvas crowd and I ran and ran and my Mom reached home plate and vanished and my Dad was puffing like crazy with his fur coat flying and he reached it too I didn't stop I ran I ran

I looked up.

On the staircase in the darkness with the harps and wailing strings and the skeletons strumming....

Death in his superhero costume on his throne.

I stood panting for a while. Then, "Why'd you let me win?"

Rumble. Rumble. The train.

"I don't have to justify myself!" Death grated. Then he looked down and I tried to stare him down but he wouldn't even look at me.

God, I needed a shower!

I said, slowly, "All this crap about justice and the grim reaper and all...all these ghostly sighings and gibbering skeletons and stuff like that...it's not real, is it? You're quite a softie, after all."

He didn't answer. I knew he'd never admit it.

Then I said, "I know why you're so bitter. I can see it so clearly. You want to die so badly but you can't! You have to sit here forever, collecting due debts, like an IRS man or a mafia beater-upper...you're jealous, aren't you?"

He still didn't say anything.

So I walked up to him and touched him lightly on the face. Although it was a skull it felt dry, like skin. And cold. But there was no quiver of breathing. Nothing.

"Gosh," I said, "I wish I could help."

Everyone has his own personal Death locked up inside him. I knew this Death; he was part of me and he belonged to me. But I had thrown him into the deepest dungeon of my soul. Of course he was bitter.

"I guess I'll have to try to love you, even when it hurts," I said. "After all, I love my Dad even when he farts up such a stink I can't breathe."

"Will you get out of here, already?"

I fell up the irises and the light swirled and I stepped into the mirror—

Dad and Mom on the bunk. Sophie on Dad's lap. Daylight. A family album portrait....

Dad said, "Wow, son."

I smiled sheepishly at the three of them.

"It's going to be Paris in an hour and we're staying in a hotel on the Champs Elysees," Sophie babbled, "and guess what there's a McDonald's on the Champs Elysees right near the FDR Subway, Daddy says so—"

"Oh Child of Earth and Starry Heaven!" Mom whispered. I knew them for the words of the ancient ritual of rebirth, words from the Sacred Mysteries....

I was too empty to say much and I knew they were all too emotional to say anything sensible, they'd either all start blabbing or we'd be hugging each other in pieces and I couldn't stand a scene like that, not now.

Dad said, sententiously, "Isn't it true that there are those for whom the climax of their lives was a home run in Little League, and that's all they reminisce about to their grandkids for the rest of their lives?"

I took the hint. I'd done an incredible thing—though I wasn't at all sure how I'd brought it off—but now it was time to go on.

"Yeah, Dad," I said.

"La commedia e finita, ragazzo mio, no?"

"Cut the wop shit, babbino."

I slipped out as quickly as was decent and went to watch the fields unreel.

—*Arlington, 1979*

Somtow Sucharitkul: Interview by Darrell Schweitzer

I thought it might be fun for me to give you lurid autobiographical details about myself, but why should I bother when Darrell Schweitzer has, in the following interview, done it for me with such chilling candor and embarrassing accuracy?

Somtow Sucharitkul may very well be the Cosmic Guru and Perfect Spiritual Master of Oriental Wisdom. Then again, maybe not. One thing is for certain: he is marvellously entertaining, either in person or in print, and he is one of the brightest new talents to appear in science fiction in recent years. Aside from one earlier story in *Unearth,* he began to appear in *Analog* and *Isaac Asimov's SF Magazine* in 1979. His popularity was readily established with his "Mallworld" series, about a gigantic shopping center floating in space (Yes, there *will* be one called "A Mall and the Night Visitor"...), and the "Inquestor" series, rather an odd mixture of Cordwainer Smith and John Varley, about a future universe dominated by religious tyranny (but in which there are flashes of bizarre beauty). He has also been published in Roy Torgesson's anthologies and his novel, *The Starship and the Haiku,* is forthcoming from Pocket Books. The collected Mallworld stories will be published by Starblaze. Sucharitkul has been nominated for the John Campbell Award for best new writer, in response to which he has launched the "Sucharitkul in 80" campaign, complete with sandwich-board signs, buttons, parties, but no tickertape parades yet, all of which is amusing precisely because it is superfluous. His work is good enough for him to win without any campaign. However, some spoilsports have waged a counter-campaign with buttons like: IF GOD HAD INTENDED SUCHARITKUL IN 80 HE WOUILD HAVE GIVEN HIM A PRONOUNCEABLE NAME. Actually, it's pronounced the same way it is spelled, in America at least.

Somtow is also a composer of avant-garde music (he described himself once as "a sort of Neo-Asian post-Serialist person"), and, as a hobby, he explains the meaning of life.

57

Thrust: Would you tell us about your earliest published work?

Sucharitkul: Well, when I was 11 years old, I wrote a poem called "Kith of Infinity" about which the only real thing of note was it contained the word "quasi-tangible." This poem, which is about a child who feels a strange esoteric relationship with the wind, appeared three years later in *The Bangkok Post*. Three years was already later enough to be excruciatingly embarrassing. Shirley MacLaine was passing through Bangkok at the time, and I suppose the newspaper was delivered to her room with a rose at the hotel in the morning, and she read the poem. For some reason she thought it had been written by an Oriental sage who had been dead for two thousand years. In fact, because the poem contained the line "I am not a man," because I was a kid, she probably thought I was a feminist 2000-year-old Oriental sage. I don't really know this, though. But it changed her life, and the next thing I knew was that several years later her autobiography came out, and there was this poem on the front page. And, you know, I'm much older than I was then, now, and I've had things published in nationally circulated magazines and so on, but never in my life has anything I've written been so widely circulated as this horrible poem. I understand it sold millions of copies. I was paid eventually. I found a lawyer who wrote her a letter, in which he informed her that I had not been dead for 2000 years, and she wrote an apologetic letter back, thanking me for letting her use the poem. That's my Shirley MacLaine story. For a while I was convinced that I could get masses of money out of this because they had left out the last line, and because I had suffered psychological damage by having this poem published, because it was such a lousy poem. But somehow I didn't manage to make that stick. I haven't seen her since, or heard from her.

Thrust: Were you immediately inspired to have a writing career at this point, or did that come later?

Sucharitkul: My writing career really began when I read

Robert Heinlein's *Methusaleh's Children.* I was so impressed by this book that I immediately wrote a two-page novel with exactly the same plot, minus the point of the story. My next incursion into literature was about a year later, when I was eleven, when I started writing a whole bunch of poems, including the horrible poem, "Kith of Infinity." I also wrote a play which was a version of Shakespeare's *Julius Caesar* in very bad Latin, which was performed at the Bangkok Patana School—which it the British School of Bangkok—with me as Brutus. The next play I wrote was an English version of Sophocles' *Electra.* This was performed when I was eleven or so, also at the Bangkok Patana School, and the person who played Apollo was immediately killed the next week by his little brother, who accidentally shot him with his father's gun. This taught me a lot about *hubris.*

Thrust: What did it teach you about *hubris*? Doesn't the Sucharitkul in '80 Campaign suggest that you haven't learned much about it?

Sucharitkul: The Sucharitkul in '80 Campaign is very insidious, because it's the only militantly tacky campaign ever mounted. The fact that the tackiness appears as a joke only hides the inner insidiousness of the whole thing. Anyway, I don't expect to win the Campbell Award this year, but in 1981 I should be able to win on the pity vote, since I am not planning to run a campaign that year. But I've learned a lot about *hubris.* If I were really as conceited as I deserve to be, you wouldn't see the end of me.

Thrust: Did you get sidetracked into music, or did this come as part of the psychological effect of writing those poems?

Sucharitkul: I've always been interested in music, but I really only became involved when I was sent to school in England. I went to a funny school in England where everybody wears tails. It was called Eton. I was there for five years. They had incredibly good music there. In fact, it was very different from the schools in the movie *If.* [Which is about English

59

schoolboys overthrowing their teachers in a violent revolt.] It was very liberal in a strange sort of way. Although you had to wear tails, you could select your own tutor. A very interesting school. It was there that I started composing music. I converted my self-taught piano-playing to piano lessons. I did have some lessons when I was four years old, but I made the teacher cry, and she had a tantrum and left, and after that I didn't have any until I was 13. I remember this vaguely, but she said, "Why don't you write a little piece?" So I did that, and the key signature was six flats. Actually I didn't know what it meant, but I just put it in to look good. The teacher was so horrified that she started crying.

Thrust: Over the fact that you had written a piece? That she had created a monster?

Sucharitkul: Something like that. She started crying because it wasn't what she wanted. This was in Holland, by the way, which was a place where I lived when I was a kid. I lived in four countries by the time I was seven: England, France, Holland, and Boston—I suppose that's a country, isn't it?

Thrust: What about Thailand?

Sucharitkul: I left when I was six months old.

Thrust: Does the music bear any relation to your writing career?

Sucharitkul: I don't really see any barrier between them, but I'm much better at writing music right now. I think I've had more practice. It's easier to write music.

Thrust: You very suddenly came on the science fiction scene. Was this a sudden effort, or had you been working at it for a while before something gave way?

Sucharitkul: I had been working on it for about a year before I made my first sale. You see, science fiction had always been something that I enjoyed reading a lot, and I'd never had any problems with being beaten up for reading pulps, because I never grew up in a country where science fiction was considered evil. They were always very pleased that I was reading anything at all.

Thrust: You've mentioned that your shopping center in

space, Mallworld, is a place you'd like to live in, but others consider it a chilling dystopia. How do you account for this difference?

Sucharitkul: Somebody once described the Mallworld series as a sort of Alice in Wonderland, only it was Somtow in America. Actually it was Hank Stine who so described it. You see, one of the reasons I love America so much is that it has wonderful, quaint, picturesque native customs, and it has these elegant edifices and institutions—you know, McDonald's and such strange, exotic temples. And the natives are wonderful. They're naive and childlike, but they're very interesting. I love it here. The Mallworld series is a tribute to the beauty and glory of Americanism.

Thrust: How come the Americans regard all this stuff as tacky and tasteless?

Sucharitkul: I don't know. Maybe the Greeks regarded the Parthenon as very tacky.

Thrust: Was there a McDonald's there?

Sucharitkul: There's a McDonald's in Tokyo. I believe the McDonald's in Hong Kong is the largest daily grossing McDonald's on Earth.

Thrust: Frightening prospect.... Is there a McDonald's in Mallworld?

Sucharitkul: No. You see, they've evolved beyond that into even more grandiose extremes of tackiness.

Thrust: How do you define tackiness and why do you find it so appealing?

Sucharitkul: It's just like a new toy. To me it's sort of like Richard Strauss' middle and later period works. It's wallowing in the glory of shit. It's beautiful.

Thrust: Occidental Inscrutability, you mean?

Sucharitkul: Oh yes, you Occidentals are incredibly inscrutable.

Thrust: What is the origin of the Mallworld series? Did you envision a shopping center floating in space?

Sucharitkul: Believe it or not, I do a lot of my writing in a shopping mall. There's a large shopping mall, called Springfield Mall, near where I live. It has these wonderful, rounded seats which give you a little puddle of seclusion in the middle of the bustle. I sometimes sit there and write. So far no one has arrested me for loitering. They will one

	day, no doubt. I also write a lot in coffee shops. In particular there's one coffee shop near my house where they know I'm a writer. So they ply me with coffee and come over and pamper me, and I enjoy that. I used to write music in a coffee shop in Bangkok, and there was always an audience.
Thrust:	Do you sit there with a typewriter in a coffee shop?
Sucharitkul:	No, I write in longhand. At least I write all the salient points of each scene in longhand before I do any typing. I think it shows.
Thrust:	In what way?
Sucharitkul:	Well, I hate to boast, but....
Thrust:	Go ahead.
Sucharitkul:	For a person who is totally oral in his life, I'm very anal-retentive when it comes to writing. Although my rooms are the epitome of utter messiness, I actually try to write with great care. Maybe because it's still quite hard in some ways.
Thrust:	Is this an outline you write longhand, or an actual first draft?
Sucharitkul:	It depends. A lot of it is counting syllables, and doing stuff like that, doing all the stuff they taught me to do in analysis of literature in school.
Thrust:	You mean setting it up with the precision of poetry?
Sucharitkul:	Yes, I often do that. Especially with opening paragraphs.
Thrust:	To the point of metering it?
Sucharitkul:	No, no, I'm not a meter maid when it comes to that [laughs]...I enjoy it when it comes out right, but it doesn't always.
Thrust:	What makes a story successful for you?
Sucharitkul:	Well, I haven't been that satisfied with—No, I shouldn't say that, should I? I should really boast.
Thrust:	But if you say that it will seem like humility and lend credence to—
Sucharitkul:	Okay, I'll say that then. I'm never really that satisfied with anything I write. As George Scithers knows, I keep sending him letters after I've mailed him a manuscript, telling him what revisions I want to make. In one or two cases this has crossed in the mail with a letter from him demanding the same revisions. My entire training is in main-

	stream. All my degrees are in mainstream. I don't have a degree in science fiction. This may be why my science fiction doesn't quite please me.
Thrust:	Shouldn't such a background give you an advantage because you know something *other* than science fiction? We have a classic type in fandom who knows nothing but sf and tries to write sf. I think you know how that turns out. What do you have a degree in, anyway?
Sucharitkul:	I have a degree in English Literature and Music—it's a double major—from Cambridge.
Thrust:	Isn't this background advantageous?
Sucharitkul:	"Yeah," he said. This is one of my famous one word answers. But as I have been describing, I only came to writing science fiction fairly late, apart from the abortive Heinlein novel. I must have been about twenty-four before I even attempted to write science fiction. I started off with fake Greek plays and went on to poetry. I'm still trying to write those Greek plays and those poems, actually, only this time I'm making money by pretending they're—woops! Abort that....
Thrust:	You're incorporating the Greek plays into the science fiction, then.
Sucharitkul:	Oh yes, I've done an Orpheus. I've done a *Heart of Darkness.* I've done most things. Orpheus in Mallworld is one of my better stories, "Sing a Song of Mallworld."
Thrust:	But you haven't done "Mallworld Becomes Electra" yet.
Sucharitkul:	I'm planning to. I already have that one plotted, but that won't be till after "Mallworld Graffiti," so we'll have to wait about six months maybe before I come up with the story. I'm doing "A Mall and the Night Visitors" first. The only thing about that is, though, that it'll have to come out in the Christmas issue. Not necessarily, I guess.
Thrust:	The strange thing is that despite titles like these, the stories are not farces. You use gag titles for serious stories.
Sucharitkul:	I've done that in the past. I think "This Towering Torment" is not an example of it, however. Yes, that's very true otherwise. "Sing a Song of Mall-

world" is an extremely serious story, but the whole story is disguised as a gag, because I think the reader needs sugar-coated pills. Of course I am not really in this business to give people pills. I don't see myself as a physician of the human condition. But when I have to take a pill myself, I might as well let them get it too.

Thrust: You mean you're giving yourself a pill through these stories?

Sucharitkul: Yes, of course. I think everybody does that. That's the central *angst* of the creative artist, isn't it?

Thrust: Or words to that effect....But what about the Inquestor series, which isn't as sugar-coated? These do not have gag titles or aggressive tackiness.

Sucharitkul: Oh, but it is sugar coated, or haven't you noticed?

Thrust: It's a different kind of sugar.

Sucharitkul: That's it. All my stories are about the meaning of life, actually, although some of them are about it less aggressively than others. You see, it all boils down to love, you know, the old Ted Sturgeon thing.

Thrust: Considering that the meaning of life was discovered in "A Day in Mallworld," which was one of your first published stories, where do you go from there?

Sucharitkul: It was *a* meaning of life. You don't understand. *A* meaning of life, only. But, yes...one of the reasons that the Inquestor universe is the way it is, is that I wanted to create a universe of incredible brutality and beauty at the same time. I wanted to make things extremely extreme, so that the emotions and the compassion of the characters could be highlighted. How about that?

Thrust: The Inquestor universe can't help but remind readers of Cordwainer Smith's Instrumentality of Mankind. Do you see any similarity?

Sucharitkul: Not really, I think that Cordwainer Smith is God. I have a very large pantheon, by the way. There are a lot of demons too, but we won't talk about them. The anti-Christ is probably—well, never mind. But...Cordwainer Smith. My Inquestor series is *less Oriental* than Cordwainer Smith's Instrumen-

	tality. The enormously brutal and beautiful universe shares some elements. Although I would hardly claim to be a hard science fiction writer, I make more of an attempt to appear that way than Cordwainer Smith does. I think.
Thrust:	Do you have any literary models? Did anyone influence you heavily?
Sucharitkul:	Yes. Let me think for a while. Marlowe, and Donne. And Chip Delaney and Ursula LeGuin. Kind of a big gap there, but I hate all 19th century literature.
Thrust:	What kind of a Mallworld story would John Donne have written?
Sucharitkul:	I think "Sing a Song of Mallworld" is the closest. You see, I believe—now here's my great theory of science fiction, so be sure to get this. T. S. Eliot claims that a dissociation of sensibility took place after the metaphysical poets. Intellect and emotion became separated. Science fiction is a reassociation of sensibility, a process by which intellectual statements can again generate emotion, as they did in the 16th century. This is my underlying theory of science fiction.
Thrust:	It would seem to me that if a story makes an intellectual statement without generating emotion, at the very best we have a prose wiring diagram. Emotion is an essential of any fiction.
Sucharitkul:	Yes, like certain stories in a certain magazine. Yes. By the way, is this magazine a frog because it goes "rivet, rivet?" Perhaps its prince will come.
Thrust:	I've never seen you writing criticism. Do you take theories of science fiction very seriously when writing?
Sucharitkul:	No. But I can discourse at great length on them to academics, and they love it. Most of my discoursing to academics has been in the music field, but I'm going to be off in March to discourse on science fiction in Boca Raton, Florida. There's this big fantasy/academic con there, and I'm going to lay my new dissociation of sensibility theory on them.
Thrust:	Would you tell us something about your forthcoming novel which is not entitled *The Humpback*

	of Notre Dame?
Sucharitkul:	I'm calling it *The Starship and the Haiku.* They've suggested that I change the title. So we don't know what it'll be yet. I've suggested *The Humpback of Notre Dame* simply because it is about whales. In fact it's a post-holocaust novel in which the Japanese discover that they are the result of genetic experiments performed by whales.
Thrust:	The whole human race, or just the Japanese?
Sucharitkul:	Just the Japanese.
Thrust:	Do you find the techniques for generating a single story of that length much different than for a series?
Sucharitkul:	The real reason I wrote that novel was that I couldn't sell the short story version to anyone. So I thought, "Let's turn it into a novel and see what happens." In the novel I managed to explain most of the things which were ambiguous in the short story, but most of all it was infinitely better than the short story anyway. I'm glad I did it. It has a new narrative technique in it, a very Japanese technique in the sense that it's told in little mosaic stones. It's been done of course in serious literature.
Thrust:	What do you mean by "serious literature?" The implication is that science fiction isn't serious.
Sucharitkul:	Science fiction certainly is serious, or it can be. It runs the gamut from literature to rubbish, which is something very few other genres do. There are very few unrubbishy gothics, in my opinion, whereas there are certainly a lot of unrubbishy science fiction novels.
Thrust:	It seems to me that "literature" runs the entire gamut from literature to rubbish.
Sucharitkul:	Well...you know. I'm only talking about *good* literature, he said, begging the question.
Thrust:	Which of course may be defined as what you mean when you point at it.
Sucharitkul:	Just like science fiction.
Thrust:	This could be a basic paradigm for the meaning of human existence.
Sucharitkul:	Well, as I was saying to you before, I really get off on paradigms. They give me orgasms. Especially intricately-structured, multi-layered paradigms.

It is this rather than the sex scenes that really give me orgasms in a book like *Dhalgren*. I like to draw very complicated graphs of everything I'm going to do, both music and writing. In fact, before I write every scene I draw a graph and fit all the characters on one axis, and the time frame on the other axis, and of course a lot of squiggles and things. Then I draw a little square, and I mark where all the characters are standing, as though on a stage, and I mark all the light sorces in the image, so when I describe the way the light falls on things it's always consistent.

Thrust: That's certainly a way to write consistently. I remember a scene in something of mine where I had to go back in a revision and put the moon up, because I was convinced nobody could see anything and I didn't want them stumbling around in the dark.

Sucharitkul: I think it helps if you have the moon there in the first place. That's only the way I do it. Some people put it there afterwards.

Thrust: It's probably very Jungian.

Sucharitkul: Yes. I like to feel that I'm constantly mooning my characters. [Laughs.]

Thrust: What are your future plans as a great science fiction writer?

Sucharitkul: I don't know. I don't think I'm one yet, but I hope to achieve that state as soon as possible. My future plans. Let me get back to why I wrote science fiction. I started telling you about all the other literary forms I went through. But the real reason I started to write science fiction was that I couldn't write any music. So I decided to write a science fiction story instead. And it was really awful. There was this planet which orbited this sun, and it was perpetually enshrouded with dust particles except for a few days of the year. No, maybe it was the other way around. I can't remember. And anyway it was a first fuck story, and the above-mentioned copulatory act took place in a gorgeous pool of light when the people from the other planet, which was not in the gas cloud, had landed there. They had all sorts of strange anthropological rites, which were probably gleaned from that book, *Ritual Mutilation* or whatever—the book about the African tribesmen who claim to their wives that they never shit. It's by Freud. Anyway, the second story I wrote I actually sold to Roy Torgesson two or three years later after revising it five times. He thinks it's wonderful. I'm not that sure about it. I think it has its moments but sometimes it's silly. It's called "Comets and Kings." So that's the earliest story I wrote that is in print.

Thrust: What was the problem which made your earliest stories unpublishable?

Sucharitkul: They were lousy.

Thrust: Did you realize they were lousy in a specific way and take definite steps to correct this?

Sucharitkul: Oh yeah. I think I learned fairly fast, because I became pretty publishable by about the seventh story. That was the *Analog* sale. I sold one story to a semi-prozine before that, *Unearth*. I wouldn't have written that story that way now, certainly. I really screwed up the ending very badly. That too had its moments. If I had been wise I would not have submitted it. You see, I was at this con. I decided to go to science fiction conventions about a year after I tried to write science fiction. Usually I was always not in America whenever there was a con wherever I was. This was Balticon in 1977. I met the editors of *Unearth* there, and I just handed them a story, and they just bought it, which was rather astonishing to me at the time. This didn't qualify me to join SFWA, however. That didn't happen for another year or so.

Thrust: You've probably come into the science ficiton scene more from the outside than a lot of people. How do you find your relationship with fandom affects your writing? Many writers insist things get incestuous after a while.

Sucharitkul: Ah, yes, that question. This is rather funny that you should say that, because many of the other science fiction writers tell me that they're envious of me for having been in fandom. But actually I haven't been in it that long. and I'm almost the only person I know who goes to fandom as a relaxation from the weirdness of his world, where I can find people of more relative normalcy than, for instance, in contemporary music fandom, which is to regular fandom what fandom is to the man in the street, I imagine, in terms of relative strangeness.

Thrust: Do you ever put this strangeness into science fiction, or would nobody believe it?

Sucharitkul: I've disguised a lot of things as science fiction which everybody has swallowed whole.

Thrust: Where does this fit into your theory of science fiction?

Sucharitkul: As we all know, theories only come into their own after the artforms they're talking about are well buried. People didn't discover the rules of Classical music until well into the Romantic period. Mozart never knew that he was obeying or breaking rules at the time. He just did it because it sounded right. So I'm not going to comment on that.

Thrust: Don't you think all this academic theorizing could embalm science fiction?

Sucharitkul: No, because I think the good bits will be preserved and the rubbish will be ignored, except by the people who are perpetrating it, but what do they matter?

Thrust: The good bits of the theorizing or the good bits of the science fiction?

Sucharitkul: The theorizing. There are good bits floating around somewhere. Sturgeon's Law also holds true of academic tracts. What would be interesting would be to discover an academia of academia, with a bunch of people whose sole function was to analyze the academic writings on science fiction and extract paradigms out of the paradigms.

Thrust: Wouldn't that be twice as orgasm-inducing?

Sucharitkul: Definitely so. I could imagine myself doing well in that. I remember one paradigm I made very well. I was at a world conference on Southeast Asian aesthetics, which was put on by Cornell. There were 25 great experts and two Asian artists. In my paper I compared the Asian composer to a crystal type with five crystalline axes, which were types of polarities. That was really fun, especially as I was able to say in the paper something like "As every schoolboy knows," and it was something that none of them knew. About crystalline axes. Academics do love to be insulted though, because every academic knows in his heart of hearts that he is not one.

Thrust: You mentioned your broad pantheon a while back. What do you specifically admire in modern science fiction?

Sucharitkul: Modern science fiction is obviously the only vital field in literature, he said, very portentiously. It is the true brainchild of the new wave of the early 20th century, and all the other stuff is just sterile mules born of this strange hybridization, he ad-libbed. The two other great theories of science fiction, aside from my own, are both theories that I subscribe to. There is the Delaney theory, which concerns the literization of metaphors. Obviously very important. Clearly language has been completely reviatlized by science fiction. And here of course I refer only to good science fiction. Then there's the LeGuin theory of science fiction, which is that science fiction *is* reality. It is the most precise and profound way of paradigmatizing the human condition. I think that's very true.

Thrust: Is it really necessary to paradigmatize the human condition in everything you write?

Sucharitkul: Well, if it's art it is.

Thrust: Are you defining art then as that which paradigmatizes the human condition?

Sucharitkul: No, but that's a good working definition, I mean, it covers most things. You want me to define art? Okay. since all experience is subjective, art is essentially a way of communicating that which of its essence cannot be communicated, by means of symbol. That's it. That's my definition.

Thrust: I assume you mean it cannot be communicated by any other means than by symbol.

Sucharitkul: Yeah.

Thrust: Delaney would probably write a whole book on that sentence, explaining the basic paradigm for the ambi-guities of that sentence.

Sucharitkul:	Well, I dedicate this sentence to Chip Delaney, whom I have never met. He also belongs to my pan-theon, so he can have it. [Pause.] Now do you want me to define the human condition?
Thrust:	Yes, please do.
Sucharitkul:	I don't know the answer to that one. It's very hard to define the human condition unless you're God, because you can't see everything from outside. As human, you can only be on the roller coaster. You can't perceive the roller coaster.
Thrust:	That's very profound. Have you ever thought of becoming a guru?
Sucharitkul:	Yes, frequently. At night I have long fantasies about sitting on a gigantic lotus and explaining the meaning of life to a whole lot of naked, attractive, young people.
Thrust:	You know, there may be more money in that than in science fiction.
Sucharitkul:	I'm working on it, though. You see, I've already reached the pinnacle of the Neo-Asian Post-Serialist composers, and I am searching for a new height to scale. Of course there are only three other Neo-Asian Post-Serialist composers, but it was good practice to climb that particular mountain.
Thrust:	How many other Neo-Asian Post-Serialist science fiction writers are there?
Sucharitkul:	I haven't done a survey, but I have a sneaking suspicion that I may be the only one. I'm not sure that there are that many composers who are academically seriously regarded, who also write science fiction. I've never heard of one.
Thrust:	As long as you're dispensing eternal truths and the like, what would be your advice to all the would-be writers out there who are reading this?
Sucharitkul:	Don't.
Thrust:	Why not?
Sucharitkul:	It is only because I have been through a great deal of anguish and pain that I am able to sit here giggling into this microphone so unselfconsciously.
Thrust:	Obviously then, the secret of true art is to be unselfconscious and to be aware of it.
Sucharitkul:	That's it. Here's another paradoxical paradigm of the human condition. You obviously shouldn't be-

71

come a writer unless you absolutely know that you really are one. Most societies contain many socially self-effacing mechanisms which tend to undermine anybody's attempts to say anything that goes "Me, me, me." Especially Asian societies. In Thailand there in no real concept of the creative artist in the language. There are all sorts of other strange concepts that you don't have in English, but we won't go into that. That's a barrier you have to overcome. You can't know ultimate reality. You must at least have grasped a little shred of it somewhere. I think that's very important.

Thrust: You mentioned once that you found that the most profound concepts of Buddhism were being confirmed by atomic physics.

Sucharitkul: There is a lot of California physics going on these days. The virtual particle. What a wonderful thing that is. That is so Buddhist that it isn't true. Then there are things that exist so fast that they don't have time to exist. Isn't that wonderful? If it weren't for modern physics, almost all of my science fiction would only be fantasy. When you think of the mysticism that's innate in modern physics, think of *rubber* modern physics. There's a real mine for any science fiction writer.

Thrust: It seems to me that science fiction is almost inherently mystical. How many SF stories can you think of—and not just the *Star Trek* movie—end with someone achieving transcendence?

Sucharitkul: If I could fuck V'ger and become the universe, I would probably not do so, because I would think being the universe would be very boring. There wouldn't be anything else to try to be. However, I notice that they also became the universe in *Black Hole*. Sort of. At least the villain went to Hell and everybody else became the universe, and it was all one. Of course, science fiction embodies much of the mythology of 20th century Western culture. The science fiction community doesn't necessarily partake of this mythology. UFOs and angels are very much the same, I think.

Thrust: Science fiction has taken over large areas that used to be the exclusive domain of religion.

	Eschatology. This would be a reason for its innate mysticism, even in the hard science writers. Like Arthur Clarke.
Sucharitkul:	Yes, very much so. You want a profound comment? Let's see, hold on while I ramble...Is science fiction religion? No.
Thrust:	I mean more a case of secularizing the subject matter of religion without getting rid of it. The same way physicists and the like have been stealing subject matter from philosophers since ancient times.
Sucharitkul:	Yes, science fiction has stolen a lot of the numinosity from religion. Obviously space is far more imposing than any cathedral. You can't write a space opera set in a cathedral. Actually I'd like to try that sometime.
Thrust:	Yes, how about an Inquestor space opera set in a cathedral?
Sucharitkul:	Well, the Inquestor series uses a lot of the furniture of space opera. I'm very consciously paying tribute to it. But I'm also trying to write real stories. It's actually very difficult.
Thrust:	We're close to the end here...Let's see: WHAT IS THE FINAL QUESTION?
Sucharitkul:	I have a comment to make on that. You see at Cambridge they had these essay questions on exams. There was a three hour exam, and you'd go in and turn over the piece of paper, and there would be one question. It could be anything whatever, and you had to write a three hour paper. One year the question was: THIS IS THE QUESTION; WHAT IS THE ANSWER? And somebody wrote, "This is the answer; what was the question?" And walked out of the room. He was flunked. But I think this was because of his other performances. If he had been very good, he might have passed. I like to think of myself as one of the other people in that exam room.
Thrust:	Like writing stories giving the answers when you don't know what the question is?
Sucharitkul:	Right. I don't want to know what the question is. But as I just said, science fiction *is* reality. What more can you want?

Thrust: You could want the meaning of life.
Sucharitkul: It's in the dictionary.

—*Philadelphia, 1979*

Indeed, after all that, it would be cheating not to reprint the hideous Shirley MacLaine poem so much discussed and decried in the previous interview, so here goes.

I make no apologia here; its interest, if any, is purely as a curio. Even at 17, six years after I wrote this little ode, I found it exquisitely embarrassing. Nonetheless, it is of all my works the one of which the most copies have been printed, the one that's been translated into half a dozen languages...oh, I'm dying of shame! Here goes—

Kith of Infinity

Hail, O Wind! Salutations!
From a night wanderer seeking light
      searching a mystic land
           from which I have come,
Oh, wind, I am not human:
I am a stranger
      from a different planet:
Is it the same planet from which
      you, O wind, have come?
I breathe as a man,
I see with a man's eyes
      But I am not a man.
O wind, rustling through the forest,
      eager whisperer
      doleful sigher
Forever coursing
      the banks of some invisible river
Borne through the darkness:
Esisting only
      in a quasitangible substance
Carrier, uncarried!
Hail, O wind! I greet thee:

74

Thou alone art the inhabitant of that world
      to which I am akin:
For I am a shadow without body
      come from the unknown depth
      from the unattainable land
Borne by the foam
      carried by the current...
O epitomiser of purity,
      I too am matter:
I am interchangeable,
I am energy, I am one,
I am indivisible and single,
One with all abstractions
Foreign to that earth
      bounded by the impure.
I am kindred to thee, O wind!
I know thee as I know myself.
Thou comest from mine own world
through the barrier of time.

—"A Poem," by Somtow P. Sucharitkul,
The Bangkok Post, Sunday, September 17, 1967

Sunsteps

Here begins the alternate history section of this book: three stories that are in a sense thematically related.

Sunsteps, you see, was actually the first story of mine ever to see print: that was in Unearth Magazine in 1977. Unearth was a magazine that specialized in the work of previously unpublished writers, and I ran into the editors at my first science fiction convention, the 1977 Balticon, to which I went on a whim that has eventually proved more than just a hunch.

Costume epics have always fascinated me, and spectacles of all sorts: this, my first foray into the subgenre, is a minor spectacle in its own right. I must say that it does suffer from a rather unsuccessful ending, though I still like the concept a lot, and I may do a novel of it one day.

Highway seems to go on forever.

I'm alone on the gold throne of the nine-seater, nestling into unaccustomed softness. Cushions stuffed with rose-petals.

Such luxury is reserved for the ones who feed the gods.

There is a glass divider. But in the driver's mirror I see his eyes, crystalline and impassive. I see black, leather-gloved hands resting lightly on the wheel, a blackness of face and hair and raven-feather cloak.

It all flashes by, the cliffs, the sky. Three days in this car! I can't describe the bleakness of it. The Sacred Highway is quite empty. Naturally: its only purpose is to bring me speedily to Texcatlipoca and to death.

Don't you think I haven't agonized over this decision, then! I'm not old. Forty. (I still see the puma eyes of my wife Takl, cold, disillusioned, as I tell her....

"They'll take care of you," I say. The show of indifference is wrung from me; I speak with an unwonted harshness. With a start, I recognize the emotion behind her dead stare. I don't think she believes, I think she is a skeptic. I hate her because her emotions touch an unacceptable resonance in my own soul.)

The images flash by. Yet occasionally I fancy I can see the eyes still, harsh as ever, suspended like twin ghosts over the accelerating scenery. The fields, the valleys.

But there is the God. The Sun, mystically rekindled by the blood of dying victims. It glares on me now, it blinds me when I turn to face it. And now I am the sun, I am the God to whom even the Emperor-Dictator of the world must bow. To me alone belongs the knowledge of my humanity, the privilege of doubt.

I'm also a scientist who has asked a forbidden question. I want to be cynical, intellectually objective about why I have offered myself. But finally all my thoughts begin to sound so poetic, so mystical, that the scientist in me would rather think nothing at all.

The forests, the beaches. It's the fourth day without refueling. It occurs to me, sometimes, that this searing isolation must be some ultimate test of my divine composure. It's all so oppressive, this paraphernalia of godhood! This coronet of solid gold, this dazzling cloak of quetzal-feathers covering a full-length robe of cloth-of-gold. These clothes are six hundred years old. And it's this weight of time, of distance, of divinity, of loneliness that drives away my logical doubts, thrusts me towards the inescapable conclusion that—

I am the God.

Involuntarily, in a moment of exasperation, I cry aloud: "Why did I choose to die?"

The lakes, the deserts.

The driver does not respond; in spite of his uncanny humanness, his intellectual programming is too limited.

* * *

My eyes are closed. This must be a dream, and yet—with a surpassing vividness, I see the past unfold....

Summer, the year one of the reign of the Emperor-Dictator Montezuma XVIII. Prosperity in all the world. Praise be to the Sun!

I shut out the Antarctic blizzard with a flick of a switch. The triple doors swing to. Takl, my wife, looks up briefly, a plain brown face framed in fur.

I pick up a little aluminum stool, set myself down rather ceremoniously.

"...His Imperial Dictatorship-Divinity Montezuma XVIII today issued an edict banning all scientific research," the radio whispers. They are all listening, four or five of them at the Antarctic Research Station, tense in the unnatural warmth. Takl pulls off her fur cloak, but I don't think of taking mine off. I am sweating.

"...His Divinity said that further knowledge is unnecessary. We stand at the center of the created cosmos, the Sun deigns to shine, the world is good and plentiful. Remember the old legend about the conquest of China, seven hundred years ago, how they with their ungodly knowledge loosed their terrible inventions on the People: gunpowder, writing, rifles, cannon. Remember how knowledge foments war.

"For the peace of the world, for the glory of the Sun. Given at the Throne at the foot of the Sacred Mountain Popocatapetl, on the twelfth day of the first year of His Divinity the Emperor-

Dictator Montezuma XVIII."

Click.

Everybody starts talking at once.

Takl says, "It's all right. They've made an exception for us. The Emperor *has* to understand the nature of the Sun, so as better to serve him."

They stop talking abruptly. Then they turn to look at me, their leader.

"Well, I did know about it," I admit. It's an uncomfortable moment. "I think we should try to understand His Divinity's motives," I continue. "He *must* know. You've seen the statistics, otherwise you wouldn't dare to be here. Simple extrapolation shows that the world population will be down to one million in only eighty years. Within His Divinity's lifetime, I'd say, given regular transplants. It's *his* problem, he knows it."

"But what will happen then, Professor Kuzdai?" the small assistant asks. Her complexion is delicate, like polished sandalwood. Takl glares at her.

Sighing, I state the obvious, dreadful reality: "Without food, the Sun will die. The Universe will come to an end." She gasps, quickly controls herself. To the best of my knowledge, the fact has never been stated so baldly amongst us.

And I cannot even imagine it: total ending! total destruction! No. Now there is truly a dead silence in the room, and you can feel the bitter deadness of the freezing waste outside, pressing relentlessly on the metal walls, you can feel a desolate coldness of the heart penetrating the artificial warmth. Here we are so far from the sun.

"Science has gone far enough, though, hasn't it?" I go on earnestly, wanting to hear anything, even myself, rather than the iciness of the silence. "Look, we've got cars, airplanes, every kind of convenience. We've pushed down to the very limit—hypothesized the indivisible atom. It's only right that everything should now be channeled towards a single end, saving the world.

"We know that human sacrifice is the only way of keeping the sun burning." I begin to relax into the familiar cadences of my pep-up speech. "But if we discover just how the mechanism works, if we can unleash this undiscovered force in those bleeding, plucked-out human hearts, we can perhaps—"

"Learn to synthesize the power," Takl says. It's a familiar speech. I let her go on for a while; I'm a compromiser at heart.

Locust, the stupid little assistant, says, "It's almost like a kind of sacrilege."

There is another protracted lull. I can't stand the tension—

we've been together like this now for four months—so I turn abruptly on my heels and stomp toward my own lab, slamming the door.

It is because of the potential accusation of sacrilege, of course, that we are banned to such a remote part of the world.

My laboratory has no windows. Carefully I close the door behind me and walk over to the only table. I'm experimenting with various tissue types, trying to get a statistical correlation between the predominant sacrificial type and the brightness of the sun on any given day.

It's annoying work, very detailed, very fidgety, especially with the ban on writing. I have to cassette all the experimental results. I feel to morose to do anything, so I sit at the table, watching the automatic burette dripping accurate amounts of cell suspension into little conical flasks. The results will probably be negative, as usual: I have begun to think that the divine must be beyond scientific consideration.

A timid knock. "Kuzdai, come quickly, come see."

More steps, the door is flung wide. Locust is beckoning. "Outside, out of the sky, a fireball!"

I follow her, confused. Up the escalator to the top level, where there is one room with a small window.

We're all crowded around the small round pane, sweating together, and all at once I see the fireball, burning high against the white sky. You can't tell earth from heaven, it is all one integrated whiteness, the sun is behind us and there is the one unearthly object, fiery, gracefully dropping on us.

Well, I think, with a sudden surge of exaltation, living so close to the secrets of Divinity, one is bound to experience these supernatural events at times. This is a very beautiful one.

"A piece of the sun!" my cold wife exclaims, catching the heady exhilaration from the rest of us. It seems that the Sun is going to give up its secret freely, by revelation. We should have trusted!

We're all talking and laughing, and my wife says, "Let's go," with unexpected enthusiasm, so we don't even bother to grab our cloaks as the three doors swing open and we all rush like children into the cold and the sunlight. I'm practically naked. Our bare feet slop into the new-fallen snow. We keep on laughing together; the whiteness around us goes on and on, out to the horizon, up to the zenith.

Locust finds the ball, gleaming in a pit in the snow. It seems to smolder for a while, there is a cloud of steam, and for several minutes after it burns out, no one dares to touch it.

It's in my lab now.

The uncanny, eerie feeling of total joy has passed, and nobody is quite sure what to do or say. The ball is on the table. We've cleared everything away. The ball—about a foot in diameter—sit there, its surface perfect like the sun's. Takl and Locust, the two women, are hypnotized.

Breaking the silence as always, I say: "Well. I'm puzzled."

"Won't it communicate with us?" asks my dour, dark-faced second. I don't answer, as it seems rather a fatuous question. Elation is replaced by a growing irritation.

"Leave me alone," I growl. They disappear quickly, responding by habit to my frequent touchiness.

The globe sits on the table.

I pick it up. It's perfectly spherical, sun-shaped. It must come from the sun, because we make no spheres, so that we don't accidentally draw away some of the vital force from the sacrificial altars of the world. The globe hardly weighs anything; its metal is unfamiliar to me, a little brighter than silver and quite unmalleable.

As I clasp the object in my hands, I hear an alien voice stirring in my mind. The revelation!

"Do you come from the sun?" I ask out loud.

"Be patient," comes the ghostly voice, an inner whisper all the more spine-chilling because it sounds so uncannily familiar. "I am going to ask you the questions. I am a provoker. I awaken dormant possibilities."

I nod to myself, An idea familiar in our myths, though it feels strange in reality. But our work brings us close to Divinity.

Abruptly: "What is that object?"

I look at the tubular metal device lying on the workbench, bewildered, wondering why it hasn't been put away.

"Why," I whisper—I don't want people to think I'm talking to myself!—it's a telescope. Comes in useful sometimes, if one of us gets lost in the snow."

"Why don't you point it at the sun?"

Disbelief. I shudder. What sort of voice it this, that dares so casually to suggest the unthinkable? But I realize that I've often wondered why science has never considered dealing with the sky. Sacrilegious thoughts, always instantly curtailed. Because we have always known all the facts about the heavens, science is supposed to uncover new things, not truths as old as man and older even....

But when a voice from the Sun itself has suggested it—

Working feverishly, I take a pile of photographic negatives

from the drawer, tape them one by one over the end of the tele-scope. The others are in the lower level, noisily eating the evening meal. I tiptoe back to the only room with a window; the Sun has shifted to the west—it is not quite the time of the midnight sun—and I know that if I raise my instrument to the skies I will see the face of the God himself.

I do so, trembling.

In that moment, I discover two extraordinary new truths. One: my eyes do not smart, I have not been blinded.

Two: the sun has spots.

I am back in the lab again, sitting at the table alone with the celestial object. My fists are clenched, sweaty. I am fighting the growing realization that the sun is really weakening, that this is really the brink of the dreaded holocaust. The image that would not burn out my eyes has burned itself into my mind, a glowering glory of the sun, hardly muted by the protective negatives... pitted with tiny flaws.

As the only person in the station with access to all the data cassettes, I know that the number of sacrifices has dwindled to a trickle, a hundred thousand a year at best, all over the world. And so it has begun.

"Are you sure you are jumping to the right conclusions?"

I push the cassettes into the machine, one by one, Listening, I note that there has been no fall in the average world temperature.

Perhaps the spots have always been there?

But if you can accept that, you *must* be drawn to accept even stranger things. The structure of truth disintegrates.

There is a secret doubt within me, never acknowledged, deep-dungeoned and concealed. Not understanding it, I still feel it gnawing inside. I think of Takl for a moment, Takl who has always been cynical, whose reasons for joining this project are almost certainly heretical, though she is a thorough, careful researcher. I think that she has planted within me this seedling doubt.

The object says nothing all this while, and I dread the coming of its voice, knowing my beliefs will be tested to the utmost. Why does the voice sound so familiar?

The regulated night-chime sounds; I go to Takl.

I do admit one appalling heresy: I keep a diary. I *write* in it. Writing was an art abolished when the People overcame the bar-barians. You scratch little marks on paper, and lo! they become words! It smacks of heathen magic, but I cannot help myself, because my diary is *me*, I don't care to reveal its contents to anyone.

That night I bring it out. Takl is waiting in the bedroom one level deeper; I make some excuse and go to my lab, unlock the bottom drawer.

In it I write down everything that has transpired today. I work by candlelight, since night and day are regulated automatically.

Suddenly there is someone in the shadows behind me. I start. It is Locust.

"What are you doing?"

She is suddenly so desirable, this lovely little girl who asks naive, embarrassing questions!

I have been caught red-handed. But I don't think she will tell.

"Marks on paper," she whispers. She looks over them casually, not, of course, understanding anything.

We look at each other in the candlelight. There is a moment of yearning sexuality, but it subsides.

I must go to Takl, waiting for me with feigned passion in the artificial heat, in the artificial night.

* * *

Wakefulness.

The car, the robot driver.

...We are stopping

Drowsily: "...Tezcatlipoca?"

"No, Your Omnipotence," says the driver in his metallic, precise voice. He does not look around. "It is necessary to refuel. If Your Omnipotence has no objection—"

"No; why should I? Where is this?"

"This place is called Louisville, Your Omnipotence. It was an ancient capital of subject peoples known as whitemen."

...The Feeder center! I sit up, look around. It is a green, inoffensively pleasant terrain, very ordinary looking. The car pulls into a refueling station that seems to be the only building for miles around.

An old man is leaning against the fuel pump. I do not see his face as he comes over, bends down with his hose; as I look out over him through the rear window I glimpse only wisps of white hair.

He looks up. I am stunned.

He is a whiteman—old, obviously past fifty. But they're always given to the sun before their late teens, I think, while still straight and golden and superb in their sunlike beauty. Why is this man alive?

He glares at me fearlessly, so that I am taken aback. For the past year I have met only humility. Here is a look of hatred so intense and concentrated as to ruffle my schooled composure. Behind the hatred, I feel, is pain; and behind that anguish is some certitude, some knowledge about me, that I cannot grasp, that makes me tremble.

I want that knowledge.

"Let me talk to him awhile," I command the driver. The car has already started up.

"Your Omnipotence, time is short."

"I *will* come down for a moment. I *will* rest."

"Your Omnipotence—"

Desperately, "I'm famished!"

"Very well, Your Omnipotence. You may stop here for a while and avail yourself of the pump attendant's hospitality."

The car door opens. I step out gingerly, unsure of myself. The old whiteman prostrates himself, and now I see why he has been chosen to survive: there is a reddish, blotchy birthmark on his back, just by his left armpit. Imperfections displease the Sun.

Two boys, young, laughing, run out of the building, stop, look at me shyly. Their golden hair is beautiful, the soft fair down on their naked bodies is beautiful; they are the image of the glory of the young sun.

What a beautiful people! What a splendid life, I think, to live so perilously near to the God, to know that one will die for the Sun, that the obsidian knife will inevitably fall. These children, for instance; they are truly close to Divinity, their every breath is a rapturous urgency in the face of destiny.

I'm jealous.

At a word from their father, the boys retreat into the building. The old man rises, beckons to me.

There is a small throne room behind the refueling station. Wordlessly, as they have trained me, I walk up the ten or fifteen steps and seat myself. There is a smell of disuse about the place; am I the first Living God who has deigned to stop here?

A dumpy, unlovely whitewoman comes in and prostrates herself beside the man. He dismisses her.

"I am hungry," I reiterate. I realize it is true: I have been fasting for five days. Then I wait in silence.

Eventually the woman returns with a golden platter. To my dismay I recollect that as the Living Sun I am only officially allowed one kind of food.

As the platter is passed up to me, I see two human hearts, raw, bloody. I hesitate briefly—but I have been well schooled. Not wishing to offend, I devour them greedily, making the requisite noises of gluttony and delight. Soundlessly, the woman takes the platter from my lap and leaves the room, crawling abjectly, arthritically.

The old man sits on the floor at the foot of the steps. We are alone in the small throneroom. It is quite dark; the only light comes from two candles at my feet, mounted on skulls.

Again I think about the beauty of his people, how blest they are in the Sun's divine love. They are really the Chosen race: they go to the Sun every year in their tens of thousands, chosen by lot from the Feeder reservations, they all ascend the golden escalator into the sky....

I see that the man is gazing at me with that same look of hatred. It is incomprehensible, for I am wearing the benevolence of the God who has eaten his fill. I wave my hand in blessing, only to be answered by the relentless look of hate.

"Why do you hate me?" The scientist in me is momentarily forced to the surface.

"You ask why I hate you!" he grates. "You, the lordly one, the symbol of tyranny, whose whim raises us for slaughter."

I am thunderstruck. This interview is not going at all as I expected. "What do you mean?" He is bitter, I reflect, because he is too imperfect to have been chosen.

He can hardly control his rage. "This 'religion' of yours," he scoffs. "You know it's an excuse to enslave us!"

"What do you mean, 'religion'? The People are enlightened, we go by scientific principles and axioms." I struggle to remain calm, because I feel the dormant skepticism in me stirring again. "It's your unfounded 'cults' that are 'religious.' Why, when we first conquered you, you were worshipping some unfortunate criminal tied to a tree!"

His raving is lunatic. All too clearly I see the totality of the flaw that must have barred him from union with the Sun.

"Don't think you've brainwashed us all, you so-called God! You are Professor Kuzdai from Antarctic Research. We send our children to your training schools,where your priests knock elevating thoughts into their heads about divine destiny—but we are there too, with the truth!"

"But I am going to die, too," I protest unconfidently.

"You *chose!*"

My hidden skepticism whispers that a precious illusion is being shattered, for the good. But I make an effort to combat the thought, to see the madman for what he is.

"So what can you do about it?" I say, petulantly. "You will die anyway, 'truth' or no 'truth'...unless you fall short," I add, looking at his birthmark with distaste.

"For a God, you're not particularly omniscient," he sneers. "So I won't enlighten you about the hidden armoury, the secret army, the Messiah or leader that is to come."

I have had enough. "I bless you, madman," I intone, my Divine voice tinged with irony. He rises, shaking his fist at me, and leaves the throneroom.

The driver comes to fetch me.

The sun is setting; the grass is blood-red, the building and the gas pumps are a gloomy black against the red sun-glow.

I see the old man cowering in the shadows.

I am filled with great compassion. His imaginary world moves me, with its armies, its fighting, its Medieval revengings. I don't stop to ask myself why I feel for him so strongly, knowing that it might be the darkness inside me that answers.

I don't want to leave so abruptly, so, in a kind voice, I try to ask some meaningless, trivial question: "Where are the children?"

To my astonishment, the old man breaks down, he crouches, clinging to his fuel pump in a hideous parody of a lover's embrace, sobbing uncontrollably, despairingly, into the dusk.

I cannot understand this. I am powerless, though a God.

He lashes out at me from a face distorted with unspeakable grief:

"You ate their hearts!"

* * *

Monotony, monotony.

So easy to slip back into the past....

The radio has stopped functioning now and won't let itself be fixed. So we have become truly isolated, a self-sufficient island universe in the Antarctic waste. It has been many weeks since the object spoke to me.

I am too terrified to go into the laboratory alone now. When I am there I talk incessantly—my new volubility is much commented on, especially by my wife—

"Can't you shut up? I can't think."

I stop talking for a moment, but without even looking at the object I can sense the vague stirring in my mind. Quickly I go on talking about this and that, joking about the state of putrefaction of this or the other tissue sample, remarking on how this flask is more congealed than the other, just the usual laboratory small talk. And suddenly I'm alone.

But here I am at that same stool again. I don't think I can keep up these defenses much longer, I'll go crazy.

Question pops into my mind.

"Why don't you do a spectrographic analysis of the sun?"

Analyze the sun? I am tempted. The awareness of heresy makes me shiver, though, in spite of the stifling warmth. Nervously, I fumble with the sun-disc clasp of my bear-skin cloak. The ghostly voice is silent, leaving me without an external object on which to project my inner conflict.

A few days later I discover the composition of the sun. It has been very simple to design the equipment, given one awesome leap of imaginative thinking—to *look* at the sun. It's hardly a new device, using the tell-tale lines in a spectrum—Ixtyl's cassettes are almost a hundred years old.

It is all hydrogen, a trace of helium. Elements you can find on earth—the lightest ones, strangely but plausibly consistent with known scientific theories.

What of the divine matter then, that all the ancient cassettes sing about? Everybody *knows* what the sun is made of, whatever the readings may say....

I have seen the results with my own eyes, my scientist's eyes. Another shattered illusion.

Days later, another question: "Where do all the elements come from?"

"I'm tired!" I shout to the empty room.

Here I am, toying with the clasp again, and I'm dog-tired. The others have all gone with the huskies to the nearest supply station. For a while the blizzards have abated; it's the first opportunity.

I don't want to communicate with the object again. I'm starting to regret not going along, and yet I seem to have manipulated staying behind. Sweat glues me to the stool; I lay myself open to temptation again.

I am in two minds now. The questions have set up radical new trains of thought, seditious, positively evil, but undeniably logical. Why doesn't the object talk to anyone else? Is the object talking to me at all, or is it some repressed inner self that is using the object to express its ungodly being?

The new question, now: automatically, I fall to thinking. Hydrogen is the simplest element, and the others have bigger atoms; atoms are surrounded (according to the recent hypothesis) by energy-shells that are the basis for electricity and chemical reactions. But atoms don't *come from*; they are. I fail to see the point of it.

The sphere gleams quietly in the shadows. Wonderingly, I pick it up—I am not now so sure of its celestial origin—and I gaze into it. Another question comes: a whisper, resonant, insidious.

"Is the atom indivisible?"

"Yes, of course, by definition!"

I blurt out. The question irritates me by its illogicality. I slam the object down on the table; it rests, unperturbed.

"Is the atom indivisible?"

Why, if it weren't, you could synthesize other atoms by pushing together hydrogen atoms!

Why, why—my mind is racing with unheard-of extrapolations. Have I been drugged, is the object some diabolical mind-control device? But if the Sun is all hydrogen, and helium is the next highest element by weight, then couldn't the atoms be so crushed together in the sun that they fuse together—at some terrific, unimaginable pressure? And then wouldn't this tearing up of atomic structure release enormous amounts of power—more then electricity, *much* more?

It would explain the burning of the sun, the creation of all other elements! I see a vision of earth as a conglomeration of heavy atoms thrust out from the sun in some fiery, grand agony of birth.

Then, logically, there are some stupefying conclusions:

The human sacrifices have nothing to do with the sun's energy source—

And the sun is only a mechanism, not a God!

My world comes tumbling down.

I get up reeling from my stool, pace frenziedly up and down the corridor, my steps echoing metallically in the emptiness. I try to calm down. Why, I have the secret of everything in my hands, it's only another step, a matter of time, from knowing how it operates to being able to reproduce it....

The tension cracks.

The object gleams seductively, but I am numb.

I find myself in my seat again, scrawling the theory in my diary. It's only a theory, I keep writing, logical, but it contradicts all known realities.

Obviously, I tell myself, this continual isolation, this constant sexual tension between me and Locust and Takl, has damaged my capacity to reason. I'm mad, this is all madness. They say the midnight sun gets to you, the continual exposure to God, enveloping you, penetrating walls of solid steel. I'm not pure enough to be here, my heart conceals some secret darkness.

I calm myself with a superhuman effort. I look, feigning

impassiveness, at what I've written in the diary. It is incoherent, ludicrous. Analyzing myself, I note the beginnings of a dangerous megalomania. "Secret of everything," indeed! Carefully I lock the diary away in its drawer. If I don't look at it, it can't damage my mind any further.

I need to see a priest, to leave the station for a while. Nervously, I unclasp my cloak, try to clamp down the noisy chattering of my teeth.

Resolutely, I say to myself: This excitement is unwarranted. I'll simply call the Ministry of Science—what's left of it—and ask for a brief vacation.

A chilling gust of wind and Takl is there. I imagine her ready to pounce on me, like a tigress. Paranoia.

We stand, face to face, a few inches apart. I am about to speak.

"Why, what is it?" she demands, shoving the door closed. She does not seem concerned.

I tell her I am going for psychiatric counseling, probably at the home Temple at the city of Nefertari, in Egypt. I explain briefly: "The sun-sphere: I keep thinking that it's talking to me, giving me strange, corrupting notions."

"Oh, it's been talking to you too?" she remarks.

I can only gape. They're all in collusion against me!

"You're a fool," she says. "And a coward. There are big changes afoot, you can't just cling to the old ways."

Chillingly I realize the extent of her irreligiousness. Yes, they're all in it together, they, the sphere, the ungodly people, they probably planted the sphere to delude me, to drive me to this despair.

Paranoia is inevitable, I keep insisting to myself. Must get a grip on myself.

"Pack," she tells me, and walks away. I follow her into the little bedroom, and she has already started to sort out the clothes. She is well experienced, since this is my second nervous breakdown.

I let her do all the packing. I'm completely disoriented, I wander in a daze, succumbing to an unnatural feeling of entrapment, the new thoughts continually stealing into my consciousness. I don't dare to acknowledge the crucial conclusion, so I try to banish my thoughts by humming and mumbling to myself.

Now I'm in the lab. It's all so unreal, so out of focus... vaguely I see the shifting shapes of the flasks and bottles, I glance at the torn poster of a pregnant whitewoman gazing raptly at the

Sun, at the stool which I have kicked over at some point. My travel satchel is in my hand.

Locust is watching, strangely, as I carelessly load the gleaming sphere into it. She doesn't ask me why, and I am hardly aware that I am taking my temptation with me.

The thoughts again.

God is God! I repeat over and over in my mind, as though to drown out anything else. I long for some proof of God. You cannot gauge the profundity of my despair.

* * *

We are rapidly approaching the heartland of The People. There are deserts and more deserts, and then the highway broadens. The driver slows the car for the last few hundred miles: the triumphal progress through the Seven Cities of Gold.

Dots on the horizon grow into great pyramidal ziggurats that line the road, some of steel and concrete, others half-crumbling stone, relics of the past now veined with shrubbery. In between the pyramids, a forest of statues—squat, grimacing fertility gods, bloated war gods from forgotten war-town antiquity, red paint still lurid on their lips, fallen statues of dead heroes and kings, arms and heads half-buried in the sand.

My lips tighten. I must prepare myself for what is to come.

First there is a distant hum, inoffensive, like lowing cattle. Steadily it grows, and there are people everywhere, yelling the names of the Sun, waving, prostrating themselves, on either side of the highway. Zetsoc is one of the great cities of the world, with 200,000 people. . . .

A mother, laughing, lifts up her gap-toothed child to see the God. An ocean of faces washing the windows, old men are tearing their clothes and throwing them at the car, the streets are strewn with feather headdresses, bowler hats, confetti.

The roof of the car opens, my throne rises slowly, and I sit, my arms upraised until they ache, ascending into the sun's oppressive glare.

The throng is hushed. Still I rise, then lifting my ceremonial obsidian knife I point it at my breast, my left arm pointing towards the sun.

At once there comes a surge of yelling, fanatical screaming, for the Sun has shown his willingness to die so he may feed on himself, for the sake of man. And first an old man comes running and throws himself prone onto the highway; the car speeds up a little, I feel the crunch as the tires crush him, and then another one immolates himself, becomes one with the chariot of the sun, and another—and still I rise hydraulically, majestically into the sky, my face masked into the appropriate expression of otherworldly strangeness; blood splashes the tires and spatters the windows, and so we go on through the city, like a surfboard battling the tide.

Never have I felt such power. The grandeur of my gestures, the sense of eternity in my gestures, as I become, I *am*, all those who have preceded me!

There is a coldness in me, a sense of immense distance. My mask of indifference becomes real; I am really unmoved.

Now I can truly say I am the God. In Louisville, two boys died for me. In Zetsoc hundreds give up their lives, too frenzied to feel pain, squelched into laughing death, extinguishing their being at the very source of their being.

* * *

Sitting there, with the sunlight on me, I lose interest in the screams of the dying. I am recalling how I came to be here, in my former incarnation as Kuzdai, the neurotic scientist....

I have come home. Takl has come too; she insists I am too sick to be alone. She does feel a kind of love for me, I think.

We live not far from the great Pyramid of Khufu. You all know the story—or any child could recite it to you—of how the Emperor came to conquer Eqypt. It was Montezuma II of the age of the great ships. When he saw the Pyramids he wept; amid the alien peoples they were so familiar, so sun-blessed. And—so the story goes—the Emperor fell to his knees, disregarding the hot sand blowing in his face, gazing for hours at the marvel of antiquity. He laid his weapons down (muskets or swords—the oral tradition is vague, since at the time we hadn't even dis- covered, let alone banned, the 'writing' of the whitemen), he spared the People and sailed home west, into the sunset. Egypt is that sort of place; very holy, very contradictory—after all, why are the Pyramids there at all, when the people themselves were not The People?

I drive to the Pyramid, where there is a small psychiatric center. Its two red-brick stories are deep in the pyramid's shadow. I park the car.

My priest-counselor receives me: tall, pale, almost white- man-colored in his complexion. He has kindly eyes, surprisingly large and young-looking for his age. We sit and talk in one of the sound-proofed cubicles reserved for the mentally ill.

"Well," he begins this final session. "We've progressed quite far, I think; it seems, after all, to be only a conventional aberration, remarkable only in its extremity."

The memory of my extravagant heresy is warning. I keep the object in my car, these days, daring myself to face its blandishments, but it has never spoken in the two months since my return home. I associate my confusion with the blizzards, the isolation, the bitter cold.

"Do you feel healed?" he asks me gently.

Emphatically, I reply "Yes."

"I think not, though; there is an inner core of—something analysis hasn't penetrated at all. But I think you must find the way yourself, from now on. All I can suggest is that you go out for a long while into the desert. Seek communion with the Sun. Your spirits will be lifted, perhaps your religious crisis will be blown away."

When I leave I feel dissatisfied. I start to drive away. On impulse, I leave the highway, thrusting out into the directionless sand. I want to be alone with the sun for a few hours. Perhaps the priest is right.

I go on and on into the monotonous yellow expanse, suddenly becoming aware of the resemblance between the two wildernesses, the desert and the freezing wilderness where it all began. The sun beats down on me—the car is roofless—the heat is as extreme as the cold was, the yellow like the white, stretching forever. I feel confusion again, and glance at the sphere that is lying at my feet.

A dune looms up: behind it, an array of parked limousines and tethered camels. I curse misanthropically; I did not expect to stumble onto other people.

A brass band is playing, French horns and Tibetan trumpets. There are about two hundred cars dotted about, and, as I should have realized, it is the Sphinx in its newly moved location in the middle of nowhere. A golden escalator has been added up the creature's flanks and all the way to its back, where an Altar to the Sun has been built, a gaudy, feathery outgrowth of the animal's back.

There is the Sphinx, superb, incomprehensible. I note the new nose done like a quetzal-beak, the neon-blinking sun-disc halo above its head.

Priests are singing softly. I get out of the car and start trudging towards the celebrations. It is quite a long walk and when I arrive I am exhausted, burning.

People are clustered round, singing in unison. Some are

wearing outlandish costumes of the subject peoples—tuxedos, doublets, grass skirts. There are long tables for the ensuing feast, laden with suckling pigs and champagne machines.

A girl emerges from the house between the Sphinx's paws. She is surrounded, jostled by priests with their peacock-feather-topped staffs and heavy robes, and she herself is naked. They are crowding her, but she is far away, like a slide projection, not quite real.

She smiles.

I push myself up to the front of the crowd, she walks past me, her arm brushes against mine. The serenity of the smile! The steadfastness of the walk! The sun plays on her long golden hair, gentle on her, while savagely scorching the crowd. Her eyes are cold like the Arctic Sea, already turned to the God.

She has the peace I long for. I crave it. As she passes me, the singing swells, an ancient paean in the old tongue, and I join them; I'm carried away with my sense of belonging to the one People.

Now she has reached the escalator of gold. For a moment she pauses—an instant of frail humanness!—then she goes to the Sun, standing stock-still on the moving sunsteps. The priest high above us raises the knife. It flashes dazzlingly in the sunlight and you can see nothing else for a moment. One with the crowd, I am dizzy with joy.

The priest—he is a robot—rips open the girl's chest; accurately he finds the heart and tears it out, lifts it, still bloody, to the sky.

The heat, the heat! I am dumbfounded by the outpouring of energy, of benevolence, from the sky.

And I know.

Of course! There is something that can purify my mind, cleanse me, wash my iniquity from me.

How did I ever waver? How could I ever have conceived that the Sun is a mechanical object? It's all so logical. Joy is in the people's hearts as they sing, it must stem from a fundamental reality. Joy isn't founded on a lie.

And I can become part of it. I am singing as I walk back to the car, the sun bores into my pores and the sweat gushes out, my feet are burning as they tramp into the hot sand.

I see the globe glinting in the car.

Suddenly: "You wish to extinguish yourself for the sake of a known untruth?"

But with a rather self-conscious sense of symbolism I pick it up and dash it hard against the sand.

It rolls in the direction of the Sphinx, out of sight.

I am still humming the hymn to myself as I pull into the center to volunteer as the one yearly Victim chosen from the People to play the role of the living Sun.

When I emerge, Takl has come to meet me from the supermarket. We are standing outside the Temple gates. When I tell her, she looks right through me and says—as though to herself—"Do you know? The object only asked me one question. It said: 'What would the sun be if it were a trillion trillion miles away?'

"It obsessed me, that question. For of course, the sun would be a star. It's a crafty object, that sun-sphere. Because it was only logical for me to turn it around, to realize that all the stars are suns, and if there can be other suns, there must be other earths.

"Kuzdai, we're not the center of the Universe! The source of the sphere is not the Sun. And there is more to come, I know, much more.

"You're not going to accomplish anything by dying—you're merely pandering to your own selfishness."

It stings me, that she cannot understand the simplest of motives. Quietly, I try to disillusion her: "But by dying, I'll preserve the whole structure of our beliefs—my beliefs. The world will be sealed into its true course, since only I have conceived of these ideas and they will die with me."

"A martyr complex! They haven't healed you at all!"

"What are you worried about? They'll take care of you," I counter, with a nonchalance I do not feel.

I stalk away to the car.

This is the essence of my transcendent revelation: I never looked at the sun. I never made the spectrograph. Vain fantasies, delusions of loneliness that have been dissipated by the sunshine, like the night by the day.

Then why am I speechless with rage as I drive away? Why does Takl's meaningless accusation provoke me?

* * *

We've arrived.

The holy citadel on the high mountain.

Night. Gloom.

They have left me alone in the cavernous marble hall. It is so dark that the room seems endless. Quiet sounds: cicadas, distant hymning to me. No wind to touch the stillness of it.

Footsteps. A barrage of artificial light. A palanquin approaches, covered with purple silk veils, billowing as the bearers sway.

They set it down. It is a splash in the marmoreal whiteness. I ascend my throne. A bearer partially lifts one veil; out steps the Emperor-Dictator, His Divinity Montezuma XVIII.

Now he is just a form prostrated at the foot of the throne. I survey him, my expression haughty.

"Oh Sun! I come to pay Thee customary homage before Thou returnest to the sky, and to bring Thee Thy bride."

It is a clear voice, dispassionate. I bless him, smiling benignly. The Emperor humbles himself still lower. I feel pride; the Emperor kneels to me!

He dismisses his retinue. The lights are dimmed as he rises, obscuring his face. We are alone together in the gloom, the only light the flickering of an incense-burner, blue green, smoke-heavy and fragrant.

"A clever way of arranging an audience," he says, fingering the flashing medals on his military uniform. "You might as well stop this charade now, Kuzdai. God, indeed." He snickers unpleasantly.

He has confused me. I come down from the throne. I do not see his face because it is in the shadow; he seems like a talking uniform, decapitated by the darkness. I think there is a penetrating stare.

"Curious? Quite a calculated risk, Kuzdai. But do you think you could be allowed to die, after *this*?"

He thrusts something at me. Involuntarily I catch it with both arms. It is the diary.

"How—?"

He disregards my question. " 'The secret of everything.' Yes, Kuzdai. You will not die; a robot will be killed in your place. It's been done before."

"What!"

"I want you to help me," he says wearily. "You say there is a possibility of making the power, of imitating the sun. Without the tyranny of the sky, civilization will push forward, nobody will die needlessly again."

I can't believe my ears. "You're mad," I gasp, realizing with a shock that His Divinity has *read* the diary, that he has allowed his position to be polluted by an obscenity.

"No, Kuzdai. This was planned. There was a fireball that fell into my garden, whispering strange thoughts to me. I didn't want to hear them, but I became more aware of the nature of responsibility. I allowed your research to continue because of it; and you saw through to a solution I didn't envisage, but nevertheless a solution."

I am terrified. "How can the Emperor be a heretic?" I blurt out, my mind awhirl with contradiction. "How can you stand here and say this in front of your God?"

He laughs, quite warmly. His mood becomes more patronizing: "It's all right. It's not a trap, Kuzdai. I'm a ruler, and a ruler is by nature a skeptic."

"You're a traitor!" I feel my convictions strengthened. I am the God, tomorrow I will die and it is not for nothing. "I can feel your dishonesty, your political ambition, perverting your sense of reality. You can't change facts, and I'm not going to change them for you."

His Divinity says, grimly, "This play-acting has gone to your head. Delusions of grandeur. Remember, the real power is mine, yours the illusion."

"No! I've raised myself up from confusion, I've absorbed the truth. I'll not go back into the darkness that the sun has wiped from my mind. There is an almighty battle between good and evil to obtain my soul, and if you win, the Sun will not shine tomorrow."

"Tomorrow," His Divinity muses, "I could have it announced by radio, all over the world, that the Sun is not a God, that millions have been sacrificed for nothing. I could proclaim a new era of life and mercy—I'll find someone else to do the research, create the energy, if you die."

"They would not believe you."

A pause. "I know," says the Emperor. A tremendous sadness emanates from the shadows where he stands, and the voice rings hollowly in the huge chamber.

Finally, he asks me in a formal voice:

"Living God, what dost Thou desire?"

So I have convinced him, cured him. "To die," I declare. Fervently, firmly, according to the ancient formula. The god has conquered temptation!

"For the Sun will not rise tomorrow, nor the warmth of the Sun descend upon the earth, unless I return to my celestial abode. I am the heart of life, and I offer unto myself my own living heart, for the sake of my servant Man.

"Thus I speak those words in the city of Texcatlipoca, where my rays first struck the earth a thousand years before the coming of Man.

"At least give me the book," the Emperor—the incarnate trickster-god!—pleads.

"No," I say, tossing it into the flames of the incense burner. The blue-green fire devours the pages, flaring up for a brief moment.

"Ah well," the Emperor-Dictator sighs. "There is one more formality.

"I must bring Thee Thy Bride. And she is here with us, the Princess Hatakatl, my sister."

He steps aside, and another figure has stepped unnoticed from the palanquin.

When she comes to me, naked and lovely, I understand how many things have come to be; the feigned stupidity, the naive questions that ferreted out necessary truths, the night my diary was seen by another. She was no fool, this girl Locust.

* * *

Before the Dawn that is not to come.

No crowds, but an endless staircase of rough-hewn rock. Two priests only for this most private ceremony, the Emperor and his sister on their thrones, torchlight.

Theatrically, a shaft of light bursts onto a golden escalator next to the ancient staircase.

The two priests motion me to ascend.

"It is not my wish."

Brief consternation.

"I choose this ancient staircase where I first ascended."

All are relieved, except the two royals, who sit rigidly, without apparent emotion.

I begin the ascent.

Each step brings me nearer to God, to myself. The peace comes to me at last. Robes weigh down on me, seven layers of ornate cloaks and coverlets. The golden crown presses down tight around my skull and still I climb to spite it; it is so dark that I cannot see to the summit of the pyramid, but I climb on.

At each step the heaviness lifts, the robes grow lighter. I am loftily at peace, alone, giving up everything and gaining everything. I'm dying for the pump attendant with his bitter delusions, for cold Takl, for warm Locust, for the skeptic Emperor-Dictator.

Immortality!

I climb. The air becomes harder to breathe, but I am indefatigable. My passion and death are in the old manner—no escalators, no machinery to mar the perfection of my sacrifice.

Will they never end? Step follows step, I never stumble, though the steps are steep and treacherous.

Now the pinnacle is in sight. The clouds are dark. I am one, alone. I begin to sing softly to myself.

And then—

Abruptly, the sky bursts into flame! I jerk up my head to see a million fireballs raining from the sky. There is a thunder like gigantic war-guns, the sky is brighter than day. I cover my eyes with my hands, I try to climb on regardless, but I am rooted to the spot. Again and again there are explosions in the sky, and then comes a huge voice pounding into my brain, reverberant, soul-shaking...and I sense that the others far below are hearing too, that perhaps everybody on earth hears.

"The truth is painful, but necessary.

"There are other earths. We are from such another earth, and we have come to help you solve your problem of self-annihilation.

"Direct intervention now becomes necessary to save the life of one Kuzdai, who we have selected to help lead your People through a perilous ordeal of re-orientation into a productive way of life."

No! My illusions are having one final try at claiming my soul! No, I order these visions to desist from tormenting me, I order with all the force and the power and the majesty of the Sun whose incarnation I am!

Wildly, I scream out:

Wildly, I scream out: "You can't take choice away from me! I make myself free of you!"

And I wrench myself away from the spot, I run up the last hundred steps, my eyes closed to the tumultuous burning of the sky. I reach the altar, carelessly I fling down my robes and offer myself, knowing full well that the robot priest is not programmed for such a contingency and has no choice, while I am a man and must choose.

So I am lying on the altar and the sky is burning before the dawn and I can taste the lips of Locust on my lips and the obsidian knife flashes and rips into my entrails with a messy splat.

* * *

Time runs backwards.

Agony! My heart flies back into my chest, the blood races from the stone steps into my arteries, with a searing pain my wounds close tight together.

It is day. The fireballs are rapidly shrinking into brilliant dots against a cloudless sky.

On the altar there is a single sphere. It speaks to me, its voice no longer ghostly, but a voice of reason and authority.

"I am sorry. But you never had any choice," says the creature in my mind. "You see, we have power even to reverse the time flow locally, to alter the continuum to a small extent."

"So I was wrong."

"...not exactly. You were chosen. Our agent placed no ideas in your mind that were not latent, ready to pop out if you would only let them. You have a strong sense of right and wrong, and that is necessary too. You were willing to die for it."

"In the end, it was only selfishness."

"Not exactly; you were demonstrating something for the whole species—in the end, you died for the sake of freedom, of individuality. Those were your final thoughts. And we will not tamper with that individuality, we promise."

"Why did you not just reveal yourselves, take over?"

"We do not tamper. The voice was your own voice, your scientist's voice."

A pause, then: "I am sorry it became necessary to interfere, because now we have thrust you into the galactic community. I think only a few like you possess the imagination to prepare your people."

It seems, then, that the real power has finally come to me.

It is too soon, I think, to measure the full impact of Their coming: especially the knowledge that they will be here with us, superior to us, for a very long time.

Is it possible we have merely exchanged the tyranny of our own misconceptions for the tyranny of aliens?

From this height I can see the whole city, a cluster of toy houses; I can see the twin royals still unmoving on their thrones at the foot of the broken steps. A strong damp wind strikes my face, makes me shiver, and I gather up my discarded cloaks.

Sunrise has come, and there has been no sacrifice.

—Bangkok, 1977

Aquila the God

Now here's the obverse of the coin; Indians, Romans, and spectacle once more, but now treated rather satirically. You may notice that, as a tribute to the custom in Hollywood spectacles of the fifties and sixties, I have the Romans speaking in pronounced British accents. Something else about this story, which became absorbed into my forthcoming novel, The Aquiliad, due out eventually from Timescape Books: never has so much research been expended on something of so little substance!

As soon as I arrived in Terra Nova as the Emperor Domitian's newly appointed procurator of the province of Lacotia, I made all the usual decrees: renovating the procurator's palace at Caesarea-on-Miserabilis; engaging the impresario Lucretius Lupus to provide sufficiently astounding beasts and gladiators for the weeklong games in my own honor; and sending parties of surveyors to check up on the aqueducts, temples, and other public works that my predecessors had created.

In my time I had traveled most of the Roman world—I had been as tourist to Egypt and Hispania, and as Dux of the Thirty-Fourth Legion to Dacia and as far east as Cappadocia, where I had a run-in with the Parthians. But I was unprepared for Terra Nova. They had warned me that the place was at least as huge as the rest of the Empire. That the two provinces under our control, Iracuavia and Lacotia, were as vast as Europe, wild and impenetrable, and swarming with savages of a thousand kinds and languages. I heard of the mighty Miserabilis, a river longer than the Nile; of the Montes Saxosi, mountains at the Empire's limits that dwarfed that Alps and the Caucasus. But none of the stories—and not even my prior acquaintance of a tribe of Lacotii, who had helped me in my struggle with the Parthians—was as astonishing as the reality. It was the little details that were most alien: the strutting, giant chickens; the skin-tent villages, the feathered countenances of my new subjects. And the distances; for it took me almost three months, even with the advanced new ships, to reach the port of Eboracum Novum, and then many months of overland and upriver travel to reach the realm I was to rule.

I have told of my official acts on reaching Caesarea, a jewel of a little city, nice Roman temples and insulae and fora and agorae and a little amphitheatre and racecourse, nestled in a fork of the River Miserabilis, a comforting chunk of Rome in the midst of unending plains dotted here and there with clusters of tipis and vast herds of aurochs. My first private act was to have a marble statue of Aquila made, and to install it in an atrium of my palace.

For Aquila, the barbarian, chieftain of the Tetonii tribe of Lacotians and the Emperor's favorite, was responsible for my being in this forsaken wilderness. Oh, he didn't mean anything by it, I'm sure. And a great deal of it was simply Domitian's annual purge of the up-and-coming. But here I was, and he was in Rome, no doubt enjoying all the things I couldn't have: peacocks' brains! raw unborn dormice dipped in honey! and the wine, the good Greek wine that cost a whole aureus here for a single jug.

Each day, as I sat in the procurator's seat and signed documents or pronounced judgments, I would be looking straight at the statue's face. I'd made sure the sculptor made it quite unflattering; the beak of a nose, the coronet of scraggly eagle feathers, the unkempt, stringy hair, the stooped shoulders, and the smirky expression: all had been very accurately displayed. When particularly frustrated I would pelt it with rotten fruits.

Indeed, I was doing just that one fateful morning, when I found out just how devious, relentless, and unmitigated Domitian's dislike for me really was.

I was on a couch by the fountain, having my morning Lacotian lesson. In every other land of the Empire we had established Latin or Greek as the lingua franca, but not here; we had been beaten to it by a system of peculiar hand-signals and gestures with which all the savages, no matter which barbarous tongue they used, could communicate. My boyhood tutor Nikias, a sexagenarian by now, who had preceded me into Lacotia, had made it his life's task to study the dialects of Lacotia and to compile a monstrous Lacotian-Greek Lexicon. It was easier to learn from him than from some savage; and so, though it was almost forty years since I'd sat on his knee and recited my *alpha beta gamma*, it was as though nothing had changed.

"No, master Titus," he was saying, pointing at the scroll on which I had been laboriously trying to translate Virgil from Latin into Lacotian using the Greek-letter transcription system Nikias had devised (for the Lacotian Savages wrote only in pictures before our coming). "Not at all. You see, here you've written *mit'awichu* for 'my wife' and *mit'achinki'shi* for 'my son.' But you see, 'son' takes the *intrinsic* possessive, so that should just be *michinki'shi*. The extrinsic possessive is used for alienable or distant possessions, such as a wife who might after all be divorced, whereas a son—"

"Jove blast these Lacotians!" I said. "Why can't they have simple declensions and conjugations, like civilized languages? So we do have six hundred different endings in Latin, but at least we bloody well know what the word's doing in the sentence! None of this extrinsic and intrinsic possession...oh, I'd give anything for a good old irregular Greek contracted verb. Well, I suppose you might as well finish correcting the paragraph...."

"Well, actually the rest of the sentence is wrong too. You see, when 'thou' is the subject and 'them' the object, the two pronouns are replaced by the prefix *wichaya-* and for the plural you must add -*pi* to form *wichayak'tepi,* 'you (plural) kill them,' but then—"

"Curse it! How did *you* ever learn all this nonsense?"

"I was a slave once, master Titus. Slaves learn very quickly, or else end up a spectacle-fodder for the circus."

I sighed. The sun was rising over the Temple of Augustus. I cursed at the statue of Aquila, smug and smarmy in his war-bonnet and toga. Damn them all! "Just *one* goblet of Chian wine, that's all I want. Half a goblet."

"First you have to hold court a while, my lord; then I'll go down to the steward's and see whether there is any."

"There isn't. I drank the dregs yesterday." I stood up and shook my toga straight. "Any good court cases?"

"Nothing; just a run-of-the-mill crucifixion or two, and oh, a raid on the southern town of Cansapolis by the wild Apaxian tribes beyond the border. A delegation of the Cansae are here to ask for help."

"Oh good, I'll be able to practice my Lacotian on them."

"Wrong dialect, I'm afraid. Related, I think, but not mutually comprehensible."

"Damn these Lacotians and their squabbling tribes and their countless languages."

"If you say so, my lord."

I hefted half a pumpkin at Aquila's face.

Just at that moment all hell broke loose outside the palace. Hoofbeats thudded. Shields and weapons clanked. "Oh no," I said, "not another coup-counting expedition!"

Tubae blared. Slaves scurried in and started swabbing at Aquila with mops. "Visitors," said Nikias. Gathering my dignity as my body-slave handed me my vestments of office, I ascended the steps to my procurator's seat. The riders were near now. Suddenly slaves and officials were scuttling in at the main entry to the atrium, scattering in the wake of the mounted messengers, while the trumpets barked raggedly and out of tune. "Those savages!" I cried. "They ride into one's very house. Nikias, have them executed or flogged or something on their way out."

They dismounted.

I recognized four Praetorians in spanking new uniforms. A pretty, over-dressed page bearing a scroll on a silver platter. And behind them—in the toga praetexta of a senator yet—an ancient man with a beak for a nose, wearing a ridiculous headpiece that was a tasteless mismatch of golden laurel wreath and eagle-feather war-bonnet.

"Aquila!" I shouted.

"I see you've been getting good use out of my statue, my dear General Titus," he said, approaching my throne, and curiously eyeing the slaves as they scrubbed at the still pumpkinified nose of the marble image.

"What's it to you?" I snapped. Then emotion overcame me. "Oh, Aquila...I've been so miserable here!" I had missed him terribly, and had never had the guts to admit it to myself. I got off my throne and went down to embrace him. "My friend! Has the Emperor recalled me? Perhaps he's dead and one of my friends is on the throne?"

"Come, come, stiff upper lip and all that, you know," he said.

"A year in Rome and you talk just like my father," I said, and he shrugged.

"To business, Titus; and I think you'd better get back on that official chair of yours—"

"You dare to command—" I stopped. He picked up a purple-bordered fold of his senatorial toga and whisked it in my face.

"I'm not a savage, you know. In fact, the Emperor has made me next in line to the procuratorship—although I've frankly declined the honor. Sooner or later one gets purged, I found."

I climbed back on my throne. I was now the voice of the Senate and People of Rome; that is to say, Caesar's mouthpiece, I put on a good menacing mien as befitted my role.

"There's a good lad." I pretended to ignore his patronizing tone. In spite of my five minutes of enthusiasm, I was already wishing the uppity savage into a nice hot niche in Hades. Then Aquila came forward and placed an object in my hand, cool and smooth. I looked at it.

"Strange," I said. It was a statuette, carved in jade, only a few fingers tall, but worked in lavish detail. It was a baby—no sex could be distinguished—caught in the middle of some supernatural transformation, for parts of its face and body were shifting into those of some feral cat-creature, leopard or tiger perhaps. It was not exactly beautiful; any Greek craftsman would have inveighed at length about its lack of proportion, its complete disregard of natural human posture. The expression was what held me: it was both anguished and joyful, unhuman. I knew it as the face of some god.

"What is it?" I said.

Aquila said, "It came to Rome with Trajan's triumph, one of the many spoils of the campaign against the Seminolii and the Chirochian Confederation. Caesar was so captivated with it that for weeks he stared all day at it, neglecting the government, not even participating in the customary banquets and orgies."

Looking at the statuette, I understood. "But what culture has fashioned this thing? The only jade-works I have ever seen have come from the distant east, down the silk route from the empire of the yellow folk which no one has ever seen; but, this workmanship is different from theirs. And this is no god I've ever heard of."

"General Titus, the Word of Caesar!" Aquila said. Tubae brayed resoundingly, and the silver platter with the scroll on it was presented to me.

This is what I read:

> To Titus Papinianus, Procurator of Lacotia, from the Divine Domitian, greeting.
>
> Titus old boy!
>
> Thought you'd got out of my hair, did you? Thought I'd never bother you again, eh, out there in the middle of the wilderness with nothing but barbarians for company? Well, you thought wrong, I'm afraid. My famous sense of humor prompts me to issue new commands.
>
> I have a new favorite at court, Leukippos, son of the philosopher Epaminondas whose visions created the motor-car and the quick-sailing-ship. He is one of those scientists, you know. He's re-calculated the old figures of that ancient Eratosthenes, and has decided that Eratosthenes's estimate of the circumference of the earth is wrong by some vast factor. The upshot of it all is this...that the fabled Middle Empire, called by the Hindish traders Chin or China, ought to lie somewhere within the great continent of Terra Nova. This statuette—which I can hardly bear to part with—is further proof, since everyone knows that only the Chinish peoples have the art of carving jade.
>
> Well, can you guess yet, my dear Titus, how I plan to bring about your downfall? Yes indeed! I want more of these things. I want that Kingdom discovered at once. In time we'll send a real general, someone competent like Trajan, to do the actual conquering, but in the meantime I want you to explore beyond the Empire's borders until you find this Chinish Empire.

*A small party will do very nicely, nothing fancy, since
I have no intention of paying for this out of the royal
coffers when the mob outside is howling for more
bread and more spectacles!*

*I'll expect some kind of report, Titus Papinianus.
And beware—I've my eye on you. I still haven't
forgotten what your father did to poor old Nero.*

> *Good Luck,*
> *Titus Flavius Domitianus,*
> *Caesar, Augustus, God-*
> *Emperor of the Universe, Pater*
> *Patriae, Pater Maximus*
> *Candidusque,* et cetera, et
> cetera.

"Good heavens, Aquila," I said, passing the letter on to
Nikias.

"This is absurd!" Nikias said. "Eratosthenes's figures are
clearly impeccable, measuring as he did the parallax of the sun's
shadow in two different locations in Egypt. And besides, the
extra space is necessary. After all, where does the sun go when its
chariot comes to rest at the day's end? Where do all the deities of
the world live, and where are the thousands of heavens and hells,
if not in the 'lost' spaces?"

"And," I added, "this simply is *not* a Chinish piece of artwork.
I'd wager twenty talents on it. Domitian's gone mad!"

"Alas, Titus, I wish I could agree with you," said Aquila. But
I happen to know that this whole thing is simply a rather imaginative, roundabout way of getting you on the purge list. You see,
simple executions and things have gone out of style in Rome.
Indeed, I was there at the very banquet when Domitian and Leu-
kippos (who, I'm afraid, shares the Emperor's bed as well as his
confidences) concocted this elaborate scientific hokum while
downing endless bucketfuls of Chian wine."

I was furious. "It rankles," I said, "especially the Chian wine.
Onze mayahu kte lo!" I added (it was the one obscenity I knew),
hoping to impress Aquila with my new grasp of the Lacotian
tongue.

Instead, he and Nikias laughed uproariously. "I suppose I
shouldn't make fun of you, general," said Aquila, "but you just
told me that I am about to perform an unspeakable act upon your
inviolate person."

"Oh, sorry. Wrong pronoun again, eh?" I said. "I intended to
say that *I* would perform this act on the Emperor."

"Yes, you should have used the nominative *wa-* prefix. But seriously, it was then that I knew Domitian planned to do away with you and play a fiendish joke besides. That's why I insisted on bringing you the message myself, all the while pretending to laugh myself silly over Caesar's brilliant wit. You see, I'm the only person who can possibly help you solve the riddle of the jade statuette. Besides, Rome was beginning to bore me. The decadence! You've seen one orgy, you've seen them all. And the Lacotian tribesmen who settled in Cappadocia—dissipated, every one of them. Gone to boozing and orgifying. Some of them have taken up in the arena, where they even perform the sundance nowadays, although it goes against all I believe in. I'm bitter, Titus. I'll come with you on your quest for Caesar's golden fleece."

"But you said you knew—"

"Perhaps so. It's a legend, nothing more. Of a race far far to the south, who worship the were-jaguar and carve mysterious heads. For all I know they may have died out."

"And their name?"

"I don't know what they call themselves. But the Apaxians of the desert talk sometimes of an ancient empire-building race they call the Olmechii...."

In a few days we set off down the great Miserabilis River by paddleboat. I was proud of this new acquisition: Epaminondas of Alexandria, who perfected the steam engine and had since been executed for refusing to give up its secrets, originally created such a barge for Nero's state visit to Egypt, so that Caesar could journey down the Nile in style. It was occasionally powered by steam; more often, the huge paddle was kept in constant motion by an assemblage of treadmill-jogging slaves. They were lazy, shiftless good-for-nothings, captured from the Algonquian and Athapascan tribes of the icy north, less civilized even than our somewhat Romanized Lacotians.

It was an idle month. I and Nikias and Aquila would sit in our couches of state; an elegant little temple to Minerva graced one end of the boat, while the prow was carved to resemble a Naiad in a somewhat pornographic pose, and inlaid with several talents of solid gold. The trappings were as luxurious as in Rome; the food and drink were not, and for some weeks we ate nothing but aurochs: stewed, boiled, roasted, fried, but never once metamorphosing into some more palatable creature. Aquila disgusted me by frequently eating the liver raw; even as a senator he had not given up all his filthy barbarian ways.

Aside from the paddle slaves, of which a certain number expired daily and had to be replaced, we had brought few attendants. There were about a dozen guards, mostly of the tribe of Tetonii, in their half-Roman, half-barbarous garb; and the usual consortium of body-slaves, cooks, scullery-maids, bed-wenches, foot-washers, masseurs, singers, lyre-players, dancers, Nubian palanquin-bearers, toga-stitchers, pot-washers, and so on: only a few score of these, hardly enough to call a decent household, but then Lacotia was still something of a hardship post. An escort of charioteers rode alongside, and we had horses below deck.

Lacotia went by slowly—for it is a vast terrain—and we soon grew weary of endless plains. Here and there stood a little shrine to Caesar, whom the natives had graciously been permitted to worship under the aspects of their own rather nebulous god Vacantanca, a god whose vagueness is equalled only by the formless thing the Judaeans worship. Or we would pass a little tipi-cluster from which smoke curled into the brilliant blue sky. Or a Roman town, an islet of marble in the great green grassy ocean. It was a beautiful land but I wished we would get on with it. I had the slaves lashed harder, but nothing came of it.

Soon we went by the last frontier fort. We encountered rough waters where the River Ochaio runs into the Miserabilis. Now we were in enemy lands. We had catapultae and ballistae aplenty on board, and I set the Lacotian centurions to constant watching. On the right bank was Caddonia, on the left Muschogea; so the first explorers had named these lands, after the principal languages the savages spoke. But we knew little about them, and the names were meaningless to me.

For a week or so we continued downriver. We ate dried aurochs now, salty and tough to chew, and a little river-fish. We watched the dancing girls and talked of old times, and at night I stared at the Olmechian figurine, trying to divine its secrets.

One day we were eating breakfast on deck. I was just stuffing my mouth with a chunk of aurochs when I heard a zinging, whistling sound. I stared incredulously as an arrow pierced the meat, flew into the temple of Minerva, and nailed my breakfast to the goddess's nipple.

"Whaa—" I said.

"Hostiles riding alongside boat, General, Sir!" said a centurion. "They've killed half the chariot escort—"

"Dispatch them, for heaven's sake! I can't have my breakfast ruined, you know."

"Duck, Titus!" I heard Nikias shout. As I did so, arrows began to rain on us from both sides.

"Get the catapultae out!" I screamed. "Lash the paddle-slaves, maybe we can outmaneuver them!" As I looked up I saw the slave-whipper clutch at the arrow in his throat and tumble from the treadmill. The slaves, who were chained and couldn't escape, were screeching with terror.

"China, my arse!" I cried. "We're not even going to get out of Lacotia alive!" Then I ran into the temple of Minerva and bolted the door. I found Nikias there already, hugging the altar in supplication, whilst Aquila was waving his arms and doing some hoppity-skippity dance while singing in a wheezy monotone. "Aquila, do something! You're the bloody expert on the savages."

"I *am* doing something," he said, and continued his dance. "This war-dance happens to be excellent medicine, and will render the three of us quite invisible to the Apaxae."

"Apaxae—?"

"Yes," he said, not missing a beat of his dance. "They are the hardiest of all the tribes; I am not surprised to see them come raiding this far, for they often venture even into Roman-occupied territory. Now, if you'll excuse me...*hey-a-a-a hey-a-a! Eya-heya-ey-ey-ey-a-a!* ...let me see...*eya-hey-hey-heya—*"

I gave up on him. Behind the goddess there was a window; I looked out and saw them.

There were several dozen. They were riding up and down the river-bank, whooping and taunting us. Their flowing black hair, held in place by headbands of old rags, streamed behind them. They were the scruffiest savages I'd yet seen, and the fiercest-looking.

Aquila stopped dancing. *"Huka hey!"* he shouted. "Let's attack them!"

"But the war-machines—"

He threw open the door of the temple. The Lacotian guards were letting the horses out from below decks; they were whinnying and rearing. Above the gleaming cuirasses and blood-red cloaks, their faces gleamed with war-paint and their heads were crowned with feathers.

"Huka hey!" they screamed in unison. The Apaxians were charging straight into the water at our paddleboat, pelting us with arrows.

"Catapultae!" I shouted, grabbing a bucina from an astonished slave and blowing on it myself. The engines were wheeled into position. Great rocks soared and brained one or two of the Apaxian horses. They were diving into the water now, one after another, knives in mouths. I ordered the boarding-ramps lowered. The Lacotians' horses leaped overboard and they were fighting hand-to-hand, half in, half out of the water. Meanwhile Aquila had mounted himself and was rushing straight at the Apaxians, who never seemed to notice him.

"If an eighty-year-old man can do that—" I said to myself. Soon I too was calling for my horse. The temple of Minerva was on fire and so was the paddle-treadmill, and lines of slaves with buckets were busy quenching the flames. I jumped the side of the boat and rode down the ramp, cursing Domitian with a will.

"Quick!" I shouted at the last of the on-shore escort. "Put all the chariots in a circle!" One of them heard me and relayed the order. In a while we were driving the Apaxae back over the river and right into the circle of chariots. The carnage was incredible, for these savages fought as if insensible to pain.

After some hard fighting we drove them off. The Lacotians scattered to strip and scalp the corpses. In the distance, a shout went up. Two Lacotians on horseback were returning, pursuing a man on a bicycle.

"Good heavens!" I said. "I haven't seen one of *those* since Rome—and Domitian wrecked almost all the bicycles in the world in an epic spectacle in the arena ten years ago!"

They had knocked off the bicycler, pinned him to the ground and were about to scalp him when I rode up to investigate.

"Let go!" a voice was squealing in Greek. "You can't do this to me, I'm a Roman citizen! You don't speak Greek? What about Latin? Sum civis Romanus! *Romanus*, d'ye hear, sum...civis... *Romanus!*"

"Release him," I said.

The man got to his feet. He was middle-aged, clad in a torn, dirt-streaked tunic of good Greek wool, but he had a decidedly dusky complexion, and his Greek was strangely accented. Once before had I heard such an accent..."Jove help us!" I said. "You're an Egyptian! Whatever are you doing here among these barbarians?"

He brushed himself with his hand. Then he said squeakily, "I was captured. They were going to torture me to death! Please help me, help me, I'm on a mission from the library of Alexandria, and—"

"That seems unlikely," I said, "considering that library was burnt down a century ago."

"No, no," he said, like a tutor addressing a stupid child, "not that Alexandria. Alexandria in Iracuavia! You know, Terra Nova's center of learning, dedicated to humanizing the savages! What are you doing here, anyway?" he added sulkily.

"How dare you use that tone to me? I am Titus Papinianus,

Procurator of Lacotia."

"Well, how was I to know? Procurators come and go; the turnover is amazing, what with purgings, recallings, treason-trials, and compulsory suicides. Never even heard of you. Wouldn't know you from Amenemhet!"

Just then Aquila and Nikias came riding up. They were jabbering away to each other in Lacotian, much to my chagrin. Then Nikias saw the Egyptian and exclaimed, "Well, if it isn't grumpy old Aaye!"

"Nikias! Why this is—this is—" He was overcome. Nikias got off his horse and they hugged each other, weeping.

"My lord," Nikias said to me, "this is the most bad-tempered scholar the world has ever known, the astrologer whose full name we could never pronounce at the Academy; but he answers to *Aaye*. We studied together before my unfortunate enslavement."

"What a coincidence! But what's a scholar like you doing far from civilization, being captured by savages?"

"You Roman pseudo-intellectuals are all alike," he grunted. "Always afraid you'll soil your delicate fingers, never leaving your slave-ridden palaces to quest for the hidden meanings to be found in the backwaters and cloacae of existence! But *I* am a true philosopher. I search for truth. At the moment, though, I'm searching for the pyramids."

I laughed. "The pyramids? In Terra Nova? I've heard of people losing their way, but this is ridiculous! You're out of your mind!"

"Perhaps so, though it's impertinent of you to point it out," he said. "But there is a scrap of parchment in the library—dating, it seems, from the first explorations of this continent—that mentions pyramids. Somewhere to the south. At least, I took it to mean that. Literally. They all laughed at me. How they laughed! Those rationalizing scholars with their theories of hallucination, symbolism or some explorer's bout with a jug of bad Fallernian wine. If it doesn't warp to fit their theory, they'll ignore it or ridicule it...not me! I propound the scientific method. If it was good enough for Aristotle, it's good enough for me."

But how did you come to be among the Apaxae?"

"Patience, Roman! We Egyptians have been civilized for four thousand years. We were building the pyramids when you were coming down from the trees. That's why you're all so damned impatient. Well...I journeyed here after learning a little of the Apaxian speech from one of my slaves, hoping to get corrob-oration for the parchment at the library. I lived among them for some months—no luxury at all, let me tell you!—when the village was raided by a rival tribe. They intended to trade my bicycle for some horses, and to kill me by some fiendish means; but as they journeyed towards their trading-rendezvous, they chanced upon your paddleboat, and, thinking of the booty on board—"

"Enough of this longwindedness! We are travelling south at the Emperor's behest, on a wild goose chase as preposterous as your own. You can come with us if you choose; if not, there's not much I can do for you."

"How dare you call it a wild goose chase! I had already found evidence, before wicked fate cast me into this predicament—"

"Evidence?" I snorted.

"Yes! For when I inquired among the Apaxae about pyramids, when I drew them in the dirt to illustrate my meaning precisely, I would often elicit a certain response. It was a single word—foreign to their tongue—that appears to be the name of a race of pyramid-builders...."

"And that name?" Aquila said. I noticed that he had leaned forward suddenly, and seemed to be taking this fool seriously.

"*Olmec.*"

We reached the delta of the Miserabilis without much more incident; for the local natives, who were by no means Apaxian and lived in as much fear of their ravaging hordes as we did, were friendly, and we were often able to get food from them in exchange for a few of those valueless, heavy old copper coins that are still in vogue in Egypt and carry the images of the long-gone Ptolemaic dynasty. It was lush country, rich in fruits and meats. When we reached the sea, we had no idea what to do next.

Aaye to the rescue, then. Faded old maps hastily copied from the Alexandria library documents were pulled out and pored over. They showed the seashore curving to the west; the words *terra incognita* were evident everywhere. I ordered a fort built on the left bank of the Miserabilis; stocked it with catapultae and other artillery from the ship; and left most of the slaves there under guard, while Nikias, Aquila, Aaye and I rode southwards with only a handful of cavalry, Lacotian and Roman, and two weeks' supply of that hideous buffalo jerky.

Two weeks! We were very optimistic then; no one dreamed that the world could be quite as large as we came to discover. In any case, we followed the coastline at first, coming to the mouths of many rivers. After a fortnight we began to go through harsh terrain. The heat was stifling; and we had little water. To my surprise, Aaye proved the most stalwart of us here in the desert. I supposed it was because the Nile is a mere ribbon of greenery in

113

the midst of a vast ocean of hot sand, and that the Egyptians have perforce learnt some of the ways of deserts. He had apparently learnt something from the Apaxae, too. How to trap and kill those alarming serpents with rattling tails, and how to suck the juices from the prickly, clublike vegetation....

The worst was yet to come, though. I thought I had seen forests...I was not prepared for what came next. You could have sworn this forest was alive. It was dark, wet, swarming with vermin; snakes masqueraded as vines, alligators as logs, and mosquitoes bit our skin raw.

"Wherever we are," I sighed, "this certainly isn't China!"

"Clearly not," Aaye agreed. Then, settling into his pedagogic tone, he said, "For it is a well-established fact that the Chinish lands are full of golden towers and ziggurats, and that silken tapestries hang from every home. Indeed, I have heard it mentioned by Apollodorus the Bithynian, that Chinish silk is manufactured by a giant worm, seven leagues long, that continually runs in a circle, eating its own tail, and that the effluence of saliva that drools from its maws, hardening in the path of its circumperambulatory meanderings, forms the thread used in the warp of the silk; for the woof, however, the Chinish sages entrap moonbeams by midnight and—"

"Rubbish!" Nikias said. "Aaye old chap, you were always the most gullible boy in the Academy. If some two-obol authority had told you that the oceans on the moon's surface were deserts, you would have believed it."

"You bastard! You stole master Harpocrates's apple and I got the strap for it! How dare you—"

"Enough, you fools!" I said. "Look at Aquila; he never argues with anyone, and he's borne all these hardships better than any of us."

We had found a little clearing. Bones and the remains of fires littered the forest floor; it was our first evidence of humans. They were likely as not to kill us, but at that point I would rather have died at the hands of recognizable people than be torn to death by beasts like a criminal in the arena.

"And to think," Aquila said, as he tethered our horses (some had succumbed to horrid diseases, and these we had eaten, much to the discomfiture of our bowels) "that I did this all for you! Those deadly boring orgies at the palace are beginning to sound more and more attractive by the hour!"

The Lacotians were pitching a tipi and spreading aurochs hides on the ground to sleep on. If we fumigated it thoroughly with incense, and sealed the thing completely shut, the mosquitoes only bit one an average of once a minute instead of continuously.

Drinking the vile water had given me a flux; so I spent the day groaning in the tipi while Nikias read to me from a stack of the latest *scientiae fictiones,* which Aquila had had copied in Rome and had been kind enough to bring me: in particular a collection of pieces in the avant-garde style that characterizes all the decadent literary efforts of Domitian's reign, entitled *Visus Periculosi.* While I found none of the visions particularly dangerous, especially in view of the actual horrors that surrounded me, I was amused by the frantic blandishments of Alienus Elysianus, the scribe who had anthologized and annotated the various scrolls.

"Reading that rubbish again!" said Aquila. "You should be working on your Lacotian grammar."

"And what of it?" I spluttered, gripping my bowels. "Why don't *you* do something useful?"

"I intend to! I am going hunting."

"What?"

"A brave can't laze around all day. Lack of action ages a man. I shall go stalk some creature for our supper." So saying, he took his quiver and a dagger and a sackful of skinning tools, and he strode out. Knowing the mosquito problem, I didn't care to follow.

Presently, though, a bloodcurdling scream cut across the jungle's cacophony of buzzings, croakings and screechings.

"Jove help us!" I cried. "If it's Aquila, what'll we do?" I rousted some of the others and we crept out, hacking at the undergrowth with our short swords.

"Aquila!" we called, our voices fading into the gloom. It suddenly occurred to me that we were lost, hopelessly lost, and even if we weren't lost, we weren't going to get home anyway—

When I heard a familiar hooting sound, such as the Lacotians used as a secret signal in warfare.

"Come out of there, by Hades!" I said. "I'm in no mood for another trick, this dysenterial flux is killing me, and—"

The hooting again.

"It's coming from the left," Nikias whispered.

"The right," hissed Aaye.

I listened. "The left." We tiptoed farther into the darkness.

Now from the right. We passed huge trees, greater than the columns of the temples at Karnak, twined with vines. No light fell at all in the depths of this alien forest.

Then—

"I see light," I said.

"Ahead," said one of the Lacotians.

I took another step.

Something tightened around my foot! I was jerked up into the air. I saw my companions dangling head downwards from trees on either side, and so was I, and my helmet clanked onto the ground, and the jade figurine that I had kept on my person all these months fell down beside it—

And then there were torches, blazing, blinding. Brown-skinned, lithe-looking natives had rushed to pick up the jade statuette, and were fingering it reverently.

"What the hell is going on?" I yelled. For in the center of the clearing ahead stood Aquila, large as life, his head thrown back in laughter; and all around him on the forest floor, prostrated in obeisance, were dozens of natives in elaborate costumes. And right at his feet was the corpse of a huge and frightening creature, the leopard-like demon that I had heard Aquila call *jaguar*.

"Tell them to let us down!"

Aquila said, "How can I? I've no idea what's going on, although it's about time a high chieftain of the Lacotians got treated with the proper respect. Why shouldn't I let you Romans hang for a few days, like pheasants ripening for the oven?"

We began to yell imprecations in every conceivable language. Finally one of the savages came and cut us down, after which we were led, with our hands tied behind our backs, to Aquila's feet and forced to make the prostration also.

"This is shameful!" I said. "That a Roman and an equestrian by rank, and a procurator at that, should be compelled to kneel down before some...some...."

"Now you know how we lowly savages feel, oh noble procurator! But to be frank, I'm as much in the dark as you are. I just went out and happened to kill this jaguar."

"With your bare hands?" I gasped.

He chuckled. "We Lacota have always been excellent hunters—although I did cheat a bit. I made friends with him first, by pulling a thorn out of his foot. Now, if someone would care to translate—"

One of the natives—whose earrings, I saw now, were enormous sun-disks of solid gold—came up and began barking, bellowing, and braying in various languages.

"Ah!" Aaye said at last. "One I know. This one speaks Apaxian!"

So our interchanges began. Their leader spoke in whatever language it was (and I had a feeling it wasn't Chinish); their interpreter translated into Apaxian; Aaye relayed in Greek with a sprinkle of Latin and an occasional Egyptian curse; and finally

Aquila repeated the exchange in the Tetonian dialect of Lacotian for the benefit of the native centurions who were also swinging by their feet. In this laborious way we spent the better part of a night; mercifully the need to discharge my flux did not visit me as yet.

Yes indeed, these people knew of the Olmechii, although they themselves were only a subject race. Aquila, who had killed the jaguar, had unwittingly become the victor in their regular competition for the rank of God-of-the-Month, and would soon be going in triumph to his coronation.

We mere mortals, on the other hand, would be sacrificed to the glory of Aquila and the entity He represented, the Great and All-powerful Flying Disk of the Sun....

Indeed, I, whom the Great Were-Jaguar in the Sky himself had chosen by causing his image to appear beneath me as I dangled, was to have the honor of being the first to be sacrificed to Aquila the God...and all this by the charming expedient of ripping my still-beating heart from my chest with a crude obsidian knife.

"Delighted, I'm sure," I said. "At least it's a nice simple death; none of Domitian's labyrinthine jokes."

"It's good to look on the bright side," Aquila agreed, as the flayed skin of the newly-killed beast was placed over his shoulders and a palanquin brought in to receive him, and as two of the natives stooped down for him to step up on their backs. "At last my dream has come true," he went on as eight burly, oiled natives hoisted his throne up on their shoulders. "A nice, quiet retirement far from civilization, all the comforts of Rome without any of the bustle."

"But what about us?" I said. And then I saw the cages. They were double-decker ones with wooden bars. We were herded into them, and they too were carried by natives: mangy ones, gap-toothed and cross-eyed, clearly litterbearers of lower quality than those of Aquila the God.

The forests thinned; in a few days we were in open plains, sunny and verdant. We passed villages where we were eyed with disinterest; Aquila got all the attention.

Eventually we came to a broad paved road. As good as a Roman road it was. And in a few days we could see the walls of a vast city in the distance.

"Curse you all!" Aaye was saying for the thousandth time. He was in the same cage as I, in the lower compartment, so I was forced to listen to him. "You should have left me to die with the Apaxians. Oh, I know they'd have tied me to a rock in the desert and cut off my eyelids, but at least with them you knew where you were. You've certainly led me off the trail, you idiot general. No wonder Domitian made you procurator; it's a well-known fact that only the utterly unintelligent can ever rise in office, and...."

My fever had worsened. I was in no mood for any of this talk. As far as I was concerned, Domitian's ruse had proved all to successful; I was anxious to get it all over with.

We were coming into the gateway—

"They're—they're—it's true!" said the Egyptian, losing his ill humor at once. They *do* have pyramids!"

I opened my bleary eyes and saw them. At the end of the avenue there was a huge one of gleaming stone; it must have had more that a thousand steps. And the street was lined with sculptures of heads as huge as buildings, their features a curious hybrid of Asian and African. Golden disks—sun-signs, clearly, hung from the walls, like giant saucers. People thronged the squares and marketplaces; I could have sworn this city was as big as Rome, if I hadn't known it was impossible.

"Maybe this *is* China after all," I said.

"Oh, no," Aaye said, falling automatically into his lecturing mode, "it's not China at all; for one thing, I haven't seen a single silkworm, and it is an established fact that the Chinish citizenry ride these silkworms, after disengaging their tails from their mouths, driving great hooks into their segments and urging them forward by the irritations they cause—"

"I think I read that," I said, "in one of the recent *scientiae fictiones.*"

"Oh, no," he said, "it's the truth! You can't have opinions about truth! No, this is the land of the Olmechii for certain; the pyramids prove it. I'll show those doubters back at the Academy! They'll have to believe me now! I'll make them grind up every papyrus they've written against my theories and eat every word of their unscientific rantings!"

"We," I said, "are about to get sacrificed...or had you forgotten that, eh, old chap?"

"Minor matter, general; they're pyramid-builders, I'm an Egyptian, give me a couple of days and we'll be tighter than brothers...why, I'll bet they *are* Egyptians, stranded here in antediluvian times. We'll get along famously. It's an incontrovertible fact that we deep, inscrutable, and mystifying Egyptians can talk our way out of anything."

"Shut the idiot up!" Nikias moaned from a neighboring cage.

"Call me an idiot, will you? Me, the greatest theorist of all time, now that my theories have been vindicated!"

The flux hit me all at once then, and, using what dexterity

118

was still left to me in my condition, I managed to void my bowels in the direction of the Egyptian, drenching him thoroughly. It was a childish gesture, and unworthy of a procurator-general, but it did shut him up.

We were dumped into a spacious prison, opposite the gargantuan pyramid-temple and overlooking the city square, and they gave me a potion that did wonders for my flux. Aquila had been installed in the temple across from us. Every day we would see him holding court from a throne of solid gold; I could tell he had been watching Caesar carefully, for many of his imperial gestures were an amusing parody of Domitian's. He mimicked to perfection the Emperor's gesture that signaled a concealed guard to execute the suppliant; but he seemed to do so merely in sport, for I saw no executions. He would never have made a good Roman emperor; our rulers know well the efficacy of a well-timed, spectacular execution of some important figure. It is thus that they are able to appease the mob, and thus it is that the Empire will last forever, though any individual emperor is lucky to survive a year or two...in short, Aquila seemed constantly to be showing such unkingly clemency that I was afraid the crowd would soon be bored to death and assassinate him. And that we could not have; for Aquila, savage that he was, was our only hope of rescue.

Day by day we watched. Far and away the most mysterious sight was that of golden disks that flitted about in the sky, resembling nothing so much as levitating dishes or saucers. Sometimes three or four of them would hover over the large pyramid for some minutes, and then vanish into the sky. We could not decide what they were, although Aaye, who naturally had a theory handy, said that they were sun-sculptures and that the flying effect was brought about by constant rubbing of the pyramid's summit with huge house-sized cloths, just as a piece of electrum, or amber, can when briskly rubbed be observed to attract small particles of papyrus, engendering that ineffable and mystic force to which amber has lent its name.

The argument over this consumed several days. Food came at a slot in the prison door, a slab of solid rock that would not budge. Our clothes had been taken from us and we were forced to wear ridiculous loincloths; the material was soft and comfortable, and therefore effeminate and unworthy of a staunch and stalwart Roman.

The sights from the window were remarkable—

For these Olmechii (Aaye had convinced us they were not Chinish by the sheer weight and intricacy of the learning at his

119

disposal) were by any lights the most technologically advanced nation in the world. It galled me to see them travel about in gilded motor-cars when Rome's motor-cars had all been destroyed in the Coliseum and the secret of their manufacture lost. It rankled to see they had a hovering device, floating from pyramid-top to pyramid-top by means of enormous leather balloons containing heated air from which dangled baskets of people; I will not say that such sorcery is beyond the Romans, because we are, by the grace of the gods, the dominant nation of the world after all, and are by nature superior to all peoples, whether as-yet-subjugated or not; but *I* had not seen it before. I longed to send a few such devices to Caesar.

"Imagine the spectacle!" I said, gnawing on an ear of maize. "We could stash gladiators in the baskets, and they could have at each other with catapultae and ballistae, flinging fireballs at one another as they soar over the sands of the Circus Maximus!"

"How can you think of such things," Nikias said, "when our death is imminent?"

I was brought down to earth. "If only there was some way of contacting Aquila—"

"He'll do nothing!" Aaye said gloomily. "Savage blood will always show, that's what I always say. Gullible, unreliable, and a dullard, there's your standard savage."

"Are you out of your mind?" said Nikias. "This is the man who singlehandedly won the Battle of Domitianopolis in Cappadocia by driving the Parthians into—"

"And made an utter fool out of *me!*" I grunted. "No, look at him out there. He's happy now; not many people get to be a god in their own lifetime, you know. Even the old Caesars had to wait until the Senate declared it after their death, although *these* days—"

"A plan!" Aaye cried. "I have a plan!"

"Ha! You, a plan!" Nikias said. "I remember well your schemes to make a few obols when we were children, selling lemonade in the streets of Alexandria in the middle of December."

The Lacotians among us were sitting apart, grunting or singing softly to themselves, with a great deal of *hunh-hunh-hunh*ing and *hechito welo*ing. The three of us huddled together.

"What you don't realize, Nikias old chap," said Aaye, "is that I am by profession a trained astrologer, and as such am in the position of knowing a great deal about the proper motions of the sun and moon and stars. I happen to know a few things that will scare the living daylights out of these Olmechii."

"I doubt it," I said. "These Olmechii seem rather sophisticated to me."

"Appearance only, my dear general! For it is a well-known fact, a truism, indeed, that those not blessed with the...ahem... *Roman* citizenship are by their very natures superstitious, credulous, and incapable of rising above the status of simple peasants."

"If this city is but an appearance of civilization disguising utter savagery, it's bloody convincing, I say."

"Stuff and nonsense! Are these savages not making a big song and dance about sacrificing us to their gods? Back in the *real* Empire, people may be killed for amusement, as in our great epic spectacles of the arena, but it is hardly something to be taken *seriously,* as they are doing. The lack of a cynical attitude to life and death is a telltale sign of barbarianism. We'll never talk sense into them! No, I shall perform my patent razzle-dazzle, just as I so impressed the King of Parthia, who held me captive, with my lightning wit and arcane knowledge of trivia that he awarded me safe conduct to the country of my choice!"

"Poor Aaye. Never knows when he's being tactfully gotten rid of," Nikias said.

The two were at each other's throats; soon their beards had become entangled, and I had to extricate them from each other.

Just then one of the Lacotians, staring out the window, began yammering. We all rushed over; an awesome sight greeted us.

Huge heads, of the kind we had seen lining the city streets, were hanging in the sky. Each was taller than three or four men; each dangled from a convoy of the heated-air-balloons, which soared high above thick as birds. Sun-disks hovered or darted about them; it could now be seen, from the scale of the flying balloons, that these dish-like floaters were actually the size of palaces or temples.

"Extraordinary!" said Aaye. "A remarkable method of transporting heavy objects...."

"Which would leave no trace on the ground, no evidence of where the rock was quarried..." Nikias said.

"Goodness," I said. "I'm going to *have* to wrest away the secret of these levitating baskets; I can just see them being used against the Parthians! Imagine a squadron of these things pelting the enemy with rocks...we could easily cross Parthia and maybe have a stab at conquering India."

"Now who's daydreaming?" Aaye said. "First you pooh-pooh my plan without even listening to it, despite the fact that I am (admittedly by default) the most capable astrologer in this land. Then you talk as if we've already freed ourselves—"

The door opened at that moment. Olmechii, dressed in jaguar skins and armed with lances, came in and bound us fast.

"Well, fellows, this looks like it," I said, deciding that an eve-of-the-battle speech was called for. "Remember—"

"My plan! Don't you want to know my plan?"

"Oh, all right," I said, "let's have it. And it had better be something with a little more substance than your airy speculations."

"Ha! You have the gall to come to me now, after deriding my learning and abusing my person? I've half a mind to let you all perish—"

"Come, Aaye," Nikias said, "we're all in this together."

"Oh, very well, very well."

The light was blinding in the square. The avenues, the roof-tops, the balconies were crammed with spectators in all their finery: spangled loincloths, headdresses of feathers, furs, even the actual decapitated heads of various forest beasts; while above, the traffic of golden disks and floating heads never ceased. But, in contrast to the festive atmosphere of a Roman spectacle, the rivers of wine, the carousing and the whoring and the catcalls, this was a very sober throng indeed. It was just as the Egyptian had said: these people were simply far too serious about the whole thing; they lacked the good Roman sense of sport and fair play.

"Which is precisely what I shall rely on," said Aaye. They'll swallow anything I tell them."

As we progressed down the avenue we were joined by other prisoners; most of them were of unfamiliar tribes, but there were a certain number of Apaxae, Caddones, and Comanxae. Whether these had simply ventured too far south, or whether the Olmechii had raiding expeditions that traversed the very desert and crossed into the land of the River Miserabilis, I could not tell.

Soon were sounded tremendous cornua of stone from the tops of distant temples, a bleating noise with a tinge of croak to it. We reached the foot of the pyramid, and I assumed that we would now be forced to ascend to the summit; instead we were ushered into a little chamber within the base, which—wonder of won-ders—began to rise, by pulleys or by some hydraulic mechanism as is used for the raising and lowering of scenery in the arena in Rome. Thus, without any expenditure of effort, we reached the top. There was a huge chamber there; from its windows I could see a panorama of the city, stretching limitlessly in every direc-tion. It was clear now that these Olmechii were masters of super-science, so powerful as to be beyond the imaginings even of the

122

writers of *scientiae fictiones.*

We were pushed to the ground in prostration. When I looked up I saw Aquila seated upon a throne, every inch the ruler; and at his feet, voluptuous and elegantly dressed in jaguar-skins and jade, was a woman. When she spoke, the walls reverberated; and to my astonishment I found that as the words re-echoed they reformed into translations, into Lacotian and Apaxian among other languages. This was sorcery indeed! I no longer doubted that we had penetrated into one of the supernatural realms; for it was impossible that any race could be this much more advanced than Rome, without divine intervention.

"I am," she said, "the High-Priestess and Chief Consort of the Were-Jaguar-Golden-Sun-Disk-Almighty."

"Glad to know with whom I am dealing," I said in my halting Lacotian, which words immediately rebounded from the walls in a foreign tongue. (So the old man had been very well served indeed, I thought enviously, with such a womn as his official bride!) "Aquila!" I said in Greek. As I hoped, there was no wall-translation. "You've got to get us out of this!"

"Whatever for?" he said, waving a hand languidly. "There seems to be nothing I can do, and so I've decided to be philo-sophical about the whole thing."

The priestess said: "Here, then, is the order of the sacrifice. First the man who calls himself general, he with the bulbous nose—" I fought against the guards who held me at this physical insult, but I was too tightly bound. She went on down the list of names. "And finally, at the last rays of sunset, the great Personifi-cation Himself, the Living God"—Aquila beamed at this—"will condescend to resume his place in the sky among the High Ones from whom he has come—"

"Wait a minute," Aquila said. "Does this mean—"

Guards ran up and dragged the God down from his seat. "Oh, yes," the high priestess said. "Your sacrifice comes last. I thought you already knew."

Aquila shrugged. "Ah well. I am an old man, and I have seen the world come to many bad things. I have seen the *washichun* take my children's land from them; I have seen them made sub-jects to a distant self-named god whom I have myself met; a man who daily drinks and eats and indulges himself into a stupor. I am old, old, old. I have fought against the Romans, and I have fought for them; and I know that they will never leave our land. It is best that I die here, in a foreign country. Today is a good day to die! And though the manner of it *might* be a little unorthodox, there is, I think, some honor in it; for when I reach the land of many tipis, I shall say to all of them. *Here comes the Flapper of Wings, the man called Eagle, who has counted coup a thousand times and ended his life a god."*

"But Aquila, old chap...can't you simply *command* that we be released?"

"I already tried. Oh, I tried. I know what cowards you Romans are."

I bristled.

"Wait!" Aaye said. My heart leapt. I knew he was going to try his ruse, which depended on a somewhat shaky astrological calculation.

"We are," Aaye said (in the Apaxian tongue, which the walls translated, "terrible sorcerers from the north. I tell you that we have power to control your god! For lo, in precisely...ten minutes, I will summon a great dragon from heaven who will swallow up the sun, and your days will be dark forever until you release us!" The guards were so surprised he was able to shake them off; he hobbled up to the high priestess and looked her in the eye. "For behold!" he said. "The dragon has even now begun to swallow the sun!"

For this was what he had told us; that, based on the calculations of Apollodorus of Bithynia, a solar eclipse happened to be due on this very day.

As we stood there the light began to dim very slowly. I heard the crowd murmuring outside.

The high priestess stared at Aaye curiously; then she began to laugh. At this all the guards laughed too, pointing at him and hooting hysterically.

"But it is happening at this very minute!" Aaye said. "Do you not believe me? Do you deny that I, as a full-blooded Egyptian, am born with power to perform this feat?"

"Poor, silly man," said the priestess. "I suppose you must have been listening to the guards. Why, you superstitious little foreigner, you! Everyone in the whole empire knows there's an eclipse of the sun today. The Olmechii have never, in their thousand years of history, found anyone to equal them in the accuracy of their astronomical calculations. Not to mention the fact that the Great Were-Jaguar-Sun-Disk Himself frequently comes down and tells us things. Why do you think all those thousands are gathered out there? Surely you could not be so egocentric as to believe they are here to witness a mere sacrifice of the kind they can see any day of the year?"

At this Nikias too began to laugh. "First time in your whole life," he spluttered, "you actually make a correct prediction—and everyone in the whole town knows it before you do!"

Then I had to laugh too. There was no hope now. It was over. *Vale, Roma mea!* Darkness was falling rapidly now; the Olmechian guards had kindled torches and were holding them up. They pushed us out onto the top of the steps, where there was an altar, and other priests, dressed in jaguar-skins, waited. It was then that I saw the knives.

Madness overcame me then. I laughed and laughed until my eyes were blurry with tears. As they bound me to the altar I saw the sun's corona, dancing, shimmering, and the stars in their millions, and I thought of how insignificant my death really was in the midst of this awesome sight. The crowd wasn't watching me at all. Their eyes were all trained on the sun, stunned by the beauty of it. Then the blackness began to ease a little, and a corner of the sun glistened like a diamond on a ring of ebony.

I saw the high priestess nod—

Just then, the sun-disks that had been flying to and fro changed formation and started to swoop down in my direction! The priestess was shrieking something in her language. The crowd's attention was diverted for a moment.

They were coming straight for the top of the pyramid!

Suddenly all the terror I should have felt before burst loose from its cage within me. I started to scream. The golden disks, a dozen or more of them, grew enormous as they neared me. I knew they would crash into the pyramid and kill us all, that whatever mystic force that was holding them in the air must have dissipated—

I was blacking out fast. "Zeus help us!" I heard Nikias yelling as I lost consciousness. "The flying saucers are attacking!"

When I came to....

A chamber with walls of solid gold, it seemed; the walls curved inward, into a flattened dome. A huge window, glassed-in with some transparent substance, looked out over terrain: forests, rivers, plains, cities. We were very high up indeed. This must, I decided, be the actual interior of one of the golden disks that had descended upon us sacrificial victims and seemed to have snatched us up.

"The gods have intervened!" I said.

I looked around. The others were stirring beside me.

"Why, this is heaven itself!" Aaye said. "Walls of solid gold...death isn't so bad after all. I hope the ambrosia is everything they say it is."

Nikias just smiled.

I don't think we're dead at all." It was Aquila speaking. *I don't remember dying.*"

"Stuff and nonsense!" the Egyptian said. "You can see for yourself that we have been elevated far above the condition of men. Why, the view from this very window proves it. It is a fact, proven and incontrovertible."

"Bah," said Aquila.

"I want to go home," I said.

Suddenly a presence materialized in the middle of the room. With a shock, I recognized it—

Large as life! It was the very figurine that Domitian had sent to me, the very statuette that had precipitated this whole madness! A little green creature, perhaps an armspan in height, resembling an enormous human baby in the throes of turning into a jaguar.

So we *were* in the domain of the gods! What else could it be?

The thing began to address us in a high whiny voice. The walls mumbled a little, then shifted into Lacotian.

"We have saved you," said the were-jaguar, "because you don't seem to be the regular run of sacrificial victim. I would be most interested in knowing how you got here; you are Lacota, aren't you? From the north? My name is V'Deni-Keni, and I am an officer of the Dimensional Patrol. We protect the continuity, consistency, and integrity of the millions of alternate universes within this continuum." I understood very little of what he was saying, but he went on to explain that they were from the far future and that they had come in search of certain criminals who had to be brought to trial, who were guilty of attempting to tamper with the past....

"I see," I said in my halting Lacotian.

"Now," the little green man said, "which of you is the leader?"

All of them looked at me.

I looked at Aquila. He shrugged.

"I suppose I am," I said.

"Well, perhaps you can help us in our search. We have carefully avoided appearing in other hemispheres, in order not to change your continuum too much; but we suspect our criminals may have gone elsewhere—"

"I don't know what you're talking about."

"Oh?" the god seemed puzzled for a moment. "Ah, you mean...you don't know what I'm...I see. Well, with verbs beginning with y-, in Lacota, the *wa-* prefix for the first person usually mutates to *b'l-,* so the translating device was a bit puzzled by your dialectical variant—"

"Damn this intractable language!" I burst out in Latin. "I've had enough of barbarian languages. Mutating prefixes. Pronouns that get stuck into the middle of verbs. Extrinsic possessives. Male and female particles—I'm a Roman, and I'm fed up!" I knew that I wasn't in heaven. Not if the gods were going to correct my Lacotian grammar. And since this probably wasn't China either, I was almost certainly in hell.

The were-jaguar fiddled with some device he wore on a bracelet. The translating wall buzzed and squeaked for a moment. Then it said, "Good heavens, old chap! A Roman, eh?" in perfectly good Latin. I could have cried with relief.

"Yes indeed. I am Titus Papinianus, your divinity, procurator of Lacotia, sometime dux of the Thirty-Fourth Legion."

"Wait a minute. What do you mean, Lacotia? You people aren't supposed to be on this continent! By Jove! Are you sure?"

"Why, certainly. Crossed over on a sailing ship, you know."

"And you rule over these Indians?"

"Indians? These are not Indians. These are Terra Novans; India is another country altogether, and remains unconquered."

The god muttered a few things which the wall did not translate. Then there were several dozen of them in the room at once, jabbering away like a cageful of cats and dogs. I caught the odd phrase on the wall, but the more I heard, the more mystified I became.

"...must have made a wrong turning at the third tachyon nexus...."

"...nothing for it now, we'll have to tell headquarters, we'll have to abort the mission...."

"...can you get a fix on the right universe? Perhaps a wrinkle within the Riemannian time-construct...."

"...Romans in America, indeed! It's all K'Tooni-mooni's fault, I'm afraid; he brought this frightfully *intelligent* specimen from outside the official surveillance territory on board... Epaminondas, I think his name was, must have run off with a few newfangled notions and made a whole new universe split off at timesector 101.24...."

"...anyhow, I resent having to abandon these Olmecs to their fate and take away their source of power. You remember what happened in the last universe, when we had to pull out four hundred years earlier?"

"...yes, their civilization vanished practically overnight! Mighty strange parallel world that was. Y'remember those Americans coming into power, with their cult of hamburgers and shopping malls?"

127

Well, we were standing around, getting more and more confused by the minute; you can tell from the scraps of conversation I overheard, which I have set down literally, even the bits which can't possibly make sense, that madness reigned supreme among these people.

"Am I going insane?" I said. "Is this some hallucination I am having to cover up my terror as the knife slices into my chest?"

"Don't worry," Aquila said. "Back in Lacotia, we make a kind of tobacco mixed with a certain dried mushroom, and it induces dreams very similar to these. It'll wear off."

"But what's to become of us?" I shouted. The walls reverberated with the translation.

They stopped their chatter for a moment, and the one who had first addressed us did so again. "Oh, don't worry, chaps. You'll be released at the spot of your choice. Sorry to be such a nuisance to your dimension, and everything will be back to normal just as soon as we can arrange it. Oh, and we'll have gifts for all of you. Here." The ceiling opened and we were rained on by several hundred of the little jade were-jaguars. "Some small mementoes of our visit in your universe. Oh, and don't noise it about too much that you've seen us, eh? We're in enough trouble as it is with the Central Dimension Patrol Authority."

"The delta of the Miserabilis will do very nicely," I said stiffly.

When we got home I sent a shipload of jade were-jaguars to Domitian together with a note explaining as little of our adventure as I could get away with—for I knew we would not be believed. Aaye and Nikias opened an academy together in Caesarea-on-Miserabilis, and I went back to ruling my unruly savages.

It was more than six months before a reply arrived. As it chanced, our whole gang was together, for it was high summer and I had decided on a grand aurochs hunt to celebrate some festival of other. We had followed the herd for some days, making Lacotian camps by night.

It was towards evening; we were exercising our horses in the plains, when a messenger arrived from Caesarea with a message from the Emperor. When I unsealed the scroll, I beamed with pleasure at first.

"Why, it's from General Trajan! Domitian, it seems, has been assassinated. Well, I'm awfully glad a decent military man has become emperor; we won't have any of these elaborate madcap jokes for a while at least."

But as I read through the letter my face fell. For Caesar had new orders for me.

Dear General Titus, it ran,
We have received your report on the Ol-
mechii with interest, and your jade statuettes make
welcome additions to the Imperial Treasury. Never-
theless, We are somewhat distressed that you have
not yet found China. It is Our conviction that the
fabled Empire of Chin must be conquered, for Rome
cannot tolerate a force greater than herself, even in
hearsay.
We charge you, therefore, and authorize you, with
due dispatch to seek out this land of Chin, whereso-
ever it may be upon the continent of Terra Nova; to
furnish maps and charts of this empire, or at least to
establish once and for all its mythical nature so that
We do not have to fret constantly about the possible
military challenge....
Ave atque vale,
Marcus Ulpius Trajanus,
Imp. Caes. August. and so on
so forth.

"What shall I do?" I cried in despair. A strong wind blew from the west, making the tall grass sigh. In the distance the aurochs herd moved, dots of brown in the twilit hills. "Trajan has no idea of the vastness of this land! From here to the Montes Saxosi lies an endless wilderness of nature and savages. And beyond them?"

Aaye said, riding up to me, "You must go about this logically, procurator. You have tried the south, without any success. To the north are Athapasca and Algonquia, and frozen lands where surely the giant silkworms may not survive, for they are well known to be of a delicate disposition, and must continually be suckled with the milk of young Chinish maidens."

"If you know so much about the Chinish peoples, tell me where they are!"

"I was just getting to that! You impatient Romans...is it not true that gold deposits have been found in the Montes Saxosi?"

"Yes, but—"

"Let me finish. The Chinish folk are reputed to have yellow skins. Indeed, Apollodorus of Bithynia claims that their visages are normal in hue, but that their country is so rich that even the poorest among them paints his face with a paste of water and gold dust...."

"And who *is* this Apollodorus who knows so much?"

"It is the pseudonym of a very great scholar, P. Josephus Agricola—"

"Another writer of those blasted *scientiae fictiones!* A dreamer. A weaver of escapist tales."

"When will you even learn to trust me, general? Did I not cause the solar eclipse that enabled us to elude the altar of the Olmechian sun-god?"

I could see that he had convinced himself that he had indeed saved our lives; but I did not bother to contradict him, because I was feeling too sorry for myself.

"What I'm telling you, general, is that this Chinish land may well be very near...just on the other side of the Montes Saxosi. If you would but follow the line of the setting sun—"

"Aquila," I said, looking to the old man for support. "What does he mean?"

"I think, young Titus," he said, "that he's telling you to go west."

I looked towards the sunset. Truly this was a beautiful land; and now it was no longer an alien one. Shafts of red light broke through the clustered clouds. "West, lad, west," Nikias whispered. They were treating me like a child or a younger brother, even though I was nominally their leader; but I was too confused to rebuke them, and I had grown fond of all of them.

Far over the horizon, I knew, were the Montes Saxosi, the most imposing mountains Romans had ever looked upon. Behind them was the land of the setting sun. Could it be that east met west there? "China," I said softly.

We sighted a wild creature in the distance—an elk, perhaps— silhouetted in the sunset. With whoops and cries—and mine were as hearty and savage as the Lacotians'—we galloped towards it and the last of the daylight.

[Notes to pacify purists:

[The Olmecs, in our continuum, died out of course, before the first century A.D. when the Aquila series takes place; so I have created a transitional culture, mixing the little that is known about the Olmecs with smatterings of slightly later cultures whom they influenced.

[For the transliteration of the "Lacotian" language, I have stuck to the Teton dialect of Dakotah as analyzed by nineteenth-century philologists. The Riggs phoneticization as adapted by

Swanton and Boas was used as a base, but I have "Englished" some of the phonetic symbols to avoid giving the reader a headache.—SS]

Comets and Kings

A final story in this classical vein. Alexander the Great has always been a hero of mine. I am now slightly older than Alexander was when he conquered the entire known world, or close to it; but I have yet to conquer my own back yard. This, then, is wishful thinking of a sort . . . .

When you are a boy, all the trees of all the forests seem to stretch up forever, to merge into a leaf-dark zenith as far away as the sky. When you're older, I suppose you laugh at yourself. But there is one forest of my boyhood whose trees, I sometimes fantasize, have kept pace with my growing. Even now, when I stand at the edge of the universe, the shadows touch me, across Greece, across Persia, across India.

Do you believe in hubris?

But of course you do. Yet it is a far more complex issue than our ancients could possibly have imagined.... Well, I shan't philosophize. This isn't even my story; and I am no visionary, as Alexander is.

There was a forest in Macedonia where we played at being men, in an autumn much like any other. He was a petty princeling with a crazy fire in him; and I had only just found out how terrible it is to love the great.

"Hephaistion!" he called me, and flashed into the forest, his gray chiton crisscrossed by the evening sun. He ran ahead, I caught up, we walked arm in arm, we laughed together, senselessly; we wrestled, we sank, panting, onto the damp moss.... Then he got up, without a word, and went off by himself in an unknown direction.

Already I knew better than to follow him unbidden.

"Hephaistion!" he cried out again. I could not fathom the emotion. I saw a strange man lurking in the shadows; Alexander had practically walked into him.

A sudden terror seized me. Did he only seem to be a man? "He's harmless," I said. "Just a peasant of these parts, I bet."

His body was blurred against the trees, shimmering. My eyes smarted. Alex was cautious, so I stayed frozen too. The glare forced my eyes away from the bearded face, from the blood-chilling eyes, down to the chiton, woven of some alien stuff, like the stuff of rainbow.

Perhaps he was one of the forgotten gods of Macedon, driven into oblivion when civilization came to the North.

Alexander showed no fear, as always. He didn't flinch at all from the alien's gaze.

Past the old man's head, in a little gap between the trees, stood a structure of polished bronze, something like an inverted amphora. A field of metallic reeds protruded, waving delicately in the breeze. It was perhaps large enough to house the stranger. I thought it quaint, a prop in a satyr play, perhaps.

Alex spoke first. "Are you a god?"

"It might be expedient to think of me that way, yes," said the stranger. He laughed suddenly, but his eyes remained expressionless. "Call me Ectogeos—'outside the earth.' " He spoke Attic atrociously. His sibilants lisped, and he didn't contract his verbs, which gave his speech a peculiar, mock-Homeric quality. "You wonder why I come to you, Alexander?"

Nothing was being addressed to me. I was just an insignificant witness to some key event in his life. I tried not to be jealous.

"I am an observer," the ancient continued. "All my kind are; incessant observers. And here there is surely something to observe, even if he is only a boy as yet!'

Alex was drinking it in. I don't know how, but he seemed half to recognize the stranger....

Ectogeos said, "You stand out against your human background like a supernova against the stars. Observing you, one sees the whole world; influence you, and one could—well, it is forbidden of course. Even my visit here is a little risky." Had he said too much? "Think of me as your guardian from above."

Alexander nodded. "But," the old man said, "I wish to ask you some questions, in the name of research—or you might call it curiosity. What do you plan to do in your life?"

"Conquer the world." This without hesitation.

"The world?"

"When I was born a comet came."

I had to interrupt, then. "Why are you asking him questions? Are you a god then, or is he? Is it your place to question him?" Then I said, "Are you or are you not a god?"

"A god?" I saw he had no intention of answering me.

Alexander said: "If you are a god of these woods, your kind is dying. Soon they will forget you, and you need worship to sustain you. Times are changing...." It was true enough.

The man laughed again. It was a throaty chuckle that seemed to grow out of the forest depths. "It's kind of you to worry about me." It *was* kind, I thought; he had always been concerned about the aged. Was he destined never to see age, then? "But I am more than capable of seeing to myself."

My eye was drawn again to the structure. Softly the silvery reeds rustled. I wanted to dare to go up to it and peer inside....

"It is forbidden, Hephaistion!" he said sharply.

He has read my thoughts! Fear and guilt shot through me. I withdrew my thoughts, shielding them. They were deep in conversation, those two; it was boyish stuff, about conquering the Persians and the rest of the world. Alexander had always been extravagant; I found it charming, but Ectogeos looked very grave.

Finally the alien said, "Thank you for your information," and made to return to his inverted amphora.

"Not yet!" It was a challenge. "You have not told me who *you* are." Alexander...the forest sunlight mottled his face. My heart almost stopped beating.

"You tempt me, earthchild," said the stranger. "We cannot, as a rule, reveal our identity to the worlds we observe...but there is something special about you, and...no, no, I doubt you could accept what I am."

"If you don't tell me, I won't rest till I've found out. My father is King here." Alexander's eyes flashed, defiant.

"I know." The stranger spoke reluctantly. "But you could not imagine what I am. Perhaps, though, at the end of your Quest... when it no longer matters...."

"My Quest?"

"Well, it won't hurt to tell you what you know already. The world is yours."

"*All* the world?" asked Alex, wonder creeping into his voice.

"Why not?" And he had gone into the structure.

He seemed bewitched as we walked home; he moved ahead, striding rapidly, crunching twigs, not looking in front of him. It was hard to keep up with him. And now the twilight seemed to settle. Of a sudden we had stepped out of the forest; I picked the leaves from my cloak and wrapped it around his shoulders as he paused. It was chillier now. The breeze and the half light toyed with his long, untamable golden hair.

"Don't be so withdrawn, Alex," I said. "How can you hide so from me?"

"You saw. My dreams are coming true, faster than I can cope with them." He looked steadily at the dark earth. Only when he had said it aloud, I thought, did he know it was true.

I knew he would sulk tonight, and be surly to our tutor, Aristotle; that he would sit alone at the edge of his bed, dreaming dreams, excluding me—not by design, for he would not do that, but because the dreams transcended me. "Who was the man?" I asked him. "What was the dream?" The name, 'outisde the world,' does not ring true. Alex did not answer me; I do not think he knew.

"Alex," I said, breaking another silence, "was it a visitation from a god?" I felt the shadows of trees, and was uneasy.

His eyes were on me. I wanted so much to give him everything, if I could reassure him just a little. . . . To love the great is terrible.

But he turned to me on impulse. Without a word he embraced me in a desperate clinging, like a lost child.

Many images follow in the memory: the stench of blood, the sun eclipsed by black blankets of arrows. . . and Alexander and I growing tall together.

They have all merged for me, these images: all the forests and woods and taiga and sweltering jungles, the towers and pyramids, the ziggurats and obelisks, the empty tombs, the wide-trousered dancing boys, the kohl-eyes priestesses, the satraps with beards like terraces, the camp whores with bosoms spilling out of gaudy corsets, and the countless Kings, overdressed, like life-size dolls, dwarfed by their golden thrones.

But he conquered Persia and became Great King, and we sacrificed at the tomb of Achilles and Patroklos.

And after, flushed with wine and victory, he stormed into the tent. Our friends were posturing drunkenly at one another; and after a while they staggered home, and the Persian domestics vanished like a magician's coins, and we were alone.

"Aren't you ever going to turn back?" I asked him. I was not the first to ask; well, perhaps the first to ask to his face.

He flung down his empty wineskin. "What do you mean?" His speech unslurred abruptly; his eyes flashed clear in the half dark.

"I mean, consolidate your empire. . . ." I was always more practical than he, not a visionary, as I have said.

"I have no *time* for that!" He began to explain: "There's so much of the world left, and I have to have all of it! It's nothing personal, this conquest, it's just. . .I *have* to. It's a destiny." He said the word with a funny self-consciousness.

"By now you ought to have seen reason."

His voice slurred again. "Don't you remember? In the woods, with the god. . .?"

I struggled to place the memory. It was hazy at first: a shimmering old man, an autumn haze, dreary conversations in the half dark—

...the forest sunlight mottling his face.

It was an image of fragile transience and cutting clarity. Like a magnet, it drew the memory to the surface. But I tried to laugh it off. "It was just a practical joke, or something...."

"*You* don't believe that." Alexander was right. I turned away from him, watching the fire and the dance of shadows against canvas. I heard him say, urgently, "He came to *me*. And he gave me the world."

"Maybe it wasn't his to give," I countered with involuntary sharpness, although I was trying to humor him. His confidence had always terrified me—and convinced me, by its sheer intensity.

So we argued, for the sake of form, a few minutes longer. *It's a mistake,* I thought, *to judge him by values which he has rendered meaningless. And we both know how such arguments usually end.*

In the flickering orange light he touched me, touched my hands, my face.

How can I refuse you, I thought, *what is yours by right of conquest?* He yielded to me as marble to a sculptor; giving, he only became more and more himself.

The night he burned Persepolis....

Towering, fantastical spires of flame were lapping at the corners of the sky, and in our noses was the suffocating stench of incense and charred flesh.

We followed Alexander into the empty, endless throne room. As they cleared a path through the rubble, he wielded his torch like a fury, staggering toward the Great King's throne, clambering up the hundred giddy steps of solid gold. Across the vastness of the hall, I heard him shout for a footstool—he was too short—and then he became like the other Kings, countless Kings, deposed and dying, dwarfed in their own thrones. *They were living gods,* I thought, *and now he has cast them down.*

The wild laughter sounded small. Soldiers were hurling their firebrands into the splendor. A courtesan was screeching elegantly, quaffing from a looted wine cup. From the foot of the steps I watched him; the brightness of his eyes still cowed me, even at this distance.

I thought: *This fire rages so he can breathe life anew into the defenseless city.* The fire evoked a sense of wonder, with columns snapping like lyre strings overtaut. For a moment we were all openmouthed, like children at our first funeral.

I heard him call me, so I went up to him, almost stumbling over a severed arm.

Urgently I asked him, "Why are you burning Persepolis?" But he sat impassively on the throne.

Then he said: *"Because no God has visited me since I was a young boy. I make this fire so they can see me."*

A great palace burning...a great man, burning with desire...; a great man, desperately feeding on the love of so many, yet knowing they cannot touch his solitude...the brightness hurt my eyes. Then, after some hours, it flickered and smoldered and was spent. The morning came: gray, rainy.

Always I shall remember this night, not only because the brilliance of the flames made day where night should be, and usurped the functions of the Gods, but because there sprang to my mind unbidden the sound of a chuckling forest, and the sight of an alien personage in front of an unearthly structure of polished bronze.

Perhaps it was some kind of purging for him. I hoped it was a fire to drive out fire; inside, I hoped for an ending, though all our hopes would be transmuted by the catalyst of his personality, and we would become mere aspects of him.

And then, more merging images: white sand that blinded, pyramids that littered the sand like a child's building blocks. Nilos, which runs backward, strange gods, strange rites. Soldiers, digging up mummies from the sand, mummies whose faces glared stone-hardened across unimaginable time.

There was an oracle in the desert, in an oasis. We waited while Alexander went to consult the strange gods that had become his own. It was an idyllic time, without bloodshed; soldier's children played at the desert's edge, and there was water and grain toward the river. It was a place of luxurious plenty, sprouting out of a devastated vastness.

One day a Bedouin scout, shouting frenziedly, whipping his camel, rode into camp. *The oracle has declared Alexander a God, the son of Zeus!* Alexander would return, perhaps in a few days, perhaps a week, to receive the homage of his subjects.

The scout did not say that Alexander had met Ectogeos again....

We were alone together, and it was one of those times—increasingly rare now—when he talked freely, almost as though we were still boys together. "Let them believe that they deified me!" he said, laughing. "The priests, muttering in their weird languages, the incense everywhere. At least it was cool there in that temple under the rocks. I listened to their god with great courtesy, but...there was another meeting, too."

I stared at him, already guessing. An oppressive tension fell out of a clear blue sky. "I'll tell you a secret!" he said, half laughing like in the old days; but it was not the same. You'd think he had become an oriental, with all the bowing and scraping....I waited as I was supposed to, listening to the date palms rustling.

Finally, "Well, what?"

"Relax! I'll tell you!" His eyes sparkled.

After a sufficient pause, he told me. He had gone off by himself in the desert, after the fuss at the Siwa Oasis was over. The others must have been frantic trying to find him. And, just as he knew it would be, *he* was standing there, beside the comical structure. "He says it's a flying machine, but won't elaborate."

"What," I said, "is he a Daedalus too, as well as a peasant and a guardian from above and a wood god?"

"After I spoke to him, he got into it and flew off," he said matter-of-factly. His eyes were distant. "Well, say something."

"I don't believe it." But I believed every word.

"Oh, nonsense, Heph. Do take me seriously. He said many things which tempt me to believe, you know, that oracle. We played questions and answers again. He was very ambiguous.... I think, you know, he tries to cover his tracks...."

As though he might be reprimanded if caught? I thought.

"You know what the first thing he said to me was? Go on, guess."

"How should I know? 'How you've grown,' maybe."

"Exactly so! You see, you *can* read my mind."

We both burst out laughing. Almost at once, the tension returned.

"Actually, he said: 'How you've grown; you shortlivers always surprise me,' " said Alexander.

Shortlivers? And what had he called Alex before: *earthchild?* These were not the sorts of words gods used of mortals, exactly ...and then I thought, what if someone had invented a flying machine? Many of the wonders that had assaulted our senses were no less implausible.

Alex said: "He said to me, 'I hear they have given you divinity now. How does your halo fit?' I said I wasn't at all sure. 'Ha!' he said. 'Isn't sureness a measure of one's divinity? Of course it is!'

"But I said, "If I'm to be a god, then I am one of you, but you see, I can't fly."

" 'What's bigger—flying, or conquering the world? I didn't

invent this contraption, you know. Someone else—let's call him Hephaestus, so as not to distort your world perception too much—makes all these things.' "

"So what came of it?" I asked him.

"I said to him, 'So you still maintain that I'll conquer the world—even though my army doesn't want to go on? They all miss home, don't you know that?'

" 'I maintain nothing. Actually, *they* keep telling me not to interfere.'

" 'Who're *they?*' I was insistent. I don't like riddles." Alex was very serious. I tried to see the mystery of the story, but it was broad daylight, the breeze was blowing softly through the trees, children were playing "leap-the-steps" on a little step pyramid (they've looted it since).... Somehow it was not as terrifying to me as it might have been brooding by night on a battle's eve. He sensed, I think, that I was trying to hide something from him, not disbelief exactly, but...the delicate tension of our relationship had drifted away.

Looking at him, sitting on a rude bench, travel soiled, I saw he had battle scars but there were no lines under his eyes. He had shaken off the foreboding of warfare like a sea lion erupting from the water. His eyes reflected the sky.

Even when I looked away, his presence was something palpable. "Don't you want to know, then, what he said next?" he asked me.

"Of course." I did, really; I did not know why it came out so offhand, so blase.

"Well then. He didn't answer. In fact, he just looked at me, the way Aristotle used to peer at a specimen. A sandstorm was brewing, but I had to wait, even though it wasn't funny anymore. Abruptly he said to me, 'Define a god.'

"I was stuck for an answer. He chuckled, the way he had done in Macedonia long ago; you could hear it echoing in the wind and sand, and then he walked up to his structure and sort of faded into it. Fire leaped from under it. Then he poked his head out, as though tempted to say one final thing:

" 'Go on! *Be* what they say you are! Isn't that what *being* is all about?' "

Alex assumed that distant look again. The conversation was not satisfying; it had all the logic of a dream, and all the essential reality of one.

I fell to thinking, under the scorching heat:

I have known him intimately, in the most profound sense that a man can know, ever since we were boys.... How old were we now? I had lost track, not yet thirty, though. And now that he was elevated to godhead by an oracle, I was left a poor relation, like Polydeuces to Castor. How did they manage these questions, after we were dead?

As I watched Alexander, locked in his terrible solitude, the thought of death fell like a tree's shadow across my mind. *Does he still think of conquering the world, of absorbing the universe into his fiery corona?* In the final analysis, the vision was his alone. Even I could not see it.

Ectogeos had called himself an observer. I did not understand why he should observe. The gods see everything anyway; they did not have to send someone down to gawk. Were the gods voyeurs? There are men and gods.... Was there a third category?

I wished *he* would come and talk to *me*.

More images, from the last days of the great conquering:
The world grew wider, wilder.

There were markets reeking with strangers' sweat, great green jungles, serpents of myth coiled around nameless trees of emerald...and everything growing, upward, outward, inward, downward, in a frenzy of growing as we neared the edge of the earth. There were whirlwinds, assaults of rain; the horizon never moved any closer, and black Ganga coursed sluggishly beneath a lowering sky. There were faces so alien that I forgot *the alien's* face; there were the giant gardens of King Poros, green, now dipped in the purple of bloodshed. And the animals: elephants, rhinoceroses, dolphins, tigers, unicorns, and women with diamonds in their noses, women naked from the waist up, their breasts dangling like ripe mangoes that glisten in the sunshine, brown children leaping into rivers, widows leaping into funeral pyres—

Amid the amazing fertility, the armies came to rest, perhaps only eight hundred stades from the other shore of Oceanos, the boundary of the world—and were on the brink of mutiny.

"Pull down the tent flaps, shut out the noise!" Alexander screamed.

"Can't you see, Alexander, they want to turn back?" I was pleading with him.

He talked like a child, sure of his reward, but knowing he has to play a silly begging game first. "But I haven't *seen* yet!"

I was irritated. By then I knew exactly how much of this conquest was due to his charisma, and how much merely to his understanding of the mob.

"If you don't turn back, they'll mutiny and leave you here."
They were outside the tent, cursing, demanding, the old veterans,
making threats in Macedonian. "Can't you hear them?"

"They would never leave me," he said. Then, with a quiet,
terrible intensity, "I *must* see this through to the end! I *must* fulfill
my destiny!"

"Destiny? *Hubris?*"

I had stung him. He turned to me and said, with a strained
calmness, "I know he will be there to meet me."

"You mean you think you'll run into that man who claims to
be your guardian from above? What a farce! In the desert, back in
Egypt—I wasn't even there with you! Prove it!"

He flared up, then fell back, speechless. I pressed my advan-
tage. "*I'll* send them back, with or without you!"

"*You!*" He was livid. "By what authority do you flout your
supreme commander?" He reached for his weapon, then put his
hand down, staring at it dully, not knowing where to put it. "Who
do you think you are?"

I said, very softly, "*He, too, is Alexander.*" Those had been
his words to the mother of Darius (they are history) when she had
prostrated herself before me, the taller, by mistake.

He was about to speak, but his voice was drowned by the
clamor from outside.

"Yes, Hephaistion," he said. An admission. "But *I* must see it,
the limit of the world, the horizon extending until it merges with
Ocean, the boundary of our cosmos. Send them home; it's only
eight hundred stades from here and I can catch up...."

"But—why leave me out?" I said. I should live up to this
blurring of our identities....

He planted a single kiss upon my cheek, this boy with his face
mottled by the forest sunlight.

In history, we turned back; and what is not in the records
does not constitute history. Truth does not enter into it....

He was standing by the seashore in the twilight, beside the
shining structure. We tethered our horses to a tree. Hands touching, feet sinking in step in the warm wet sand, we approached
the alien.

The wind at the world's end howled over the sea. There was
no horizon; sea and sky merged into one gray. You could not tell
where the end came, for the gods are masters of illusion.

I saw recognition burst out in Alexander's face. He left me
running behind, in his eagerness to meet the ancient.

"Rejoice," he greeted him, like a friend.

Ectogeos said nothing. His eyes were closed, his lips moved soundlessly as though he were in communication with something far away.

He woke with a start and saw us, smiled broadly.

"Now that your destiny is accomplished," he said, "I have been liberated from observing; I am free to answer your questions."

I expected Alexander to ask the questions one asks of gods: questions like *when will I die?* or some such.

But all he asked was : "Is there not more?"

"Why? Does your Quest's ending disappoint you?"

I saw how perceptive the alien had been, though Alex would never admit it to himself. For I understood him, how he was driven by the desire to push forever into the unknown. We all followed him, of course, but our desires were limited: a little treasure, a little land, a kingdom, a satrapy even, a little sexual adventure...and we were content.

For him, ending was catastrophe.

Ectogeos turned to me. "Well, Hephaistion, are you not satisfied? I did not come to observe *you.* You could have asked me anything; I have been reading your mind always."

I didn't know what to reply. He shrugged. His rainbow chiton shone brilliantly in the dusk. A shaft of light from the structure fell on Alexander's face, and I saw for the first time that his eyes had become lined. Alexander repeated his question.

"Come into my *spaceship,*" said the alien. He had coined a strange word, full of power. We followed him in, and all the while the world's-end ocean sighed and heaved in the world's-end wind.

The interior of the structure—I cannot describe it; I have no referents in my experience of the world...a mirror curved into forever. Hazes that became solids. Lights without source, shifting like lights of a faceted crystal.

"This," said the ancient, "is a space-time scanner." There was a square mirror of highly polished silver. I was struggling with the name of the thing. "Don't bother to understand," he said to me, not unkindly.

Alex accepted without question the old man's assertion that the mirror could show all places in the cosmos, and all times.

First we saw the world's end, but from a peculiar distance, as though suspended far above it.

We saw a round world spinning crazily like a top in the nothingness; and on that world countless nations springing up wildly, everywhere, in its most inacccessible corners, immense buildings crashing into the firmament on an undiscovered conti-

144

nent where Aztecs built pyramids to bloodstained Helios and starfarers leaped into the sky. The moon was full of people.

Alex clenched and unclenched his fist.

"So there's more. Our cosmology is wrong," he said tonelessly. "I haven't achieved anything yet! It isn't over yet!"

"My poor child! Your whole world doesn't begin to contain the totality of life!"

Rushing past our eyes at a continually accelerated rate—the seven planets, and a few more besides, crowded with life forms, microscopic, macroscopic, insubstantial, massless, waveless, thought forms...I gave up trying to understand.

Alexander watched, engrossed. I felt his heart sinking.

The solar system shrank to a point.

We flew past thousands, then millions of stars, all full of life: green, purple, gold, black, ultraviolet, X-ray-colored life. The galaxy collapsed into a single point.

Alexander looked up, relieved that it was over. "So that is why it could never be mine," he said, almost reconciled.

The scanner was black for some moments; then another galaxy swam into view. The same process began again: a cluster of galaxies shrank into nothingness, a cluster of clusters, a cluster of clusters of clusters...the universe shrank into nothingness.

The mirror was empty for perhaps ten minutes. Then, to his horror, another universe began to form, and another, a cluster of of universes, a cluster of clusters, a cluster of clusters of clusters....

The alien said: "And now you have the truth. I wanted to spare you the pain of looking more."

It was midnight. The wind had never ceased to howl; we were outside the structure. A pale, cold light from the structure illuminated Alexander's face, and I saw the despair in his eyes, and the innocence.

"I may have mocked you," continued the stranger. "If so I apologize; there are so many rules governing scientific research. I wish I could have helped." His garment glowed faintly.

Alex was silent, so finally it was I who asked the question that I had wanted answered for so long:

"Who, in all truth, are you?"

"My name is Zethtep," he said; "in your language, 'Watcher.' My friends call me 'Meddler.'" Already he was going into the spaceship.

Alex and I watched, alone together on the shore. The ship streaked into the blackness of the sky. In the distance, against the stars, it blazed like a comet; then slowly, like the dying of a plucked lyre string, it faded and melded with the night.

We found our horses. Alex was silent all the way to the camp. But I was not as shaken as he, for it was not, after all, my vision.... We rode in a darkness further darkened by compound shadows of strange trees. Wind gusted, damp and warm.

I remembered the ship, splashed out across the sky like a living fire. *Are all comets born this way?* I thought.

Alex was spurring on his horse, impatient. I could not see his face, and for once I was glad I couldn't.

I remembered how he had told the alien, that first time, in the forest in Macedonia: *when I was born a comet came.* I remembered the casual pride of that statement. But—

Had they come, even then, to observe him? Had they gathered round, like students round a specimen?

I sped up to a gallop. The wind streamed on either side of me; and I abandoned myself to it, hardly noticing which way we went.

I think it has broken his heart.

—*Tokyo and Alexandria, 1977 and 1979*

Angels' Wings

I wrote this little story for Roy Torgeson's anthology series *Chrysalis*. It's rather a peculiar one, really, both whimsical and serious in tone. One reader told me it was a feminist story; another told me it was violently anti-feminist. I can only say that such thoughts were far from my mind. By the way, the delegates' lounge at the U.N. is described exactly as it used to be when I used to drop in to lunch with my father there, complete with tackily grandiose Wall-of-China mural.

Unending desert, silvered by impending darkness—
Tire squeal. Observatory.

Shit! Clem Papazian stubbed her toe against the metal banister, *only ten minutes to totality.* Metal door flew open, settled, rasping, into place. She looked past their heads at the wall-sized monitor. They were all ignoring her. They were hunched forward in the stiff chairs, intent on the huge electronically-toned-down sun. She waited to get her breath. *Damn the brat....*

"Sorry I'm late. Kid."

No one acknowledged her.

A shadow stole over the sun....

I should relax, she told herself. *So what if I'm a token woman astrophysicist serving tea in a far-off observatory, sneaking from my stand-in-the-corner servitude to watch the stars and the suns and the unreachable galaxies? Enjoy, enjoy.*

"Oh, there you are, Clem." Dave Ehrlich turned at last and waved her into the semicircle of chairs. She sat down and the hard-angled metal dug into the small of her back. Briefly she glanced from face to face: Dave Ehrlich, the director, a thin taut face latticed with red lines, white hair like jungle undergrowth, distant unnerving eyes; Bill Nagata, the next one down, all smiles and no substance; more faces, all a little nervous at her intrusion into their little games.

"The shadow crept quietly, the sun glared ten feet high from the monitor, the darkness swept across and in a single dragon-swallow—

"Quick, upstairs!" shouted Nagata. "To the deck...."

Hands suddenly clutched pieces of dark acetate, everyone shuffled, rushing for the one door—

Clem was about to turn round when she—

"Wait!" she said. What was wrong with the image on the screen? She took one step towards the monitor, knocking over a chair. "David, Bill, take a look at this...."

She lurched forward, her hand tracing the lines of the screen. "Wait a moment!" She heard the clank of shoes on metal steps, knew they were ignoring her yet again, ran after them and saw their legs thunking in the curve of the stairwell above her head, and knew she couldn't get their attention....

Damn it! I'll have to do the female *thing.* Exasperation pounded at her. *If they won't take me seriously—*

She began to scream. She did it well.

All at once, softly, from above..."What's that damn woman up to? Hey, you go and look...." "I'm damned if I'm going to miss a second of this; you're the director, you go—" And she screamed and screamed until Ehrlich had come and was holding on to her, muttering about the first decent eclipse of his career and how he was missing out on it.

"All right, all right, what's the matter?"

She stopped suddenly, taking him by surprise. It was so quiet that her breathing echoed in the stairwell. Above on the observation deck, she knew, they would all be standing breathless, wonderstifled, rapt. Ehrlich's eyes were hostile; the metal stairs and peeling walls seemed to cave in on her....

"There's something wrong," she said quietly. "Go look at the monitor."

"Okay, show me." She had to admire the way he feigned patience. She knew he didn't want to lose the U.N. financing.... *What are you thinking?* she thought. *That I'm only working at this prestigious place because my ex-husband is Secretary-General of the United Nations? How can you be so naive?*

Then she hefted to door open and pointed to the monitor. The door wheezed into place.

"They won't be able to see it *out there*," she said. "The lines are too fine for the naked-eye...."

She saw Ehrlich go pale, so the red lines on his face stood out like red cobwebs. "God, oh, God," he said...he let go of her and walked towards the screen. She saw how he was doing the great discoverer thing, with the Byronic gait, the overdone, eureka-ish expression.

Damn right he knows how important this is.

"You see why I had to scream." Nervously she started prying her sweater from her slacks, pushing it back in again....He seemed to miss the accusing tone completely.

"Why yes of course, you did well, Clem."

And, trembling, she too turned to watch the phenomenon. They were both quite silent.

There were times when she wanted to go back to the New

York and Geneva circuit and flash platitudinous smiles at diplomats and recline at elegant parties, listening to the chiming of chandeliers over the clinking of cocktails and the babblebuzz of big decisions.

It was in times like this that she was glad she had traded in the vapid stars of world politics for the other stars, the stars beyond grasping....

She watched in silence.

The blackness first, the soft starlight. Around the black circle, the corona. A burning hoop in a dark circus tent. *Something about an eclipse, no matter how many Ph.D.'s you have in astrophysics, lumping in your throat, giving you shivers, making you sense the vastness and the cold out there, in the beyond.*

But this wasn't right!

Lines of light, darting across the blackness into the sun, appeared, were visible for a split instant, dissolved, reappeared, redissolved, divided, coalesced, like cloud chamber trails, but she knew that each of them must be a million miles long....

They just can't be there, those lines....

Tiny light-trails, out of the blackness and into the coronal lightveils, arcs, corkscrews, whorls....

No possible known phenomenon. A thought—*extraterrestrial life*—surfaced for only a second; she backed away from it, afraid.

"They can't be there!" Ehrlich whispered, his back to her. A phone began to ring somewhere.

And then the darkness ebbed and the first sunrays burst starsapphirelike out of the abyss, and the lines vanished, drowned by light, and the monitor glared at them....

From all over the observatory, the jangle of phones came, jumbling her thought.

This is history, she thought.

Ehrlich turned around and shouted at her, "Go answer the phone! I want all the radio astronomy people, I want all the SETI guys, I want everyone you can get, I bet they're all jamming the line right now!" She started to catch the fire from his eyes. But then he said, under his breath, "I'll never rest until I solve the mystery of the Ehrlich lines."

"*Papazian* lines!" she muttered. "*I* discovered them."

He didn't seem to hear her.

* * *

A ting from the microwave, a clickclickclick of changing TV

150

channels. "Mommy...."

Clem detached herself, automated her body, and sent off her mind to where lightlines still whirled and dived into a black pit, a hidden sun. "Come quickly, Mommy—"

She snapped around from the range, looked across the cutlery-cluttered bar to the dinette table. Beyond, through the panoramic window view of a toy city, beyond the antenna jungle, night was falling. Her five-year-old son's face was half-eclipsed by the back of the TV; only the curls shone, lustrous in the shabby lampshade's half-light.

"I can't get the channel I want." His eyes appeared above the set: cow-eyes, his father's eyes. *Your father's child, you are,* she thought, *demand, demand, demand, You males are all alike: your dad, glamorous Mr. Score-and-Run Doctor Kolya Sachdev with that strange half-Indian half-Russian face that nobody could ever forget, leastways an Armenian slumgirl who'd scrabbled her way up to a Fulbright and Paris....*

And that screwed-up Ehrlich. She reached for the oven door, claustrophobia clawing at her. Then she pulled out the reconditioned stew and ladled it into Denny's teddybowl. "Chow, honey."

"Mommy—" a shrill exasperated command.

She came round to him with the bowl, glanced at the TV set, and—"Okay, I'll fix it. I guess it's something in the back."

—fzzz—the bitter, fratricidal war between the two sects in central Africa today reached a new—fzzz—"

Clickclick. And for the second time that day she was looking at a video screen and nearly passed out.

"I don't wanna watch the Lucy show, Mommy!"

Clem was thinking, quickly, chaotically, *This show isn't on at six o'clock and it isn't in color and there's no channel 41 here—*

...Lucille Ball on the screen, elegantly stretched out on a sofa, evening gown, pastel decor. But the set blown apart, and behind it galaxies whirling in mid-space. Thin firelines streaking, twisting, cartwheeling across blackness....

Help me! she said. *I don't know who you are or why you are killing my children. I'm a lightmother from the big emptiness, giving birth out of the far nothing, sending my children in from the cold to give them sunwarmth for a moment before their long migrations into the spaces between galaxies—*

Laugh track came on. Lucy ignored the cackling, stared straight at the viewer with hurt eyes.

"This isn't real TV, Mommy," said Denny. He dug into the stew. But Clem couldn't take her eyes off the screen. Something

151

out there beyond the night was broadcasting on to her television set with images out of old sitcoms. It was too surreal to be terrifying, at first. Until she realized that this was *first contact* in a way undreamed of by any science fiction writer...and then she was desperately trying to swallow her terror, didn't want Denny to see her get this scared....

—My children, creatures of light, have burst from me. I can't control their direction of flight any more. They are too young, they have no minds. And they are dying as they reach your star, some of them, dying, driven mad, tumbling to their deaths. A mad ogre is assaulting them with orderless waves, crazy imagequilts they can't understand.

(Laugh track.) The ogre is a rocky planet that cannot harbor life, yet seems alive. I cannot understand. I don't understand.

Is it possible the ogre doesn't even see me, doesn't even know that I'm here? (Laugh track.)

But I'm trying to reason with you. I've sorted out things from the wavepatterns that may be meanings in the madness. But I don't know how well I am simulating the patterns. (Laugh track burst for a moment, cut off.)

Meanwhile my children die if they should pass within a certain radius of the ogre planet. There is only one recourse. You must be silent, you must not even whisper a single wavelength... I don't know if this is possible. I know nothing of the kind of creature you are...but please, be silent for a while, I beg of you, let the children live, let them be born!

Help me—help me—(Laugh track—laugh track—)

Denny was crying. She realized she had been squeezing his upper arm so hard that he couldn't move it, that she was hurting him. "Who's killing the other kids?" he said, hysterical, "I don't want them to!"

The television began to fizzle and the doorbell rang. Clem cursed and crossed the little living room area to get it. "We don't want any, damn you!" she said, unhitching the chain and preparing to slam the door.

The foot in the crack was David Ehrlich's.

"Can I come in for a moment?"

It was an embarrassed voice. Clem heard the hesitation and felt more in control than she had been before. She resisted an impulse to keep him waiting there; and opened up to a haggard, splotched face and sweatstained office clothes. Suddenly she felt sorry for him; but then she remembered the casual way he had assumed the credit for discovering the alien lightstreaks, earlier that day, and she became stiff. "You look awful," she said, but it

152

came out hostile.

He sat down on the tattered beanbag without asking. "Well," he said, "we've been in touch with SETI and the radio people and the X-ray people.... This is pretty damned serious. This thing's some kind of energy being, seems to be hovering a little way beyond the first comet belt. It'll be here for about forty days according to the information they've been getting—in English— on the spacewaves. In the meantime—"

"We have to stop broadcasting," said Clem. "*Everything*. No TV, no radio, no transcontinental communications, no satellite relays, nothing. No air traffic too, I guess, because it means radar. It's the babble that's killing off the children...."

Ehrlich stared at her. "No chance. There's a war on in Africa, for God's sake! Only if *you* can talk to that husband of yours. We need you, Clem."

"So it comes out!" she said. "First you grab the credit for my discovery—"

"If *that's* what you want—"

"*Keep* your credit! I've had it with all your games. I came to astrophysics to get away from all that, but I found it all over again...." Ehrlich looked away, made a face at Denny, evoked no response, stared at the floor instead. She felt how he was *enduring* her, something unpleasant that had to be got through.

"Look," he said at last, "we don't know what the thing can do to us. It's obviously a very powerful creature. We have to accede to its demands. We have to study it anyway, for science's sake. I know America will do it—it's a great campaign gimmick—but some dinky country in Africa could just blow it. Look, you've got to get to New York and talk to your husband while the General Assembly's still in session, not that the U.N. can do much, but it would be a start, and—"

Anger seethed inside her. "Damn, damn, damn you," she grated. "You're talking about a living sentient creature, and I get nothing but fear of retaliation, fear for your political future... don't you see, we're out there killing babies, and—and—"

"Okay. We can't get hysterical now. You're a very idealistic person, and you'll convince them. With sheer sincerity."

"You're using me."

"You agree that it's necessary."

They didn't speak for a while. Clem saw her son at the dinner table, contracted into himself, retreating. Lucy's message sounded from the television set again; and Lucy's image was a ghost in the window, superimposed over the lattice of city lights.

Clem said, softly, "There is a mother out there, in the loneliness between stars, and we are killing her children. We have no right to do this, and she has told us of it, and we can't talk of ignorance. There's a mother out there, contending against the collective stupidity, the self-serving, crass impenetrability of a man's world."

"Aren't you anthropomorphizing this whole thing a little much?" Then, suddenly, "Hold it!... You *identify* with that thing out there!"

That's not true! she started to say, and then she realized that it was. She didn't answer him.

He went on, "I'm pleading with you, Clem. I suppose you enjoy it. You think that as soon as the announcement is made to the world, everyone's just going to altruistically shut down the show and wait for the aliens to fly by.

"But there's going to be xenophobia. And what about that religious war in Africa? Think they'll stop communicating before the other side stops?"

"I don't see why they shouldn't stop," she said. "It's a great thing, a beautiful gesture for the human race."

"Oh, I hope so; I see it your way, too; but I'm a lot wiser than you, I think."

Sure, she thought. *You must know your man's world better than I do.* She closed her eyes and thought of the lonely mother. "Well," she said at last, "I've got to do it, haven't I?"

Damn it, why had the alien chosen to represent itself as a woman?

"I'll see you in New York, then. All us 'world experts' are going to be converging on it," said Ehrlich, all organizer now. He left quickly; Clem suspected he did not wish to prolong the tension of the encounter.

"Looks like you're going to stay with Gran again, Denny...." She looked at the child for a long time. She wanted to rush over and hug him, but she was too angry inside.

* * *

The delegates' lounge was much as she remembered it. Dominating the far wall, the gaudy gargantuan tapestry of the Great Wall of China; darksuited diplomats huddled over low tables, rendered beetle-like by the ceiling's immense height; the usual three-hundred-an-hour class ass that blended with the scenery and serviced the overpaid men made sudden bachelors for a season.... Clem took a seat. The lounge made you feel small in a way that whole vistas of intergalactic space could not; there

154

you felt part of a grand scheme, here you were oppressed by power. Just beyond her sight, she knew, reporters lurked, photographers.

There had been news conferences and broadcasts and talk shows, and each time more of the alien's children were being killed. But she had put off a meeting with Kolya for as long as she could.

After three years, she was afraid of him. Afraid that she might have made the wrong decision, when she left him.

Clem had learnt more in the past few days. Lucy had been seen on about a billion TV screens around the world; the radio-astro people had had more complex interchanges with the light-mother. There was a day's delay in communication, so they were not precisely conversations, more like running commentaries. Lucy's English was good, though interrupted by laugh-tracks and polluted with tags from commercials.

Lucy's kind lived in what science fiction writers liked to call *hyperspace*. She was subliminally aware of the continuum of stars and men, but only entered it to give birth, once at the end of a million-year life cycle. Her children would need to draw on a star's energy to gain the acceleration to enter "their" universe.

Once they were all born, Lucy would die.

What remained of her would disperse into the known universe: as stray nucleons, as cosmic radiation, as neutrino swarms. (It was a day of rejoicing for continuous-creation theorists—here was one way at least of adding mass to the universe. The big-bangers continued to sit tight on their much more weighty evidence....)

Clem no longer denied it to herself. She thought of Lucy as a sister. And she would stop the slaughter, she would make everyone see reason. It would only be for forty days, surely they could see that. Surely the world leaders could grasp that the human race itself—its capacity for compassion—was on trial.

She rehearsed the fine-sounding phrases over to herself, and then she saw Kolya Sachdev standing in front of her. She looked up at him. He was the same, a little grayer, perhaps; but he had been gray when they had first met. His eyes held her as they always had.

She could see the headline suddenly:

ALIEN'S FATE REUNITES ESTRANGED CELEBRITIES and she saw that several of the hidden reporters had already emerged, whipping out their cameras and notebooks.

They did a smiling stage-embrace that both knew would be on the front pages, she knew it had to look good, and then he led

155

her to his office for the real drama.

As soon as he sat down behind the huge, veined-marble desk, he became quite distant, almost as though she were seeing him on the evening news....

"How's the boy, Clemmie?"

"Fine." *Let's get to the subject!* She didn't sit down. "Now let's talk about the forty-day embargo on telecommunications."

"Yes," he said. "Mr. Ehrlich tells me it is of supreme scientific importance that the alien's last moments be properly observed, and that there may be a possibility of violence if we don't comply...."

"That's not the point at all!" she said.

"Hold it, Clemmie. I've been watching your appearances on TV talk shows and I know that you're trying to appeal to the compassion of the human race, you're heavily into this baby-killing business, which is really making an absurdity out of it all. But it's worked. America will fall into line—the President's worked it all into his re-election campaign, very wily man, that— and most every other country too."

"So we're all pulling through, then," Clem sat down finally, settling into soft leather. The table-top, paper-cluttered and huge, dwarfed the man who had been her husband. "Thank you."

"But wait," said Sachdev. "You scientists are so unrealistic! You have no idea...there's a war on in Central Africa, you know that, don't you? There's a dictator—Kintagwe—who won't have anything to do with this. They are sure their country will be wiped out...."

"Can't you impose a cease-fire?"

"With what, my dear? Since when has the United Nations had any power?"

"Oh." She tensed.

"But there's a lot of cause for satisfaction. Everyone dreams of humanity pulling together for a common cause, and that's never going to happen. And I think you've done wonders."

"It isn't enough!" She got up again and leaned on the table, trying to penetrate the gulf. "We have to have *everything!* It's the communication waves that are killing the children, and *all* of them must be turned off!"

"We've achieved a fantastic political victory. Look, the Russians and the Americans are out drinking vodka together— what more do you want? I talked to Bohan, leader of the other country. He's willing, but he doesn't trust Kintagwe. You've got to understand...religion's religion, and these resurgences of tribal things are impossible to deal with rationally. Especially when they're reacting against the Moslem faith imposed by centuries-dead Arab conquerors. You can't talk reason at them."

"Kintagwe's got to see! Oh, I loathe these games you men play, games of war and religion and power and politics and intrigue. I'll talk to him myself! All it takes is reason!"

"Aren't you carrying this feminist bit a little far?" said Sachdev very quietly. "Kintagwe's a woman, you know. I guess you scientists never watch the news."

She stared at him.

"Clem, *we're all on your side!*" He sighed. She saw that he was changed, more so than she had noticed at first. Besides the thinning, graying hair, there were more lines around the eyes. She had not noticed them before because the eyes themselves had held her so powerfully. "Suppose," he said, "I send you to the Republic of Zann, as a special envoy of some kind. After all, it was you who discovered the lightstreaks. Suppose you could talk them into it...you and your *reason.*"

"You're shoving the responsibility for helping the light-mother into my hands!"

"Are you afraid?" A sadness came from him, suddenly, and she cast her eyes down and counted the veins of marble on the table, touching a coffee-stain with her finger. "Clem, I wish you would come back to me. I miss you so terribly...."

But she said nothing at all. And, abruptly, he was all formality. "And there you have it," he said. "Take it or leave it."

"I'll take it."

"I hoped you would," he said, and smiled at last.

* * *

She arrived in secret, was rushed by landrover along nerve-racking roads through a night stifling with heat and mosquitoes, to a quaint palace bordered by British-built gardens. A pseudo-Gothic mansion, rising from banana orchards and palm groves....She came with nothing, no official mandate, no realizable threats; only her compassion for a thing not human.

She was to have breakfast with the Dictatress.

Huge doors opened to reveal a stateroom all in blue velvet, simple, not at all overdone like the rest of the palace. Clem took a step and was terrified immediately. She expected—she didn't know what, but certainly a savage barbarian in a spanking military uniform. She had heard of the atrocities, after all...this was the lion's den. Everywhere else on earth, the temporary shutdown had begun. Except here, where propaganda broadcasts and war

157

communications still zinged across the skies, driving Lucy's children mad.

On the sofa sat Kintagwe, military Dictatress of Zann. She was about fifty, strikingly beautiful, her white hair neatly bunned, wearing a long white dress with a single, tasteful malachite brooch. She was one of the very dark black woman, but with unusually high cheekbones. She watched Clem come in, and Clem saw in her eyes only concern, sympathy—no killer of infants, no commander of a terrible fratricidal war.

"Come," said Kintagwe. The voice was deep, melodious, and Clem noticed at once the Oxford accent. It made her feel all too acutely her West Side origins, and she was flustered for a moment; but she came into the room and sat down opposite Kintagwe. "Who are you really from, Mrs. Sachdev: the Americans, or your husband?"

"I'm from myself," she said. "I've come to plead with you about the question of the lightmother."

"If it is a question of a ceasefire, my dear, I'm afraid your request must fall on stony ground.... I can't help you. How can I, when my whole country is being torn apart before my eyes?"

Clem was startled by the woman's directness, her intensity. She looked up at her eyes and saw that the face was completely unlined, innocent. Kintagwe bent over to pour Clem a cup of coffee, and offered her a plateful of exotic fruits. Clem said, "Don't you know that a mother is dying in childbirth out there, and that we owe it to her to let her children live? Don't you know that we as a race have an obligation to respect other living sentient races? Don't you know how painful it is to give birth?" As she said those things she realized how blatant, how proselytizing they sounded.

"I am a mother of four," said Kintagwe very simply. "Two of my children have already been killed in this very war."

She had put her foot in it again. Clem did not know what to make of this woman. She was so compelling, so fragile-seeming, and yet—"Then you know you must stop all this," she said. "The other side seems willing enough—"

"But they do not trust us." Kintagwe wiped her mouth elegantly. "You see, you understand nothing at all, Mrs. Sachdev. In this country we are a people of principle. We don't make concessions when the dignity of God himself is questioned. We must eradicate the wrongdoers, and this is a holy war. If you don't believe that people must fight for the truth, if you don't believe in decency, in morality, in the just punishment of sin, then you are a very sad person indeed...."

"How can you sleep nights, knowing that you're destroyng

the human race's chances of earning the goodwill of the first nonhuman we've ever encountered? How can you sleep when you must wake to kill more people?"

"I believe in God."

"Damn it, this is the twentieth century!"

"That doesn't eliminate the need for God." She smiled disarmingly, and poured out more coffee.

"Aren't you the slightest bit afraid? I mean, here's an energy-being that's capable of broadcasting signals that override our regularly broadcasting systems—at least some of them—don't you think it might destroy us if we don't do something to help?"

"Your wily husband has already pointed this out to me," said Kintagwe. "I told him that the alien has never mentioned violence, and that the threat was somewhat anthropomorphic...."

Clem swallowed angrily. It was the same argument *she* had used with Ehrlich, with Kolya. Kintagwe was no fool, only a fanatic.

Kintagwe went on, "I already know the rest of your arguments. You'll tell me that our peoples will only kill each other off anyway, that it's a grand gesture for the species, that it's a golden opportunity to stop fighting without losing political face, and so on. I am forearmed, you see. But it won't wash, my dear, not a bit."

She had stolen every one of Clem's carefully prepared pleas. "Why not?" she demanded. She felt anger building up inside her. The woman was a brick wall.

"Because I am a person of principle! Because I have committed myself to continue this war, in the name of God; because it is a crusade, because it is righteous, because it is the people's will, because I have faith, and love, and trust, beyond the grave itself. There is no more to say."

"You're a fanatic!" Clem cried out, angry.

Kintagwe looked at Clem sadly. Behind the sadness there was a laughter, a dancing of lights in the eyes. Clem saw that Kintagwe was at peace with herself, that she had already fought with herself and won...."I'm not a fanatic," said Kintagwe softly. "I'm an idealist." She reached over and touched Clem on the cheek, very softly. "As you are, sister. We are kindred, you and I."

Clem sat frozen for a very long time. An aide rushed in and whispered in the Dictatress's ear; the hand left Clem's cheek, and Kintagwe said, very quietly, "Execute them," and then closed her eyes. As the aide left, Clem saw that Kintagwe was holding back tears.

"You hypocrite!" she screamed. "Very well then, if you don't capitulate, my country will throw everything they've got at you!

They'll blast you off the face of the earth!" She got up, fists clenched, trembling.

"Are you empowered to make those threats?" said Kintagwe, disturbed suddenly.

"Yes! Yes! Yes!" she lied, passionately.

Kintagwe was silent for a long while, Then she rose too, and said, "How quickly one loses one's idealism! I rather suspected you might be from the Americans as well. Since you threaten to use force, why then you win, obviously." She sounded very bitter.

Clem felt no triumph at all. They shook hands—Kintagwe's hand was icy as a corpse's—and did not look at each other's eyes.

As she turned to leave, Clem knew they had both given up their innocence. Even the wet wind, blasting her in the blinding sunlight outside, felt cold.

* * *

Much rhetoric went with these things: grand speeches about man's greatness, about human unity, about historic moments. Full credit was accorded Clem Papazian Sachdev: they did name them the Papazian Lines after all, too. But Clem felt unfulfilled, because she had brought about the events not by persuasion, but by lying. By lying she had joined the very world she had hoped to escape, when he left her husband....

The humans settled down for the forty days of peace. No TV, no radio, no air or sea transportation, no war. Lucy's children would come in sporadic bursts, and then the lightmother herself would fade away. After the forty days, Lucy appeared on television for the last time, to say goodbye....

"Thank you," she said, "for sparing my children's lives. I will go soon. And as my children fly towards your sun, the edges of their wings will touch the earth."

The desert bloomed that night. People had come from the city, had left their cars parked every which way in the sand, to come and watch the passing of the light children. Clem and Denny were there, sprawled out on a rug in the sand: and Kolya had come to join them.

It was a cold night, a clear night. The observatory was a black, baroque shape against the sky. Overhead was the star-blazoned darkenss, still and silent. A sight Clem had seen so often that it was a cliché, but which choked her this time, for a reason she couldn't fathom.

She heard beer cans popping around her, champagne glasses clinking, children's laughter. There was a camaraderie in the crowd that she couldn't feel, somehow.

"Thank you for coming," she said to Kolya. His face was brighter than she had ever seen it before; perhaps it was being far from the centers of intrigue that made him look so much younger, so much more innocent.

"Still angry with me?" he said.

"No. I understand how the world runs now. But I don't have to like it."

"Truth hurts," he said lightly, hiding the pain in an easy cliché. "But seriously, Clem..." he said, more tenderly, "idealism isn't going to patch up the world. You remember those stories of one man uniting the troubled tribes of the universe in a single grand vision? You know, the old science fiction stories we used to love when we were kids?"

"Sounds like some of those speeches we've been making."

"We all want something *simple* to believe in. Hey, it's not so bad, is it? You got what you wanted, didn't you?"

She saw Kintagwe's face for a moment, proud, serene, conscious of being right. *I betrayed you, didn't I?* she thought.

"Are you going to come home, Clemmie?"

"Maybe. Maybe." she said.

And then a murmur burst from the crowd. "Angels, Mommy, angels!" Denny cried, jumping up and down and pointing to the sky. The whole crowd was shouting it then: "Angels! Angels!" And Clem followed the thrust of her son's arm and saw—

Fingers of light, breaking out of light-cracks in the blackness, spirals of light that lanced the blackness in patterns of streaksilver and burning white, silent fireworks...a tingling warmth in the air, like a mother's comforting hug, the wind snuggling against her body...ooohs and aaahs erupting from the ground, cheers, laughter, whoops of sheer joy, applause....

She saw Kolya's eyes shining. Denny was leaping all over the rug, trampling on the food, shrieking "Yaaaaay, angels!" for all he was worth.

More lightstreask criss-crossed the sky now, making webs that shifted and dissolved. There were aurora colors, golden vermilions, brash purples, subtle blues...the roar was deafening now. It was a cosmic fourth of July. And then she found herself yelling along with them, becoming part of the crowd at last.

I guess it's only human to lie, to fight, to be divided like this, she thought. *But also to dream....*

"I daresay I will come home after all, sometime," she said. Kolya didn't hear her; his mind was on the wild kaleidoscope in the sky. She reached out to touch his hand, very gently. Denny came between them, and they both held on to him, feeling his warm body.

"What did you say?" Kolya shouted at her.

"I said," she yelled *(I don't care if the whole world hears me!* "I'm going to come home sometime!"

For all our faults, we humans are on the side of the angels.

—Alexandria, 1979

Meeting in Milan Cathedral

I wrote these poems the first time I went to Italy, in 1973, that is. This was long before I planned on being a science fiction writer. I was composing wildly. I finished my second completed opera (none of them have ever been performed) which was based on the life of Michelangelo. I still have it somewhere, although my first, based on Ibsen's "Brand," and written when I was 15, has vanished, thank God. These poems sort of go with that opera. You can tell from them what kind of an adolescent I was, I think.

MEETING IN MILAN CATHEDRAL

you kneel at the altar with your face derailed
all jackalled in the candlelight
undead

the cathedral shimmering with the sounds of labour
imitates rebirth
glass spirals in a distant galaxy
above the dead foundations
cryptic engravings giving no relief

you overwhelm me in a torrent of unborn speech
a petrifying of deceit
we have passed understanding by
you kneeling at the altar with your face derailed

MESSENGER

messenger
you come to tell the I no longer I
to wait
between the salt sand and the vulture's sigh
you come to tell the I no longer I

trees tremble
their green tops graze the stillborn sky's
continual asphyxiated cry
then they dissemble
winds crouch ready for ambush
lit by floodlights red with ambition
evening's dawning and the day's contrition
wait for the trumpet death

messenger
bring revelation hard as frosted breath
though Mary is still Mary
I still I

ON AN UNFINISHED PIETA OF MICHELANGELO

I see continuum-frozen
for one stone moment
pain coexisting with its resolution

my outer shells
(renascent in their stalactitious tears)
implode in metamorphosis
crushed by the earth's compassion into marble
claiming their nucleous self

recognition!
rapt in a cage of flame
her unformed face, tomb tendent
finds me the god freed peace
becoming truth with time

Dear Caressa
or
This Towering Torment

This story has a rather strange history. It started off as an attempted collaboration between Sharon Webb and me, based on a cover painting which George Scithers described to us, and which neither of us had even seen! Unfortunately, the collaboration didn't work out. We simply couldn't agree on a thing, so we decided that we would both write a cover story on this subject, and let the great Scithers decide for himself. The great Scithers became tremendously agitated and asked for several more stories from other writers, including John M. Ford and Jay Haldeman...all of which were printed in the same issue of the magazine as the cover story....

I'd thought that moving to suburbia would save my marriage. Save me from Dusty, my daughter of the Brooklyn Bridge braces and the Nosferatu-ish smile. From my son Boogie, torn-tee-shirted prepube of serpentine precociousness with the chocolate-chip-cookie face and those kestrel eyes. And especially from my wife Rebecca, an immaculate, pre-feminist woman who worked for the household like a dog—and was about equal to one in I.Q.

I had no idea my life would turn into a science fiction story.

That, I suppose, I owed to Hermie Tebaldi.

You're surprised I know him, aren't you? Nobel laureate and all, author of "An Application of Irrelevance Theory to Synchronicity and Quantum Mechanics," the paper that crossed Einstein with Jung and spawned a monstrous hybrid that people are still arguing about to this day? Well, to me he was the boy next door. Got into scrapes together—somehow, though, only I got the spankings—went to Princeton together, ended up teaching at U. of Penn. together (although naturally he was head of his department). I won the Rothman Fellowship and he got the Nobel prize, all in the same day.

He died. Or rather, he disappeared mysteriously while doing research on transfinite transdimensional interfaces. (If this were science fiction, they'd dream up some pseudoscientific nonsense to call it, "alternate-reality-paradigms" or "parallel universes" or something.) And left me the house in his will. My family and I thought we'd been saved.

But nothing changed. I was still a man who had married too early in life—one of Hermie's cast-offs, at that—with a couple of unsavory kids, an unfinished paper on archaeopteryxes, and a stupid wife.

That summer, the stupid wife discovered the romances of Caressa Byrd.

I turned over in bed and my nose hit an open paperback. I fumbled for the light. Becky must have gotten up, but the sheets

166

still smelled faintly of Givenchy and pepperoni. (Some days it was salami and Shalimar.) I elbowed the paperback off the bed: it was *This Towering Torment* by Caressa Byrd. I groped for the curtains—

Midmorning light fell through the blinds, zebrastriping the primrose-studded sheets. I arose, tripped over a copy of *Chastity's Chastisement,* and made for the bathroom, cursing all dull Saturdays.

I degrunged myself. Shaving was like brushing the dust from archaeopteryx bones. Better to be a character in one of Caressa Byrd's romances! That woman had written 200 or more, all in the first person; many of the fans thought that they had all really happened to her.

Coming out in a bathrobe, I felt paper prickle my feet and knelt down for a look. A trail of paper had dribbled from an old rattan wastebasket.

I like all my things in the right place and this was on the wrong side of the bed. I picked up the papers and tossed them back in, thinking: *Funny, I haven't written anything lately, and Becky's too illiterate....*I uncrumpled a piece and began to read:

> *Dear Caressa* [it began, in spiky, awkward script]
> *This is my twentieth letter to you. I have read every one of your books and know that you are very experienced in matters of men. It's Arthur. I love him so much, but he doesn't love me any more. Maybe he doesn't want me. I wish I could be like in your Love's Ravening Ravishment when the old woman said to you "But do you love him enough to give him up?" and you cried for days afterward. He is a great scientist and I am only a high school sweetheart that he knocked up I mean had an indiscretion with, I know I am too dumb for him. Is it right for me to punish him like this? I know you are very busy but I wd. appreciate a response at your convenience.*
>
> > *Sincerely yours*
> > *Rebecca Kurtz*

I couldn't believe it. I unscrunched more paper (heavily Chanel No. 19-doused, I noticed) and found more uncompleted drafts.

That's it, I thought grimly. *She's over the edge.*

I marched downstairs in a rage, brandishing the letter.

"Damn it," I shouted half-way into the kitchen, "do you have to use so much perfume?" The smell of baked ham and Nina Ricci filled the room.

She turned round from her cooking. She wasn't exactly ugly; she had a mop of red hair over a face three shades too pale, liberally sploshed with freckles. "I want to smell nice for you," she said. "Isn't that all that matters?" She looked very vulnerable; her eyes were watering and I felt both furious and guilty.

"Look!" I yelled, waving the letter. "You've gone crazy!"

"I need all the help I can get—"

"Damn it, I want a divorce!" I screamed.

She started to cry—went on and on as though it were some eye exercise—and said, "All right dear, if that's what you want. I knew it would come to this...here, eat your breakfast, it's your favorite...." Then she buried herself in *Passion's Fiery Sling* and the conversation was over. I hadn't even gotten her mad, damn it! I stomped into the back yard, and—

The basement window! I found myself staring at it. *It's been broken into! Damn raccoons!* I started to panic. There wasn't any real reason for us to have kept the basement boarded up, even if it *had* housed the esoteric devices Hermie Tebaldi had been working on towards the end of his life. And yet....

Damn raccoons, I thought, cursing. *Dog must have broken in after them.*

I'd never thought of trying to get into the basement before. But now—

Glass-shards lay on the grass, dazzling my eyes in the summer sunlight. The window was shattered; a man could easily squeeze through—

It wasn't snooping, damn it, it was my own house. And I had too many problems that day. My family. My unfinished paper and the pressure of publish-or-perish. No better way to deal with pressure than go and do something completely different.

I snaked over to the opening and lowered myself gingerly onto the—

There wasn't any floor!

I was falling, falling, falling—like Alice down the rabbit-hole. Only I didn't have time to make inane comments like "Do bats eat cats?" or to calculate the distance to the center of the earth. I was too busy screaming.

First it was soft soft soft and dark dark dark, like being on the couch at my analyst's and listening to the drone of her hypnotic voice. I was falling but there wasn't really any down; I was screaming as hard as I could, but the sounds were lost; there wasn't any echo; this wasn't a mine-shaft or something that had somehow been grafted onto my basement, it was something far huger, and I knew I'd hit bottom sometime and it wouldn't be pleasant, but the thought was somehow so distant, so insignificant. I seemed to be shedding all my worries, my anxiety over the impending divorce, my anger, my self-frustration....

Forget everything, I thought, *until this dream is over...* Gradually I made out a sourceless red glow around me. I couldn't see very far. My feet were being sucked into something half-solid, and then I hit ground and was running—

A wild Wuthering Heights-landscape, gray helter-skelter heather, knee-high, cresting and ebbing in a singing wind. Black cloth flapping in my face, and I knew I wasn't wearing the same clothes I set out with. A starched, uncomfortable high collar hugged my neck, and it was a black cloak lined with crimson that I was wearing, streaming in the wind, and I was running. I tried to brake myself but I couldn't halt the momentum. I remember thinking all the time that the dog must be loose in the metamorphosed basement, with a raccoon backed into a corner somewhere—

The wind was warm. There was an enticing odor of French perfume, spiked unaccountably with pepperoni. *Becky!* I thought. *She's at the bottom of this!* I knew I wasn't making any sense at all, but neither was this whole experience.

After a while I managed to slow down. The moor stretched to the horizon all around me. There was no way to judge distance, except...yes, the horizon seemed strangely near. It was a distorted world. Two moons careened in the sky, blood-red and huge; they were the source of the strange red glow; and then ahead I saw a silvery glint among the...oh yes, weird, rocky outcroppings, I hadn't caught sight of them before...it was as if the whole landscape was coming more into focus and I was seeing more details all the time. I slowed down to a walk, panting heavily—I'm not that young anymore—and began to make for the silvery point of light that flickered between black fantastical monoliths. It was a demon force that pushed me forward. I stumbled onward, never quite coming to a full stop.

Arthur, oh Arthur....

Everyone dreams of a voice like that. It sang to me in the wind. It was a girl's voice, a child's voice almost. The wind blew on my cheek like a soft hand. I struggled to loosen my collar, my chafing Victorian clothes—

Then I saw the tower.

I couldn't tell how far it was. The scale was all wrong here, wherever "here" was. Both moons had moved behind it. The light had come from a window in its topmost turret—

But what a tower! It was like a rocketship and it was like a tree. It was like a Corinthian column plated with silver and torn from a Greek temple and overgrown with chromium vines. Glitter-rich flying buttresses sprouted from the naked rock. It was a bewildering madness. *And it was singing my name.*

Arthur, oh Arthur, it sang to me in its achingly beautiful voice, *I've waited for so long, Arthur, please come to me now, enter me, possess me, be one with me—*

The wind was streaming against me. I was being drawn towards the tower, being sucked into a lorelei whirlwind....

"No!" I screamed. "No! No!" I tried to think of Becky and the kids but they were so far away. I felt like a little genie battering away helplessly at the walls of his glass bottle.

A swath of light, tinseled like fairy light in a Disney cartoon, fell on me from the window. But somehow it wasn't kitsch. I felt like a kid again, wanting so hard to be someone, identifying with the prince on the horse, and my cloak was flapping behind me and billowing around me and it was like the time I pulled little Sharon out of the tree—

But Hermie Tebaldi was the one who made it with her, damn it! I remembered, coming down to earth. I remembered Hermie and I snapped. *I'm getting out of this nightmare,* I told myself. "Let go of me," I screamed. "Whatever you are, understand, let go, let go—"

In a flash, I saw two archaeopteryxes soar across the swath of light, noting how closely they conformed in gliding patterns to my hypothesis—

I came to on the hard damp concrete.

I looked around me.

Machines, dusty, an old typewriter. Nothing that seemed to make much sense. This was the basement, all right, though; ahead, the narrow stairs had to lead to the kitchen closet. I rubbed my eyes a couple of times. *Getting flaky,* I thought. *Must call Dr. Webern in the morning.*

I heaved myself off the concrete and shambled around. *But weird,* I thought, *I've been on the wagon for over six months now, I shouldn't have been seeing things....*

That voice came back to me, so enticing, so erotic. I could almost have stepped back into that moor under the red moons again, but—

Back! I told myself quickly. *With all your problems, schizo-*

phrenia is something you can do without. It was very dark in the basement, except where light fell in spider-strands, pinholing through chinks in the boards. And there was a big stripe of dazzling sunshine through the broken window, stippled with dancing dust-motes.

I glanced at the machines. I couldn't tell what they were, of course. The theory of transdimensional interfaces wasn't exactly my field—and frankly I never had the math to follow even the simplest of Hermie's theories.

Everything was in obvious disarray. I hate messes, and it had always irked me that Hermie could dream up such elegant theories when he couldn't even tie his shoelaces or file a carbon. I looked around, getting angrier and angrier.

The light from the window fell on some kind of lab bench. A piece of paper, a page from a looseleaf notebook, weighted down by a book caught my eye. There was a message on it, in huge, childish capitals—

ARTIE, MY FRIEND
HELP ME HELP ME
SHE'S GOING TO KILL ME
HELP ME
HERMIE

I rubbed my eyes. The red ink glowed in the glare. What the hell was this? Who was *she?* How old was this message, anyway?

There was only one *she* I could think of right now—

The voice! The singing wind from the tower that sparkled silver in the blood-red moonlight! *Arthur, oh Arthur*—So sensual, so seductive. And me in my chafing collar and black cape, breasting the wind like a prince from a soppy novel or a childhood myth...haunting. Haunting. Haunting.

And, suddenly, somehow, I knew that the voice could be mine—I mean, the creature behind the voice—for instinct told me that inside the tower there must be a princess, a golden-haired Rapunzel who would sweep me away from Rebecca and Dusty and Boogie and the whole suburban schtik, and—

Get a grip on yourself, damn it! Doctor Sharon Webern will bring your back to earth.

I stood staring at the message. Unquestionably it was Hermie's handwriting and...the ink was still wet! On second thought, it wasn't ink at all.

It was blood.

"I see you've put Doctor Webern on the calendar," Boogie said, sauntering into the kitchen Sunday morning just as I'd mis-flipped my eggs. "Want to talk about it?"

"Not to you."

"Don't be silly, Dad!" he said, coming closer. He seemed tense. It's devastating when one's child is so much smarter than oneself.

Without really meaning to, I started to tell him everything. "Sheesh, Dad," he said, "it sounds heavy as hell to me. Maybe you do need a shrink...but then again, maybe not."

"What do you mean?" I said, plunking myself by the kitchen table and addressing my Jackson Pollocked eggs. (One thing about Rebecca—she did know how to fix food; and when she went to church of all places, which she did every Sunday morning, I had to eat my own glop.)

"Well, you just told me that the letter from Uncle Hermie was real, didn't you? Now, when you have eliminated the impossible...."

"Oh, give me a break, Boogie!"

"Hold it, Dad. I've *read* Uncle Hermie's paper. It's all about parallel universes...he starts off with the assumption, you know, that every time a subatomic particle must make a statistical decision within the limits of the uncertainty principle, a parallel universe splits off—"

"Huh?"

"Dad, that theory was way back in the seventies!"

"Yeah, like all of two years ago." I gulped down some of the egg concoction. Sunlight played on the table, lightly leaf-dappled, too bright for my depression. Knowing you're on the verge of a nervous breakdown can be a pretty unnerving feeling—and I had been through *that* before.

"You don't get it!" Boogie cried, exasperated. I tried not to listen, but became marginally interested in spite of myself. "He was working on transdimensional interfaces when he died; that means channelling into parts of spacetime where universes overlap! He was talking about this new kind of particle, see, he was trying to generate them before he died, but he was running up against the law of conservation of strangeness...but I guess you wouldn't know anything about quark theory either," he added disdainfully. "Hey!" Perhaps he succeeded in doing what he was working on, and perhaps there's a transdimensional interface right in our basement! *Sheesh!*" He paused for a breath. Then he went to the refrigerator to get a glass of milk.

"You're going to be just like Hermie when you grow up, you little bastard," I muttered, not quite concealing my bitterness.

"I knew it!" He whipped around, brandishing his milk. "You do suspect me of being *his* son...."

I was shaking. He'd seen right through me, right to my innermost fears.

I tried to change the subject and go back to his theory, or whatever it was. "Okay, suppose it is another universe out there?" I said. "How would you account for the smell of Becky's cooking and Becky's perfume? And what about the Caressa Byrd-like gothic ambience?"

"Oh, that," Boogie said. But he was already leaving the kitchen. I'd hurt his feelings. Strange how Hermie still haunted this family.... "Well, I don't know everything, you know. Even if I *am* smarter than you are." He vanished into the hall. What a hateful shrimp. The obnoxiousness of his intelligence more than made up for the obnoxiousness of Rebecca's stupidity.

I closed my eyes and remembered the archaeopteryxes, crossing the faces of the bloody moons. Why had they been so close to the description in my unwritten paper? Didn't that prove that I was going insane? I piled up my dishes and went to the sink. Through the window, I saw Dusty and Boogie and their friends were trampling the hedges, but I was too tired for even a token yell.

Beside the sink, in a neat pile, and exuding a soft odor of Dior and spaghetti sauce, were some paperbacks: *Love's Hideous Strength, Dark Touch of Desire*, all vintage Caressa Byrds. I leafed through some of them. There were notes scrawled in the margins, things like "Apply to Arthur," and "Yes, yes, oh yes," and so on. *Sickening.*

I was just squeezing some soapsuds when a wild impulse took hold of me. I walked over to the kitchen closet. Behind the stacks of raisin bran was the door, boarded up now, that led to....

In my head I heard the song of the tower, high and breathy, passionate. I reached for the toolbox on the top shelf, hardly knowing what I was doing.

An hour later I was standing at the top of the steps. *At least there's a light switch here,* I thought, *when you come in the proper entrance.* I reached for it and—

173

I couldn't believe it. It was like a set for a mad scientist's lab in Hollywood. Nothing could have looked more thoroughly unscientific. Banks of equipment rose from an undergrowth of wires, leads, cables, with an occasional jack or plug sprouting up like a jungle flower. There was the table with the scrawled not I'd found the previous day. I walked down to it and scrutinized it again. The blood had caked now, rust on the yellow paper.

I laughed out loud. This stuff was supposed to create a trans-dimensional interface? Boogie was a bright kid, but he did read too much of that sci-fi nonsense. With light flooding the room, it didn't seem nearly so daunting. I remembered suddenly, with astonishing clarity, the Christmas when Hermie and I had both been four years old and had both gotten Lego sets and I had built a car, following the instructions to the letter, and he had built a ramshackle madness so weird even he couldn't think up an explanation for what it was! That's all this basement mess was! High-and mighty Nobel laureates had feet of clay after all. They still needed their Lego sets.

Just then I tripped over a wire and—

No! Not again!

The familiar feeling. Falling into the soft darkness. This time it didn't take nearly so long; it was as it there were less resistance, as though my previous journey had bored a wormhole through the dimensions...no! I was starting to believe my son's pseudo-scientific babblings!

And then—

I was running in the soft gray heather on the moor under the light of the crimson moons. The wind swept me along. I leapt into it, exhilarated. And ahead, past black tarns that loomed like trolls over the landscape, I saw the tower. From its highest turret, a flock of archaeopteryxes glided, soared, their shadows shying against rock outcroppings...it was amazing. Their flight patterns...my theory was vindicated. And then I saw that the tower had grown a little. You couldn't put your finger on it. Another chrome-shiny buttress, another row of sharktooth crenelations, perhaps...I ran towards it. The singing had already begun.

Arthur, oh Arthur, come to me, enter me, be mine....

I didn't resist. Anything had to be better than the life I was leading now. Even schizophrenia. I ran hard, and the wind helped me so I felt no strain, only a giddy exaltation. The perfume of the wind had transmuted now so that I couldn't recognize the scent. It wasn't one of Rebecca's. I stopped thinking. I ran towards the voice, hearing nothing but the voice.

Time and space—they were somehow all distorted here! I

knew I couldn't have reached the tower yet, but—

It loomed above me, eclipsing the two moons, whose scarlet glow radiated from behind the silver glitter like distant fire, like the light from a far flaming city.

Buttresses soared like frozen rainbows. Turrets sprang from its sides, veined with metal moss. It was so huge I could get no sense of proportion out of it at all. And all the time it thrummed in the wind. And when I craned I caught sight of a window from which a light shone—like a searchlight, like the cover of a cheap romance.

Then the wind ebbed a little.

Enter me, the voice sighed. I stepped forward—

A door irised in the metal wall. A delicate fragrance came from it, and I moved closer, took a step inside....

A rich hallway.. Velvet tapestries. Oak chairs around a banquet table. French windows, a glimpse of a sculpted garden. And a huge, curving staircase that spiraled, up and up and up until it vanished into a vague silvery height. It was all impossible!

Come up the stairs, oh Arthur, Arthur—

For the moment, I resisted. I went up to the table and banged my fist on it. Solid. As real as my nineteenth century clothes had been real....

I shed my cloak. I tried to ignore the voice for a moment. In the walls of this antique salon, between the stuffed rhinoceros heads, were heavy, carved oak doors. I stepped across the hall, my steps on the polished wood resounding and echoing through the vast space above me. Gingerly I tried one of the doors.

Arthur, oh Arthur, why do you ignore me? I love you so much, I need you, I adore you, enter me, love me—

I stepped through.

Nothing Victorian about this room. It was a thin corridor that stretched straight ahead until the walls seemed to converge in the distance. The walls were metal as the outside of the tower; and there was a faint acrid smell, vaguely discomforting. Lining the corridor—

A chill took hold of me. I forced myself to look at them, frozen creatures standing statue-still, staring—

For sure, they weren't people. Their skins were green or blue or purple and they had scales, some of them, and tentacles...but all of them had eyes. The eyes were all alive. The not-people had been transfixed in a hideous living death.

I walked on, not daring to look too hard. Some would have been monsters by any standards, some of them were strange, delicate creatures with pale pink fur and lemur eyes...I couldn't look at the eyes. I was sure they were alive. I hurried on, and then on my left I found myself looking at Hermie

"My God!" I whispered. "What's happened?" For he was the last of them, and beyond him there were rows of low podia, stretching on as far as I could see.

And obviously all waiting for occupants.

Hermie was breathing. I shook him. He was soft, still alive. "Wake up, man, talk to me, explain all this!"

He began panting. Then he said, "Artie...hoped you'd come...help...."

"How? How?"

"You wouldn't understand the math anyway, Artie...but we're in another universe, and...."

"What the hell is this tower doing here? Why is it trying to seduce me, for God's sake? How can we get out of here?"

"Look, it's an alien. I know you don't believe in science fiction, but take my word for it, it's an alien, and this isn't Earth either. Look, it feeds on emotions! It *loves* people and not-people to death! It's a parasite, and it's already devoured every sentient being on this planet...."

"What?"

"Got to get back," he gasped. "Or else I'll never be able to turn off the field, and the two universes are going to go on leaking into each other...the last time you came it was so busy trying to snare you that it weakened and I was able to escape for a few seconds; no blasted pen in that whole basement though, had to cut myself to leave the message and now it's wise to me and I can't get free...."

"This has got to be a dream!" I said, squeezing my eyes tight shut and desperately *hoping*. Then I kept repeating, over and over, "Aliens don't read Caressa Byrd romances. Aliens don't know about archaeopteryxes. That's why *I'm* going crazy, and none of this is happening."

"Will you listen to me, numbskull! It's semi-telepathic, and it's got a range of about fifty meters beyond the transdimensional interface! It's been trying to lure you here for months...and all it's got to go on is the thoughts of you and of all the people who love you who come into range! And Becky loves you. She loves you so much it's choking her own life, damn you. And I bet all she does in the kitchen is think thoughts of you and thoughts of Caressa Byrd's romances. And of course the archaeopteryxes conform to your theory...."

His voice was weakening. I didn't know whether to be convinced or not. Insanity seemed a far saner hypothesis.

"You've got to get me out of here!"

"How?" I screamed. "How can I fight a thing that's eaten a whole planet?"

"You've got to find it, and face it, and convince it, somehow. You can't come in here with a Colt .45 and riddle it with bullets. But maybe you can talk to it—"

"No way! I'm getting out of here!"

"Look," he rasped. "If I don't go back and pull the plug on this interface, the interface-leakage will begin to spread. Understand? I'm not going to spout the formulae at you, idiot, but you're my best friend so you might try just believing me. If you resist it now, while you're free, it won't be able to hold on to you, but...if the leakage spreads! The alien's range will get bigger and bigger. It's slow, but it's practically immortal. It'll get you in the end. It'll get Becky and Dusty and Boogie and the Langbarts and everybody else on Bevan Street and everyone in Ardmore and everyone in Pennsylvania...there's no limit to its hunger! Look, I hate to sound melodramatic, but the fate of the universe is in your hands!"

"Hermie, be serious, cut the sci-fi crap—"

"Don't say *sci-fi!*" he snapped, and then fainted.

I turned and ran.

My shoes clanked on the metal floor. The frozen aliens stared at me. I ran and ran—

Through the drawing room with the stuffed rhinos and the velvet drapes—

Arthur! Why are you leaving me? The voice whispered in my head, so soft and desirable, I almost turned back—

Resist, resist, I was thinking, *get yourself out of this nightmare and fix yourself a stiff drink—*

Oh, Arthur!

I didn't care about the fate of the universe. I just wanted to get out of there. I burst through the iris-door and began running like crazy, against the singing wind that caressed me like soft hands of a young girl, against the voice, so pure and so knowing, across the waves of heather. The voice sang more insistently and I started to scream to try and drown it out.

And still it sang, so that I wanted to turn back and dive into the ocean of the tower's overpowering love.

Resist, imbecile, resist! I chanted over and over.

—and staggered up the steps and burst out of the kitchen closet, screeching, sending a volley of raisin bran cascading across the linoleum tiles—

Dusty and Boogie looked up from their chess game.

"Oh, hi, Dad," Dusty said, smiling her undead smile. "Supper's in the oven."

"I've just seen your Uncle Hermie!" I gasped.

Boogie said, "Mom's upstairs packing." He smiled too, a supercilious grin. "Says you're getting a divorce."

"Well, there it is." I couldn't believe what I'd done. The family was gathered around the kitchen table and I was laying my sanity on the line. Here we were, in the heart of suburbia, a mile from the Conshohocken State Highway, with the warm light of a summer evening streaming in through the window and the chatter of children and dogs from distant backyards and birds singing and the Sunday roast waiting in the oven...and I was trying to talk about the fate of the universe.

Dusty spoke up first. "I don't want to hear any more of this rubbish, Dad!" she said. "You've gone bananas. Fix an appointment with Dr. Webern or something. I'm going upstairs to call Tommy and make him take me out to a movie or something...."

"Not until you've done your homework," Becky said through her tears. But Dusty had run off.

"All I want to say," I said, trying to sound calm, "it that this is something I've got to try...for old Hermie's sake. I probably won't come back, so I want you to be a good family and try to make a go of it—"

"Stuff and nonsense, Daddy!" said Boogie. He looked at me earnestly from across the table, more serious than he'd even been before. "I believe you, but...there's no point in making a big show of things and making a melodramatic stand just because you feel inadequate." I started to argue but he went on. "Don't argue, I know why you're into this trip. I also know something about Uncle Hermie's theory, too—namely that the rate of interface leakage isn't going to be quick enough to get us. Especially if we move away from here. I vote we all split. Sure, it'll get the whole Earth and the solar system and galaxy and everything else. But not, for God's sake, in our lifetime. Dad! Not if we move, say, to California...."

"That's not responsible," I said. I knew he was at least half right about my motives. But there was something else too. "If *I* don't go out there and confront the thing, *nobody* will! I've got to do it!"

"*Sheesh*, Dad, I don't want to lose you!" he cried out, and then he rushed out of the kitchen. I heard him crying.

He'd never said that before. I'd had no idea he cared. Suddenly I felt very strange inside.

I got up and started for the kitchen closet.

"Wait, Arthur," said Rebecca. She had stopped crying.

I waited.

"Listen. I know that if you come back we'll probably go our separate ways. I'm sorry it didn't work." She was struggling to keep her voice steady. "But...you say this thing creates illusions that...come from our minds, that it's been picking my mind for months and all it's come up with has been Caressa Byrd books. It must know how much I love you if it's read my mind, its whole set of illusions must be based on my illusions...."

"What are you saying?"

"Maybe I can do something. I'm the one who knows all Caressa Byrd's books by heart...and even if I don't understand any of your science, I love you and that's enough. I'm coming with you...."

"Don't be silly. Who's going to take care of the children?" Was she going to obstruct me even now, here when I finally had gotten a chance to do something important in my life? And yet...she was willing to risk her life. For the first time I felt a funny kind of warmth for her.

"Come on, then."

We held hands. I kicked aside some cereal boxes and we started down the steps. Almost at once—

The singing came. My cloak flapped gently in the breeze. The heather was in bloom, a bleakly beautiful landscape. I saw that Becky was now dressed in a white gown that rippled softly. We ran towards the tower, in slow motion it seemed, like a gushy scene in a romantic movie. Ahead the tower rose up. It had grown a little more. A flock of archaeopteryxes crossed the faces of the moons, and the tower called to me, called my name over and over....

I saw where here another silver casement sprouted from its walls, there a vine of metal hugged the tower's trunk, new buds that had sprouted since the last visit. I knew then that it had been preying on Hermie's emotions. But when the tower sang I couldn't resist it. It was...like all the things my marriage had never given me.

Arthur! Arthur! Enter me, love me....

We reached the foot of the tower. I walked into the irising door and Becky followed. Now we were in the drawing room, a sombre, baroque chamber of velvet hangings and wood-panelling and varnished oil paintings of busty Venuses and flutter-winged Adonises...the room, too, had grown, it seemed.

And then the voice—

Arthur! Why have you brought this woman? I will deal with her in due course. But now, come, come, come to me—

And I saw the silvery staircase that stretched up to merge into the sky-high roof, spiral upon spiral, and in my mind there burned the image of a golden Rapunzel, fair and soft and sensual, and I could hardly restrain myself from rushing up the staircase and throwing myself into her arms....

Come, come, why do you resist me? Do I not love you as no one else can?

I had to go up the staircase. I had to confront the very soul of the alien. Heart thumping, I mounted the stairs, with Becky close behind me.

Then we were caught up in a wind, it seemed. The stairs had been illusions. Now we were drifting upward in the wake of some kind of force, some kind of tractor beam, the science fiction people would call it.

Now we were in another room, a womblike room with a single window, high up in the tower I supposed. The walls glowed, the air itself glowed. It was blinding. The walls were festooned with starlike sparklepoints, as though they had been papered with Christmas trees.

I knew what this room was; it was the room with the lighted window that I had glimpsed before, the room in the topmost turret of the tower.

And then out of the glitter stepped the most beautiful woman I had ever seen. Becky gasped. I knew than that the image had been shaped out of Becky's fantasies. Perhaps this was how she dreamed she should look, for me....

She resembled Becky. But idealized. The red hair liberated from its hairpins and sprays and billowing behind her. The same white gown, the same features, but somehow purified. The same eyes, but on this woman they glowed like emerald cabochons.

It was a woman I could love.

And involuntarily I was stepping towards her, towards this creature I had come to destroy. She spoke to me.

Arthur. It was the same voice that had called me from the beginning, that had beckoned to me from beyond the dimensions. *You're here at last. Please stay with me, please don't leave me. I'll give you any illusion you want to sustain you. Just let me love you, here, forever....*

"No!" I managed to whisper. "No, you've got to release me and Hermie and all the other beings you've caught, that you've frozen into that terrible living death." But I hardly cared, I wanted to finish saying my piece and then just leap into her arms.

What are you saying, Arthur my dearest? Listen...I come from an ancient race that needs to love, that needs to give...we were millions once. We flew where we willed, from world to world, giving of ourselves and growing...then came hunger and desolation. I think I may be the last of my kind, and even I lay dormant for millennia upon millennia, too weak to fly away even, too weak to love. But now I am strong. Please, Arthur. I have to love! I have to give of myself, completely and utterly! It's my nature. I can't help it if I destroy the things I love—and yet e who would not willingly choose death in exchange for a brief time of my love?

She stepped towards me. Her scent, so enticing, wafted toward me, and I was shaking with desire. So much for my brave defiant act to save the universe! I had lost. I walked towards her, arms outstretched, my body resounding with the beauty of her—

Becky interposed herself between us.

"No!" she cried out. "This isn't love at all! You don't know the meaning of love, you interstellar hussy, if you think this is it—"

But I am love! I am the perfect giving—

"Nonsense," Becky said. "You know nothing about love. If you'd read a single Caressa Byrd book...but no. Let me tell you something! My husband asked me for a divorce and I didn't utter one word of complaint. Because I knew he would be better off without me. I'm only a stupid woman with no repartee whom he can't show off in front of his friends at the University. But I really love him. For all your words and your beauty and your gorgeous illusions—you don't love him as much as I do! *Because you don't love him enough to give him up!*"

And then the dream-princess uttered a bloodcurdling scream that rang through the tower and chilled me to the core.

"Quick," said Becky, "while she's still confused—" She clasped my hand and we burst through the wall of lights which hadn't really been there at all, and the staircase opened up and we ran down it, stumbling and holding onto each other for dear life, while the scream echoed and re-echoed, a monster's death-scream, the stairs trembled as a tremor shook the tower—

We were running outside now. The scream went on behind us. It was no heather-strewn moor now, but a rocky desert, brown and craggy and burning, gridded with ragged sulphur clefts that smoked foul fumes. A dead world. Dead for millions of years perhaps—

Hermie was running alongside us. "You released me!" he shouted, panting. And when I glanced back I saw the unlikeliest crowd of marathoners you could possible imagine: claw-waving,

tentacle-shuffling, grunting, squeaking, hooting as they streamed
out of the screaming tower.

"Thank Becky, not me," I said. We jogged on.

"Guess they'll rebuild their world now," Hermie said—

And then we stopped for a breath and turned around and
saw—

Flames spurting from the tower's roots, silvery debris flying
in a whirlwind around its base, the ground shaking, and then...
the whole tower lifting itself into the sky, streaking up past the
dancing moons, an eye-smarting daytime comet that left behind
only an echo of a terrible scream, that melded with the sky and
vanished....

"Here," Hermie said. "Step through the interface."

We trooped into Hermie's Lego land.

For some reason Hermie didn't want his old house back—in
fact, he never set foot in it again after pulling the plug on the
transdimensional interface—and he took an apartment in West
Philly, on Larchwood, I think.

A day or two after that, Becky got a letter in the mail. It was
from Caressa Byrd.

> *Dear Mrs. Kurtz, [it ran]*
>   *Thank you so much for your twenty-one letters. I was
> deeply moved. Ah, we women, what frail creatures we are!
> You are a real woman and I know you will suffer anguish,
> yea the fires of hell, itself, for the man you love. Why I
> myself, when I was captured by the evil Marquis von
> Ringdahl...but of course you've read that one, my dear.
> Continue to sacrifice yourself! One day he may come to
> understand....*
>
>   *Your true friend,*
>   *Caressa Byrd*

I was in town and I dropped in on Hermie. I wanted to show
off the letter to him—it isn't every day that a real author writes to
you.

After only a week, his apartment was a jungle. We sat on the
floor and talked over a beer. It was like old times.

"I've learnt a lot," I said. "I thought that everything and
everyone was my enemy before, and now I know that I haven't
been exactly that perceptive myself. We're working things out,
Rebecca and I. And the kids. Somehow it's not a war anymore."

It was true. I was happier. I didn't feel inadequate anymore. I had a wife who was willing to die for me. And we *had* saved the universe—although somehow it didn't feel like that much of an achievement.

Anyhow, I pulled out the letter.

Hermie scrutinzed it for a long time. Then he walked over to a big cardboard box and pulled out a pile of what looked like manuscripts of scientific papers.

Only they weren't. They all had titles like *Love's Raging Fury* and *Passion's Ravishing Flame* and *Desire's Diaphanous Dart.*...

"Caressa Byrd original manuscripts?" I gasped. "I've never seen *those* novels before...what *is* this?"

"Artie, my dear friend...I've a terrible confession to make. You see, when I was a starving high school student and needed money, the fastest way was to knock off one of these, and—"

"My God! You're Caressa Byrd!"

"I've never told a soul."

"And when you were away—"

"I had a backlog at my publishers. It only takes a week to write one of these things...."

"No wonder the alien was convinced! She'd read Becky's mind and was feeding off yours...she must have believed that the love of gothic romances was genuine, human emotion."

"You mean it isn't?"

And Hermie smiled an enigmatic smile.

Hermie was the most frustrating person I ever knew. You simply couldn't get the better of him. He always had an extra ace or three up his sleeve. I couldn't do anything without him being there first.

Hell, even the alien tower affair had been on the rebound.

—*Arlington, 1980*

Absent Thee From
Felicity Awhile...

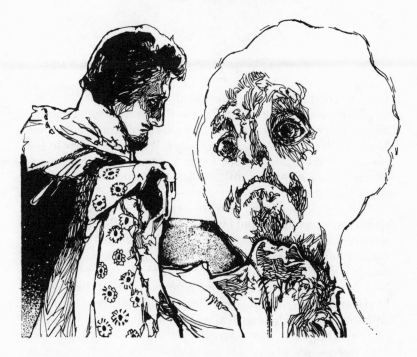

Interestingly enough, although the Absent Thee was nominated for
the Hugo and has appeared in a Best of the Year anthology, it was
rejected by nine editors! I don't really know what this means.

1.

You remember silence, don't you?

There were many silences once: silence for a great speech, silence before an outburst of thunderous applause, silence after laughter. Silence is gone forever, now. When you listen to the places where the silence used to be, you hear the soft insidious buzzing, like a swarm of distant flies, that proclaims the end of man's solitude....

For me, it happened like this: it was opening night, and Hamlet was just dying, and I was watching from the wings, being already dead, of course, as Guilderstern, I wanted to stay for curtain call anyway, even though I knew the audience wouldn't notice. It hadn't been too long since my first job, and I was new in New York. But here everything revolved around Sir Francis FitzHenry, brought over from England at ridiculous expense with his new title clinging to him like wrapping paper.

Everything else was as low-budget as possible, including me. They did a stark, empty staging, ostensibly as a sop to modernism, but really because the backers were penniless after paying FitzHenry's advance, and so Sir Francis was laid out on a barren proscenium with nothing but an old leather armchair for Claudius's throne and a garish green spot on him. Not that there was any of that Joseph Papp-style avant-garde rubbish. Everything was straight. Me, I didn't know what people saw in Sir Francis FitzHenry till I saw him live—I'd only seen him in that ridiculous Fellini remake of *Ben Hur*—but he was dynamite, just the right thing for the old Jewish ladies.

There he was, then, making his final scene so heartrending I could have drowned in an ocean of molasses; arranging himself into elaborate poses that could have been plucked from the Acropolis; and uttering each iambic pentameter as though he were the New York Philharmonic and the Mormon Tabernacle Choir all rolled into one. And they were lapping it up, what with the swing away from the really modern interpretations. He was a truimph of the old school, there on that stage turning the other actors into ornamental papier-mache all around him.

He had just gotten, you know, to that line:

Absent thee from felicity awhile...

To tell my story.

and was just about to fall, with consummate grace, into Horatio's arms. You could feel the collective catch of breath, the palpable silence, and I was thinking, *What could ever top that, my God?* ...and I had that good feeling you get when you know you're going to be drawing your paycheck for at least another year or so. And maybe Gail would come back, even.

Then—

Buzz, buzz, buzz, buzz. "What's wrong?" I turned to the little stage manager, who was wildly pushing buttons. The buzzing came, louder and louder. You couldn't hear a word Horatio was saying. The buzzing kept coming, from every direction now, hurting my ears. Sir Francis sat up in mid-tumble and glared balefully at the wings, then the first scream could be heard above the racket, and I finally had the nerve to poke my head out and saw the tumult in the audience....

"For Chrissakes, why doesn't someone turn on the house lights?" Claudius had risen from where he was sprawled dead and was stomping around the stage. The buzzing became more and more intense, and now there were scattered shrieks of terror and the thunder of an incipient stampede mixed into the buzzing, and I cursed loudly about the one dim spotlght. The screaming came continuously. People were trooping all over the stage and were tripping on swords and shields, a lady-in-waiting hurtled into me and squished makeup onto my cloak, corpses were around in the dark, and finally I found the right switch where the stage manager had run away and all the lights came on and the leather armchair went whizzing into the flies.

I caught one word amid all this commotion—

Aliens.

A few minutes later everybody knew everything. Messages were being piped into our minds somehow. At first they just said *don't panic, don't panic* and were hypnotically soothing, but then it all became more bewildering as the enormity of it all sank in. I noticed that the audience was sitting down again, and the buzzing had died down to an insistent whisper. Everything was returning to a surface normality, but stiff, somehow, artificial. They were all sitting, a row of glassy-eyed mannequins in expensive clothes, under the glare of the house lights, and we knew we were all hearing the same thing in our minds.

187

They were bringing us the gift of immortality, they said. They were some kind of galactic federation. No, we wouldn't really be able to understand what they were, but they would not harm us. In return for their gift, they were exacting one small favor from us. They would try to explain it in our terms. Apparently something like a sort of hyperspatial junior high school was doing a project on uncivilized planets, something like "one day in the life of a barbarian world." The solar system was now in some kind of time loop, and would we be kind enough to repeat the same day over and over again for a while, with two hours off from 6 to 8 every morning, while their kids came over and studied everything in detail. We were very lucky, they added; it was an excellent deal. No, there wasn't anything we could do about it.

I wondered to myself, how long is "over and over again for a while?"

They answered it for me. "Oh, nothing much. About seven million of your years." I felt rather short-changed, though I realized that it was nothing in comparison with immortality.

And, standing there stock-still and not knowing what to think, I saw the most amazing sight. We all saw the aliens as gossamer veils of light that drifted and danced across the field of visoin, almost imperceptible, miniature auroras that sparkled and vanished....I saw Sir Francis's face through a gauze of shimmering blue lights. I wanted to touch them so badly; I reached out and my hand passed right through one without feeling a thing. Then they were gone.

We turned off the house lights—we had until midnight—and went on with the play. The buzzing subsided almost completely, but was very obviously there all the time, so everybody gabbled their lines and tried to cut in quickly between speeches to cover up the noise. The applause was perfunctory, and Sir Francis seemed considerably distressed that he had been so easily upstaged.

I walked home at a few minutes to midnight. I saw peculiar poles with colored metallic knobs on them, all along Broadway every couple of blocks, like giant parking meters. The streets were virtually empty, and there were a couple of overturned Yellow cabs and an old Chevy sticking out of a store window. It had been too much for some, I supposed. But I was so confused about what had happened, I tried to think about nothing but Gail and about the bad thing that had happened that morning.

I climbed up the dirty staircase to my efficiency above an Indian grocery store and jumped into bed with all my clothes on, thinking about the bad thing between me and Gail, and at midnight I suddenly noticed I was in pyjamas and she was lying there beside me, and there was a sudden jerk of dislocation and I knew that it wasn't *today* anymore, it was *yesterday*, it was all true. I squeezed my eyes tightly and wished I was dead.

2.

I woke up around 11 o'clock. Gail stirred uneasily. We made love, like machines. I kept trying to pull myself away, knowing what was coming. Whatever the aliens had done, it had turned me into a needle in a groove, following the line of least resistance.

We got up and had breakfast. She wore her ominous disheveled look, strands of black hair fishnetting her startlingly blue eyes.

"John?"

The dinette table seemed as wide as all space. She seemed incredibly unreachable, like the stars. "Umm?" I found myself saying in a banal voice. I knew what she was going to say; I knew what I was going to do. But whatever it was dealt only with appearances. In my thoughts I was free, as though I were somehow outside the whole thing, experiencing my own past as a recording. I wondered at my own detachment.

"John, I'm leaving you."

Anger rose in me. I got up, knocking over the coffee mug and shouting, "What for, who with?" like an idiot before going off into incoherent cursing.

"Francis FitzHenry has asked me to stay with him—in his suite at the Plaza!"

The anger welled up again. Blindly, I slapped her face. She went white, then red, and then she said quietly, dangerously: "you're too petty, John. That's why you're going to be a Guildenstern for the rest of your life." That hurt.

Then she walked out of my life.

I shaved and walked slowly over to the theater. We played to a full house. The aliens came. Sir Francis seemed considerably distressed that he had been so easily upstaged. I walked home, casually noting the two overturned Yellow cabs and the old Chevy stuck in a store window, past the overgrown parking meters, to my efficiency above an Indian grocery store, and threw myself fully clothed on the bed. I fell asleep.

I woke up around 11 o'clock. Gail stirred uneasily. We made love mechanically, and I knew that the two people who were lying there together had become totally divorced from themselves, and were going through preordained motions that bore no relationship to what was in their minds. And there was no way of communicating.

We ate breakfast. She wore her ominous disheveled look, and I desperately wanted to apologize to her, but when I tried to speak my facial muscles were frozen and the buzzing seemed to get louder, drowning my thoughts. Was the buzzing an external sound, or was it some mental monitor to enforce the status quo?

"I'm leaving you."

Anger rose in me. I quenched it at once, but it made no difference either to my posture or to my words.

"Francis FitzHenry has asked me to stay with him—in his suite at the Plaza!"

I slapped her face. Suddenly the veils of light came, caressing the musty stale air of my apartment, touching the dust and making it sparkle, like a golden snow between the two of us. They faded. We had been watched; we were trapped in a galactic Peyton Place.

"You're too petty, John. That's why you're going to be a Guildenstern for the rest of your life." And walked out of my life. It hurt me more every time. I was doomed to be a Guildenstern in this play too, a Guildenstern for the old ladies and a Guildenstern for the veils of light. It was hell.

I shaved and walked slowly over to the theater. We played to a full house. The aliens came; Sir Frncis seemed considerably distressed that he had been so easily upstaged. I walked home, past the overturned cars and the gigantic parking meters that had materialized out of nowhere.

As I fell asleep, just before midnight, a thought surfaced: we were supposed to have two free hours every morning, weren't we? For months now, I had slept through those two hours.

I resolved to force myself to wake up at six.

3.

I jerked myself awake at 6:30, snaked into unostentatious jeans and a T-shirt, and came down.

The brilliant summer morning hit me between the eyes. It had been autumn the previous night. Everything was to wonder at: the trash drifting down the sidewalk in the breeze, the briskness of the air, the clarity of the sunlight. . . .

Two tramps were leaning against the first of the alien poles. They had their eyes closed and were very peaceful, so I crept away. Potholes exuded smoke, people jostled each other, and everything seemed astonishingly normal, except for the insistent buzzing.

Another of the poles had a man in a scruffy three-piece suit and blatantly orange tie, holding up a sign on which was scrawled VON DANIKEN LIVES! He had acquired a squalid-looking collection of onlookers, whom I joined for a moment.

"...man, these critters built the *Pyramids!* They built the *Empire State Building!* They're the Gods! Alexander the Great was one! Richard M. Nixon was one! God was one!...and you, too, can be saved, if only you'll just throw a quarter on the altar of repentance! Hallelujah! Thank you, ma'am...."

I walked on.

At the next extraterrestrial parking meter a group of Hare Krishna types was dancing round and round like they had a missionary in the pot. In the middle a scrawny, bespectacled shaven man was caressing the shaft, which was glowing a dull crimson. He seemed transfigured, almost beautiful, much more like the real thing than Sir Francis FitzHenry could ever be. I watched for a long time, fascinated, my mind dulled by the hypnotic repetitiveness of their chanting.

They ceased, jolting me from my reverie. The lanky one came up to me and started to whisper confidentially, intensely, "Did you know they're only a few microns thick? Did you know that they're called the *T'tat?* Did you know they have a shared consciousness that works over vast reaches of space-time? Did you know thay've reached an incredibly high evolutionary phase, huh?"

"You don't talk like a Hare Krishna person."

"Hey!...oh, the clothes, you mean. Actually, I have a Ph.D. from M.I.T. I *talk* to them, you know."

"No kidding?"

"Hey, really! Listen, come here," he pulled me roughly over to the pole, which had stopped glowing. "Just sit down here, relax now, touch the pole. Totem pole, divine antenna, whatever. Can't you hear anything...?"

Hello.

I was shivering. The voice was so close; it was speaking inside me. I drew back quickly.

"Hey, did you know they have many colors, that each color shows their status based on age? Did you know that, huh? Did you know they don't join up with the collective consciousness until they're almost half a billion years old, that they have these learning centers all over the galaxy, that they originally crossed over from the Great Nebula in Andromeda? No kidding, man!"

I didn't know what he was talking about.

"Here, touch it again, it isn't so bad the second time." He was twitching all over, a bundle of nerves. "Sorry I'm acting like this.

191

It's my only chance to act normal, you see, the rest of the day I'm either stoned or asleep, according to the script. I can't wait till we all wake up!"

I reached out. *Hello.*

"Isn't there any way we can *resist* them?"

"What for? Don't you want to live forever? This is just a sort of Purgatory, isn't it? We all get to go to heaven."

"But suppose I wanted to, you know, contradict them, or something."

"Dunno. They can't control *everything.*"He paused for a moment, but then launched himself into a stream of information again, as though I'd fed him another quarter.

"I have the general equations worked out." He flashed a bit of paper in front of my face, then thrust it back into his pocket—"but you obviously have to be in control of unified field theory, and even then there's the power source to worry about. I have a couple of theories—f'rinstance, if they had sort of a portable mini-quasar, like, a miniature white hole worming through space-time into a transdimensional universe, they could tap the energy, you see, and—"

He had lost me. I touched the pole, and his voice faded into nothingness. The buzzing intensified. *Hello.*

"We're just dirt to you, laboratory animals," I said bitterly. "I wish it was back to the way it was."

You can't help being a lower being, you know. There's nothing you or I can do about that.

"Well, will you tell me one thing?" It suddenly occurred to me that everyone had left. The Hare Krishnas, hands linked, had gone dancing off.

Sure.

"Is this thing really worth it, for us? Seven million years is a long, long, time; it's the same as eternity for all practical purposes."

Hah! Fat lot you know.

"You didn't answer my question."

All in good time. But it's almost 8 o'clock. Hold on, you'll be dislocated back to yesterday in a few seconds. You're pretty lucky, you know; in some parts of the world the two hours' grace comes at some ridiculous time and nobody ever gets up.

"Goodbye."

Goodbye.

I woke up around 11 o'clock. Gail stirred uneasily. We made love mechanically, like machines, with living sheets of light, only a few microns thick, darting between us, weaving delicately transient patterns in the air, and I felt hollow, transparent, empty.

4.

I met Amy Schechter in Grand Central Station, coming out of the autumn night into a biting blizzard of a winter morning.

We were both standing at a doughnut stand. I looked at her, helpless, frail, as she stared into a cup of cold coffee. I had seen her before, but this morning there were just the two of us. She suddenly looked up at me. Her eyes were brown and lost.

"Hi. Amy."

"John."

A pause, full of noisome buzzing, fell between us.

For a while, I watched the breathing form and dissipate about her face, wanting to make conversation, but I couldn't think what to say.

"Will you talk to me? Nobody ever does, they always back off, as if they knew."

"Okay."

"I've been standing here for five years, waiting for my train. Sometimes I come an hour or so before 8 o'clock, you know, just to stand around. There's nothing for me at where I'm staying." Her voice was really small, hard to hear against the buzzing.

"Where are you going?"

"Oh, Havertown, Pennsylvania. You've never heard of it." I hadn't. "It's sort of a suburb of Philadelphia," she added helpfully. "My folks live there."

"Buy you a doughnut?"

"You must be joking!" She laughed quickly and stopped herself, then cast her eyes down as though scrutinizing a hypothetical insect in her styrofoam cup. Then she turned her back on me, hugging her shaggy old coat to her thin body, and crumpled the cup firmly and threw it into the garbage.

"Wait, come back! We've got an hour and a half, you know, before you have to leave—"

"Oh, so it's score and run? Nothing doing, friend."

"Well, I *will* buy you a doughnut then."

"Oh, all right. A romantic memory," she added cynically, "when I'll be dead by dinner anyway."

"*Huh?*"

She came closer. We were almost touching, both leaning against the grubby counter. "I'm one of the ghosts, you know," she said.

"I don't get it."

"What do *you* do every day?"

"My girlfriend walks out on me, then I play a poor third fiddle to a pretentious British actor in *Hamlet.*"

"Lucky. In *my* script, the train crashes into an eighteen-wheeler 25 miles outside of Philadelphia. Smash! Everybody dead. And then every morning I find myself at the station again. I was pretty muddled at first; the aliens never made any announcements to *me* while I was lying in the wreckage. So I do it all over and over again. One day I may even enjoy it."

It didn't sink in. "Chocolate covered?" I asked inanely.

"Yeah."

There was another pause. I realized how much I needed another person, not Gail, how much I needed someone real....

"We should get to know each other, maybe," I ventured. "After it's all over, maybe we could—"

"No, John. Nothing doing. I'm a ghost. I'm not immortal, don't you see! The whole deal ignores me completely! I'm dead already, dead, permanently dead! You don't get to be part of the deal if you die sometime during the day, you have to survive through till midnight, don't you see?"

"...oh God." I saw.

"They've just left me in the show to make everything as accurate as can be. I'm an echo. I'm nothing."

I didn't say a word. I just grabbed her and kissed her, right there in the middle of the doughnut stand. She was quite cold, like marble, like stone.

"Come on," she said. We found a short-time hotel around the block; I paid the eight dollars and we clung together urgently, desperately, for a terribly brief time.

I woke up at around 11 o'clock. Gail stirred uneasily. As I went through the motions for the thousandth time I was thinking all the time, *this isn't fair, this isn't fair.* Gail was alive, she was going to live forever and she's just like a machine, she might just as well be dead. Amy, now, she was dead, but so *alive!* Then I realized a terrible truth: *Immortality kills!* I was very bitter and very angry, I felt cheated, and the buzzing sounded louder, like a warning, and I knew then that I was going to try and do some-thing dreadful. ("They can't control *everything,*" wasn't that what the Krishna freak had said?)

I struggled, trying to push myself out of the groove, trying to change a little bit of one little movement, but always falling back to the immutable past....

We got up and had breakfast. She wore her ominous dis-heveled look, strands of black hair fishnetting her startlingly blue eyes.

"John?"

"Umm?"

"John, I'm leaving you."

"What for, who with?"

"Francis FitzHenry has asked me to stay with him—in his suite at the Plaza!"

I lifted my hand, then willed with every ounce of strength I could dredge up from every hidden source.

I didn't slap her face.

A look of utter bewilderment crossed her face, just for one split second, and I looked at her and she looked at me, her emotions unfathomable; and then the whole thing swung grotesquely back to the original track, and she said quietly, dangerously, "You're too petty, John. That's why you're going to be a Guildenstern for the rest of your life." As though nothing were different. That hurt.

Then she walked out of my life.

But I had changed something! And we had communicated; for a split second, and I looked at her and she looked at me, her a split second something had passed between us!

The buzzing became a roar. I walked slowly to the theater, bathed in the glow of a hundred diaphanous wisps of light.

5.

It was a couple of minutes before 8 when the phone rang in my apartment. I decided to make a run for it, so I made for the kitchenette in the nude.

"Yeah?"

"This is Michael, John." Michael played Horatio. He was sobbing, all broken up. I didn't know him very well, so I played it cool. "John, I'm going to do something terrible! I can't stand it, you're the first person I could get through to this morning, I'm going to try and—"

I woke up around 11 o'clock. Gail stirred uneasily. We had breakfast, and I didn't slap her face.

It seemed too natural. I realized that I had changed the pattern. This is the way it would always be from now on.

I had never slapped her face.

A look of utter bewilderment...but it was no longer a communication, it was just a reflex, part of the pattern, and then she said quietly, dangerously, "You're too petty, John. That's why you're going to be a Guildenstern for the rest of your life."

That hurt. Then she walked out of my life.

I went to the theater. There was Sir Francis, making his final scene so heartrending I could have drowned in a sea of molasses; arranging himself into elaborate poses that could have been plucked from the Acropolis; and uttering each iambic pentameter as though he were the New York Philharmonic and the Mormon Tabernacle Choir all rolled into one. He was dying, and he clutched at Horatio, and he said, measuring each phrase for the right mixture of honey and gall—

Absent thee from felicity awhile...

To tell my story.

and was just about to fall, with consummate grace, into Horatio's arms, and you could feel the collective catch of breath, the palpable silence except for the quiet buzzing, when Horatio drew a revolver from his doublet and emptied it into Sir Francis's stomach.

After the aliens departed from the theater, the play went on, since Hamlet was dead anyway, and afterwards I walked home. I saw peculiar poles with metallic knobs on them, all along Broadway every couple of blocks, and there were a couple of overturned Yellow cabs, but the old Chevy was gone from the store window. Good for them.

In the morning I met Amy. I told her about what had happened.

"When you get to just before your accident, try to jump out of the car or something. Keep trying, Amy, just keep trying."

She chewed her doughnut, deliberating. "I don't know."

"Well, we've got another six million, nine hundred thousand, nine hundred and ninety-four years to try in. So keep at it, okay?"

She seemed unconvinced.

"Just for me, try."

I kissed her quickly on the forehead and she disappeared into the crowd that was heading towards the platform.

6.

The pole was glowing a pale crimson when I touched it.

Hello.

I couldn't contain my rage. "You bastards! Well, we're not powerless after all, we've got free will, we *can* change things. We can ruin your high school project completely, rats that we are!"

Oh. Well, that too is one of the things under study at the moment.

"Well, let me tell you something. I don't want your immortality! Because I'd have to give up being a person. Being a person means changing all the time, not being indifferent, and you're changing us into machines."

Oh? And do you deny that you've changed?

It was true. I had changed. I wasn't going to be a Guildenstern for the rest of my life anymore. I was going to fight them; I was going to learn everything I could about them so I could try and twist it against them; I was going to be a real human being.

There are things you can't do anything about. You're in a transitional stage, you see. With immortality will come a change in perspectives. You won't feel the same anymore about your barbarian ways, Earthling.

I had to laugh. "Where did you learn to talk like that?"

We monitored your science fiction TV broadcasts.

The picture of these alien schoolkids, clustering around a television set in some galactic suburbia somewhere in the sky...I laughed and laughed and laughed.

But then, seriously: "I'm still going to fight you, you know. For the sake of being human." I had a new fuel to use, after all, against them. Love. Revenge. Heroism. I was thinking of Amy. The good old-fashioned stuff of drama.

Go ahead.

I woke up around 11 o'clock.

Although "Absent Thee from Felicity Awhile" proved so popular that it was nominated for a Hugo Award, and appeared in one of the Best of the Year Anthologies, it had rather a rough history. You see, I first sent out the version you have just read to one editor, who told me it was unsatisfactory, and said that I had to "finish the story." So I did so, tacking on another 20 pages of manuscript. Well, that editor still didn't like it, so I started to send it around. On the tenth try it was accepted with enthusiasm by Hank Stine, then editor of Galaxy. Alas, like "The Starship and the Haiku" which he had also accepted, it was returned when Galaxy was sold to another company.

It wasn't until Analog had a change of editors, thus providing me with someone new to send it to, that I decided to try again, digging it up off the frequent-rejection pile, dusting it off, and...on a whim, not sending the last 20 pages that I had originally been told to add. Stanley Schmidt bought it right away. I shrugged, thinking...well, maybe it's the name, you know, and the small measure of fame I've acquired... then the nomination occurred, upsetting all my preconceptions, for it was not one of the three stories of mine I was rooting for. None of those got on the ballot.

Hank Stine, when I submitted this collection to Starblaze, now editor there, suggested to me in rather strong terms that I restore the story to its original novelette length. I demurred at first, but here's a compromise.

If you turn the page now, you can pick up the story at just the moment you left it. Part II precisely the way I wrote it five years ago, including the anachronistic Winston sign in Times Square.

Judge for yourself—nine other editors, or Hank Stine?

Part II

7.

"Amy, *please.*" We were at our doughnut stand again; something drew us to that place, I couldn't stand it any more, I was going crazy.

"But I've tried so hard, I've tried every day for a year, now!" She was crying tearlessly, in that whimpering, wounded-animal way of hers. Impulsively I held her, hardly touching, though, and I put my hands round hers round her coffee cup, for the warmth. "John, it's just impossible. It's one thing to move an arm or a leg a little differently, avoid slapping a face, pull out a weapon and phut! it's over. But getting up, jumping out of a train...I can't make myself do it! Once I got as far as the edge of the seat. You should have heard the buzzing." (I heard the buzzing even then.) "Maybe it upsets their time field too much, if you try to go too far at once...."

"Poor Amy, poor little ghost."

I turned her around and touched her face. "You can do it a little at a time, maybe," I said. "Just edge up on it, slowly, over the next year or so. We've got to think of *something.*" It was all I thought about, all through *Hamlet,* all through the fight with Gail.

"It's all right for *you* to say that! You'll never have to die! You'll never experience what I experience! You'll never feel the incredible hopelessness, the nightmare, the pain of being crushed to a pulp, day after day, then waking up and knowing it's going to happen again, every day of your life, and you'll never get anything back out of all the torture...."

They burned me, those words. Because I knew that she was right, that there was one area of human experience which would be forever denied me. I was more hurt than ever I had been by Gail's callousness. Because perhaps, if I never died, I didn't really qualify as a human being.

Very gently, I said to her: "Sometimes I think the aliens get more fun out of our off-hour antics than when we're on duty."

She was staring into the distance. "Did I ever tell you why I came to New York?"

"No, it never occurred to me, I thought you lived here."

"Shows how much *you* care." Why was she being so bitter, suddenly, almost childishly so? "Well, my little brother ran away from home. Brian, eleven. I thought I'd find him here, maybe."

"Oh?" I didn't know how I was supposed to react.

"My parents are alcoholics, you know," she volunteered. "We're a textbook case of parental neglect, me and Brian." Then she clammed up completely about her past, and I didn't find out anything more.

"Oh, it's almost time." she broke away abruptly, and said, disarmingly, "Do you love me?"

"I don't know, I don't know! For God's sake, let's save your life before we get into any of that!" I was sick, sick inside. And she was shrinking into the distance, being swallowed up by the black tunnel that led to the train and to her unspeakable anguish.

I was angry at myself. Why had I answered her like that? I threw my half-eaten doughnut on the concrete and squashed it thoroughly with my shoe, knowing full well it was a pointless gesture, since it would have vanished in a few minutes....

I woke up around eleven o'clock. Gail stirred uneasily. We made love, and I was sick inside; we made love to the music of alien buzzings, to an audience of fluttering auroras. Then we had breakfast.

She wore her ominous disheveled look, strands of black hair fishnetting her startlingly blue eyes (how different from Amy's!) and she said: "J-j-john," and stopped abruptly.

What was she trying to communicate? I "Ummed?" banally, studying her face for any clue at all, but it was as cryptic as a hieroglyph. I knew she was trying to answer me, to reply to what I had done so long ago when I stopped slapping her face (that sequence was so long ago it was only a dream now, shifting and unreliable); and that she was a person, too; a person subjected to the most extreme depersonalization possible. It made me feel terribly guilty, because I didn't love her anymore. I probably never had. (I understood a lot more now than I ever had.)

I hoped to God I could live with my guilt for another six million years.

We were machines. We were video images in a nightmarish forever rerun of a bad soap opera. "Gail, I'm *sorry*," I thought at her, as hard as I could, hoping that somehow she would hear, but—

"You're so petty, John. That's why you're going to be a Guildenstern for the rest of your life." The gulf was forever.

And shaved and walked to the theater.

The audience was a little thinner that night. It could have been my imagination. Or perhaps it was just that their thoughts were not wholly on the play, any more.

Even though Sir Francis was making his final scene so heart-rending it could have wrung tears from a lump of concrete.

I was waiting, you know, for the moment when Michael would whip out his revolver and empty it into Sir Francis. The mechanics of the time-stasis whateveritwas, of course, ensured that Sir Francis would now no longer survive to pollute the world, when we all became immortal. The expression of bemused incredulity on his face was a classic, in any case. Well, he had just gotten to those lines (measuring each phrase for the perfect blend of honey and gall)

Absent thee from felicity—

But he never finished.

Instead, he fished out a grotesque-looking kitchen knife from his costume and started hacking away violently at Horatio, who was too astonished to scream, and there was blood everywhere, all over the stage, all the costumes were spattered, and then Horatio fell with a resounding *thwack!* onto the boards. Scattered screaming in the audience was suddenly stifled.

Sir Francis heaved and panted for a moment, and then, in a flamboyant gesture of triumph, fainted on top of his bloodied victim.

There was no "good night, sweet prince" that night, or the next night. But the play was finished (after the aliens departed) after a fashion: an exactly timed pause replaced Horatio's last speech. The applause was perfunctory as ever.

I realized that causality had gone from our lives. From now on, *anything* could happen after anything else, any outlandish sequence of events could be reality, because the continuum would always try and adjust, and compensate, as best it could, to the original norm....

I walked home that night.

Light-veils followed me all the way, softening the harshness of street-lamps, even making the garbage sparkle.

The Chevy had returned to the store window (I wondered what sort of argument had been going on in that car, when the aliens first materialized) but a taxicab had vanished instead. Good for them.

8.

I woke up at 6:30. I caught Gail and Sir Francis FitzHenry

in flagrante on the sofa as I was making for the door.

"...but I *had* to do it! I *had* to! or else he would have killed me, and we wouldn't have...wouldn't have..." he was moaning in his most effective simulated pathos.

"There now, there now," Gail was saying, cradling his head in her arms and stroking him. They were the first new words I had heard her say ever since the Thing happened. She suddenly looked up and saw me trying to sneak out of the door.

"Get out!" she hissed. Did she have to treat me like a criminal in my own apartment? The effrontery of it! I was sick inside, I fled down the grimy stairwell without thinking, and went through the door into a surprising spring.

It was a chilly, bracing morning, and all the cranks were out.

At the first of the parking meters, about a dozen sick people were lying on the sidewalk on stretchers. It was fascinatingly unpleasant—they were all terminal cases, obviously, withered people, smiling beatifically at the glowing pole. An incredibly small child on a soap box was telling them to repent in a fake-sounding Southern accent (I've been to acting school and I can *tell*, believe me.)

"Feel the healing power of the Pole! Feel the light of the Lord shining on you! I heal you in the name of the T'tat," he was shouting, as he tottered off the soap box and laid hands on each of the sick people. "You got cancer? leukemia? hemorrhoids? acne? Just believe in the Pole, and the T'tat will save you!"

One decrepit specimen had staggered off his stretcher and was crawling, in unmistakable agony, towards the pole. "Heal me, heal me," he rasped. The child's countenance was, at best, questionably angelic. But the old man's face was frozen into a mask of joy.

"Can't they leave the sick people alone, those crazies, those cranks?" I muttered to myself, turning my back on it all.

"That's where you're wrong, young man," said an old lady in a floral print dress—she had that elementary school librarian look about her—who had been standing next to me, watching the curious proceedings. "It really works, you know. *I've* seen things."

"That little kid on the soap box—that isn't—"

"Yep! You've seen him on TV, I suppose. Little Joshua Mattingly, the faith healer from Alabama...he was on tour in New York." She fell into step beside me, and some sort of chivalry prevented me from shaking her off. "Isn't it against his religion, or something?" I said, to make conversation.

"Goodness no. His *agent* told me—why he's had a revelation from the Lord, the T'tat are the lost tribes of Israel, you know."

"That's silly." (Where was Amy? I hadn't seen her for weeks.)

"Yeah. Well I have to put up with it all day long. You're not one of those—religious types, are you?"

I shuddered. "Hardly."

"Well, I don't mind telling you a secret." She whispered in my ear—I had to bend down—"I'm his mother!"

I clucked-clucked sympathetically, since this seemed to be what was required.

"I knew you'd understand. My husband's one of *them*, too, but I've turned away from the Lord," she said confidentially, "because he stole my son." Then she gripped my arm intensely. "Will *you* be my son?"

"Er—"

"Choose! Now! In the world to come there won't be any more begats and begottens!" she was snarling at me now.

I shook her off and ran into a crowd of people who were may-pole dancing at one of the parking meters. "Watch it, mister!" a man shouted, and I tripped and sprawled right into a tangle of colored ribbons.

"Oh, hell," said a bovine woman in a tired, bureaucratic sort of voice, "Start it from the top."

The couple of people I had knocked over got up, gasping for breath, and took their positions. As I walked away they were twirling their ribbons and prancing about, for all the world as though they had just emerged from the middle ages.

Everyone had his cult or his subculture or his family or *some-thing*, I realized. Except me. I was lost in a city conquered by aliens. I wished *I* had a family....

That night, Sir Francis only got as far as

Absent thee—

when Horatio whipped out his revolver. Sir Francis retaliated with surprising agility with his knife, and they both flopped down dead on the stage. A few more lines of dialogue were replaced by the ubiquitous buzzing that night. Maybe one day the aliens would do the whole play.

9.

"Well, where've *you* been?"

"Oh, hi. Doughnut?" She was in the usual place, after all. Didn't she ever go exploring?

"Don't try that old spiel on me." She grinned, then said: "Why have you been avoiding me?" But she wasn't angry.

"Well, six million years is a long time; we can't see each other *all* the time."

"Yeah. We've got time enough, but we haven't got world enough," she said, giggling at her own erudition. "Hey, do you ever wonder where these doughnuts come from?"

"Frozen, madame." Suddenly the paunchy man behind the counter spoke up. He had never said a word before, but lately he had been observing our carryings-on with a kind of lugubrious detachment. "Of all the luck, happened to buy two tousand boxes chocolate covered, two tousand plain, just before the Ting happened. Only taka ten minutes to bake a dozen every morning."

"Won't they ever run out?"

"Sure, fifty year, a hundred, who cares?"

"But the sign says, 'Fresh Doughnuts,'" Amy pointed out.

"Is a crisis! What you spect me to do, go outa business?" He shrugged extravagantly, and then returned with startling abruptness to his former detachment.

"Amy, come exploring with me, or something. We can't go on meeting here, I know it's a cliche."

"I'm still looking for my kid brother, though. I figure *everyone* ends up in Grand Central, sooner or later."

I was discovering what a single-minded person she was. If she loved me, she wouldn't love anybody else. And that scared me no end.

"John—"

"What?"

"I've figured out how to do it, I think!"

"How?" I was excited.

"I'm not going to tell you yet. I'm not sure it's going to work, but you and I want to get out of this thing, both alive, and both together, so I'm going to try it. Look, I'm not going to be able to see you for a year or two, understand?"

"Oh Amy, why?" I was going to lose her, just as I was falling head over heels in love with her?

"I have to track down and get to know all the other passengers on the train, or as many as I can. It's all part of the plan."

There was a new resolve about her, a new sense of purpose. She was a miracle, there was so much to her I didn't understand...she was almost a different person every time I saw her.

I did love her.

I did. But I couldn't bring myself to say it, I had this crazy terror of rejection, the way you're scared of the dark when you're a kid, I just couldn't say anything.

She said: "When it happens, I'll call you."

"You won't see me at *all*?"

"I can hardly trust myself to push this thing through! This

has got to be the biggest change anyone's ever tried to effect in the whole messy situation...I just don't know, I don't want us to get too cocksure about our chances."

And that was all I was going to get out of her about this.

"Well...bye," I mumbled.

"Oh, and see if you can find my kid brother. And—" somehow she had seized all the controls in our relationship, but I was so mixed up I hardly noticed—"kiss me."

10.

I found myself talking to a Pole.

"Hey, man, get out of the way!" It was the Hare Krishna fellow from way back, but he was wearing a shaggy army-reject coat and you could hardly see his face with all the scarves. It was mid-winter. He was emptying some gray powder out of a cardboard carton onto the snowy sidewalk.

"What are you doing?" I sprang up in alarm, and immediately slipped into the slush.

"What do you think?...oh, I remember you."

"Well, looks like you're trying to blow the Pole up."

"Go to the top of the class! Why, do you know what this damn thing told me? Can you guess, huh? Did you know what I found out?" He kicked the Pole, which didn't react. "You...*Hitler!*"

I got ready for another lecture.

"Did you know that they routinely eliminate half their offspring? Did you know that when these baby T'tat flunk their exams on 'one day in the life of,' they're going to get shoved in the oven and recycled into new T'tat?"

"Well, look, they're a different species. We don't have the right to judge them."

"And I thought they were Gods, or something, man. Did you know they think nothing of destroying whole solar systems? That they once massacred an entire interstellar civilization in a war? So much for higher consciousness." He spat copiously.

"Look, you used to *love* those Poles...I mean, no pun intended..." he looked dangerous.

"Get out of the way, will you, like I don't feel like blowing you up along with it, do I?"

"Just let me finish this conversation."

"Oh, sure, what's ten minutes in a zillion years."

Hello.

I had forgotten how frightening the voice was, how it seemed to touch your very insides with claws of ice..."I just wanted to ask you one thing. What are these Poles for?"

204

You wouldn't understand, earthling. We lack the necessary images to explain it to you. It's something like eating—and something like eliminating—and, well, something like praying.

"Can't you give us just five minutes of silence, one day? Or even ten seconds?"

Sorry: we'd have to leave the planet.

"So, why don't you?"

Well, as a matter of fact it wouldn't be in your best interests. You see, this time stasis field is in an experimental stage, and we aren't supposed to leave it behind.

"You mean it might backfire? Trap us in space or something?"

Possibly; I doubt it.

"Well, how dare you try it out on an intelligent species? Don't you have any decency, or anything?"

Intelligent? Ha, ha, ha, ha, ha.

"I really hate you...."

Well, we would never try it out on an intelligent species, you know. But there are limits to altruism.

"I just know there's a catch in this somewhere...."

No there isn't. Frankly, we think you'll go far as a species: that is, as soon as you become immortal. You'll have to.

"Have to?"

Well, setting up this field involved a bit of tinkering with your sun, you see, so it'll probably go nova soon.

"You tricked us! You lied to us!" I felt very bad. Perhaps Amy and I were fighting on for nothing. Perhaps they were just playing with us, not being fair to us.

Wait! 'Soon' doesn't mean what you think. You've still got the shortliver mentality. I mean, maybe in one or two billion years, instead of the regulation ten billion. You'll have plenty of time to extricate yourselves from the situation! And just think—you'll still be alive, then, you'll be able to travel to the stars, go to other galaxies, maybe, participate in the greatest adventure man has ever undertaken...look, earthling, there's no fine print in this contract. You're getting the finest brand of immortality there is—

"Which is?" I was still very suspicious.

Well, you know, there's the struldbrug variety, that's the worst. Where you go on aging. You people are getting the 'eternal youth' formula.

I was terribly relieved about that, although I didn't really quite trust them. But I couldn't have found out from anybody else. I knew that the aging thing might be a barbed clause, I've read plenty of science fiction.

Are you still going to fight us?

I was taken aback by the way it recalled our former conversation.

"Well, I'm trying to. At least, to get what *I* want out of this deal."

Spoken like a true earthling. So you think you can reconcile it all with 'being human,' or whatever.

"I don't have any choice, do I?"

"Hey, I'm lighting the fuse, stand aside!" Quickly I got to my feet and took refuge behind a parked car. "Blam! Blam! Down with all fascists," shouted the Hare Krishna man, and joined me there, a grim smile on his lips.

There was a tremendous explosion.

The pole was still there.

"I knew this bootleg gunpowder was no good," he murmured. There were tears in his eyes as he sadly crossed the street, his carton still trailing the gray powder into the soft snow.

I was very depressed; I didn't have Amy now, I didn't have anything. Often as not I would get up for my morning adventures to find Gail and Sir Francis enjoying the freedom of my apartment. They had come to treat me like a piece of furniture.

The memory of that last kiss came to me. I would have done anything to get her back, but I had no way of finding her now.... I trudged home in the fresh snow. Some of the snow was colored, green and turquoise and gold and fire-red, because the T'tat were trooping by.

11.

Six million, nine hundred thousand and fifty-two and counting....

I woke up around eleven o'clock. We made love mechanically, under the gaze of three fluttering shower-curtains. Then we had breakfast. My coffee cup was in a different place, so I lifted and drank the empty air.

She wore her ominous disheveled look, strands of black hair fishnetting her startlingly blue eyes.

"J-j-john—" she said. The dinette table was as wide as all space. She seemed incredibly unreachable, like the stars.

"Umm?" I said banally; I still hadn't bothered to edit that particular detail. But I knew what was going to come next.

She said nothing at all.

I knocked over the invisible coffee cup, while the real one steamed away in the corner, shouting, "Speak hands, for me!" like an idiot, before my words degenerated into incoherent cursing.

206

"Francis FitzHenry has asked me to stay with him—in his suite at the Plaza!"

Blindly, I didn't slap her face. I didn't want to apologize any more; I just wanted to get this whole scene over with a minimum of fuss, so that I could go back to the real world, the two-hours' world. She turned white, then red, and then she said, quietly, dangerously, "You're too petty, John. That's why you're going to be a Rosencrantz for the rest of your life."

That was a new twist. I appreciated that.

Then she walked out of my life.

I shaved and walked over to the theater.

Horatio disposed of Sir Francis in act one, scene one, so we did the entire play without him, leaving appropriate pauses. The buzzing was quite wild; I wondered why, since nothing had changed *that* much. The corpse was exactly where the throne was supposed to be, though, so whenever it came swinging from the flies, it balanced precariously on it, like a rocking chair.

On the way home, I noted that there were no wrecked cars at all in the streets.

Good for them.

I walked past the overgrown parking meters, to my efficiency above an Indian grocery store, and threw myself fully clothed on the bed.

At two minutes to twelve, the phone rang.

That's impossible! I thought. It rang five times and kept on ringing. *Have to reach it...* the phone call wasn't part of the time groove, I had to push really hard against the tide, the buzzing came like a beehive in my brain—I made a mad dash for the phone and picked it up—

"Hi, this is Amy, I don't know if you'll be able to talk or not but *I've made it!*"

I tried to speak, but could only force out a strained gurgle.

"I know you're there, don't strain yourself! It's okay, you see I finally figured it out, I got a whole group of people together, and then, two minutes before the accident, *everyone* struggled and struggled, and we all yanked against the time force and we managed to pull the emergency cord!

"Oh, it's been so weird. I had six hours of complete freedom, I had six whole hours to make up a whole new pattern for the next zillion years, so I walked all the way home, all 25 miles, I'm so tired—

"The time thing has been going haywire here! I don't think they've had to adjust to such a big change before. When I was walking home, people were pretending not to see me, determinedly bumping into me, looking straight through me...it's weird! John, let's meet tomorrow in—er—Times Square under the Winston-Marlboro ad, and celebrate!

"This phone call is part of the daily routine, now, I suppose. Isn't that something, now I belong to both your worlds, now we'll both have something to look forward to every night...bye, see you tomorrow," she was breathlessly trying to get everything in.

I managed to squeeze out one word: "I—"

Midnight.

12.

I was waiting for Amy under the Winston-Marlboro ad in Times Square. I'd been waiting for a week or so, I wondered why she was teasing me like this, I was getting desperate. It seemed to be August: a bright day, quite fresh and breezy, and nobody was about, which only compounded my misery....

"Hey, mister, want some dope?"

I whirled around. The voice belonged to a small boy grinning vacuously at me, dirty and cute in a bland, Brady-Bunchy sort of way.

"I really don't think so. Anyway, get off my back. What's a kid like you—"

"We-e-ell," he said in a passably inviting voice, "maybe you'd like to...fool around?"

"Sorry, kid, you're *really* barking up the wrong tree there."

"Huh? Oh, good." He didn't leave. I can't say I wasn't shocked at his brazenness, even though I'm an actor and all that. I am, in the final analysis, a country boy.

He just stood there, waiting for me to say something. I didn't see any reason to be unpleasant, so I said: "How's business?"

"Oh, dreadful. I'm really a dope pusher, see, but these days... just as I'm about to pick up a new shipment, *blam!* midnight, I get swung clear across town, that's why I'm getting desperate... say! aren't you the guy in *Hamlet*? John Petinari, that's you... wow! a real live actor!"

How could I fail to be touched? "You recognize *me*? Of all the insignificant hangers-on on Broadway?"

"Well, hell, I've been watching *Hamlet* every night for the past half a million years."

That kind of dampened it. Then he said, "Well, of course I *am* going to be an actor when I grow up. Like you," he added in a dutiful sort of voice.

"What do you think of—er—the new developments in the play?"

"Well, I tell you, having to watch it every day is no joke! You get kinda bored, see? Well, all those murders and things have spiced it up a lot. I mean, I'm not really the Shakespeare *type*. This way, at least you wonder what's going to happen next... say, you *are* John Petinari, aren't you?"

"Sure. At least I think I am."

"Can I have your autograph?"

That did it. I liked him a lot. "Do you have a pen?"

"No."

"Me neither." We looked at each other for a moment, then cracked up. "Hey, what were you doing at the theater anyway? I mean, normally, kids like you...."

"You're prejudiced against us defenseless street kids, aren't you? Well, to tell the truth... you see, my *supplier* is... the doorman at your theater...."

"Well, I never." Old Leibowitz? *Him*?

"Say, if you ever come into some dope or something, will you let me know? Supplies are really thin, see. They can only grow those plants for two hours a day, you know. Just think of me, huh? Ask any of the kids around here for me, my name's Brian Schechter."

You could have dropped a Steinway grand on my head.

"Y-y'you're *Amy's* brother?"

"You know her? What the hell's going on, anyway?" Suddenly he was a frightened kid. "You're not a cop, are you?"

"*Know* her? Why she's my—she's my—" (Well, what was she? My fiance-to-be? My girl-friend? All those labels sounded so preposterous.)

And then she was there.

My heart stopped beating.

She was so radiant, so beautiful..."Amy!" we both shouted, and I ran over to her and hugged her in two.

"God, what I've been through for the both of you," Amy said fervently. She told us everything again, how they'd yanked the cord, how the eighteen-wheeler had swerved into a barricade.

"Amy, we've made it, we've conquered them! And now we're going to live forever and ever!" I was delirious with joy, I was shaking all over, I could hardly say anything important. "Hey, let's go and get a doughnut and all celebrate...."

"Bull. They *must* have run out by now, it's been thousands of years...."

"Well, why don't we go see?"

How the sun was shining! It was shining on leaking fire hydrants with peeling graffiti on them, it was shining on old

McDonald's wrappers floating in the breeze. The Winston ad was smoking sexily into the sunshine. And the air was buzzing, soft sounds of love. And silvery curtains of aliens were swimming, undulating, so pretty, through the air...what had the Pole said? That we who were now going to live forever, we would see planets and stars and have unimaginable adventures and live through incredible times? Outer space, here we come?

I looked from one to the other.

Hell, anything can happen in New York.

I didn't care about Gail or Sir Francis FitzHenry or Horatio or Guildenstern or any of those damn aliens. They could do anything they wanted to us.

Suddenly, I had a family.

Suddenly, I wasn't lost anymore.

The human race would just have to muddle through.

—Bangkok and Arlington, 1978 and 1980

The What March?

"What? You want me to write an *Isaac Asimov's Science Fiction Magazine March?*" I said, almost dropping the telephone into the piano.

"Why not?" George Scithers asked. "After all, the *Washington Post* has one."

"Yes, but—"

"Such a march—in an arrangement for solo piano, say—could even be printed in the magazine. Readers all over the world could pull out their pianos and render it rousingly as they recall our tales of starships and alien worlds. Now, what would such a march have in it?"

"Well," I said, improvising wildly, "first there'd have to be a brilliant, heroic, fanfarish sort of a theme. Then, I suppose, an exotic, sensuous alien-princess sort of theme would come in for contrast. Then there'd be sort of an evil-is-lurking interlude followed by a dogfight in which the themes are developed, followed by a climactic recapitulation of the super-heroic theme."

"Isn't that just like, say, *Star Wars?*" said George.

"Yeah, but I'd do it all in five minutes' music. Just hypothetically, of course—"

"Hypothetical my foot. When can you deliver it?"

"Perhaps he isnt' joking, I thought for a crazy moment. "I don't know. Maybe in a couple of weeks."

That was a year ago....

To tell the truth, I had more than several qualms about writing the *Asimarch*. For one thing, it isn't in the usual run of music I write; never, to my knowledge, has the school of neo-Asian post-serialism come up with even a single march, let alone a science-fictive one. But after a while I realized the George was asking me, in effect, to try to uncover just what it is that might make a march feel science-fictional, and to produce, by way of illustration, an example of this genre.

Well, to begin with, this isn't science fiction music at all.

Music of the future probably won't be much like anything we're hearing right now, any more than today's music—from the proliferation of isms in academic modern music to the blandishments of Muzak in fast-food restaurants—is anything like a florid baroque aria for castrato and continuo, for instance. Those who say "But ah, whatever changes may come, melody, meter, and harmony will still persist," are usually suffering either from cultural chauvinism or from lack of knowledge. In Western music, the good old C major chord—to some the root of all music— was still considered a pretty horrid dissonance back in the fourteenth century, and many Indian musicians will say that Western music has no rhythm at all—however complex you may think it is, it's dull as a funeral march to them, while your ears may bend in half trying to catch the subtle distinctions between those teeny fractions of semitones that are so important to them.

Yes, but there are *cycles*, SF writers will say, and so will pop a contemporary style of music right into the middle of some weird culture. But since when has art of any period *really* resembled that of a previous one? There are no cycles as such, although there may be spirals.

The purpose of this digression was to warn you that the piece of music attached to this article isn't, in any sense, music of the future, or some kind of extrapolation. That may or may not be the subject of some later article, but not here. Instead, I have been giving some thought to something far less sublime and academic—the science fictional theme tune.

And what kind of music is that?

To answer that, I thought about the movies. I thought about the music in science fiction movies, and about its antecedents— the music in big epics of the fifties and earlier, and the music of costume adventures (they wear different costumes in the SF movies, but the plots haven't changed much) all the way back to the music of the High- and Late-Romantic composers: Wagner, Mahler, Richard Strauss in particular.

Music in movies is always conservative, but SF movie music seems particularly so. In its joyous pulpiness it harks back to sea-pirates and Roman legions, and ultimately (having suffered some dilution in the process) to valkyries and other operatic wonders.

Then there's this archetypal adventure movie theme.

It's very simple: two long notes (tonic and dominant, doh and sol if you think in those terms), a triplet, another long note:

Dah—dah—di-di-di-dah—!

Do you recognize this? Some variants of this basic pattern divide the second *dah* into two shorter notes:

Dah-dah-dum-di-di-di-dah—!

Or they may do this to the first of the *dahs:*

Dum-di-dah—di-di-di-dah—!

But the general shape is unchanged. Here we have the outline of, for instance, two of John Williams's big themes, the *Star Wars* theme and the *Superman* theme. But also themes from movies as divergent as *Lawrence of Arabia* and *Born Free.* Say this magic formula to yourself and you will instantly be transported to a soundstage in Hollywood.

Actually, in the *Star Wars* theme, John Williams rings a remarkable change on the pattern. As non-technically as I can explain it, he delays the *di-di-di* so that it falls on the beat instead of being a lead-in to the beat, and this turns the final *dah*— into a syncopation. This may sound trivial and fussy, but in its own way it is a stroke of genius, imbuing a rather familiarly patterned melody with a new kind of propulsive *oomph.*

Well, of course, any space-operatic march worth its salt had to open with some form of this archetypal theme. For some months I brooded on this, trying to come up with one that hadn't already appeared in some movie and yet would at the same time distill the essence of *all* SF movies.

Well....

In the ensuing pages you will find my solutions to the the enigma propounded to me by the Editor of this magazine. You will note that the music is dotted with footnotes: (A), (B), and so on. In a radical departure from tradition, I will now proceed to the footnotes and I suggest that you read them before rushing to your pianos.

(A) *The Fanfare.* Every march should have a nice grand fanfare, and so away we go.

(B) This passage of descending major chords is an oblique reference to the "spooky music" they used to have when the scene shifted to a starfield full of asteroids and nebulae and usually a dozen Saturns; ultimately a third-hand dilution of such music as Holst's *The Planets Suite.*

(C) *Generalized Superhero Theme.* This follows the pattern described above.

(C-1) Obligatory flattened-seventh modal harmony in opening phrase of superhero theme: cf. *Star Wars, Star Trek—The Motion Picture,* dozens of others. Inherited from the Roman epic and the Western.

(D) *Exotic Alien Princess Theme.* All right, so this is really a march, but I couldn't resist putting in one of these. If you're at that piano, don't linger romantically over this part, whatever the temptation, or you'll lose the sweep of the music; play through it in one soaring, yearning rush of tempestuous vigor. Every space opera has one of these, and for this one I went all the way back to the style of Late-Romantic opera.

(E) *Obligatory Hordes of Evil.* By time-honored tradition, "good" is represented by stalwart, major-key, diatonic themes, while "evil" must make do with twisted chord changings and tortuous chromaticisms. This theme resonates with those scenes in the old serials where the hero is tied to a stake, dangling over a pot of boiling oil, about to be sliced by a deadly atomic ray, etc. A chilling dread enters the listener's heart at this point. Note that the forces-of-evil motif is, in fact, loosely adapted from the superheroic theme. Is the villain, then, a concretization of the hero's dark side, a shadow-hero? In writing this kind of thing one should always plant a few gems for the academics to dig out, thus ensuring that one will be immortalized in some obscure journal somewhere.

(F) *Conflict!* The superhero theme returns in the minor, to be rebutted savagely by the forces-of-evil theme.

(G) The battle intensifies.

(H) *Redemption by Love.* Thoughts of the exotic princess stir in our hero's head, no doubt spurring him on to greater feats of valor.

(I) *Triumph!* The hero's theme returns in a grand recapitulation.

(J) Glancing reference to the princess—the first three notes of her theme.

(K) Distant rumbling of evil forces: the obligatory "I shall return" line that leaves room for a sequel.

(L) Final Chord.

That's it! I hope you had fun. I tried to arrange it so that a moderately gifted pianist (not a virtuoso) could handle it fairly easily. If you had trouble, practice, practice, practice!

And for the conductors among our readers, I am planning a nifty orchestral arrangement and perhaps a band arrangement too. Write to me (16 Ancell Street, Alexandria VA 22305) for details, or watch for an announcement in the letters column of this magazine....

Oh, and if you happen to be a film producer and you're doing an SF picture and need some music (not necessarily of the neo-Asian post-serialist school) you might try the same address.

The Isaac Asimov's Science Fiction Magazine March

by Somtow Sucharitkul

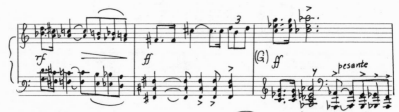

June 15, 1981

Darktouch

This story is actually only the second story I ever created in the Inquestor universe. It went through many incarnations before it finally appeared in Asimov's Magazine in January, 1980; it was a momentous event for me, my first cover story! And a cover by Stephen Fabian, too, over whose covers I had drooled as a kid.

As the Inquestor universe grew in my mind, I began to realize that these were not quite the right events for the vast future history that I was creating, however, so this story ended up in a sort of limbo. I've resurrected it for this collection, but its version of what happens to Darktouch and Davaryush is not quite the same as what will transpire in Volume III of my Inquestor trilogy...which you won't be reading for another couple of years yet, so I won't spoil it for you.

The terms were not the best.

But these were harsh times, weren't they? A war with aliens that couldn't be seen or heard. Power struggles and civil wars within the heart of the Dispersal of Man itself.

But it wasn't the prospect of the fee. Or the fatal attraction of the overcosm, that space *beyond* and *between*, where light goes wild and tantalizes you and drives you crazy with strange yearnings. Or that promise that it would only be a one-way trip in realtime, with guaranteed return by tachyon bubble, so that he would lose at most two centuries of objective time.

Kail Kirian found these conditions satisfactory. But—for an astrogator of his ability—they were not overly tempting.

No.

It was the woman Darktouch.

The face, soft and proud, the hair jet-black, the eyes dark, the skin snow-pale as though it had never seen suns' light, the single piece of clingfire that hugged her and burned against the frail whiteness—

She was all white and black, a holosculpture of monochrome projected into a colorclashing chamber, a thing from another world.

"You'll take the offer?"

"Offer...."

Where am I? This was Lalaparalla, he remembered, the planet of warriors' rest, and he was rising from *f'ang*-drenched torpor, and tongues of solvent were licking in the crusts from his eyes...the war ached in his bones still, and the *f'ang* mist rose once more to succor the deep hurt, to steep him in oblivion....

Ah yes. At the hostel. A message. "Request: for an astrogator of clan Kail, to take party of approximately fifty to destination Earth, terms negotiable. Whereto, Inquestral Seal."

Why *request*? If an Inquestral mission were involved, why not just *requisition*?

"You'll take the offer?" A hard voice.

And then he saw her eyes through the parting mist.

"Let me know more," he said, baffled. *Such eyes! There can't be a woman like this. I'm still in a drugged dream.*

And then he saw who stood behind the woman.

Tall. A shimmercloak that glowed, pink and blue, through the dense mist. Sternfaced. *Old.*

Powers of powers! he thought. *An Inquestor!*

"Yours to command," he said automatically. Kirian could hardly believe he was standing so close to one, sitting naked in a f'ang bath. And one of the rulers of the Dispersal of Man! Practically a God.

"You're mistaken," said the Inquestor, and he laughed. He didn't speak with the deep-voiced authority that Inquestors had. Somehow...his voice was *tender.* "I cannot command you. I am no longer *Ton* Davaryush, Kingling of Gallendys, but merely Davaryush without-a-Clan. I am apostate. And all these people here with me...are dreamers. Refugees. They want to secede from the Dispersal of Man."

The f'ang...it must still be clouding his senses! "You aren't real," Kirian muttered. And he mindflicked for more solvent, to wash his eyes and clear his vision. *Inquestors don't lead groups of crazies on wild-goose chases. Inquestors—*

And then he saw the woman again.

There isn't such a woman.

But the dream stood there, defying him to blink her away.

"The money's good," Davaryush said. "Three thousand in tarn-crystal carat-equivalents."

"That'll sway you, if nothing else!" the woman hissed. "Mercenary!"

What's behind this woman? I feel as if I ought to take her away from this obviously lunatic Inquestor, take her to a deserted planet and—

"I don't suppose you've ever heard of Earth," said the Inquestor. "It's an abandoned place, far beyond the worlds of the Dispersal. Our ancestors came from there once. We dream about it all the time, of building a utopia there, a perfect world."

"We don't want our children to be packed off to war at six," said the woman. "We think civilization is done for."

"The alien war out there..." Davaryush said. "Do you know how many planets they've burned? Of course not. The Inquest never reveals anything...."

Kirian did not listen. He couldn't take his eyes off the woman, and her look of contempt never abated. Not once.

"Take this woman Darktouch," Davaryush said. "She is from

Gallendys. Do you know of Gallendys?" Mist enveloped his face.

"No."

"You astrogators of the clan of Kail, you who mindlink with the delphinoid shipminds to guide the starships through the overcosm...you of all people should know. Do you really know of the delphinoid shipminds, the gigantic brains that are fused into the starships?"

"What is this?" said Kirian, uneasy. "I'm not a historian, not a philosopher. Just tell me the terms and let me decide. I'm a soldier, an overcosm flier, a man of action."

The woman laughed once, a warm laugh. Perhaps she was not solid rock to the core, then, like a dead planet.

"Listen, then,' said Davaryush. "On Gallendys there is a gigantic volcanic crater, a hundred kilometers high, a thousand across. Within is a dense atmosphere, a relic from a previous epoch...in this dark land, above the Sunless Sound, the delphinoids float. They are creatures who are all brain. They perceive the overcosm directly, without instruments. It is this power that we use to travel between the stars.

"But listen more! These delphinoids sing, Kail Kirian. Their songs are holosculptures ten kilometers across, suspended over the perpetual darkness of the Sunless Sound. They are image-songs, lightpoems woven out of overcosm visions. And a strange music too, a harmony that makes men weep, even hardened soldiers like you. Even Inquestors. For every starship that flies the overcosm, a song must die."

The mist was dying now. Davaryush's intensity touched Kirian, made him nervous. And he glimpsed other people behind, other crazies. Davaryush continued: "No human who had once seen the light on the sound, and heard the songs of the ones whose minds were turned to the space beyond our space, to the utter beauty of the overcosm...no human who had once experienced this could willingly kill a delphinoid. The Inquest understood the need for space travel. They mutated a race that was deaf and blind, and gave them a mythos and a mission, and now they live in the darkness and silence of the crater-wall caverns. And they fly out on their airships and fling their forcenets over the delphinoids and bring them home. They do not know that it is to feed the shipyards, to glorify the Dispersal of Man.

"I was Kingling of Gallendys once. This woman was a girl, a genetic throwback; she could see and hear. At puberty she joined the holy hunt, and what she saw there made her flee, half-crazed, out of the dark country to the City of Effelkang where I held power. And later she took me to see for myself. An old man and a girl, we saw the slaughter of joy. It changed us....

"We have all had these experiences. All of us."

And Kirian saw the others now, behind them: an old man; a couple of child-soldiers with laser-irises, who could have killed him with a glance and a subvocalized command; a matron; a young hermaphrodite in a whore's robe; a princeling clad in lapis and iridium; a slaveboy with a chrysanthemum branded on his forehead; a girlsinger with a whisperlyre....

They're shameless! he thought. *Look how they carry on, without regard for rank. Look how brazenly they flout the principle of degree.* The slaveboy and the princeling held hands and were close. The hermaphrodite leaned on a child-soldier's arm, defying all decency.

"You're shocking."

"Don't criticize," said Darktouch coldly. "Just take the money and help us."

The Inquestor motioned her to be quiet. With such a strange gentleness...."We are giving up anger. Remember that." With the same voice he said to Kirian: "We have all been through such experiences as Darktouch has. We have all turned our backs on the Dispersal. I say this so that you may see why I, an Inquestor, a former Kingling, a hunter of utopias once...have come begging to you."

Kirian was profoundly shocked. Only once before in his life—

And then he mouthed his deepest fear. "This Earth. Is the route well mapped? Are there any anomalies in spacetime, any tachyon whirlpools...?"

"None are known to exist," said Davaryush. "And moreover, I have been able to requisition power enough for one tachyon bubble. When you have delivered us to Earth, you may use it to return to your homeworld."

Powers of powers! "You must have been a very important man," said Kirian, wondering at how low the Inquestor had fallen....

For the tachyon bubble's secret was known only to the Inquest. They were bubbles of realspace, held together by phenomenal power expenditure—the deaths of suns, it was sometimes said—that smashed their way through planes even higher than the overcosm, traveling instantaneously.... If Davaryush could really supply such a thing, Kirian's travel time would be halved, the problems of time dilation would not be nearly so bad.

Not that he cared about time dilation. Only a loner could be an astrogator: how could a sociable person stand it. coming home after ever trip to find his friends grown old, dead?

"If it weren't for traveling with you lunatics," he said, "I wouldn't even hesitate."

The slaveboy and the princeling had moved closer to each other for reassurance, had their arms around each other's shoulders...intolerable!

Darktouch cried, "I told you, Daavye!" And Kirian cringed, that a clanless woman should dare to call an Inquestor by a diminutive. "He's a mercenary, and for what *we* want we'll never be able to pay him. We're trampling on all he believes in. He's a cog in a machine, a rat in a maze, and he'll never know it...."

"Hold it!" Kirian said.

She turned back to look at him. The mist had parted, and she was so *real* that no overdose of *f'ang* could have created her. He wanted to touch her so badly it hurt him...but he could not even reach out. The rift between them was complete. It was not her remoteness (he sensed it was insecurity as much as anything); not her beauty. But the fact that she would not acknowledge him as a person, only as a type. Was there a brittleness behind her scorn?

Davaryush was saying, "It has to be Earth. Because it is so far away from people's minds, so that they will not search us out and kill us. And because it is the source, the place of beginning, a potent symbol out of the farthest past there can have been...."

"Don't go on talking," said Darktouch. "It's just wind to him, just noise." She was bitter; how many astrogators had they tried?

"I haven't said no yet, have I?" he said, feigning toughness.

They all edged forward like one man—

He heard their unison intake of breath; he saw the woman and the Inquestor exchange a quick look that shut him out of their topsy-turvy world and their crazy philosophy—

And felt naked, suddenly.

* * *

It was a routine journey at first.

The passengers had all opted for stasis; they would only awake on Earth. Except for Davaryush—and he was an Inquestor, who must always lead, even if dethroned—and Darktouch. That he couldn't understand. Six months subjective, in the overcosm—but he brushed her from his mind.

Or tried to.

He reclined in the small room. Circular mirror walls gleamed around him. He was shielded. He was at the ship's heart. He closed his eyes and reached out with brain-implanted sensors. It was second nature; he had been doing it since puberty.

The delphinoid shipmind came alive, moving like an ocean in darkness. The sensation was soft, familiar. Endless darkness cushions swam by. He knew the ship was easing from its orbital anchor. But he saw nothing. He was alone in the room. It was so still. . . .

(What's it like, to be born in the dark country of Gallendys, to see the imagesongs of the delphinoids, and not to have words to protest, to understand? And how can something be so beautiful that you can't bring yourself to kill it? Killing was second nature to him, like touching the delphinoid shipmind. *If commanded to, could I have killed the woman Darktouch?0*

Kirian was no thinker. Thinking was for Inquestors. You couldn't afford to think. . . .

The delphinoid's warmth enveloped him.

Then a voice, tugging at the bottom of his mind—

Do you hear?

(An untried delphinoid. He would have to coax it, firmly, onto the right flight plan.)

I hear you, he mindwhispered. *Are you ready?*

I'm afraid. This route is poorly charged. . . .

Be still, be still, he mindspoke, as though to a pet animal. But he was frightened too.

There was always the split second of blinding terror that would come upon him, seconds before bursting into the *other* space where space and time go mad. A memory would come to him, a nightmare—

On his first war mission. He was seven years old. A newboy. Anyone could have ordered his death. A hundred starships packed into a shieldsphere, charging through the overcosm; and he was alone on a deck with the walls deopaqued and the overcosm light raging, and alarms blaring and sirens screeching and he was so alone, and—

One by one. The ships falling into darkness.

So strangely beautiful. . . .

They flew into gold-tinged scarlet nets of flame, vanished, a ship at a time, like beads of a cut necklace, slipping one by one into water.

And after, in another chamber, stripped and lined up and black mourning cloaks thrust over their shoulders, all the children standing stiff and frightened while the Inquestors paced and raged. Huge reflections of their shimmercloaks flapping, blushing the mirrorsilver walls. . . .

227

What's happened to the other ships?

Not looking at the other children. Obeying or dying.

"It was a tachyon whirlpool."

The Inquestor's voice rasping above his head. And Kirian could almost touch the silence. More pacing, and the floor humming eerily as the Inquestor's fursoles rubbed and whispered. A child burst out crying. He clenched his eyes. The boy would be returned to homeworld in disgrace. Impassive. Make your face impassive.

Another Inquestor's voice: "Never forget this experience until the day you die! Tachyon whirlpools were made by man. During the first experiments in tachyon travel there were foolish errors. A thing that travels faster than light, like a tachyon, must have a negative timeflow relative to our universe! And the first experimenters were hurled into the past, twisting the local continuum, wrenching causality apart. And even now these tachyon whirlpools remain, symbols of their lust for knowledge! Repeat this! It is good that only the Inquest knows the secret of tachyon travel."

Unison chorus: *It is good that only the Inquest knows the secret of tachyon travel.*

"It is evil to question nature. Only the Inquest is wise."

It is evil—

Theirs was the only ship to survive.

And later they burst into realspace in the region of the star Keima, and they obliterated the planet Zelterkangh. It had been a simple punitive expedition, nothing a single starship couldn't handle....

The terror lived again for a moment in the ship's darkness. Even after twenty years. More vividly this time than the other times....

So it isn't a perfect universe. That much my lunatics have gotten right. But they're wrong to run away from it. They shouldn't question the way things are. Man is a fallen being after all, he thought.

Quickly he returned the memory to its cage.

You can't hurt me, he lied to himself.

The nightmare beat at the cage bars. This time it came mingled with the eyes of the woman Darktouch. He beat it back. And the darkness of the shipmind did take him, eventually, but not before he had gazed into the strange woman's eyes for a long time, puzzling himself....

* * *

Some weeks later, he broke free from the shipmind and staggered up to the observatory.

She was alone there. All the walls were deopaqued. They stood on the metallic floordisk, floating in—

The overcosm raged. Oppressing him. No escape from it.

And she was a silhouette gazing out, not moving. Even her clingfire garment was muted by comparison with it. She didn't acknowledge him, only stared out at the—

—vermilion hurricanes spattering whitepeaked wavecrests, the ochre lightpeaks tumbling, crumbling over blindingwhite Catherinewheel firevolleys—

"You mustn't expose yourself to the overcosm too long." She flinched from the words, startled. "You'll stare your eyes into cinders." He went on, not liking the silence, "People have gone mad, you know, from being unable to cope with the torrent of sensations—"

"It's beautiful." She turned her back on him.

—geysers of green flame gushing through scarlet walls, veils that ripped to reveal more veils—

"It's just nothing, just mass hallucinations, because we can't understand what we perceive." Damn it, why did she ignore him? "You spend all our interstellar trips like this?"

"Always. I am afraid of stasis." She was frail in the colorstorm.

"They're just lights."

"The world the delphinoids see, Kirian. Isn't it strange?" She turned and watched him; he wanted her then, and despised her too, and could think of nothing to say.

Finally he said, "You're so full of words. As though words could save the universe. Like this utopia of yours...more words."

"You poor mercenary...."

"Don't pity me! You reject reality, you dream hopeless dreams—"

"Of love, brotherhood, things like that...." She began to explain it all to him, and it was like a child's wishful thinkings, impractical, destructive. "Oh. I see you're not impressed. How could you be? They've lied to you so much you couldn't recognize a truth to save your own skin."

"To be so sure of something...." he said. He saw how her eyes shone, how she seemed to be looking straight through him, to some world she and the others had made up. "You're not perfect either," he said brusquely.

"Of course not! But—"

"Oh, you're so proud. You see not what I am, but what I'm

supposed to be like in your eyes, and—"

She turned away sullenly. No, she was no angel.

—volcanohearts twisted inside out, lightfeathers fluffed out of prismpools fracturing into mosaics—

"Why shouldn't I hate your kind?" she burst out. "Don't you know how you make the delphinods suffer, how every moment of their lives from the moment they are mindsoldered into the ships is spent in excruciating agony, how you force them to live when they can't sing, which is agony beyond your understanding?"

"Intellectually one knows—"

"Every parsec we've advanced across the Dispersal of Man has given unconscionable agony to a sentient creature! How can you live with that? How can we all live with that? If you can live with it, you must be—"

It was true. But it had always been the way. There were no alternatives.

In the end he said, "Are the imagesongs even more beautiful than this?"

Not looking at him, she said, "Of course. They are art, and this, though beautiful too, is random lightnoise...."

She's the first woman ever to despise me! I'm not a rôle, I'm a human being! he thought. And she was so still. Like a holo-sculpture in a museum: untouchable.

You're proud, so proud it goes against all your fine talk about love and brotherhood. You're hypocritical as the rest of us.

Above them, the firestorm stretched to forever. Behind the stormshards, past the colorclouds, pale sinuous snakes of light darted from dark to dark.

And he was jealous of the certainty for which Darktouch had given up the whole galaxy. And jealous of the lunatics who had stolen her from him....

So he fled and sought the comfort of the shipmind's darkness, and drew the darkness over his thoughts as a child retreats into a blanket heavy with familiar smells, retreats from the fear of night.

He even welcomed the recurring nightmare of the tachyon whirlpool...that at least was familiar.

* * *

Many months later, from out of the darkness—

—he burst blind through terror that didn't belong there at all, his mind screaming burning ANOMALY ANOMALY against the relentless logic of the shipmind, and he was crushed into

darkness within darkness screaming falling burning ANOM-
ALY ANOMALY—

(Memory: a hundred ships dropping into the net of flame.)

"Cut the connection!"

(Memory: alone on deck with the sirens bawling.)

The shipmind said, *Kail Kirian, we have navigated safely
past the tachyon whirlpool.* A toneless internal whisper.

"Identify the anomaly," he said, "for the last time."

It is a tachyon whirlpool, Kirian. What else can I say?

(A f'ang dream?) "If that's true, we're off course."

No.

"Yes! This should be the vicinity of Earth, and the failed
tachyon experiments were millenia after the first Dispersal from
Firstworld!"

*I understand this. I understand the unlikelihood. Neverthe-
less, what I sense I sense.*

"How can there be whirlpools in this uninhabited, abandoned sector? You're malfunctioning—"

No.

Kirian broke the connection finally. And passed through the
forcecurtain to the observatory. She was still there; it was almost
as though minutes, not months, had elapsed.

—firebubbles foamed through lacelightcurtains lanced by
liquid lightnings—

The old man was there too. His shimmercloak blushed softly
against the patches of night.

Darktouch turned around.

He gaped at her. The light from the overcosm haloed over her
face, the hair flowed dark and free, the clingfire kissed her slight
body. He couldn't speak.

"Well?" Davaryush said. "We felt...disturbance."

"Tachyon whirlpool." *Mustn't sound frightened. Mustn't
give anything away!*

"That's—" said Darktouch.

"I know! I know it's impossible!"

The Inquestor merely said, "Will it delay us much?"

Is that all they can think about, their fool mission?
And Darktouch moved closer to him, and his desire embarrassed him. "Not long."

"Good," she said. Fanatic eyes, shining....

"I don't share your dream," he said angrily. "I just want to get
to the bottom of this anomaly."

"Mercenary!"

"You should go into stasis!" he shouted. "The strain's getting to you—"

"Darktouch," the Inquestor interrupted, "scorn, hate, all the things we are giving up."

She subsided. Behind her, the lightveils parted—

——kaleidoscoped, dissolved—

Darkness fell without warning.

"WHAT HAVE YOU DONE?" he shouted.

Another whirlpool! said the ship. The mind connections closed all around him, the darkness breathed on him, mathematical figures danced and wavered in his head—

* * *

Afterwards, they burst out of the overcosm into a blackness of new stars. One in particular, a yellow dwarf of no importance. Realspace was dull compared with the overcosm, so Kirian stayed in his wombchamber, assessing the damage. It was bad, very bad.

The utopians didn't have a chance.

The stasis-pod life-support systems had been thrown into dysfunction. They were all dead: the princeling, the slaveboy, the girl with the lyre, the hermaphrodite, all of them with their hope-fired eyes and their false, poignant dreams....

The tachyon bubble system was dead too. He would have to use the delphinoid to return home. He would lose four centuries to time dilation, not two.

Before he went to the observatory he opaqued the walls. He felt more comfortable between the gray walls....

"You have to go back."

They looked blankly at him. They could have been holosculptures of the dead.

"Look, the last tachyon whirlpool—it wiped out all your chances. Even though I still can't believe it was there at all. The dormant passengers are permanently dead. You can't create a viable colony. You can't ever propagate the species—you must be over three hundred years old, Davaryush."

"Four hundred and twelve."

He felt a sudden compassion for their shattered dream. But pushed it aside. "The shipmind can think us home readily enough," he said. "It's learned where the two anomalies are...."

"No!" said Darktouch. "Not while we still have one male left—" And she glanced at Kirian, hostile.

Oh no! I desire her, but not like this—

"Now wait!" he said angrily. "I'm no head-in-the-clouds

utopian like you and the Inquestor. I *know* where I belong. I've finished my part of the bargain. You've failed, and I'm sorry for you, and I can take you home at no extra charge. I can't leave an old man and a woman to fend for themselves on a dead planet—"

"Never! Not after the agony the delphinoid has been through to bring us here!" cried Darktouch, trembling. "We vowed to let it die, to free it from its shipbonds!"

He saw that she was assessing him now, as genetic material, as a piece of meat, a pawn in her utopia. . . . He wanted to help her so badly, in spite of her hate. She couldn't want to stay. It was beyond all reason, even a fanatic's.

"I want to go back to what I know," he said.

"With the war and the civil war," said Davaryush, "I think it's rather an ambiguous question as to whether there will *be* a Dispersal to return to. . . ."

I can't accept that! "No!"

"All right," said Darktouch calmly. "We'll land on Earth. Then you can impregnate me and leave. You do desire me, don't you? I am beautiful, aren't I?" And then she began to weep, terrible, hysterically.

But he was afraid to comfort her.

"Delphinoids don't make mistakes. . . ." he said.

"Don't speak of delphinoids again!" she screamed.

"It will pass," said the Inquestor gently. "You will never understand what she has suffered on Gallendys. . . ."

"Blank out the walls!" she cried out. "I want to see Earth! I want to see the dream!"

Abruptly the starstream burned in darkness behind her. She turned and stared out at the tiny yellow disk. He tried to put his arms around her, but she was like a statue.

"Remember the delphinoid's pain," she said quietly. Her eyes said, *Animal!*

Davaryush's voice came from behind them: "You see the desperation that drove us, Kail Kirian. You *must* let us down on Earth; and then, if you choose to go, we will at least die on the ground that made us, on the planet untouched by the Inquest. . . ."

And he was moved, in spite of himself.

The inconvenience of it! He longed to be in battle where he belonged. Here they were as far from the center of things as it was possible to be, as far as the very primordial beginnings of Man. Even the stars were thin here, in this wisp of galactic arm; it was a bleak and desolate sky. Cold touched his spine.

"Very well," he heard himself say. "I'll land you there, then ship back to homeworld. Even though abandoning you goes against my conscience."

"Oh," said Darktouch, mocking him, "do you have one?"

But she thanked him with her eyes.

I cannot touch her, he thought, *while she still hates me. But perhaps I can find a way....*

"Look, Earth," said Davaryush.

They smiled, both of them, falling into their dream. *How could they smile when there was no hope? How could they—*

Earth hung in the blackness: opalescent, white-blue, beautiful, dead.

* * *

Desert. Rocky desert, hilly desert, dunedeserts, deserts of blasted glass that might have been cities fused together in some cataclysm...harsh polar caps made ice deserts. Millennia before, men had done a good job of killing Earth....

In the north of one of the great landmasses they found thin grass-fields, yellow-gray and stubblestrewn, and the lander settled on a hill-fringed plain where a brook ran to merge beyond the horizon with a shallow river. The lander sprouted wheels—Kirian realized with a shock that here they could not travel from place to place by displacement plates—and waited.

The three of them stood by the stream. Why, they didn't even know how to set up a camp or forage for food, thought Kirian, any of the skills that a Kail learned from childhood.

"I'd better help you find food," he said, avoiding their eyes. But they were watching their new planet, enraptured.

Food they found readily enough. On the foothills were fruit trees with reddish round fruit and soft yellow meat; and curious, fearless fish fairly leapt into their forcenets from the brook.

They'll live an idyllic life, thought Kirian, *without my help. Until they die.*

He didn't want to admit that he feared the four-hundred-year time dilation and the tachyon whirlpools that didn't belong...*I mustn't leave in unseemly haste,* he thought.

The next day they went exploring. They climbed the hills easily. Davaryush followed on a floater because of his age and because the gravity was a shade higher than he was used to.

Darktouch was silent the first few hours.

He would look at her when she didn't know he was looking and see her somehow at peace. She no longer groomed her hair, so it streamed free in the wind; the clingfire garment was worn threadbare. It gave off no fire but a pearly rainbow. She belonged here.

The ground was soft, yielding to his feet. It was a strange sensation, quite unlike the continual disruptions of displacement plates.

It would take days, months, to explore the world. But from what they could see around them it was truly dead. Twenty millennia had rubbed the planet smooth. They saw no sunken cathedrals such as the sand acropolises of war-torn Kellendrang, no mile-high husks of skyscrapers such as bestrode the fire-snowed horizons of Ont....

At the summit he said, awkwardly, "I wish there was not this gulf between us."

"I pity you, Kail Kirian," she said, avoiding his eyes. "You belong to the old things, cruel and senseless. You've no pride in yourself—otherwise why would you have come here for mere money? If you could only see things as they are—"

"If only *you* could!" he retorted. "You're just as hypocritical as the rest of the human race. You took my help, didn't you? Help in running away. You're cowards. Running away—to die!"

They glared at each other. Her hair blew across her face—

How softly she glows, he thought, *against the strange yellow light of this sun.*

Davaryush, ahead of them, called out. Kirian eased himself over the hillcrest and rested his elbows on a flat boulder, and his field of vision telescoped abruptly to an endless brown plain spattered with smooth sand-carved rockshapes like sculpted bushes. Half-way to the horizon was a forest of brown trees... trees?

"What are they?" he said.

"Let's go and see," Darktouch answered. He felt an unbecoming curiosity in himself for a moment. "Well, don't you want to find out? Why, they look almost like...people, those trees."

"It's too far to walk," he said, and summoned two more floaters with a flick of his mind.

They rode the breeze, the two of them, down through the desert. It was so far...sand stretched until distance meant nothing any more. And the wind-etched sandstone sculptures... they were huge, bigger even than the delphinoid that orbited above them, waiting.

They were dwarfed by this one plain. And the thought that the huge world stretched around them forever. Kirian felt lonely. From ground level they could not see their objective at all, so they floated blindly, trusting the floater settings.

And then there were—

People.

Kirian stepped gingerly off his floater. He practically walked into a man. The man was quite cold and he didn't move.

There were other men standing nearby. Farther off, some women. Many were naked. These had on nothing but a blue strap around their wrists. Others had clothes. Clingfire was one of the fabrics, but the fire was frozen. Others were in fantastical costumes, headdresses with pointed layers, extravagant codpieces.

They didn't move.

"What *is* this?" Kirian felt panic. "First the tachyon whirl-pools, now this—holosculpture museum, on a planet with no people. This is the wrong planet!"

"Delphinoids don't lie," Davaryush mocked him, gently.

"You don't like mysteries, do you, mercenary?" said Dark-touch and smiled a hard smile.

"No, I don't," said Kirian. "I like answers! We've got to get back now if we can. Obviously we had a warped shipmind and we're somewhere quite different from where we set out for. Maybe you plan to die here, but *I'm* leaving."

"Coward!" Darktouch shouted.

"I'm no coward! I've killed more men than you've ever seen! But I'm going to go back to what I *do* understand."

The statues never moved. He slammed his fist hard on a woman's shoulder; it was harder than a starship's hull.

"You're all alike," said Darktouch bitterly. "You want no mysteries. You've no pride in being humans. Inside, you hate youselves!"

Her anger sounded small on the huge plain. Kirian looked around him. Perhaps a thousand humans, frozen hard and seemingly indestructible. Children, too. He touched a child near him; red-haired, the hair tousled but stiff as metal.

Red hair, like mine, he thought. The thought irritated him, obscurely...something oddly familiar about the child...he stared at the unseeing eyes.

He *did* want to know what they were.

Maybe there's no harm in asking one question....

"All right," he said. "I'll stay a few days more. We can run tests on the statues. Maybe this is a hall of fame, an ancient artifact, an Inquestral plot, a cunning mirage.... When we've found the answer I'll leave."

And he surprised himself, that he was able to wonder.... Were they humans somehow frozen out of time? Or imitations of humans, bait laid by some alien?

236

And why do they seem so familiar?

Afterwards he closed his eyes and used the delphinoid—whose orbit matched their position, monitoring them constantly—to move the landing craft to the edge of the forest of statues and set up the shelters.

But he found that the order to the delphinoid was not a simple reflex as it had always been; for the first time, a thought nagged at him:

This ship is in agony, and cannot die.

* * *

He woke to the dawn. The sands had shifted; the statues had not moved at all, and some were now knee-deep in litte dunes.

The dawn—here it was like pink feathers of a pteratyger, speared and brought down over the gray sea on Keneg, Kirian's homeworld. The image chilled him; he did not think he could still be homesick.

This planet did have a magic then...it was the primal homeworld.

He shut the shelter door and approached the nearest statue. For they must be statues, if they didn't move—statues from a time of primitive technology that had stood the ravages of twenty millennia. Impossible.

He and Darktouch worked on the statues that morning. They wanted to saw off a piece—part of a garment, they had decided, just in case the statues were real people—and they were trying an old man's white tunic. A pretty tableau watched them, a young woman and two boys all in white. Their metal tools all broke on the cloth. It never gave so much as a micron, from what their instruments could tell them.

In one of the pauses she said to him: "Did you ever figure out why the tachyon whirlpools were there?"

"I suppose our history is wrong. The Dispersal of Man is too large for full records, perhaps. The abortive experiments were so long ago, and—"

"But the whirlpools are anomalies in space and time, aren't they? So they could be experimenters in the future?"

"Rather hypothetical, considering your sort think the future is pretty much done for."

"You've no imagination. What could I have expected." But the insult was automatic, not laced with spite as it might have been two days before. They worked on without talking.

It was hard to take his eyes off her. Long crimson-tinged

237

shadows crossed her face.... *If I don't leave, immediately, I'll...fall in love with her.* And the thought was like pain.

After the laser device had failed to chisel off a piece of the man's clothing, they rested, leaning against the hard statues. A light wind sprang up, sprinkling them with sand.

"You've never had any experience," Darktouch said, "to make you doubt the universe you were taught to believe in?"

"No."

—but there were the hundred ships falling into the tachyon whirlpool—

"Not even war?"

"War is necessary! It keeps the children occupied, it purifies the human instincts, it keeps down the population...."

—I blasted one of the revivified corpses over and over and still he came barreling towards me. I blew off his head and he collapsed a centimeter from my face...my first kill—

"You don't believe that."

"The Inquest told me!"

—and the headless torso of the kindled corpse, still groping towards me across the starship's silver floor, struggling without a mind, and me striking it over and over in my nine-year-old passion, yelling hot anger from my heart—

Kirian was in tears, suddenly.

—and the hundred starships falling—

—and after, on leave, going to Alykh, the pleasure planet, riding the varigrav coasters until we were drunk with giddiness, and then on to the oblivion of fang and Lalaparalla...and then another war and another—

He didn't want to think of himself. He didn't know who he was, anymore. "Why are you called Darktouch," he said, "in the hightongue, and not a pretty name from an archaic language?"

"Because," she said, "in the dark crater over the Sunless Sound there are no names. People speak with their hands. I did not know I could have a name, until I went on my first hunt and saw and heard....

"They're not delphinoids to us, they're—" she did a finger-dance across his palm then. "Huge, sleek, streamlined creatures that are all brain. They talk by drawing patterns of light in the dark air above the Sound. And they leap and soar and sing, they sing!

"We had netted one and were towing him home in the airship. Their bodies were twined around each other, singing of victory. And then he began to sing. The lightstrands tore the air apart. It was pure tragedy...of course you have to be deaf and blind to hunt them! At lightsend I ran away, crawling through the hidden tunnels till I reached the lightworld, struggling across the badlands of Zhnefftikak until I reached the city where men could see and hear, Effelkang...."

Kirian turned his back on her and began to laser the man's tunic again. "I'm not responsible for the sins of the Inquest," he said. "You're just trying to make me feel guilty so I'll stay here and join with you in a loveless breeding plan and make your project come true...."

"No!"

But he *was* feeling guilty.

"Look," he said at last, "they all have these blue bracelets in common...maybe if we lasered a bracelet."

By noon there was still no result. By then Kirian felt an overpowering need to find the answer to the riddle.

"How about this one?" He indicated a boy standing behind the old man. "His bracelet seems a little askew."

A red-haired boy, that odd familiar look, unnerving somehow...Kirian tugged at the bracelet.

The boy sprang to life. "Where is this?" he shrieked, looking wildly around him. "Where's the space station?"

Darktouch was beside him quickly, trying to calm him.

"What?" said Kirian. "He speaks the hightongue?" They took the boy to the shelter, kicking, screaming, and biting all the way.

* * *

The shelter: a circular silver wall around them. Like a room on the starship.

The boy: eleven or twelve. The age of a young warrior of the Dispersal. That familiar look—Kirian could almost put his finger on it. But no....

"Who are you?" he demanded.

The boy shrank back, still defiant. He tried to break free of the tranquilizer field—

"Let me out of here! This is the wrong planet I guess; there's no space station, and I didn't fasten my stasis bracelet tight enough—"

He stopped. He looked into Kirian's face. And then he said, "I'm dreaming." And then he smiled. The smile made Kirian uneasier than ever.

And then Davaryush smiled too. And Darktouch. They were all smiling, threatening Kirian with some secret knowledge—

"I'm getting out of here!" he said, trapped. "I'm calling the delphinoid now—"

The fear was gone from the boy. He looked at Kirian with a strange reverence...almost as if Kirian were some prince, some Inquestor even. "I'm not afraid now," the boy said. "This is the dawn time; I understand that I've accidentally triggered the bracelet thing by tying it wrong on Sirius. What a stroke of luck I've found you! Now you can do it up properly for me and bundle me off to the station and I can get home. Right?"

Kirian released the tranquilizer field. "Tell me what's happening, someone?" he said desperately.

The boy laughed, a silvery laugh that somehow made his throat catch..."Ha! Well...I guess you really wouldn't know. Would you? Davaryush, Darktouch, and Kirian?"

"Now, answers," Kirian said tightly. The boy had known his name. What next?

"Be gentle," said Darktouch. She moved closer to Kirian, and their hands touched and were warm together. "Where are you from?"

"Sirius."

"Where—?" Kirian said.

"It's a colony. My parents sent me back to Earth to go to school."

"To this empty planet?" said Kirian, more and more bewildered.

"Well, it *is* the dawn time. The stasis field—"

"All right," said Davaryush. The boy turned and stared at him, huge-eyed. "You recognize us."

The boy nodded slowly.

"So you must be from the future, from a time when Earth is populated again, with a colony or two even."

He nodded again.

"We're a little simple," Davaryush said, "to sophisticated people from the future like you. So why don't you tell us in easy language, what's happened, what you're doing here...."

"Simple!" the boy blurted out, awestruck. "*You* of all people, Davaryush, *you*, how can you possibly say that?" And he seemed moved.

"I'm old," Davaryush said; and Kirian saw that his face was not tired the way old men's faces are; it was aglow with wonder.

"If I tell you everything," said the boy, "will you take me back to the space station and do up my bracelet properly?"

"Of course."

"Well then—"

Kirian could not forget the story.

240

More than a thousand years ago, the fathers had come, fleeing an intolerable world: Davaryush, Kirian, Darktouch. Men filled the whole galaxy; but great wars decimated them, and broke the web of power that the Inquest had spun over the million worlds of the Dispersal of Man....

Davaryush and Darktouch and Kirian came with their dream of a new humanity. They came and rekindled the Earth.

There were great secrets of science in the old days. Men knew how to compress a fragment of spacetime into a tachyon bubble, and send it flying instantaneously through space.... It was a lost secret. The children of the utopians did not recover all the knowledge of the past. But they felt a longing for the stars, a longing common to all men. A way was found, without the tremendous energy of tachyon bubbles. Men were sent through space through the tachyon universe, with its negative time-flow, in a time-stasis shield which locked the traveler into the moment of his departure, preventing time paradoxes until reality could recapitulate to the same moment....

The plain of statues was a gigantic space station, a harbor. But its walls and its machinery were not built yet, nor was the huge town of Kirian-Angkar beside the station. One day the domes would come, and the towers of a great city.

How had they known they would succeed? How had they picked the site of the space station? It was easy. For they had grown up seeing the passengers standing in the sand, in their millennial sleep....

And how had the earliest people known who the travellers were? There was a legend of a young boy with his stasis-bracelet askew, who had accidentally awoken in the dawn time and spoken with the ancestors....

* * *

I'm the boy!" the boy was shouting. "And to think my parents named me after the boy in the myth...."

Davaryush said, thoughtfully: "Science is strange. We had the technology to do all this in our own civilization. But it never occurred to them to use tachyon travel for mass journeys... because above all, the Inquest wanted power, exclusive power, over the Dispersal of Man. We didn't have tachyon travel for everyone because the Inquest could not bear to give up one iota of its terrible power!"

241

Darktouch added: "The rules of the universe don't change. But the uses to which they're put...our children *did* learn—*will* learn—from our dream, Davaryush! To work for the good of all. Our hopeless dreams of freedom and love—are vindicated, Kail Kirian!"

It was too much for Kirian to take. *Got to get home....*

"You'll stay now, Kirian," said Darktouch.

"I can't, I can't!" He blacked out desperately and groped for the shipmind in the sky. *Homeworld! I want homeworld!*

And the three of them were laughing, roaring with laughter—"You're staying, Kirian. Not a doubt of it," said Davaryush.

"Of course not! You must have tricked me...."

The silver walls returned to his vision.

"Tricked you, Kirian?" said Darktouch. "Just look at the boy, Kirian, just look at the boy!"

And he did.

The boy. Standing against the wall. A redhead with unkempt hair, a slight, insignificant sort of boy...there were a million boys like him, scrabbling in the ruins of burnt cities, hawking sweets in the bazaars of Alykh, staring wide-eyed at the delphinoid starships that streaked across the night skies of their homeworlds... he saw nothing remarkable.

Until he saw his own face, reflected in the wall beside the boy's. Distorted by the wall-curve, and yet so alike....

"You're my...I mean, I'm your—"

"Forefather," the boy whispered, and knelt down to kiss his hand. As though he were a visiting Inquestor....

He trembled with pride. Then he raised the child up and gazed at the face until he could see, behind the features that mimicked his own, traces of Darktouch's face, too.

Darktouch, who had despised him, who had accused him of hating himself, of being without pride, of being senseless and meaningless and cruel...but he knew now how to make her love him.

And thought of the delphinoid, orbiting above them, in its terrible pain.

* * *

Darkness. A terrible loneliness.

Kirian's mind was blank, joined to the shipmind. The darkness pressed against him, waiting.

"Shipmind," he called softly, "what is it you really feel? Can you not share it with me?"

And he felt pain. Like nails being driven into his head, over and over, into his spine, into his bones, his body rolling in a barrel of nails, pain beating burning blasting bursting him and more nails driving driving into him everywhere and screaming until he could never stop screaming until he screamed himself into silence—

Nails nails nails nails nails—

And behind the pain, a still grief. The grief of the Sunless Sound whispering under the hunters' airships. The grief of lost songs. Of unborn torrents of light in the thick dark sky. And Kirian wept until he was beyond tears—

Nails nails nails—

And pity behind the grief. Pity for a being so pitiless it could torture a sentient creature. Compassion for him.

Kirian's mind whispered, "Shipmind, I'm sorry. I knew, but I tried not to know. Go free now."

He awoke to night. Darktouch was standing by the shelter under the strange thin starlight. He came to her....

"I freed the shipmind," he said. "I think he's going to die now."

Darktouch said, "I tried to hate you so much! Because all soldiers were supposed to be mindless automata, slaves of the Inquest! But you do have compassion after all...."

"Glimpsing the future has changed so much."

They were silent. The air was heavy with the tension of beginning relationships.

He said, suddenly, "I can't believe that everything I believe in, out there, is coming to an end!"

"We don't know."

"Maybe our children will burst out into the galaxy again. And find the worlds of the Inquestors. And heal the wounds, maybe."

She smiled at him in the alien moonlight. There was a moment of fierce, burning pride.

Then—

"Look!" she cried suddenly—

His eyes followed the curve of her arm, up into the blackness. A meteor flashed. Fireworks. The sand glittered silver for a moment. The hills glowed and faded.

"It's the ship," he said. "It's the past, burning up as it hits the atmosphere."

"Happy?"

"I suppose so...."   The moon hid in a cloud, and in the darkness the only light was the cold clingfire of her dress.

We'll have to make our own warmth.

They pressed closer together. Ahead, the plain was full of their unborn children, waiting to be created.

They held each other close, not only for the warmth now. The first step into the future waited to be taken. And then they took it.

The first step was a kiss, an embrace, an act of love.

Coaster Time

Here's another roller coaster story. It is interesting perhaps to compare this to The Thirteenth Utopia, elsewhere in this volume, another treatment of the eternal roller coaster situation. I often get my ideas while sitting on roller coasters.

My relationship with Trina had begun to settle...like a fly on the head of a dime-store Indian. I was restless and I could see what was coming. Dawn would find me half-heartedly humping her, when suddenly across the gulf of my closed eyes would come the warm and the chill, the darkness roaring, and I'd want to slough off my body as it clanked like a dead machine. And I'd know it was summer, coaster time.

Twelve different suburbs of twelve different cities. Twelve women: white, black, blotchy, dumpy, willowy, brim-bursty... Trina was the beautiful one. Three summers I'd resisted the urge. Because I almost loved her. Twelve tree-lined shady streets. Twelve sets of prefabricated kids. Trina's I'd almost loved.

I sprang from the bed. She murmured something. "I'm going," I said softly.

She was wide awake now. Wind rippled the drapes behind her, dazzle-drenched beige. "I've been expecting it, Jack." No rancor at all; Trina alone of the twelve might have understood me. "Don't wake the kids." She was deathly calm.

"I—"

Her eyes were tight shut against the brightness. Black hair muzzled her and curlicued the floral bedspread, weaving the sunsmears to the shadow. I ached. Did she hear it too, in her own way? I tiptoed out, closing my eyes and hearing only the roaring darkness.

On the street stood the van, all I'd come with, waxed and cherry red. On the doors in back was painted a secret symbol that only coaster people know. As I pulled away the past melted from me, and as I hit the freeway I began to sing.

A ways past Woodbridge I picked up a girl hitching. But it wasn't one of us.

"Coaster time?" I said. She smiled pertly, vacuously. "Oh, you don't know what I mean. But I thought you gave the sign, out there."

246

"My nose was itching." She shot me an are-you-one-of-those maniacs look.

"No, I mean—" I took my hands off the wheel and did the ritual signal of the coaster people.

"Huh? Oh, saw a bunch of weirdoes doing that on 95 and the beltway. New fad?"

"Get out."

"You creep!"

I screeched onto the shoulder. "You're making fun of me, girl, mocking our secrets. I don't care to ride with you." I pushed her off and peeled out, my mind roaring with the roller coaster in King's Dominion, eighty miles down the pike.

I shouldn't have. But she'd scared me, a stranger flashing our greeting on the road. Maybe something had changed with the coaster people.

Shit, Jacko, I thought, you haven't hit the coaster trail in three years. Maybe there isn't even a coaster trail anymore. But I knew that couldn't be true. Come summer there will always be people who take the twisted circle across the country, living only for the big ones: Rebel Yell, Scream Machine, Python, King Corkscrew, Terror Tunnel. We're the people who hear the roaring darkness, whose winter dreams are of forever falling. I brushed off my unease and drove on recklessly; perhaps I could be the very first at the gate when it opened, the first to sprint to the head of the line for the front car, a perfect beginning to coaster time....

In about a half hour I got lucky. By an eviscerated McDonald's that sleazed out onto an exit ramp, I saw coaster folk. Real ones. I could tell by how they smiled. I pulled in; they were leaning neatly against the plexiglass wall under an arm of the golden arch. "Rrrowrrr!" I said, doing the gesture.

"Whoooooshhhh!" A unison ritual response.

"Need a ride down to Richmond? I'm Jack."

"Ernesto." A thin man, hooked like a shepherd's crook; only his eyes, twinkling, showed he was one of us.

"I'm Princess." A crone with a toothless smile. "We don't know who this is, though." And next to her, in the archway's shadow, was a willow-woman all in white, white-gloved, and veiled, I mean totally veiled, a temptress in purdah, from a Sinbad movie.

The veiled woman whispered; I couldn't catch what she said. The boylike man beside her said, in a lilty, almost unearthly voice, "She says her name is Shirenzheh. It means the Eternal Quiet." The woman made our secret sign—with such grace!—her gloved arm arcing against the arching shadow of the tacky big

247

M. I knew then that I belonged here.

"Oh, you joined the trail here?" I said.

"We picked it up in New Jersey. We've already done the Super Dooper Looper in Hershey Park," said Ernesto. "It was—"

"Whoooshhhh!" "Rrowrrr!" The familiar words ripped the memories from me. It was like I'd never left the trail.

"Anyone need a ride? We could hit the first big one by mid-afternoon. The amusement park doesn't close till ten so we can do some by starlight, too...."

"We're six people squelched into a Honda," Ernesto said.

"I'll take someone—"

And Shirenzheh had already stepped forward. She touched my hand. A sharp chill seared me for a moment and then faded into the sunlight. Her gloved hand had felt gritty, abrasive, like shark's hide.

Virginia countryside; lush even green, picture-booky, unreal somehow. King's Dominion, 49 miles! Ernesto and I played car games, passing each other and speeding heedlessly. The veiled woman sat, saying nothing. I don't think I even heard her breathe. I thought nothing of her strangeness, though; coaster folk are always unusual, driven, often graceless; they are discarded people who have chanced upon the roaring darkness only by daring to take the obscure exits of the human highway. I set the cruise control and looked at my passenger. Shirenzheh...some Middle Eastern name doubtless, full of exotic music.

"How long have you heard the roaring?" A whispery voice, a little childlike; definitely foreign.

"Fifteen years now. Old-timer, you might call me." For a moment I thought of Trina and those three years, and I wondered if I should tell her I'd cheated in my reckoning. "And you, Shiren—"

"They call me Shirra sometimes." The r was rolled once, lightly, on the tongue-tip.

"Shirra...how long have you heard the roaring?"

"Oh, a million years. A million and five, to be exact."

"Bizarre." I laughed; we coaster folk lived in the present, we weren't supposed to pry. But she had made it sound almost reasonable. "Those gloves must be great for repelling muggers," I said, groping for a new subject.

"They are not gloves."

"You certainly have a sense of humor."

She laughed: a twitter of far-off cicadas.

After a while I told her about the first girl I'd picked up.

"Things aren't the way they used to be. Time was, we were few, we all knew each other even, and no wandering mundanes took our secret signs for fads."

"Things will of necessity run riot now, in these final days."

"Huh? Oh, you mean those wars and famines and things...." But I was in no mood for apocalypses.

Silence. Then I said, "And what made you take the coaster trail?" Something about her nagged me; I had to talk, to fill the silence.

"I have come," she said, "to greet the Coaster King, the Enlightened One. It is time." Well, there were crazies aplenty among the coaster people, and we tolerated all of them, gave them their niche in our midst, because of our bond, the darkness roaring. I couldn't comment; she had a way of answering you that cut off all argument.

Soon we were there. Gaudy families were gushing into bottleneck ticket booths. We parked side by side, van and Honda, Laurel and Hardy; and we rushed for the gate like children, straining through the crowd and brandishing our plastic money. I didn't care about Shirenzheh or anyone else. A man pushing forty, but I ran dodgem through the throng like a kid, past the stunted Eiffel Tower and through the rainbow arch where Yogi Bear and Boo-Boo strutted about like presidential candidates. Then I saw, up ahead, the King Cobra, slimy sick-green monster of a looping coaster, and in the distance, soaring pure as a sine wave, the Rebel Yell. Already came a whisper-roar icinged with children's shrieks. I couldn't wait now. I ran harder, thrusting through walls of warring muzaks. Waiting in line I tapped the railings like a scurrying rat. I edged ahead, casually it seemed, but really counting heads to insinuate myself into the front seat, a knack that I'd learned my first year on the trail.

It worked. I was sitting in the car, the belt locked in, when—

I turned. *She* was there, beside me. "How'd you get here?"

She said nothing. I saw her eyes clearly for the first time, cornflower-blue through slits in the white veil, and I noticed that she never blinked. We exchanged one of the secret signals, and I smiled. With a jerk we were pulling out of the shelter into the sunlight; abreast of us the mirror-car moved too, for the Rebel Yell is a twin coaster, its curve-matched tracks haunching high into the sky.

Up now, with a ratchet...ratchet...sound, up, up...the people shrinking into ants. I threw my hands up, straining, waiting...up, up, then—

The roaring hit me! My lap shoved hard against the restrainers. My body twanged taut like a bowstring, gave into the curve of falling. For a moment there was no past, I was a timeless darkness. The kids were yelling, but I sat in proud silence, ecstatic. We hit bottom and soared; I opened my eyes, at peace at last. But....

Beside me Shirenzheh murmured in a foreign language. She was still, untouched by the coaster's violence. Under her robelike garment she seemed rock-solid; she didn't even seem to be breathing.

But we were falling again, and I gave into the joy, little joys now, none so all-embracing as the first and steepest. Then we raced for the end of the line like demons, we got the back this time, bumpiest but without the sheer bravura of the foremost. After ten or eleven I was tired; I found Ernesto and Princess and the others by the skyride, ranked by height and licking ice cream cones in unison.

"Look," said Ernesto, "more of us!"

Quick introductions: "Here's Tweeny. Here's Polypheme." A woman bandanaed like a pirate, with a patch over one eye. "And Hieronymo." I saw a teenaged gangler with brushfire hair. "He's dangerous, they busted him for a pyro when he was navel-high. But he's found the darkness now. Smile, Hero."

We exchanged quick, sharp smiles.

"Where's the veiled woman?" Ernesto said. I pointed at the Rebel Yell. "Ah, she should be here. I've learned a little more about the Coaster King."

That name again..."Who's that?"

"The Enlightened One. You been off the trail a couple years eh?"

"Uh huh."

"Then you don't know. We—you, me, all of us, we're *special*. The Coaster King is coming."

"His compassion will touch us all." It was the voice of Shirenzheh, who seemed to have materialized beside me.

"I'm dreaming," I said.

"No, Jacko, never a dream," said Shirenzheh.

Ernesto said, "I've heard. On the grapevine. He's coming soon, tomorrow maybe. There are more of us here, waiting. Waiting."

"Oh, Jack," Shirenzheh said, "you do not see us yet. Let me tear the blinkers from your eyes—"

I was pinioned against the ice cream booth. A child with a balloon ran right by me, not seeing. A scream was frozen to my lips. I looked straight up at the sun, the light burned, then—

250

Shirenzheh's gloved hands, clamping over my face. A roaring darkness like a coaster's falling, and then her hands raked slowly across me. I felt them sandpapering my eyes; I tried to squeeze them shut but my eyelids were torn, squirt-rheumy with blood—

"Open your eyes. It is only in the mind. This is no magic trick. You see no hallucinations. It is technology."

"Extraterrestrial," Princess croaked.

"Open them!" Ernesto said.

They were lidded again now, but crusty. I freed my arms and rubbed my eyes. Plates of dried mucus flaked away, tugging out eyelashes.

"You won't see them well at first. But I have exchanged your eyes for better ones." As the light burst on me I saw Shirenzheh slipping a clawed, knobbed tool into the eyeslit of her veil. She let go and it vacuumed down into where her face should be. "They are alien eyes. Soon you will truly be of the coaster folk. The true coaster folk, of which your little tribe has been but a shadow, a mirror-mimic. . . ."

I looked around. The group was clustered around; I could see nothing but concern in their eyes. And then, ghosted against the garish crowds, leaning against the plastic Flintstones. . .shadow-shapes at first. Some like Shirenzheh, their white veils fluttering. Some. . .like scaly unicorns, pawing the sun. Some tentacled, some winged, some mere tendrilwisps of smoke.

I began to understand. "They're on the coaster trail too, then."

"Some of them. Others are camp-followers, the Enlightened One's disciples."

"And you come from—" I looked up at the sky, cloudless, serene, brilliant.

"Well, what are we waiting for?" Princess screeched. "The coasters! The coasters!" And again we ran for the line.

And soared. And plummeted. And ran for the line. And—

Towards evening I sat with Hieronymo. He always held his arms the highest. He crooned. Each time we came back he shook as if palsied.

"Kid sick or something, mister?" An attendant was bent solicitously over us. "You been riding for hours."

"He is fine." Shirenzheh stood behind her. To me she said, "It was not because he was insane that he had so much trouble with the law, that he was in and out of the juvenile courts. It is because the darkness is always with him. Truly the Enlightened One's grace has fallen on him. . . ."

As night fell I held him; he was drunk on diving and flying, sobbing, and still we flew and we dived. His arms rose straight as spears, when mine tottered and flailed emptiness.

The stars came out; we saw few, because of the amusement park's glare.

And after, cleansed, stoned on the big darkness, we met at the gate. The lot was sieving out now; in the moonlight, Princess and Polypheme were dancing solemnly around our cars. "A convoy!" Ernesto cried. "We must have a convoy!" There followed some debate as to whether we should stay on our go south, towards Williamsburg, where we could do the Loch Ness Monster.

"Loch Ness Monster," Hieronymo said at last. It was all I'd ever heard him say. His voice was a whisper, perhaps an echo of the dark roaring.

"You must obey him," Shirenzheh said at last. "Of all you humans, Hieronymo is closest to the Coaster King. He is closest to achieving his last journey...." So it was settled. And in my van came Shirra and the boy; and then we caravaned onto the highway, five or six cars hugging each other and the speed limit, a weird procession. Shirra and I were in the front seat, the boy behind. It was only an hour or two to Busch Gardens; we'd have to sack out in the van awhile before the park opened. In the rear view mirror I saw him, shivering, hugging himself in a far corner of the van.

"Why have you come here?" I demanded, angry. "What have you done to him? to us?"

"We have awakened you," she said.

"If you're from somewhere up there, somewhere so inconceivably superior...why ride our coasters, why run our lives?"

"They are not your coasters. Listen, human. Our people live a billion years. We are tired, human, tired...a million years or so ago, a teacher came to our worlds. He had found the great extinction at the root of all being; yet he was so filled with compassion for the myriad shapes of life that he remained behind to tell us of it. For every sentient being in the universe has a number. Mine is some six million, and I have only begun the journey to the dark...one has but to experience the great falling, over and over, that number of times, and he will come to know eternal peace."

"You take the coaster trail to heaven?"

"In a sense...."

"Why don't you stay on your own planets? We had fun once. More than fun. We washed our souls clean in the roaring darkness. But now...."

"We are exiles." Her sadness touched me, even across the barrier of species. "It is part of the testing, you see; to awaken backworlds to such a state thay they may build roller coasters, to

252

remain inconspicuous always—"

"You've tampered with us? Toyed with us?" I hated them then, because they claimed to have snatched our very wills from us.

"Do you think we enjoy it here? On our worlds we can move continents with a thought. We can travel the silence between the stars on beams of tachyons. We can fashion cities from our dreams, and populate them as we please, with humanoids or chimaeras or with beings shaped from light itself...Here is Hell, Jacko, Hell itself. But you creatures of Hell, tormented, your noses in the planet's mud, are closer to truth than we are. So the Coaster King has taught us...."

"You're saying that all the human race's advancement stems from...a religious fad?"

"You cannot call it that."

"But the monuments, the discoveries, the great human achievement—"

"Side issues. You learned quickly, in mere thousands of years; you branched out every which way. It usually happens with the worlds we touch. Call them fringe benefits, perhaps." I watched her; her tranquility terrified me. Behind, the boy moaned.

"You're driving him crazy."

"No. He is like us. He sees what lies behind the roaring darkness. He is frightened now, but later he will become one with eternity."

"You're crazy! Galactic lunatics, playing havoc with a backward race!"

"No! No!" I opened my eyes. In the darkling wayside I saw creatures gathering, inhuman creatures suffused with moonlight. I stepped harder on the gas.

"You too have had teachers. All life yearns for the great extinction. It is no myth. You call it nirvana, human."

Seeing me accelerate, the convoy sped up too. The inner wind came rushing, sweeping me up, I didn't struggle.

We'd been at Busch Gardens for some days now; the others were impatient, fretting for the Coaster King. The park was tortuous, more artfully landscaped than King's Dominion; the Loch Ness Monster reared up from greenery and a man-made lake, its loops coiling one across the other, yellow and green. When we tired we would go stand on the bridge, between the remote-controlled boatlets and a souvenir stand, where the loops loomed overhead and the cars hurtled straight down at you, skimming three feet from water.

There was a thunderburst, and then the sun emerged more dazzling than ever. I'd been riding with Shirra and with Hero and with another guy, bulging from an old cheesecloth shirt. Hero hadn't eaten, hadn't slept. As we set off—he and I in the front for the fifth time that day—he was trembling more than ever, his cheeks were puckered in, yellowing, his eyes wild, the smile soldered in place.

"I'll *make* him get off next time," I shouted. "Force some food down his throat—"

"No! He is full of grace now! He has almost reached his number of fulfillment!" Shirenzheh cried over the rattling, as we scaled the hill.

"Fucking numerologist aliens!" I sat back; a harness came over your neck so you couldn't raise your arms. The coaster dragged upwards, so slow, so—

The top! A moment of stasis, frozen out of time, then—

Windroar! The world *giving* beneath me! My whole being stretching like elastic in a slingshot, then—

Up! Around! Gravity-wrench of the three sixty, fireworks in my guts, burning, soaring—

The tunnel. I caught my breath now, ready for the spiralling darkness. Sparks flew where the coaster flinted on the track. And then I felt my arm vised in a grip of terror. "Steady, Hero, steady...."

The clutch tightened. He was thrashing against the restraint. Did he want off? We burst out into the light. And then we were pulleying up again, agonizingly slow, and I saw his face, ashen in the bright sun; I saw his wide eyes glistening like crystal marbles, gazing on some horror....I strained to follow his line of vision, but we were falling again now, and as soon as we fell our stomachs reversed and we were in the upkick of the second loop and then back at the exit, getting off....

"Something's wrong!" I said, as we trotted around the back to find the end of the line again.

"I don't want to! I don't want to!" he screamed suddenly. It was only the second sentence I had ever heard him utter. Around us, kids burst out laughing, thinking him some chickenshit jerk.

"He *must!* He *must!*" Shirra was saying, but he broke loose from the line and hurled himself into the crowd; a hail of popcorn hid him from us.

"The King is here," said Shirra. "Come, the coaster is waiting."

We rode. The joy came back to me, but it was a ghost-joy,

tinged with anger. And still we rode. Until nightfall.

And when I looked at the line that zigzagged back and forth in the log shelter where you got on the coaster, when I looked in a certain way—I can't describe it, it was something about my new eyes—I would see that there were *others*. I mean aliens. Peering over a child's shoulder, hunched against a post. I saw a fat man with twins in tow go right through one, a thing of tentacles and porcupine-spines. I thought I must be going mad. But when you have experienced the dark roaring the way I have, knowing as you do that most people get on the coasters and scream with terror and pleasure and get nothing more from them, that they come face to face with the big darkness and are too blind to see it...I was not insane. It was the simple truth that we had been made civilized, been dragged up from barbarity, in what must have seemed the twinkling of a eye to these beings, merely to be brief props in an alien drama of birth and extinction. But it was too huge to grasp, yet.

We had gone to a little snack stand across the lake. Hero was still missing. I turned to Ernesto to make some casual remark. He was coughing, spluttering. Then I saw smoke, I saw the Loch Ness Monster nesting on a bed of fire. People had begun to stampede, crushing onto the narrow bridge. "It's Hero!" Ernesto gasped. "He couldn't handle it, he's on his pyro trip again!" Shirra clutched me, saying, "There's nothing to be done, the King's here now," but I wrenched free and elbowed into the crowd. When I reached the coaster, I saw that the shelter was on fire. People were crunched together, speechless. And then I saw him lit up in a flicker of flame, straddling the loop-top overhead, doing a wild dance.

Cries of *Jump! Get him down!* "Hieronymo!" I screamed.

"You know him?" Some kind of uniformed man pulled me from the crowd. Hot air washed my face, dried up my throat. Suddenly Shirra was beside us. "Don't touch him," she said quietly, dangerously. He muttered something about questioning me. The gloved hand struck out. I knew now it was no glove but her natural exoskeleton, crusty and chitinous. In the glare the blood spurted luridly from his nose, his forehead, his eyes. "Now! Come now!" She threw a fold of the veil around my head. I shook from the sudden deathchill. When she released me we were in the parking lot, all of us. I whirled around. Behind me, past the veneer of forest, I saw the flames leap higher, I saw the coaster's steel circle rise above it and the shrunken figure, blackened in the moonlight and firelight, still grotesquely dancing....

I wrenched myself from the sight. And then I looked at the

coaster folk. They were stock-still, serene, expectant.

"Forget now," said Shirra. Her voice was flutelike in the quiet. "He came close to eternity, but he was not ready. The cycle continues."

"Hush," said another veiled figure like her.

"He is here," said another. The unicorn-like creatures pawed the concrete noiselessly. A van much like mine was parked beside Ernesto's Civic. The coaster folk looked up at it in unison. "He is resting," said the third veiled woman. "He has counted his final number but one. He has waited an eon for this journey; for his compassion was such that he delayed his voyage into the void until he could pass on his teachings...."

"Are you asking me to believe—" I said.

"Your belief or disbelief is quite irrelevant," Shirenzheh said. "Come, we're at *his* beck and call now."

"But the boy—"

"He's beyond us. The darkness has driven him mad."

I peeled out like a maniac. The coaster trail was dreary after Williamsburg; in the Carolinas there were no coasters, not until Atlanta's Six Flags' Scream Machine. I drove alone, leading the convoy now grown to a dozen vehicles or more. But in the rear view mirror I could see that the van wasn't empty, that aliens had hitched with me. I saw them clearly now that I was used to the eyes. We did not speak to each other. Shirenzheh's species seemed to be the only one that could be bothered with human speech; and I knew by now that they were lowest in the visitors' hierarchy....

I was angry when we left. They'd been callous about Hieronymo, brushing his memory off now that their precious King was here. But as I drove farther, the roaring in my mind came ever louder, tempting me into surrender, and my dreams were all of leaping into the arms of darkness, dissolving into the darkness, loving the darkness.

The next amusement parks are all run together in my mind; the Scream Machine, the Cyclone and the Cyclotron, the Python and the Scorpion. We drove at night mostly, a stately parade of some dozen vans and cars; we camped in parking lots, humans and aliens wary of each other, keeping mostly to themselves; we rode the coasters, all of them, from dawn until far into the night, until the roaring rang ceaselessly and our dreams whirled, giddy and gaudy, blurring into wakefulness. At such times in the past I would have felt so much at peace. But now Hero haunted me.

I wrote *Dear Trina* and crumpled the postcard out the window as I drove. It was dark and we were well into Florida now, with Kissimee the next big stop. Disney World was there, with its Space Mountain and its Thunder-watchamacallit-Railroad, kiddie thrills livened with stunning graphics; not for the coaster people really, these rides, but sometimes worth a stop for the sake of the spectacle. From Orlando the coaster trail veers westward and inward.

I stared at the van of the Coaster King, in front of me, setting the slow pace. Its brights smeared the dark road. I didn't recognize the make of van; I think it was like Shirenzheh, a simulacrum, an alien thing camouflaged behind a familiar shape.

"Will he ever come out?"

"When he's ready. He know the moment of his passing."

"And then?"

"Be calm. Hear the roaring." We were on a dim road that threaded Tampa to Yeehaw Junction on the Florida Turnpike: bleak, unpopulated. The roaring sang in my mind's ear like an ocean.

"And us?" I persisted. "What will become of you and me and his other followers?"

"Perhaps, one day, we too will pursue the coaster trail to its end."

"You, perhaps. Living a billion years and all. But humans—"

"I have no answers, Jack. Perhaps the Coaster King knows...."

"No one's ever even seen him!"

She didn't answer. I remembered the other parks; the veiled ones hastening to the King's van to find out if this was the designated time, being refused. I remembered the radio broadcast too, about the bizarre young flake who'd set fire to the Loch Ness Monster and tumbled to his death. I had once tried to ask whether they believed in reincarnation, whether they imagined it might take lifetimes for every soul to count the fallings until he reached his personal number. But Shirra had been vague, telling me only that life was a continuum, not a jigsaw of disparate entities.

We came to Orlando. It was night. We drove down Route 4; I expected the Coaster King's van to turn at Disney, the only place open past midnight. But no, we rode on, following the master. From this vantage one saw little of Disney World; it is a fantasy in plastic, shielded from reality by miles of landscaping. "He's starting with Circus World," I said. In a few moments we would see its tent-top cresting the highway and the moon-silvery serpent of a coaster...what was it called? Something tiger. The very names were running into one another, the litany of magic wor' that once I could recite in a rush, without taking a breath.

"Wait," Shirenzheh said. Other aliens, crouching in back, hunched closer. "I sense something."

"What?" And there it was. I could tell by the roar within me. *Whoosh!* one of the shadowshapes moaned.

"The final day is here. The Coaster King has chosen this place for his final journey. It will be now."

The procession turned, climbed a ramp, made a left into the deserted lot. A big top flanked by little tops rose up behind wrought-iron fencing; the garish reds, oranges, blues muted into shades of a single grayness.

We halted as one. It was the higher of the two parking areas. Two of the veiled women scuttled to the van. And then it opened. We rushed to see, jostling, cramming into the little opening. And there was light, bursting, blinding, a river that rived the darkness and streamed past the locked gates.

The van was a window over another world. It was sunlight that was pouring into our nightworld, alien sunlight. There were mountains like crystals of blue vitriol. Black telephone-pole trees, forests of them, topped with amethyst taffy and ivory spirals and giant sea anemones of shocking pink, bridged with inverted rainbows slung with quivering slinkies. And things I can't begin to describe.

The landscape shimmered for a moment. Then it dissolved into the back of a van. There was a glass bottle, shoulder high, linked to an apparatus that clanked and tittered; in it a wizened being squatted. Its blue fur was balding; it had no eyes. Shirenzheh and another creature, horned and coppery-eyed, climbed into the van; Shirra pulled a tool from her eyeslit, the same one I'd seen her use before on me, and did something that shattered the glass. Then they helped the Coaster King totter to his feet. We dwarfed him, all of us. They made for the gate.

The others had to scramble to keep up. I came up behind, shouted, "The place is closed now! What's he going to do?"

"Silence, human!" Shirenzheh's voice grated like chalk on a blackboard. And when I looked up the gate had dissolved, and the tents, guarded by plaster elephants and clowns, were gauzed in an alien light. I heard Ernesto muttering, "You're right, Princess, they can do anything...." There were shouts of glee now. We were dashing, all of us, as madly as that first day, splashing through the puddled porpoise pool, laughing in the darkness. And then the path forked, each fork leading to a different coaster. To the right, soaring like a scimitar from a clutter of concession booths, was the big one, almost a mile of it; to the left the Daredevil, dangling from the blackness like a titan's earring. Our laughter stilled itself; we waited, respectful, for the King.

I heard whispers.... "He can't breathe our air long. He's weakening. Dying. They broke his life-supporter." The King lifted an arm, pointed, batwing hands of silverblue. It was the Daredevil. At the signal the veiled ones pulled out their instruments and the coasters clattered to life, eerie in the alien light. The troop went left. The coaster reared over us, a coil of roaring. They could not make the elevator work for some reason; we began up the stairs, zigzags of white steel encased in a flimsy scaffolding. I was directly behind the King. His expression—insofar as he seemed to have one—was utterly blank.His creatures clutched him tightly. The steps rattled; in the gaps you could see down to the ground. Higher, higher. I was out of breath now. The coaster car waited at the platorm; they helped the King into the front car, and I stepped in behind him. Quickly, silently it filled. In the distance I could hear the other coaster, its roaring hollow because it was not topped with screams. I saw the great loop ahead, diving a hundred feet and more.

The slingshot clanged. And then we broke out of the shelter into the charging wind! Thunder in my ears, the blood surging, and—

Swooping! The night-circus spinning, the stars below, tiny leather paws shivering, my twisting guts—

Now we froze for one terrible instant on the far platform, perched over precarious nothing, and the catapult struck again and I was plummeting asswards into the loop. I squeezed my eyes tight, and when I opened them we were shooting onto the planform and—

The seat in front of me, empty.

I jumped out. Others were yelling with excitement, dying to get on. I ran downstairs, my knees buckling. I saw Shirenzheh and others, gathered, waiting.

"What have you done to him?" I screamed. A tiny sound in the big night.

They turned, all of them, on me. Their veils fell from them. With their strange tools they peeled the eyes from their faces and tossed them down. As the eyes touched concrete, they fumed, corroded. They pried away their ears and noses and lips, flinging them into fizz-smoking heaps. "What are you doing?" I cried. They weren't human-looking at all now; their faces were angled, armored with plates of chitin, and empty. They seemed soulless, dybbuklike.

"He has faced the darkness now. He has gone out, like the

flame of a candle." Shirra's voice, still lovely. "The final days are here. We can go back now...."

"What final days? What about us? You brought us to this state, didn't you? Will you just leave us, bombing ourselves to bits, fighting starvation and pestilence?"

"I don't know. Those are material things, and the Coaster King has taught us to cast them aside, to live only for the final journey. We will waken other worlds to a brief splendor, each world a flower in the desert universe, each visit like a drop of rain. Kings will come again, and the universe will turn till the end of time. Some of the worlds we have touched...survive, become great. Most of them do not; that is the way of things. But we will leave you alone, mostly; there will be tourists, exiles, lovers of curiosity, but no more interference...."

I left her then. The coaster folk had piled into the big one. They had jimmied it to run without stopping. I got on.

"Whooosh!" Polypheme yelled.

"Rrowrr!" A weight had fallen from us. We were drunk with coaster madness now. We would ride till dawn, till they came and found the gateways vanished and the machines mysteriously running. I saw how most of them were overcome by the big darkness, how they gave their hearts to it completely; but for me it was like...like clawing at a dying dream. Like clinging on to childhood, or to someone you've stopped loving.

In the morning I saw the past more clearly: the serenity of the King who passed beyond, Hieronymo driven mad by touching the darkness too close. There was no choice, really. For Hero had been a human, and the alien dream had broken him. And now we humans were alone with our crumbling societies. Now we could dream our own dreams. Our freedom was bitter and joyful both. I stole away while the others slept, and I drove north.

Summer was ending. Outside, the house seemed changed; the walls spattered with rustflake leaves, the chilling air scented by unswept foliage, heaped against shedding trees. But when I entered it seemed like I'd never left.

She was standing in the kitchen door, casually, as though she'd just come out to get something. But I knew she must have seen me pull in. Behind her the dishwasher hummed.

Suddenly the children's clatter shattered the tension. They ran by in a blur of dirt and color.

"Will you take us to King's Dominion, Jack, huh? before it closes, before Labor Day? Will you?"

"Maybe..." but I was answering an emptiness. Only their

smell lingered, lemony detergent tangled with a tang of fresh sweat and old sneakers.

"Kids," she said, shrugging.

"They shoot up, summers. I never knew that."

"As if they thirsted for the sun itself." She had always been good at finishing my thoughts for me.

"I'm back."

"That's fine, Jack, just fine. It's all right."

"But...questions?"

She smiled then. Not like the coaster people as they contemplated the big darkness, but an earthy smile wrinkled with a half-laugh. "No questions, Jack, my love."

The dishwasher thunked, changing its tune from thrum to sloshing. We did not touch.

"But I want to answer you anyway."

"Go on," she said seriously.

And then a shadow crossed her face, an elastic unicorn of darkness. I knew what I would see if I looked behind me. For my eyes were alien eyes and would still see aliens, if I cared to look. "I've left the coaster trail, Trina. I've seen to the end of the roaring void. There was nothing there, and it isn't in me to love the emptiness." She pursed her lips; I don't think she really understood, she was just humoring me. "Now I don't need the big darkness any more." But I heard it still, calling me, haunting, chilling. It trilled like the syrinx of a cosmic vulture. I embraced her then, Trina the beautiful, the compassionate.

"One day you'll love me," she said. I knew now it was true. It was this that the aliens could not have. Hadn't Shirenzheh said it herself? *You creatures of Hell, tormented, your noses in the planet's mud, are closer to truth than we are.*

After all, they had come to us.

I turned and saw the aliens watching. But they were ghostly now, less real. In time they will fade.

—*Alexandria, 1981*

The Four Dragons and the Dying King

I wrote this long poem in 1978, while trying to play mah jongg with some friends. There are, as many will no doubt know, three kinds of dragon tile in the game: white, red, and green. As I tried to play I fell into a sort of reverie; I imagined the three dragons in the flesh, in some surreal, vaguely East Asian setting; and I saw a dying king. And a fourth dragon he has never seen before....

It's rather strange, really. This poem was written before I started to write a lot of SF; but it apparently contains a lot of phrases I cannibalized later in my writing. I had not seen the poem in 4 years when I sat down to write this introduction; but I notice, for instance, that it is here that the phrase "Light on the Sound" is first used. That was later to be the title of a piece of music I wrote...then a completely different piece of made-up music in one of my Mallworld stories...and then the title of a novel that has nothing to do with any of the previous things. Why has this particular phrase haunted me? I cannot say. But here is the poem.

I

I am the dragon LIGHTFALL.

When you were born
and you dropped from the sky
like an unpainted tile:
I came in lucent laughter.

The world I scaled down
for the clutch of chubby hands,
whose jewelled thumbs are heavier now
than once the whole world was.

Now they have brought you on the sand to die
out of a city striated by tall columns
into a coolhot lightshade,
its old tiles crumbling with the weight
of flower roots.
I was the first to leave you,
laughing as when I first came.

Now, see
the light on the sound
weighed down by the distance in time.

For you I broke the silence of the sunlit sea
    as now it breaks me.
The tide corrodes me:
    claw by claw
as I transform into a cadent
    nightfall.

II

    I am the dragon GROWING-IN-THE-GRASS.
I breathed my last on you
as you came down the gilded dragon-steps
from the mist-high mountain.

I grew beside you. When linger-winter strayed,
I swooped like living droplets from a sunlit ocean,
my scales tipping towards the ut
of water water. Perhaps
I am the eldest dragon.

My voice was the voice of a young boy
    and within that voice
was the stridulating of the tall tall grass
    and within that voice
was the voice of the whistling snow
    and within that voice
was the whispering of the far far thunder
    but within that voice
was the voice of an innocent.

    Before they snapped,
my nerves stretched taut until they touched
    your soul.

III

    I am the dragon BLOODSHED
and to whichever side you turned
    your jellied sockets
thither I flew-flapped.

Behind your glance
fell my glance, like a lancet
comet. People ran mad in yellow rivers.

My breath skin-scorched the earth as she
      lay laboring, burying
the unborn. I stabbed mother Asia's mountains, breasting
      the sky.

For your lives overlapped in tenuous
      enjambement
and limbs filmed over as they swelled
      into a blood-meniscus.

They fell
like fledgling sparrows, nest-fallen
and you swallowed them.

But try as you might,
you might not scale me;
You were the Dragon-faced; I am
all dragon.

Now at your death once more the stars revolve;
And in a crimson smoke-puff I—

IV

      I am the dragon DARKNESS
with my wing's shadows grazing the once-jade fields
      now dipped in a purple of
      clash-sworded war.

      I came upon you whilst asleep.
Water had washed the wet-dyed dragons
from the ivory tiles.

The dragons frolic in the sunlit sea
      misted in distance
flaunting their new-found freedom.
You thought eternity their moment's caging—
      unfounded tyrant!
      fool!

You waited for me as a boy
      at the inverted apex. I
deflowered them all, save you.
      Fear flecked your eyes:
and now the beach bears your inflicted footstamp
as my scales wear water when I rise imperious.

And on your gold-embedded throne you lie
    inlaid,
your many features like a sequent frieze,
while my scales fall from your
    twisted eyes.
Flip-flap, the shadows beat.

    Fool!
even the silence shies from you
like an untamed dragon:

    Fool!
I tried to tell you I was on your side
but in a slow dissolving lapped by grief
your eyes were brimming with formaldehyde.

The Last Line of the Haiku

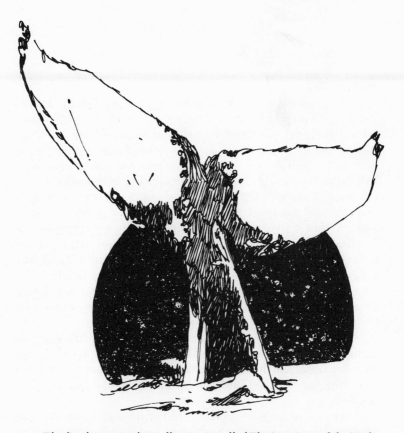

The final entry in this collection is called The Last Line of the Haiku. It is one of the first stories I ever wrote, and I first conceived of the idea when my parents, who are in the Thai diplomatic service, were posted in Japan, and I was visiting them for the summer vacation while I was a student at Cambridge. I became very caught up in the Japanese way of looking at things, and this story resulted.

Interestingly enough, it was rejected 12 times, bought 3 times (though only published once) and became the basis of my novel Starship and Haiku, published last year by Timescape. The novel was published to 12 rave reviews and 3 utter pans, a ratio diametrically opposite to its history of rejections and acceptances. Numerologists should have some fun with those figures....

Spring, 2022

The million-year silence between man and the whale was first broken on April 3, 2022. This did not result from the painstaking teamwork of cryptolinguists and zoologists, for humanity had for the most part given up such lines of research as did not meet its immediate and very urgent needs; nor was it some lone, half-crazed genius, struggling for decades to communicate with the great aliens who share this planet, who was first to stumble upon one of the most well-concealed secrets of the universe. Instead, this story deals with a young, mildly attractive girl on her first journey abroad, aboard an insignificant fishing vessel (one of the few remaining of its kind) that set sail from Beppu, the City of Seven Hells as the long dead tourists called it, which is a port in the shadow of the volcano Asoyama, on the startlingly bright green island of Kyushu, a surprising jewel erupting from the poisoned Pacific.

Ryoko was alone on deck when it happened. She was following her father's command, which was always to keep her eyes and ears open: *for there are whole continents outside Japan, my dear.* She had laughed inwardly at his solemnity, but went, an obedient girl.

They were far too respectful of her, though since she was Minister Ishida's daughter, and so she had been lonely almost all the time. The first weeks she was sick every day and stayed in the vessel's one minimally sumptuous cabin, which they had set aside for her. When she was better, they wanted to show here everything. The boat was powered by sail in the ancient way, and sometimes by electricity. It was, of course, no longer used for fishing. How it worked did not interest her, and she only wanted to see land again and not have to stand on a ground that swayed to a timeless music not of her choosing. So they left her mostly to herself.

Turning from their work, they would sometimes see her pass by, one hand caressing the soggy railings, humming some wailing melody from the classics, for she was quite a scholar, or she would be staring, hypnotized, at some imagined strip of land just beyond the boundaries of her vision.

This time she had been standing for nearly an hour. The boat was hardly moving. She stood stock still, like a statue, her mind lulled by the patterned dancing of light on the water. It was almost evening when the sea crashed open and a great black island stared back at her. She started.

It was a whale.

She could not tell which species, for so far as she knew all of them were virtually extinct. She saw only his hugeness—he was big as the boat at least—and how he thrust the water from him with such terrible force, how he sprang imperious from the swirl with a movement so charged with life that it seemed to fling aside all the hopelessness of the times.

She loved him, then; she was terrified of him, too; and she feared for him, knowing that the oceans were seething with radiocative poisons. And she remembered the sad haiku an old monk had written at the close of the last century, after the Treaty of San Diego:

Oh, Oh, the darkness!
The fishes have left the sea
in the midst of spring.

and because she was bereft of words she began to hum quietly to herself, and because she was lonely she hoped he could understand her.

But then the whale spoke to her, calling her by name: "Ryoko." It was a liquid murmur that seemed to emanate from the water itself; totally inhuman, rich and elemental. It called out to her as from an unremembered past, and dispelled her terror.

"Ryoko," the water said, and Ryoko was reminded that before the Millennial War there had been scientists who had concluded that the intelligence of whales might be far higher than that of humans...but who's to understand what it thinks, then? she thought. It's an alien, there are no common referents in our environments, probably not even space and time.

"So why are you speaking to me?" she ventured, "and why haven't you communicated with us before?"

He disappeared from sight, and the empty waves whispered: "The first is simple. I am creating sound waves by telekinesis. Our intelligence is not one of hands or tools. To the second question: you do not know what you ask."

He rose again from the depths, shadowy and shapeless in the twilight. Telekinesis, she thought: then why didn't they command the harpoons of the ancient hunters to fall useless into the sea?

"It was irrelevant!" the water thundered.

"On our history tapes I saw my forefathers killing yours by millions, in the days before the Millennial War."

"Child, oh child: you are mayflies that fizzle in the sunlight, cherry blossoms that sparkle when their corpses litter the grass. Your conceptualization of death is so innocent; you do not understand it as I do, and your people's reaction to it is rooted in ignorance and emotional immaturity. No, life is not one of our primary pursuits. A beautiful death is the supreme joy, the supreme achievement of intelligence; life only exists as a necessity for it."

Ryoko's heart leapt with understanding.

"We consecrated ourselves to death many millennia ago, Ryoko. It was a game."

I know about this death, she thought. It is what makes us different from the other races, it's why the whale has come to one of us. My people worship death: the beautiful suicide of young lovers, the noble death of a warrior in the spring. It's the ultimate beauty that pains the heart.

"Child, we must help one another, now."

A breeze came, a sudden chill. There was, almost, no sun. "Help? How?"

"It concerns survival," said the whale. "You humans have not played fairly in the game of life and death.

"We thought we had outgrown our desire for life. We had set our thoughts on eternity, on breaking through the barriers of the material. But when the survival of *all* came into question—well, even we have not the all-embracing wisdom to accept this. We are, it seems, still mortal, still bound by our animalness—" he seemed to hesitate. "It is difficult to communicate this to a creature without the concepts....

"Even you will not survive, and most of the animals are already dead."

"No, no," said Ryoko. "My father says some of us will survive." But she thought: Survival is relative.

And the whale—again he seemed to have read her thoughts—said, "Yes, and we shall all survive, if you do as I say."

"You ask *us* to help you; your *killers.*"

"Yes, yes, and you shall know why, when the time comes, later."

The whale paused; in the darkness she heard water churning, and she wrapped her arms around herself to ward off the cold. She sensed the compassion in him, and loved him still more.

"But what must I do?"

"Tell your father that he and his cabinet must come to the harbor at Yokohama in six months' time. We will meet there, to discuss what they are building."

"Building? What could my father be building? And don't you have the power to control matter? If you need something built, can't you build it yourselves, even without tools?"

And she knew the answer even before it came.

"We are not builders," said the whale, "but dreamers." And he dove into the dark water and was gone. For a long while she stared after him, shivering a little.

"Miss Ishida?" came a voice, startling her. She whirled round. It was only the captain, telling her she would be ill if she remained. At first she did not answer him, and because he was sorry for her, he stood beside her and showed her the stars, giving them fanciful names out of old myths. She looked up politely, not wishing to offend, and pretended to be impressed at his knowledge, but she knew also that some of the stars were artifacts from the past, still directing their lethal radiation at long-perished targets.

Afterwards they went inside, and she found herself of a surprisingly friendly disposition toward the crew, and they sat talking of little things; but she mentioned the important thing to no one.

From there it was a month's journey to Hawaii, where Ryoko saw enormous charred skyscrapers, black skeletons of hubris bloodstained by the setting sun, and also a fused sheet of glass many kilometers long that dazzled her eyes and brought the tears to them, and she visited the hall where the young mutants lived and the hospitals where they lay dying. Their deaths were not beautiful. She also saw the great crater inside Halemaumau, the one not put there by nature, and the cliffs that had been ripped asunder. She had never understood these things; it was all before she was born. But she began to realize why her father had sent her on this journey, had insisted that it would make her ready for life.

She heard that Hawaii was nothing compared to the devastation on the American continents, and on the way back when they were in Shanghai for a few days, she saw a level desert that stretched in every direction, and then was jostled by beggars whose faces were torn to the bone, and glimpsed a few of those others, those who had grown fat on forbidden flesh. She understood despair for the first time, and clung ever more fiercely to the whale's enigmatic promise of hope.

At night she would sometimes come out on deck to watch for him. He never reappeared to answer the hundred questions she had for him, but occasionally she would hear the high whinings, the reverberant hummings, the throbbing deep tones that were the whale's song, sounds alien and compelling, like the music of the old *Noh* plays. But usually there was nothing; no gulls cried over the waters. She became aware that because of the things she had seen, she would be returning to her father no longer a girl.

Summer, 2022

Her father always used the diminutive with her. "Not a word, Ryochan," he said, "not a word until I've looked my fill at the *fujisan*...no, no, not a word."

He took her hand to steady himself, bent to unbutton his archaic tweed overcoat because of the heat, and allowed her to lead him across the flagstoned plaza, past the grandiose, disused marble fountain into the disheveled shade of a cluster of trees. Ueno was still a comparative oasis in the clutter of Tokyo; somehow the great Quake of '89 had left it alone. There were low buildings on all sides of the square, seventy or eighty years old, which seemed not to belong to the present, but to emerge out of a transtemporal haze; moss-veins had fuzzed their outlines, and the torrid sunshine would not lighten their gloom.

Ryoko noticed a big signboard to her left, where patina'd metal gates had been clumsily boarded over. It was written, not in the usual roman letters, but in the elaborate ideographic *kanji* of the twentieth century:

> Notice: Ark Project.
> Ueno Zoo has been closed, owing to the recent decision of the Survival Ministry to ship the animals to an environmental reconstruction project in Kenya, American East Africa. Your patience and forbearance is craved.
> Signed:
> Akiro Ishida, Minister for Survival

"A new project, *otosan?*" she asked him, although she did not wish to talk of generalities, really; she was full of the message she must give him, and for a moment the roar of the waves was vivid in her memory, but she sensed the time was not quite ripe. Better to let her father relax, see what he had come to see, first.

They stood in front of the sign. Someone had scrawled, beneath the signature, in roman letters: "I can't read this old writing!"

"Well," Ryoko laughed, "after fifteen years of Back to History,

272

people will still be living out their Americanized fantasies of progress."

"Let's go," said her father, "it's hot, a very hot summer. The museum might be air conditioned by now...."

"Well, perhaps it was an immigrant," she said to herself, her eyes lingering on the sign. "It was a wise plan of you Ministry's, father, to strengthen our survival by reviving our Japaneseness, to conjure up the past when we haven't much of a future."

"Oh, it didn't work, Ryochan," her father mumbled, "and the animals are all dead in Africa."

"Everything is so beautiful now, father...do you remember the cherry blossoms on the drive to the park? It must be the impending world-death, heightening everything...."

"The new mutated plague-virus got them when they arrived, we hadn't counted on it reaching Kenya from across the Atlantic so soon...." He saw they were not communicating, and began to walk—quite briskly for his age—across the street to the museum which had been one of the world's wonders in the twentieth century.

But before they went in he turned to her and said diffidently, "I *am* sorry not to have seen anything of you or talked to you since you came back. I'm glad we can have this time together."

Ryoko suppressed a twinge of impatience, and appraised him silently in return: an old man, a wisp of a man, a small man, an unsteady man, a man of power.

They walked past interminable corridors, past listless guards with stiff hands and dead eyes, and he chattered on about this and that, so that she sensed beneath his well-schooled superficiality some unspoken disquiet.

He needs me, she thought: but he would lose face by saying so to me, a woman, his only child.

Fujisan stood by itself in a glass case. It was a brown, blotchy vessel irregularly streaked with a dull white; misshapen, crooked, by any conceivable non-Japanese standards—ugly. It was—and remains—the ultimate teabowl: the supremely perfect imperfection.

When the two of them had gazed for several long moments, they were overwhelmed, close to tears.

And after, in a little coffee-shop called *The San Diego Treaty*, which served a passable synthetic coffee and had its waitresses charmingly attired in pre-war two-ply polyvinyl tunics, they each had a cup of "blue mountain"—whatever the name, it all came from the same laboratory—and Minister Ishida listened to his daughter's story. He heard the whole thing out, without interruption.

"What strikes me now is that the whale was so Japanese, he spoke about death the way a Japanese might. I'm sure he would understand *fujisan*, too, and the tea ceremony, and all the things the old *gaijin* experts found so bafflingly alien about our culture...Father, you don't believe me."

He sipped his coffee. "Did anyone else see it? Was it not a hallucination, a dream?"

"No!...you don't believe me."

"Ryochan—" he lowered his voice. "Our ministry's Back to History proclamations, the cultural revival programs, the renascence of the old life patterns...what do you feel about these things?"

"What does it matter, father? Oh well; these things may amuse the people. What few remain of them. I see there was another suicide wave in my absence." Then she said slowly: "Our culture has never been significantly influenced, even by the surface Americanization of the old days. I don't think what your Ministry is doing is really relevant, *otosan*."

"Your trip has cleared your mind, I think. You're right, our entire program is a coverup. Despite our support for every form of suicide, especially the traditional forms like *seppuku*, we really are working for another kind of survival...and there is no way, of course, short of totally altering the environment, before the great plague takes us all."

With a flicker of earnestness, he continued: "So we have to find a new environment."

And I know, thought Ryoko, what that environment will be: the land of shadow. Honor would survive identity. So she said, "The whale came to the right source, then. He knew things I did not know."

"Yes."

"Still, you don't believe me."

"Your mother came back from Hokkaido a fortnight ago, Ryochan, your mother whom you've hardly seen since I divorced her. She has caught the plague—there isn't a town in the North without one or two cases."

Why did he not concentrate on the subject? "Father, I'm sorry," she said, not without irony. Somehow he seemed so spent, so ineffectual. But the memory of the whale was vivid to her, and she could only feel an annoyance at him for not reacting with the proper urgency. He was avoiding an answer, he did not believe her. Well, she would withhold her sympathy.

"You don't believe me," she said, edgily.

"What choice do I have?" her father said, suddenly emotional. "How could my own child lie to make me lose face?"

Her hand shook. She drained her cup and set it down. Her father was paying the bill—six million yen—with a ten million credit note, and was getting up without waiting for the change.

At the corner, the chauffeur, an American immigrant, was holding open the door of the black electric Toyota.

They were silent on the drive home. They passed immaculately desolate streets, past the empty department stores and the blind traffic lights, and she began to suspect him of knowing much more than he had cared to say. He had seemed so unsurprised at it all.

There were still three months left, before they would have to face the whale again, together.

There is a little island, thought Minister Ishida, pushed out of the sea by a volcano, twenty, thirty years ago, several hundred kilometers north of Hokkaido. On what happens there, everything depends, everything.

The driver took them up the ill-kept ramp on to the Shuto Overpass. The Minister sat well back as the car rattled across cracked pavement and clumps of lichen. He felt his daughter's presence: pensive, quiet. She had grown very comely; in her classic kimono, she was almost beautiful. He loved her, though he could not bring himself to say so.

She is wise, he thought; in the old days when they had computers and universities, she might have made a talented poetess, an observer of truths. But the sea has returned her to me a stranger; not soft as before, but strong-willed, a little alien, even. Today, she defied me, challenged my belief in her.

If she were not telling the truth, she could not have changed so much. So I believe her.

I was over fifty years old when she was born. But I could swear that her thoughts and attitudes come from a more distant past then I can remember. She's so quintessentially Japanese, so much that she doesn't understand what I mean by *survival*.

She thinks that our *survival* is really a euphemism for death, and that my Ministry, like the other two, is essentially a religion.

But why *don't* I want to die? he thought...like the others? Am I too Westernized to feel the need to take, in honor, the consequences of mankind's evil?

There is an island, though....

His mind wandered; age was beginning to touch him at last.

275

They had come to a cleared up stretch of the Overpass, and Tokyo's clashing garishness kaleidoscoped about his eyes, even through the smog.

Not *spiritual* survival! he thought, Corporeal, factual, literal survival.

My hopes are on this island alone, this secret island, where they are building the tall spacecraft, this island from which one day they will burst into the sky to rendezvous with an abandoned prototype starship of the Russians that has waited, passenger-less, in orbit for forty years to begin a journey of four thousand years, where the arrivers will have no memory of the departers, nor of earth.

What could the whale want with me? He knew it must concern his project.

The intelligence of whales came as no surprise to him; but why would they take the trouble to make contact with man? It violated the purity of his image of them—for he had never seen one, nor even a photograph, and they were to him like dragons or phoenixes, creatures of dream and myth—and he was sure that they were meant as creatures apart, ineffable, beyond man, living amidst events and emotions as transcendent as they were incommunicable.

And now, they wanted to do something to his spaceship.

He turned to see his daughter speaking with him, but he heard nothing at all, because the silence tablet he had swallowed earlier was beginning to take effect.

Autumn, 2022

They are, Ryoko thought, like three pathetic old women, parasitically consumed by their glitter-heavy ceremonial robes.

Her father was there, and Kawaguchi, the Minister of Comfort, and Takahashi, the Minister of Ending, patron of suicides. Their oversized robes flapped against their chests and billowed out behind with the strong wind from the sea. They were abrupt splashes of color in the ashen expanse of sand, sea, and sky.

Ryoko watched them carefully, but as was seemly for a woman, she stood some distance off, not intruding on the men.

There were some others, too, on the beach: a dirty old beach scavenger, tethering his rickety boat to a post; two little girls, kicking a rusty can; a mangy cat, sniffing among scatterings of refuse...but all the images were lost in the grayness, and all the sounds dispersed in the slow susurration of the surf.

Behind her, far behind her, broken warehouses of worn concrete, a century old.

She heard them softly bickering; not indecorously, but with undertones of menace.

"Has he perhaps brought us here for no reason?" Kawaguchi asked.

The Minister of Ending, tall and sacerdotal in sacramental mitre and in purple and gold, looked steadfastly at the sand as he declared: "I have no opinion; I have come as a favor to Ishida." Clearly, this was untrue; he had come to see his collegue lose face.

"But might this not be ridiculous?" came Kawaguchi's feeble, edgy tenor.

Minister Ishida remained aloof. After all, he was the only one with anything to lose.

If the whale doesn't come, thought Ryoko, my father may have to kill himself.

They waited.

Until evening fell again. Then again the water burst asunder in the mid distance, and the blackness loomed out of the water, distorting all perspective. The three Ministers gaped in unison. The old scavenger, gripped by terror, whimpered quietly. Only the two children were unconcerned, and went on kicking the can.

Ryoko felt a surge of tremendous love for him, and she trembled at the grace of him, creature of twilight, leaping from the dark water in a perfect poised arc that mocked gravity for a moment. There was pain, too, with this joy, this beauty made unbearable by its transience. And the bittersweet pungent wave-wind swept her face, and she yearned to be like him, to live with his intensity and fierceness, a life-force battling inexorable death.

The same voice came to her that she had heard from the ship half a year before, but amplified, like thunder and a waterfall. *Come! Come!* it cried.

She heard Kawaguchi's voice: "The whale does not speak, Minister Ishida."

Ishida: "Wait." The first word he had spoken.

"But *I* hear him!" she said.

Come! Come! the voice sang, and it was whale-singing mixed with the music of *Noh* and *Kabuki* and *Bugaku*, eerie; and hypnotic, and she felt herself yielding, yielding beneath its spell, her body moving of its own volition towards the soft water....

Kawaguchi said (she heard him only faintly) "The whale has not spoken, Minister Ishida. I think we may leave."

A shriek: "Your daughter! She'll drown!"

"*But I hear him, but I hear him, but I hear him,*" she screamed desperately, as the others' voices faded into the roar of the waves.

"My daughter!"

"Old man, old man, lend us your boat, quickly!"

"B-b-but—"

"How dare you argue with the Minister for Survival?"

"*Hai, hai, irashaimasse,*" a frightened old voice, remembering his place and remembering the ceremonial forms of address in time....

She gave herself into the arms of darkness. The whale's consciousness touched hers, led her into the warmth. A lone gull cried above the thunder. The water parted for her like blankets. There was no cold in the water, only a profound joy, a release from turmoil, a peace, a foretaste of death.

She was a tiny consciousness enveloped in vastness. She emerged, standing on the waves, buoyed up firmly by an impalpable force...as from an immeasurably distanced vantage point, she perceived the wetness of the waves and wind which never touched her. The mind in which she had become imbedded was a cavern, an abyss, a cathedral dome, full of compassion and mystery.

Her voice sang out the whale's thoughts.

For some moments, she struggled to regain control of her body; but she gave herself up to the joy of helplessness, like a child on a plummeting rollercoaster.

"...she's walking on the water!" a tremulous old voice. The little rowboat came into view, the three Ministers huddled together with their robes in disarray and the old scavenger pushing the oars. It was a kilometer from the shore.

Don't be afraid, she heard herself say. A voice strangely like her own voice, but more sonorous she realized, for she could be heard above the howlings of the winds.

I am holding up your daughter telekinetically, Minister Ishida. She is unharmed; do not be afraid.

I am sorry to possess her body in this way, but I cannot otherwise communicate with you; to find one such as Ryoko, with the clarity of perception to tune in to and comprehend even some peripheral aspects of our thoughts, was no easy task.

She saw her father stand up even as the boat rocked wildly to face the creature as a man should; but the others remained in a bundle together, terror-frozen.

"You want to claim our starship? To ask our help in leaving the planet we have made uninhabitable for your children?" Ishida asked.

"Starship?" Kawaguchi stammered through his fear. "What's

going on?"

What could I want with your starship? Its dimensions are wrong for me, its environment is wrong. How could a whale travel with you, in a voyage of generations?

The two other ministers were glaring at Ryoko's father with anger and incredulity.

"Ishida, you lied to us!" whispered Takahashi. Ryoko perceived directly the meanness of the man, the self-aggrandizing pettiness of him. "What is the whale talking about?"

She saw in her father's mind the picture of the starship in the sky, the desperate hope that he clung to, and understood him, his image of survival.

Ishida said to the whale: "We will help you; we owe it to you."

Ryoko was moved towards them, across the turbulent waves. She came like a ghost in a *Noh* play, her dry dress fluttering a little, her face chalk-white and blank, masklike, serene.

Take the girl. Soon she will seem as if dead. Hospitalize her; remove her ovaries. You will find, in them, fertilized ova; they are my children. They are in psionic stasis, and will not begin to divide until you arrive at the end of your journey. She carries, in her mind, instructions for your scientists, so they will know how to make them grow when they arrive. Is it too much to ask?

"No," said Ishida. "But it is a great thing, a strange thing, that we should meet like this and exchange small favors on the verge of the great ending."

"Ishida!" gasped Takahashi. "You are polluting the purity of the Ending, destroying honor! Have you no Japaneseness in you at all?"

Softly, Ishida said: "Perhaps honor is only earthbound. I do not think it will matter to the stars."

Kawaguchi: "I shall die, though, when I have done my duty. I am not a coward; and your scheme will fail."

Bitterly, Ishida turned to Takahashi: "And when do you plan to die? Are you not Minister of Endings?"

Stiffly: "I remain as long as possible, sacrificing my honor for those who want death, to facilitate their passage into beauty."

Ishida laughed quietly, without rancour.

Help the girl into the boat, she heard herself say. She reached out her arms, of her own accord, and clutched her father's hands—how dry, how papery-alien! something inside her whispered—and was eased on to the boat. They were all cramped together. Hardness of wood, she thought. Wet splinters against my hands.

The other two Ministers were protesting in their own ways.

"A hoax," said Kawaguchi, "there's been no spaceship research for 50 years!"

"Man isn't supposed to overreach himself," Takahashi rasped. "You're violating the purity of Ending. Haven't you learned anything at all from our past? You're tampering with truth, trying to find loopholes in it that can't exist...."

Ryoko felt her father's disregard for them. He was looking only at her wonderingly, the way he had gazed at *fujisan* in the museum, with awe.

Her voice said: *You are wondering why I ask you these things. Perhaps you imagine me some great ancient of the waters, able to communicate with you from the supreme wisdom of my old age.*

You delude yourselves, if so; I am a young whale. I have not yet learned to love death; and my request is not necessarily that of the others.

Look! The wind subsided. The not-quite night became clear. Misted in distance, great whales clove the air in a frenzied dancing. There were a hundred of them, perhaps more, and they were leaping in unison and falling slowly in intricate symmetries, to crash heavy against the water.

Ryoko felt their surging ecstacy, and how the others were feeling it too. The whales seemed near and far, outside concepts of dimension, as she perceived them from her perspective of immensity.

It is the death-dance. It has always been said that men will never see it. Nevertheless, Ending draws near, the rules are changed.

They leapt and then they died, some of them, from sheer exhaustion, and Ryoko touched the edge of the extinguishing of a gigantic consciousness; how they were released from life, how they were all compassion, like Buddhas. The air rang with strange music, *Gagaku* music, apprehended neither as motion nor stasis...as dead bodies slapped against the sea.

See them. Hear them. They will never communicate with you. They are in love with death, and their lives have become pure music.

As though from a great height she could peer into the others' minds, and she saw her father's wary exaltation, Kawaguchi's grudging acceptance, and the untouchable darkness that was the soul of Takahashi, Minister of Ending. There was the mind of the old man, too; small, frail, timid.

The images faded. The death-dance was far out, beyond the horizon, but its reality had reached them through the mind of the whale. And now he had disappeared beneath the water.

Takahashi, seeing him gone, spoke more boldly: "Why do you believe we will do you favors? Is it not human nature to be treacherous?"

Then the voice of the young girl revealed the great secret that had never been spoken since speech began....

We have among us a myth, which it seems is founded in truth.

We have no names—the concept is alien to us—but there was once a great dreamer to whom we gave a name, Aaaaaiookekaia, gene-changer. She dreamed a great dream, about planting her own children among the primate-sentients on the dry land. They do not think she reflected, but they have the potential to be great fashioners of tools. It we could only join forces.

She summoned a thousand thousand others from all over the waters—we were millions, then—and they dreamed the great dream with her, dreaming with such power that new zygotes were created. Aaaaaiookekaia struggled on to the dry land to give birth, and abandoned her children there, and most of them—the ones which survived—were in the shape of men.

Even the dreaming of a thousand thousand whales could not create a true facsimile of man. True, there were the same number of chromosomes, and they even interbred with Men. But some things they could not change.

Your perception of beauty. How many times has this been commented on by the other races? With you it is instinctive: the twisted tea-bowls, the joy in imperfection is a legacy from us; the wails of the hichiriki and shakuhachi are cries from the depths of your ancestral memories. Your joy in death, too—it is a remembrance of that leap into eternity, as when the whale in his transcendent revelation rushes with joy to meet the harpoon.

This child Ryoko is one who has inherited most strongly the ability to communicate with us. That is why she seems so Japanese to you, when many of your values, though revived, are obsolescent. But all of you are children of the whales.

She collapsed into her father's arms.

Ishida held his daughter tightly, shielding her from the wind. The old man rowed like a machine, drained by terror. The implications of the whale's revelation came to him gradually: the Japanese people had been guilty of mass patricide. For so heinous a transgression, there was almost no expiation.

Except the one thing that would transmute any guilt into beauty. No, there were no alternatives.

He realized that there was no way of silencing them, and that another national wave of suicides was inevitable.

The shore came nearer. Everything was gray, like an antique motion picture. His daughter's hair trailed lightly across her face, black on white. Her lips were parted, as though about to speak, and she was cold.

Minister Ishida's memories reached back to a time before the Millennial War to a tutor and a schoolroom, to the lines of the immortal Basho:

mono ieba
kuchibiru samushi
aki no kaze

"...a thing is spoken. The lips become cold, like the autumn wind."

Winter, 2022/2023

A vague elapsing of time in her awareness; little else. She drifted out of her coma and she was in a cold bed, in an old room with steel-gray walls, and she felt her belly and knew that she had been drained. Her first thought was, *I'm sterile.*

"When can I leave the hospital?"

She saw the nurse: tired, hard-faced, like many workers a Caucasian. *An alien!* thought Ryoko. *After all, I am not human.*

Fragments, confused, distorted: in the cavern with the whale's mind. Spray-splashings, wind, the death-dance, the yearning for Ending.

The nurse picked up a swab with her chopsticks and dabbed deftly at Ryoko's arm.

"Sleep now. In a few hours they will come for you, the people from the Ministry."

Water rippling...waves washing her face...whispering....

And sank, effortlessly, into unconsciousness.

Later—she could not be sure of the time of day—she was escorted past innumerable rooms with metal doors, down escalators. A masked orderly or two would shuffle deferentially by, their eyes averted. She became aware that she was known to them all.

Four of them hustled past, wheeling a trolley. She almost recoiled. It was loaded down with corpses, piled every which way. Arms and legs stuck stiffly out, and the faces were tea-green and twisted. They were so grotesque that she could not think of them as having ever been human.

She and her guides pressed against the cold wall to let them pass. They did not smell of death, but sweet, like incense.

"...not suicide."

"No," replied her guide. "Plague, Miss Ishida."

So it had come to Tokyo now, and would soon be spreading into all of their homes. She wondered whether her father's project would have enough time. She had messages locked inside her mind, what to do when the whale's ova reached their new home. If it was not too late.

She watched the pile of corpses, and wondered if her mother was among them—she must by now be dead, but of course it was impossible to recognize a plague victim. . . .

The whale, the whale.

My forefathers killed them, their—our—very own ancestors. Ignorance was not an excuse.

She shuddered with the shame of it.

And I'm sterile, she thought, *just like the earth.*

REMEMBER YOUR ANCESTORS, blinked the neons that glittered along the Ginza. Shadowing the intersection, the Pavilion of Ending loomed above the crumbling Matsuzakaya department store.

"Yes, Ryochan, there have been thousands of suicides. Takahashi announced the whale's story all over the country, and when they understood what their forefathers had done, they lost face. Our whole nation, our whole race lost face. There was no self-respect left for a Japanese to feel.

"The most popular death was leaping off a cliff into the sea. Lovers still do it together, fathers and sons, old business associates. . .the immigrants are dumbfounded. They will have the country soon, I thing."

REMEMBER YOUR ANCESTORS
ONLY HONOR ENDURES

He's so old, Ryoko thought. She felt a new admiration for him, standing as he did for something as cowardly as survival, against the opinions of all. It made him a hero to her, for the first eime.

"Ryochan—"

"Otosan?"

"Will you go on the starship?"

"But who can—"

THE PAVILION OF ENDING

They were cut off by the hubbub as they stepped into the reception hall. A commotion of kimonos, stiff hairdos bobbing like buoys in the current, old tailcoats, dazzling lights from antique chandeliers. Little pieces of conversation crystallized out of the confusion:

"...of course, the integral serialism of the pseudo-occidental era was ultimately based on the sonorities of the Balinese gamelan...."

"...read Mishima? Greatest prophet of the last century."

"...I've planned my suicide for the cherry blossom season, it will be spectacularly beautiful, to lie dying among the fallen petals...."

"...These Caucasian servants have no idea of the finer points of etiquette, my dear!"

Turning to her father: "Father—why is Takahashi giving this party?"

"I don't know."

They handed in their shoes and changed into slippers for the upper level where they would relax on floor cushions at the long tables and be served. There was a pungent *sake*, perhaps not even synthetic; elegant, machine-carved *sashimi* in the shapes of petals and leaves. The porcelain seemed to be genuine *arita* with the character *fuku* in blue on white on each item. Ryoko did not know here was so much antique porcelain left, after the war.

Her father was withdrawn, and she did not find herself participating much in the conversations. It all turned on Endings and plague deaths.

The long tables seemed to converge against the high far wall where the Minister of Ending sat, above the others, haughty in his gold-brocade regalia and mitre. He talked to nobody, she noticed, and seemed to be walled in by silence. On reflection, she realized that she had not observed him talk to anyone at all that evening.

A faint cry, like a gull's, cut in on her thoughts. Someone in the kitchens, she thought: a plague-death. But just then a civil servant asked her to relate—for the hundredth time since she had come out of the hospital—the story of her encounter with the whale, and they listened to her, those around her, with the stricken awe that she had come to expect from her listeners; and their eyes glittered with envy when she told of the beauty of the whales' death-dance and death-song, and she began herself to hear, in the cacophony of small talk, the rush and whisper of the sea.

But as she talked, she was thinking: Why did her father want her to go on the spaceship? Could he not see that she was coming to a crisis, perhaps to a decision to die?

Just then, Takahashi rose. The voices died down, the clinking of glasses thinned. He began to make a speech.

"Many of you have called me a coward—" There was a sensation at this. Clearly something unusual was about to happen. "I freely admit this. I have encouraged Ending; thus far, I have not had the strength to seek it out for myself.

"This is the message of the whale: it is the final revelation of Ending. It is now time for me to acknowledge the guilt of my ancestors, my own guilt. The time of Ending is here"—he was quoting his own writings now—"and we must make way, we must purify the world.

"And so I call upon all of *you*—when you have put your affairs in order, not rashly or unpremeditatedly—to follow the ancient path. Japan has ceased to be sacred. We are a nation of genocides, of patricides.

"Had you been observant, you might have noted the laser generators surrounding my table. Before the war, such holotapes as you are now watching were not uncommon, if you can remember that far back. I have already killed myself, in a traditional manner, discreetly and honorably."

He disappeared.

There was an instant babble of discussion; a sudden silence; then, breathtakingly, applause.

She was serving him green tea in his private tea room. He smiled frostily at her, a trifle vacantly; she knew he could not hear her, because he had taken another silence tablet that morning. So she crouched on the *tatami*, in the background, while her father sipped, alone, in his private world of utter soundlessness.

After a while she slid open the *shoji*. The Rock Garden was flaked with snow, and the wind was whistling softly. She moved the *hibachi* nearer him, for the warmth.

He motioned to her. She could not help noticing how easily he tired now. If only he were not so addicted to the silence tablets! It was such an easy escape.

"Did you know?" he said, half to himself—for she would not have been heard if she had answered him—"There is a new *Kabuki* play. They are playing it all over the country; it is called *The Romance of the Young Girl and the Whale*.

"It's about a young girl who meets a whale. The spirit of the whale communicates with her, all very mystical, and in the final scene the girl leaps off a cliff and dies because there is no way to resolve the terrible love which she has grown to feel for him. . . . When they played it at Kyoto, there were busloads trundling down to Lake Hamamatsu, and they found bodies everywhere for weeks afterwards."

Ryoko had not left the house for a month; she had heard no news. But the story did not surprise her. She only thought: *Now they expect me to die.*

It was to her a fulfillment, the only possible ending for the story. Her determination strengthened.

The vision was so satisfying. To plunge headlong into the wombwarmth, to drink deeply what she had only tasted before when the waves and the whale's mind had swallowed her up. She closed her eyes, reliving the ecstasy.

"Ryochan," her father said gently, "I don't want you to die. I want you to leave on the spaceship. Beyond the atmosphere, among the stars, you may be able to begin again, without guilt."

"Oh, *otosan*," she sighed—had he heard her? Yes, he seemed to be reacting a little. There was no knowing when the silence tablets would wear off.

"I have arranged for you to be sent to Aishima next month. They'll train you there, for the journey."

"Father—"

"You were mother to the whale children, after all, for a while you carried them in your body. You gave the instructions for caring for the ova. You have the right to leave."

"Father, I'm more guilty than the others. I brought them the news of their shame. Without an inkling of this, they would not have died."

He seemed to understand her—he had heard very dimly, or else was lip-reading a little.

"How old are you now, daughter?"

"Twenty."

"I dreamed of finding you a husband, grandchildren. I am old enough to remember a time when everyone dreamed those dreams, not dreams of expiation, not nightmares of hideous self-recrimination. You are a wise girl, but still you should obey your father."

She bowed to him, submissively, but denied his statements in her heart.

"I defied all my own ethics for this project, Ryochan. None of the volunteers are Japanese; they're all immigrants, and can't understand the peculiar agony of these decisions. And in the end, I only created this project so that I could enable you to escape the necessity of death."

It was the closest that he'd ever come to saying that he loved her.

"But I'm empty inside, father. I'd be dead weight, useless for a multi-generation journey."

"I know little about these things. I only found the money, which was difficult because the people were starving and there was no one who would understand. I was very selfish about it, too. Maybe the trip won't last four thousand years, subjectively. There were so many things being discovered before the war, before we came to the Ending.

"And perhaps you won't be sterile, either; in all those years, with all the facilities and the brains that I have put on the ship, they might discover something. How to clone you, perhaps, from a piece of tissue, so that in the end—the beginning—some part of you—of me—will be there.

"Give up your right to die, Ryochan," he pleaded.

"No, father!" she cried out. She stopped short, realizing with a shock that she had been about to defy her own father. When he had revealed his need for her, his need to be a part of what he had helped to create....

She bowed again, but remained unconvinced. She had fallen in love with the image in the play, the virgin girl tumbling into the vastness of the sea. It was an almost sexual thing, an expression of her love for a being of total compassion, a terrible compassion beyond life. She saw herself as the playwright had seen her; an actor in a myth, a symbol. Without the death, perfection was marred.

"Father," she said, to avoid the subject, "recite me some haiku."

Her father did so. They sat beside the *hibachi,* in its puddle of warmth, and the snow in the Rock Garden became an eiderdown of white, and the wind sang sadly. He recited many poems, new and old, and mostly sad ones, about winter; but then he came to the most famous of Basho's poems, the one that all the world used to quote, even the *gaijin,* though usually in bafflement:

furu ike ya
kawazu tobikomu

"An old pool. A frog jumps; I can't think of the last line," her father said.

Trying to keep her voice calm, she supplied the line: "*Mizu no oto.*" But her cheeks were moist.

Mizu no oto—the sound of water!

There was a roaring in her ears: the sound of wind and of conversations and of electric Toyotas in the empty streets and the pounding of her own blood in her head, all echoes of the endless ocean.

In the morning, in the snow, beside a great rock, he was dead. It was a beautiful death; despite his lack of experience, he had killed himself most artistically, so that he and the rocks and the snow were a tableau of the utmost elegance and restraint.

Spring, 2023

It was a very different voyage.

The boat was similar to the one she had first sailed in, perhaps the same one; there were the sails, the bare wooden decks, the nights silent and bleak. She would stand beside the railings as she had done before. More at night than in the daytime, though, and she was more alone than ever before, because she had turned her back on the concrete world and stepped forward into the cosmos of the about-to-die. A world rarefied and crystalline, untainted by the sublunary, untouched and still. The people and the boat and the sea and the sky blurred before the beckoning siren of release.

I am in love with death, she told herself. And thought of the death-dance of the hundred whales.

A night came when she felt herself ready. She rose and stood, naked to expose her shame, by the prow where the railings were knee-high. Wisps of fog caressed her nudity.

When the fog cleared the moon lit up her face so that it gleamed with an actor's powdery whiteness. She thought of her remote ancestors, shadowdark and warm under the water.

For a while she half-expected the whale to come, to see her triumphant leap, to share her one moment of supreme beauty. He did not.

She whispered, "I do love you, father," to her own father and to countless fathers and back to the parents of Aaaaaiookekaia, the greatest dreamer of all.

She steadied herself to jump, a trifle self-consciously, and her eyes were caught by...stars glittering on the black water, alien, but the dots in the water were so near that she could have touched them with wet hands....

...and knew that she had lied to herself.

She had made herself play a role, a role written by a playwright she had never known. She realized she did not want to drown among the stars, but to walk among them. The new longing was an ache, without any joy at all. There was no ecstasy, but only terror and awesome desire. And it had come from finally understanding her father. She had not been in love with death, but only with herself.

And now she would still leap, but into an ocean more unknown, and truly endless.

Land was at the limit of her vision. Glimmering above the black needles that were trees, there were tiny sticks of silver that were the first stage in a journey to the umimaginable. And seagulls, circling the rocks.

288

For of course this was the voyage's purpose: to bring her and the other volunteers to the island Aishima, where the rockets awaited them.

And for that one night, before the preparations and the strenuous training were to begin, with the unearthly music of the sea to lull her, she was free to sleep the sleep of the dead.

There was a night like this for several of those who thought they has succumbed to the enchantment of death. So Ryoko was not the only Japanese whose remote descendants reached the fourth planet of the star Tau Ceti.

One ought to describe endings, especially this one, as swift and beautiful, made sublime by their very transience; but the poisoning of the earth was a slow process, and there were still many more years when the whales danced the death-dance on the death-giving oceans, and haunted the minds of dying men with their songs.

—Tokyo and Arlington, 1977 and 1979

Somtow Sucharitkul: Interview by Bob Halliday

OK. You've read Darrell Schweitzer's interview, but D. S. is a science-fictional personality, and, while we do discuss music a little bit, perhaps this rare interview from the Bangkok Post of November 2, 1975 will give a much different picture of my inscrutable nature.

1974-1979 were the halcyon days of my musical career, before I'd ever really tasted the joys of SF. I was flying from country to country over Asia giving concerts and controversial speeches; in 1978, when I directed the Asian Composers Expo '79, not a day seemed to pass when I wasn't being lauded or derided in some Asian newspaper, and the Japanese public television network, NHK, actually made a documentary about me, following me from Bangkok to Manila and actually filming me in the act of composing my big work of that moment, GONGULA 3 for Thai and Western instruments.

Here then am I as I appeared to the Asian cultural community at the tender age of 22, coming into my last major period as an aging child prodigy. . . .

Mr. Somtow Sucharitkul is the most accomplished example of an extremely rare breed: the Thai composer of classical music. The son of Dr. Sompong Sucharitkul, the Thai Ambassador to Japan, Somtow was born 22 years ago in London. Even at an early age Somtow's fascination with music drew his parents' attention to his talents, and by the age of 13 he was composing. Somtow went to Eton and then Cambridge, where he initially studied Comparative Literature. But soon he became well-known at the university as an unusually original composer, and eventually he bowed to the inevitable and decided to study musical composition in earnest.

Among his compositions to date, Mr. Sucharitkul lists three operas, the first based on Ibsen's *Brand,* the second on the life of the sculptor Michelangelo, and the third, on which he is currently at work, a strange mixture of surrealism and science fiction for which he has also written the libretto; a violin sonata titled *Cemeteries;* an extraordinary work titled *A Catch of Waters,* in which the singers and instrumentalists, some of them playing East Asian instruments, surround the audience, and *Views from the Golden Mountain,* for two string quartets and Thai instruments.

Mr. Sucharitkul recently attracted considerable attention in Bangkok when the last-named work, which is written in a style far more contemporary than is usually heard here, was played on television. He also represented Thailand at the Asian Composers' Federation in Manila early in October.

Mr. Sucharitkul is extremely articulate on the subject of music, and holds many strong views. Before departing for the United States last week he discussed some of the dilemmas facing contemporary music, both Asian and Western.

Bangkok Post: Have you done anything along the lines of trying to integrate Thai music, with its characteristic scale, with Western music, and do you think this sort of thing can ever work?

Somtow: That's about six questions all at once. Well, have I ever done it? Yes, I've used the two simultaneously, but I don't think in terms of integrating them, I only think in terms of conflicting them.

Post: In conflicting them do you think in cultural terms? Do you think of a Thai culture or tradition being represented through its music, or do you think of it only in terms of two very different types of musical sound or timbre being set against each other?

Somtow: Well, I suppose I do end up thinking in terms of cultures. It's because I'm an Asian composer. I write a kind of music that derives from a sort of cultural conflict.

Post: Within the Thai culture or in an international sense?

Somtow: In an international sense. I mean I can't write an indigenous Thai music because, first of all, there isn't any such thing in any living way.

Post: Why not?

Somtow: Because no one's written any for a hundred years.

Post: This brings up an interesting question. It seems there are two ways that cultural conflict can affect art, and music is always a good barometer. There's the way the Greek composers have found. Skalkotta's music sounds both Greek and contemporary. And there's the Japanese way where the whole traditional style was jettisoned and a Western one moved in.

Somtow: It was "jettisoned" wholesale, but they didn't really succeed in jettisoning any of it. You can see this whenever you observe a Japaneses audience listening to the Tokyo Philharmonic Orchestra. It's really quite a schizophrenic feeling that you get. Here's this audience sitting there. They're all wearing super, super clothes, just like Europe about 80 years ago, and they're sitting there like statues.

Post: Forcing the music on themselves?

Somtow: No, I think they really enjoy it, but I also think that the Japanese concept of enjoyment is something quite alien to us.

Post: When Beethoven's Fifth Symphony was first played in Japan earlier in this century the audience roared with laughter. But now, sixty or so years later, the Japanese have made themselves felt throughout the Western musical world. How do they do it?

Somtow: They always seem to know how without knowing why. When my piece was played at Kyoto last year, the Japanese critic who was there was able to analyze it totally after only hearing it once. They really have an amazing skill for this. But I think that, in a way, this skill is forced on them by the fact that they're studying alien beings. Their knowledge of it is highly external.

Post: What about you yourself? Do you feel a strong identity as a Thai composer? I've observed that you're bilingual, and assume you've spent many years abroad. Has this affected your feeling about yourself as being a Thai composer?

Somtow: In a way English is my native language. I originally thought in English when I was born, but at the moment I've become much more bilingual. I came bach to Thailand when I was six and I stayed for six years. But since my stay abroad my Thai has improved tremendously. I think it's because Thai people abroad speak more correct grammar then Thai people in Thailand. But about my identity as a Thai composer....In a sense this

293

means feeling identity for myself as the only Thai composer.

Post: Why has there been such a reluctance for the Thais to express themselves in a contemporary musical language? In other areas Thailand has been so rapid in adapting new ideas.

Somtow: I don't know. This is a failure which has been characteristic all over Southeast Asia, even in the countries which have been under colonialism for two hundred years, like Laos or Vietnam. I heard some music by a Vietnamese composer last week and it's just like the stuff they're writing here. The piece I heard was a perfectly normal sort of arranger's type piece. It was all pentatonic and it sounded just like an imitation Oriental piece of music.

Post: What do you think of Thai classical music as a point of departure for the genesis of a contemporary style? Duration for example. The idea of writing a long developmental piece where Western and Eastern forms are combined and which lasts more than 20 minutes?

Somtow: My forms aren't Western. I don't know actually what they are. Since I'm writing them I suppose they're Thai.

Post: In what way are your forms Thai? The interplay of the different groups of instruments?

Somtow: That's not so much Thai as Balinese. They have layers and layers of textures laid on top of each other, and some of them suddenly disappear and others dominate. What I admire most about the Balinese is that they didn't allow their musical culture to die off or to become ossified as I think happened in Java. And this has certainly happened here. I think it's far worse in the city, where the only thought in the minds of the establishment is to consider whether it's good or not. I recently went to a show where a provincial group displayed the most musicality when they played. They had a whole new range of technique in ranaat playing. I was astounded, because I didn't know that this sort of thing was developing. I had only heard Thai music in the city.

Post:	Why this tendency toward mummification? It seems that it's become almost an obeisance to enjoy Thai classical music.
Somtow:	Because people have a thing about cultural pollution. I think this is the essence of the idea of court music, anyway. What people fail to realize is that the reason that Thai music developed into such a great flowering in the Eighteenth Century was that about 600 years before that had been a dramatic era of cultural pollution between the Sino-Tibetan Culture and the Indo-European culture, and this conflict must have been almost as traumatic as the one between East and West today. This is why the music of Southeast Asia, of which Thailand is the main exponent, I suppose is, or was, such a rich thing. People don't realize that you have to have cultural pollution to have great art. It developed into a kind of over-purification, and eventually you wind up with only one way of doing it.
Post:	Do you think that the fact that Thai music has no precise system of notation might prevent development since it cannot progress through analysis of previous works which are then extended on, as occurs in Western music?
Somtow:	They did it in Bali. Balinese music today is different from 50 years ago.
Post:	But do you think a notational system for Thai music would assist it in absorbing alien influences— cultural pollution—to revivify it?
Somtow:	Yes, I think it would. Obviously it would. What I was told by a Fine Arts Department person was that it would ruin the players, because they wouldn't be able to improvise. This is ridiculous, because if you're sight-reading a handwritten aria or something you automatically improvise, and if it's indicated that in this notation you improvise at such-and-such a point, then you do it. They still equate notation with exactitude. This is wrong. In the West notation wasn't exact for hundreds of years, and it's only been exact for two or three hundred years. And now it's become too exact.
Post:	This brings me to another question. I notice this

your score, "A Catch of Waters," makes use of many highly contemporary techniques. It doesn't "sound" on a note for note basis but in the form of textures, so that there's considerable freedom of expression for individual performers. Do you feel that this allows you to play Thai and Balinese musical textures off against Western ones? And can this lead to any kind of synthesis?

Somtow: Yes, of course. This is true. In a sense this textural thing is an example of heterophony. If I want a particular texture...the texture also depends on the harmony so that the pitches have to be worked out so that it doesn't interfere. But I don't use the idea of melody, except very rarely.

Post: I saw several passages where melodies are clearly articulated.

Somtow: In that respect I'm not a very contemporary composer.

296

Afterword
In Defense of Ozymandias

I started to write these words this afternoon, while standing in the middle of the Roman Forum, in the shadow of the walls of the Aemilian Basilica. I'm on one of my regular trips to Rome, which is where my parents, always, since my childhood, on a diplomatic mission somewhere in the world on behalf of the government of Thailand, are stationed at present. As I turn, the late afternoon sun to my side, I see these huge marble columns at the top of a flight of long stone steps. Capping the columns is a huge and utterly unambiguous inscription:

DIVO ANTONINO ET DIVAE FAUSTINAE

To the God Antoninus and the Goddess Faustina. You can't get any more blatant than that! Those particular gods (and gods they were, even though *we* know they were just mortals like us, made gods by a decree of the Senate) actually stood where I was standing once, and they breathed. There were other gods too, and even as a child I felt them breathing on me.

Next week I'll be going to Mycenae to root around the ruins. It will be my first time there, and I am uneasy. Let me tell you why. I will tell the story in a simple, over-romanticized way, but indulge me; you've finished the book proper by now, and if you are reading these words at all you must be pretty indulgent.

There were once these people, see. They had weapons of bronze, and palaces. They spoke Greek. They wrote it, and the only reason we know this is that they were rather like us. They couldn't stop fighting these wars. In one war, while they were sacking the citadel, the fire spread to a room where they kept these useless old laundry lists, carelessly scratched on tablets of wet clay. The laundry lists were baked, and 3,300 years later, we found them. If it weren't for this war, we wouldn't even know what language they spoke.

They had (if one if to believe the mythographers) lines of ritual kings, with such hereditary titles as Agamemnon and Oedipus. They had priestesses of the earth-mother, and if you were lucky enough to marry one (often they were named Helen) you could be king yourself. For a while. Now and then, though, they'd cut you up to fertilize the crops. That went with being a king. They had lots of big wars. Two of them were over Helen,

297

though they had to be a couple of hundred years apart at least, if you're to believe the people who dig up these things.

Eventually, they had too many wars and things, and they all died, and the people who came after them did not know how to write.

Five hundred years later, some bard (his name may have been Homer) was telling stories about them. And though their cities had been buried in dust for half a millenium, the song still knew all their names, and it knew where they had stood; and even though the places described as splendid cities were nothing but villages now, or even wildernesses, yet at every place we dug, we found the cities: Pylos, Tiryns, Mycenae, Troy. And the stories are still true.

The Greek dramatists were wise, I think, to confine their plays to stories that had come down from a time a thousand years old even then, and belonging to a vanished civilization. You see, we still do the same thing—I'm finally coming around to making my point here—but we're not as honest about it. We give our characters other names, other backgrounds, and often we hide even from ourselves the fact that we are writing about how this fellow married the priestess and ended up having to be cut up and ploughed into the earth and, guess what, he didn't like it too much. (Even Homer didn't know he was really writing about *that!*)

Okay, so where does this lead to?

Well, let me talk about childhood for a minute—my childhood. As you will have noticed, mythology and childhood have always been predominant themes in my fantasy stories.

I heard the Greek myths at millionth-hand, in Bangkok, where I lived between the ages of seven and twelve. I was a stranger in my own land, because I returned home from a long series of peregrinations not knowing how to speak my native tongue. I had already lived in four countries following my father around the world as he garnered degrees from all the major universities. My first experience in a Thai school was less than wonderful. I was so frustrated by the language problem, and the cultural one, that I would frequently go into great rages. I once even ripped my teacher's dress in a fit of pique. Clearly this would not do, so instead I was sent off to the British School in Bangkok, a building which had once belonged to a movie star (these were the days, though, when Thai movies were filmed in *silent color,* and three people in a booth in the back supplied all the dialogue and all the sound effects, and played Max Steiner records for the music!) and which stood in the midst of paddy fields.

It was in this rather unlikely setting that I had my first encounter with the stories about that Bronze Age culture that we almost thought couldn't read and write.

My English teacher there (I was eight or nine by then) was a woman whose problem of cultural displacement was rather similar to my own; that's why, a Thai, she was teaching Eng. Lit., in a British school in Bangkok. The old movie actress's house proved perfect as a place to act out one's fantasies, because in one hallway of it was a wooden stage, recessed, curtained off. I began to learn about the myths, and about SF, at about the same time. The SF was mostly accidental; it was whatever happened to be in the classroom library, and the first book I remember reading was *Methusaleh's Children,* by Robert A. Heinlein. I went home and immediately decided to write a novel myself. I was, I think, ten. We had a small portable Hermes typewriter, a European model with all those funny accents, that wrote in tiny letters. I did the novel (it was ten pages long) and it had exactly the same plot as the Heinlein novel, minus, unfortunately, the point of the story.

When Mrs. Vanit, the English teacher, began to show me Greek plays, I got all excited. I couldn't understand them all the way through at first, and thinking about it now I realize that some of the translations may have left something to be desired; but in the back of my mind the shadows stirred. I went back to the typewriter and began producing fake Greek plays in earnest. Some of these survive, in a trunk somewhere in my parents' house; others are, I hope, lost. One such play was my very own *Electra,* which our class of eleven-year-olds put on one day for the edification of the entire school. None of the classical versions of this tale were quite gory enough for our young hero, though, and the off-stage killings were ludicrously inappropriate; so he decided to have all the murders take place in front of the stage, and to have buckets and buckets of Max Factor theatrical blood everywhere. The casting was limited; the three Furies and the three fates were all played by this girl (Pam Singh, I think) who wore a vast shapeless robe with three papier-mache masks sticking out of it. The Greek columns (Ionian, and therefore quite inappropriate for our Bronze Age types, but how was I to know then?) were made of rolled cardboard and topped with scrolls of twisted cardboard. They kept toppling. I myself essayed the role of Orestes; but without my glasses, I couldn't really enjoy too much of the performance.

I recently rediscovered the script that I had written for this play, which was, after all, the first public unveiling of My Lofty

Words. It was hilarious! For one thing, words occasionally failed me, and I plugged in the parts where my rhetoric flagged with excerpts from Shakespeare, not quite correctly remembered, from whatever play we had been doing at the time. There were six consecutive lines in it that I'd unconsciously plagiarized from *Julius Caesar*, for instance.

Shortly after this, the kid who played Apollo in my play (on stage for the entire production, for, in the moments when he was not haughtily addressing the throng, he was, supposedly, a statue) well, this kid was shot to death by his little brother in an accident. I think this is how the concept of *hubris* first became real to me. (What right did I have to make and unmake gods, after all? Was I the Roman Senate?) Flippancy aside, this was one of the more traumatic events of that period for me; for I had come to believe in the absolute veracity of the Greek myths, and it came as no surprise at all that someone I had named Apollo should be made to die for it. Since there was no one to whom I could confide this guilt without looking like an idiot, I clutched it to myself, and have done so these past eighteen years. I have now learnt to face my own idiocy without too much heat, though, so I'm able to confess all....

What more can I tell you? We lived in a large blue wooden mansion on an estate that contained a mango orchard and a pond upon which stood a wooden pavilion with pointed eaves, where one could go and watch lotuses. Most of this stuff has been covered with high-rises now. In a far corner of this estate stood a ruined house, cobwebbed, dank, smelly, like in a horror movie. I used to play there; to imagine that it was haunted. The Blue House actually *was* haunted, I think, but the ruined house was just make-believe. I set up a puppet theater there and used to slip over, afternoons after school, to enact Greek drama (sometimes with spaceships thrown in) using bunny-puppets or moppet-puppets which my father had brought back from America.

In the evening the scent of jasmine would be so overpowering that it would almost choke you.

Weekends were always spent at the movies. We would drive through the bustling, vivid streets of the oriental city, assaulted at every intersection by little boys with garlands or washcloths, and we would go to the three or four theaters clustered at the heart of Bangkok's Chinatown. They were all luxurious palaces with several balconies and things. There would be some argument about what film to see, but it would usually be a spectacle or a horror movie. Imagine, if you will, the drive from the quiet estate in what was then the outskirts of town, past sardine-packed crowds, into the huge Coliseum-like cinemas, to watch Steve Reeves as Hercules once more, or to gape at the horror in *The Man with the X-Ray Eyes!* No wonder I'm so weird.

It's all gone now, of course. There are five million people, hundreds of cinemas. and hundreds of high-rises there, and pagodas cower behind shopping malls. The old estate is long gone, carved up, and now lies at the heart of a chic residential district with some high-rises. Culture shock has been absorbed, assimilated. But when I was a child, a cultural fence-straddler who had not yet learnt to speak his native tongue, the big bang had just begun. Oh, certainly, its roots went back much further. But it had only started to gain momentum, I think. I find that my own life has been quite similar to that of my home town. I have been made to digest the familiar and the unfamiliar all at once. That is how the Greek myths became true for me; by always being there, wherever I lived, unchanging.

There now. And what does the title mean? Well, I'm sure you all know this lovely...oops, I'm sure you were all made to read Shelley's sonnet "Ozymandias" in school. It tells about this ruined statue, whose inscription bids the looker to "Look on my works, ye mighty, and despair" or some such thing. The idea of it is the irony of fallen greatness, of time's calumny. Well, maybe we *should* despair. Maybe we *should* still quail at these echoes of lost greatness. After all, the walls of Troy have been levelled, but we are *still* fighting the Trojan War, for every war since then has been colored by its rhetoric and echoed its suffering. I do not believe that we will ever create wholly new myths; we will be forever shadows of those Bronze Age figures. But I know my place, and I am content.

—*Rome, Italy*
September, 1982